My Shy Alpha

Book 1

RIVER KAI

RIVER KAI

My
Shy Alpha

Book 1

Edited by Kayla Vokolek
Cover and Illustrations by River Kai

ISBN (Ebook): 979-8-9864108-4-5
ISBN (Paperback): 979-8-9864108-6-9
ISBN (Hardback): 979-8-9864108-7-6

Library of Congress Control Number: 2023916968

Our books may be purchased in bulk for promotional, educational, or business use. Please contact your local bookseller, or send a request to River Kai Art at riverkaiart.com/wholesale or PO Box 1414, Wilsonville, OR 97070.

First edition, October 2023

10 9 8 7 6 5 4 3 2 1

Riverwolf Fantasy Press
The Fantasy Romance Imprint of River Kai Art

To all those who have been made
to feel small and caged.

You matter,
you are loved,
and you belong here.

1

I'm face-to-face with my therapist, whose mouth has been hanging open for a solid minute.

I stop picking at my jeans' threads. "So, yeah. That's how my first date with him went."

Jenny's eyebrows furrow. She reverses her legs from crossed to uncrossed to crossed again. "I'm sorry, can we back up for a second? You said your date turned around and...?"

"Sniffed some woman's neck."

"Just some random woman?" Jenny's bountiful, dark curls shimmy with the rapid jut of her chin. "Did he know her?"

"That's what I wondered too! But I don't think so. She turned around and said something like, 'I've been waiting to meet you.'"

"And then they...?"

I wince. The woman's heaving moans replay in my mind like the broken porno I found lodged into Dad's old VCR - something I'd rather not remember but probably will until I die. "Then they went into the bathroom and started having sex. *Loud* sex."

"Leaving you to sit there, alone and confused."

"Yeah... Pretty much."

Jenny's deflating shoulders hurt my heart even worse than it already stings, validating that, yes, this is my life, and yes, I'm back at square one in the dating world. Again.

"You've kept a straight face throughout the story, but I get the feeling this was more hurtful than you're letting on," Jenny says.

I swallow hard. "I don't know which part hurts more, but yeah. It was."

"Is this about the dream again?"

"No. ...No?" I shake my head hard enough to convince myself this is separate.

Until I remember what I did for an entire hour after I got home, unable to stop crying as I vision-boarded away my crushed hopes for the future. And it would've lasted longer - if I didn't realize I was compulsively attempting and re-attempting to find a photo to match the sexy guy I always meet in my recurring dream, unable to find the perfect replica of his scruffy, squared jawline.

"Well, okay, maybe it is about the dream. But that's not all of it. I know some amazing guy I met in a dream will never magically show up in real life. And I know we've talked about setting realistic dating expectations and keeping my mind open. But everything has been disappointing. Like no matter what, I'm bound to feel hurt. And after how many horrific things have happened in my life, I'm scared that no one will ever—"

I choke back tears, unable to continue.

"Oh, honey." Jenny hands me a tissue, and I can't bear to look at her aching eyes. "You're scared that no one will ever...?"

"Love me."

There's a painful silence as I weep, trying to let Jenny see me upset without hiding myself. Besides my best friend Amy, Jenny is the *only* person I let see me cry.

Jenny softens her voice, leaning over her glass coffee table to rub my shoulder. "Are you telling yourself you're not lovable?"

"I just get the feeling that there has to be someone better out there. At least *one* person? But maybe that's unrealistic too."

Jenny's playful smile softens my nerves. "Or maybe the guy who has sex with random women in the bathroom while on a first date just isn't your guy."

"Maybe." I laugh. But my fears resurface, gnawing at my guts. "At least I hope he's not my guy. I hope he's the last guy like that I'll have to waste my time on. ...Or person, rather."

"Then who *is* your person? Now that you've tested the waters, what are you looking for in a partner this time?"

I stop picking at my nails. What makes Mr.-Sexy-Dream-Dude different from everyone I haven't clicked with? As my mind wanders to my last long-term relationship five years ago, my voice comes out soft and shaky. "I try hard to understand people I love, even if we don't see eye to eye. If my partner and I could try to meet halfway, maybe I'd finally feel safe with someone."

Jenny lights up.

But before I can stop myself, I say what wrecks my hopes. "If feeling safe again is possible."

"Well, what if? Maybe it isn't possible. Or maybe it is. Who's to say?" Jenny's smirk grants me a weary smile; she's poking at my "what-if" with further uncertainty like we always practice. "It sounds like, at the root of it, you want to be with someone who deeply values you. Do you think people exist in the world who value their partners?"

"I'd… like to hope so."

We share a minute of silence as I pick my nails, mulling over everything we've worked through in our sessions.

My recurring dream initially seemed like a trauma coping mechanism - my brain's way of grappling with the utter destruction my ex caused. His violence ruined sex for me. The shift was made from pleasurable to horrifying, and nothing can bring me back to how I was before Steven laid his hands on me. With how many intrusive thoughts explode within my mind around sex - detailing graphic ways I could be tortured again - I haven't been able to crawl my way back to the *idea* of intimacy with another man.

Except for the man in my recurring dream. My core heats just thinking about it: his strong hands gripping my hips over his bare body because I want them to, not because he "needs" me to.

But from the first day I had the meeting-my-sexy-soulmate dream, I never believed it would come true. The problem is that no relationship in reality ever seemed as good. Allie, the sweetheart of a botanist I went on a few dates with last month, helped me feel safer with kissing and cuddling. God, she was a good kisser and an even better friend, but she and I were always missing that spark. One I can *feel*, not search for or struggle to create.

My dream's "soulmate" wasn't perfect, stumbling over words

9

and standing stiff like he didn't know what to do with my presence. But that made me love him more. He was just my soulmate. I don't have words for why I knew he was. It was a feeling – deep, infinite love.

That I've never been able to find in real life. I'm tired of being hurt. I want to love someone who actually *loves* me. Someone I can be vulnerable with without feeling scared.

There's one thing I haven't tried to help myself let go of the dream, but I'm not sure Jenny will like it.

She gives me a soft smile. "It looks like you're working through something. Can you walk me through it with you?"

A heavy lump nestles into my throat. The whole truth feels too terrifying, so I settle for half. "I've been trying the same things and getting the same results. Of *course* it won't work out how I want it to."

Jenny chuckles. "If there were a way we could all find the greatest loves of our lives in a heartbeat, we would."

"I know, and I know I'll have to wait. But I also think doing *nothing* is ineffective."

"Does that mean you have an idea in mind?" The slow smile stretching to Jenny's eyes tells me she sees through me.

Screw it. I'll embarrass the hell out of myself. At least it's confidential.

"What if instead of pretending the dream never happened, I recreated it?"

I'm met with silence.

Then concern overwrites Jenny's curiosity. "What do you mean by that?"

Dammit. It's too late to go back. "What if I go to the forest - just one time - tracing my steps in that dream?"

"What would be the purpose? It was a dream, and I'm concerned chasing it could validate the fantasy. Not only that, but does it have that familiar sense of urgency?"

Jenny leaves no room to budge, and I shrink into her cushy couch. But her focused stare doesn't look angry. She's worried, and I don't blame her. My suggestion could sound like I'm losing progress.

"I don't *think* it's a checking compulsion, but I do feel some sort of pull to act…" I trail off, dropping my focus to my fidgeting fingers.

"I'm not trying to disappoint you or tell you what to do, honey. I'm mainly concerned this could leave you even more disappointed when your hot soulmate doesn't come looking for you in the forest." Jenny breaks into a soft smile. "Especially not one you have the immediate urge to get down and dirty with in the leaves."

I laugh with her, rubbing my neck. The heavy, incredible sex is the most unrealistic part of that dream, knowing me. I can't open up to anyone, let alone open up my *pants* for them the second we meet.

I put on my best smile. "That's true. It was just an idea. Something I've never tried."

Jenny taps her lip, thinking hard. "Given your history around avoiding forests, I want to say you could take a short walk." My heart flips, but Jenny raises a halting hand. "If! And only if - it's not for the sole purpose of checking for 'him.'"

"I'm not searching for 'him' anymore. I know Mr.-Sexy-Dream-Dude doesn't exist. I want to let this forest dream go, once and for all."

Jenny nods, but I know she's tracing my eyes for any hint of doubt. Of course, my debilitating doubt disorder is why I'm here.

"Do you feel this will benefit you? Do you have any compulsive urges to do the opposite?" She asks.

"Actually, yes. I realized I started avoiding the same forest trail you and I visited for an exposure, just because of the dream."

Jenny relaxes into her plush armchair, bouncing her foot as she re-crosses her legs. "Then I'd say go for it - using the one you're familiar with, if possible. But please, Aliya, call me if *anything* comes up around this. This isn't the only solution."

2

A heavy weight in my chest drags my feet through the dusty path home. Now that I said it aloud, tracing my dream's steps in the forest sounds silly. More like I'm in denial about how much my dating life sucks. Chasing a fever dream won't change anything. I don't think I'll be going into the forest, after all.

Light drizzling dusts Greenfield Forest as I exit the Westfield city limits, but that's nothing my hood can't solve. With fluttering bird wings above my head and a sea of swaying, green flora at my sides, I take the long way home across the countryside, lost in my thoughts. It's finally the weekend, but I'll probably spend it with my scrapbook. My childhood best friend has a third-anniversary date with her wife, whom we met in college. With how much they bicker yet gush over each other, I swear they're simultaneously an old married couple and honeymooners. It's a treat to see my two favorite people so in love.

Now that I think about it, they're my best living example of a loving partnership. My shoulders soften – at least I have one shred of proof that what I'm seeking exists.

Even though I'm now a permanent third wheel. I guess tonight is another lonely pizza Friday.

I can't say I'm too bothered about living alone after living with Steven. As long as I stayed within his lines - whether that meant curling in over myself to make myself as small as possible or to erase my voice entirely - we'd be "okay."

Then my parents died five years ago, leaving me my childhood home. My first safe escape route appeared, and my "life partner" warped into something monstrous, my traumatized mind allowing me to see reality for the first time.

He didn't like that.

I take the turn that's supposed to lead to my old, inherited cottage, but I don't find my mossy landmark tree. I freeze, knowing I can't afford to walk any deeper if I took the wrong turn.

But it's too late. I'm immersed in the forest outskirts.

Twisting every direction and scuffing my worn work sneakers even more, I slump into myself, a familiar dread seeping through my bones. Gargantuan trees shoot into the sky, obscuring the forest trails between dense thickets. The path home is nowhere in sight.

Forget losing my way in the forest outskirts; I'm deep in the thickets, with no idea how long I've been walking.

Fuck, Mom was right. Everyone was right. I'm going to get myself killed in the forest.

Okay, no, I'm not doomed yet. Maybe I just need to get out of this thicket.

I whip out my phone to check the map. Droplets splat onto the screen as they spill from overhead leaves, but as usual, there's no service beneath the trees.

I whistle out a slow breath as I analyze my surroundings for familiarity. If I knew where I started, this would be no problem, but three rivers slice Greenfield in a confusing zigzag that messes with my internal compass.

But the riverbanks can't look identical, right? I trudge deeper into the forest, veering left when I find a trickling stream - growing wider by the minute with the oncoming downpour. I blink past the rain to sniff the air, dive into my gut senses, and analyze rocks and birds for clues, but my capabilities never came close to my father's knowledge of the land. He could navigate it in the dark, but I wouldn't dare.

No matter how much he knew, Dad still died in this forest. Not anywhere near here; Mom was right, I should never trek that deep unless I'd like to face grave consequences. Maybe Dad shouldn't have either. But his death wasn't the forest's fault. At least, I don't think it was. Someone shot him. A hunter. The cops believe it was a mistake - the hunter's guilty conscience sending them sprinting in the other direction - but it never sat right with me. They left him lying there to bleed out. Deep down, I think they killed him on purpose.

I can't stop checking my phone screen. A daunting 5:47 PM stares back. Soon, it'll be pitch black. The dream and my parents' old warnings weren't the only things keeping me from trekking too deep into this forest; what if someone shoots me here too? My shoulders raise as unease crawls over my exposed back.

My feet scurry ahead on their own, desperate for some sort of clue. But all I see are trees. More trees. Trees wrapped into other trees. Even baby trees sprouting their first leaves.

The dribbling streams become mini rivers, whispering hints of my location. I jog after them, their speed increasing with me as they merge into thicker clusters.

The river's gushing roar calls to me before I can see it, pulsing between my raging heartbeat. A pebble of hope forms in my mind, betting that this is the river to follow upstream, leading to the old cottage.

But at the river's edge, I don't recognize anything.

The water threatens to swallow me whole as I peer into it. And when I lean a little too far, my sleek, black braid tumbles over my shoulder. Despite watching it happen in the river's reflection, I yelp in surprise at a snakelike "attacker" coming for my face.

I've had enough adventure for one day.

Whipping around to run back to where I came from, I stumble over a rock, catching myself just in time with a stampede of frantic steps.

Maybe the forest wants to humble me. Or maybe I'm missing something.

I face the sky to gulp desperate air, but it doesn't help; my stomach plummets at the first sign of indigo creeping over the forest canopy.

Darkness is a familiar foe. I can't get an accurate enough look behind myself to make sure no one is there, leading me to check over my shoulder compulsively - which, of course, only makes me more convinced that a vicious stranger waits in my vision's edges. Another man protecting himself from my awareness so that I can't protect myself.

But I don't think it's past trauma talking tonight. Nature is beautiful but relentless. It'll claim me if I let it.

Fuck. This is a bigger-than-fuck moment. I don't want to die out here. What if they blame Jenny for my death, allowing *me* to chase my stupid, impossible dream into Greenfield Forest? They won't find my body for days. Or maybe they won't find it at all - Mom always warned me there are mountain lions, bears, wolves, and more out here. At least I could feed them for a few days. Vivid images scour my mind of chunks ripped from my flesh when—

I groan, recognizing this pattern as my lungs beg for mercy - I'm encouraging my intrusive thoughts again, worsening my anxiety.

Plopping onto the nearest log to soothe my burning legs, I breathe into the rustling canopies that stretch into the clouds. Trees crowd me everywhere I look.

Or maybe they're protecting me. I settle into this uncertainty, allowing it to be.

Closing my eyes, I meditate for a moment. Within a minute, the chiming leaves in the wind fade into white noise. Retracing to the moment I left Jenny's office, I deepen my breath with every snapshot I can remember.

I took the long way home, passing Mrs. Jensen's farm. Her cows had already scuffled back inside, but the way the sunlight hit their stable warmed my heart.

I can't be too far from there. Maybe this is the forest behind Mrs. Jensen's house?

But I don't understand what drew me here in the first place. The long way home hardly enters the forest. I take that trail more often than not, and I'm not the type to space out. I'm in therapy for over-noticing, leading to doubt, leading to more terrifying thoughts than I should have in a lifetime. What the hell lured *me* off my usual path?

The second I question it, a bubble forms in my core, expanding by the second. But it's not just a bubble. It's an urge so deep that my eyes snap open.

Something drew me here.

My heart stutters at this, but then it softens. Relaxing into its truth.

Maybe because this sequence of events is familiar. Strikingly similar to my repetitive, alluring dream.

No, wait, Aliya. Is this seriously about that dream again?

I groan, slapping my forehead as I grip the bark beneath me.

But I can't deny it. Something deeper than my heart speaks, urging me forward. Urging me *here.*

This is irrational, isn't it? Oh, God, I'm finally losing it.

But I'm here. In the forest.

Rage smothers the initial peace in my revelation. Like most days, I'm bitter about how much of my life was stolen. Maybe I should follow this urge. End my ridiculous fantasy, once and for all.

But my gut knows more; my *soul* is calling me. And it's not letting me avoid it this time.

As I jump off the log, the bubbling urge in my torso expands until I have to fight to inhale. I've never felt anything like this in my life. I have to find out why.

I sprint in the direction of my heart. Turning a bend around the river as the sunlight disappears, I freeze; a nearby bush rustles enough to warn me it's not the wind's doing.

The animalistic instinct to run battles the urge pinning me in place, my body and heart facing off at equal measures. But forget light rustling, the whole bush quakes from an animal forcing its way through until even the trees framing it shake off leaves. Whatever is about to emerge, it's enormous.

The bush splays to reveal the animal inside, starting with a black nose wider than my head. The predator's fur blends with the brown and green thicket, more of a warped shadow in the fading daylight.

As I stare, it rises from a crouch, expanding to its full height. I blink a few times, ensuring my eyes are functioning.

I'm staring into the eyes of a wolf.

"Holy f–" My breathy whisper tenses the wolf's limbs.

I can't understand what I'm seeing. This "wolf" towers above any wolf I've ever seen - taller than a large horse. And this brown, glowering wolf is *not* what my soul called me toward.

My parents taught me about every Greenfield Forest predator, but they honed in on wolves in particular; we've heard them howling in the distance our whole lives. But besides this wolf's gargantuan form, it doesn't follow the rules Dad taught me: they likely just want to be left alone rather than waste energy attacking anyone. Which means I'm rapidly straying from Mom's rules about what to do if I encounter a wolf: don't ever, *ever* run. No, this wolf's eyes burn into me as if I've personally aggrieved their entire family.

Did I stumble into a den? I'm dead, aren't I?

I want to move. Scream. Run. But I'm frozen.

I'm never listening to my heart again.

The wolf takes a silent, prowling step, and my instincts win. Running will make it chase me, but what choice do I have?

As I sprint for my life, a stockier, darker figure flashes its teeth behind the brown wolf. A black bear of a wolf lunges for the brown wolf's neck, and I don't watch a second more.

I run and run, not stopping no matter how much I need to. I'm so winded that I'm having trouble staying on my feet, tripping and scrambling until my palms bleed.

Pausing at a rock, I cough as I struggle to inhale enough oxygen to soothe my burning limbs. Every breath feels like it's calling out to the enormous wolves, begging to be found, but I can't stifle it. I grip my aching heart muscles, preparing myself to sprint despite their complaints, when a twig snaps behind me.

Fear locks a scream from escaping my throat. From the corner of my eye, a black figure swoops for me. I swear I see fur.

3

Without looking, I start smacking. My first hand whiffs through the air, but the second hits something hard.

Someone speaks. "Shh... You're okay."

I cower from the gentle, deep voice. My pounding heartbeat nearly drowns out the stranger, but their words calm me just enough to be able to breathe.

"There you go. You're okay."

I open my eyes to find a large man. My heart flips. His stare flits away before I can see the color of his brooding eyes, but I'm hit by a sweet, luxurious scent from his hair. Long stragglers frame his shaved fade, but most of his hair on top is shoved to one side, choppy and wild like his breath. With powerful arms shielding me, he scans the forest, revealing a sharp, scruffy jawline. The one I can never find in a magazine.

This isn't Mr.-Sexy-Dream-Dude. He looks, smells, and sounds even better.

But after what the last large man did to me when we were alone, I'm way more confused about why I'm not scared of this one. As we meet eyes, his soft, teal stare enraptures me. It's rude to stare, but I can't help it. Neither can he.

"What–" He clears his throat, his husky whisper quivering as much as my shoulders. "What are you?"

With that single, demeaning question, my developing emotions embarrass me too much to acknowledge, dropping to the floor with my jaw.

"Excuse me?! How mean!"

The man flinches, his gorgeous eyes crushed by my angry reaction, and frankly, I'm fine with that.

I can't believe I just thought this guy was my soulmate. What kind of question was that? Did the wolves scramble his brain?

My ribcage locks. "Wolves!"

"...Yes."

"All you have to say is 'yes?!' No, you don't get it—"

With a crackle of dry leaves, another animal scrambles behind the man. I need to stay as quiet as possible, so I stifle my panicked breath with a sharp, vacuuming inhale.

Instead, I hyperventilate.

The man grips my cheeks, scanning my eyes for what's wrong.

All I can say is, "Wolves! There are wolves!"

His eyes widen at my wheezing lungs. "Hey, breathe!"

"I– I can't! I'm– I'm going to die—"

"I'm *not* letting you die."

His voice is so final, but so soothing, that my body submits to his words before my mind, every muscle loosening into goo. The stranger slides a hand behind my neck, cupping my head in one big palm. My teeth chatter, but his teal eyes soften as if he's relaxing in my presence despite being my lifeline.

With his fingers buried into the back of my hair, he strokes my scalp. "You don't have to be scared anymore. I'm your Alpha."

The urge in my heart explodes. I grip the man's black Sherpa jacket, struggling to breathe as intense, unfamiliar emotions seal my soul to him. He drags his nose up the side of my neck, its cold tip releasing a soft cry from my throat. The second he caresses a particular golden spot on my neck, a wave of absolute peace washes over me.

"Breathe," he whispers.

My knees buckle, forcing the man to wrap one arm around my waist. Pressed against his body, I grip for more of him, overcome by the need to let him nuzzle into that sweet, luscious spot on my neck. And he does, again and again, as we sink to the forest floor.

Just like in my dream.

"We're safe, I promise you. I scared them away." He softens his voice, only an inch from my nose.

As we stare at each other, my shoulders soften. His gaze widens until I swear I'm looking at the sweetest, most vulnerable soul I've ever seen. Before I can stop it, a slow smile creeps over my face. I don't know why, but maybe he's right; we're safe now, and something unbelievable is happening. Judging by the flustered, anxious grin gracing his cheeks, he feels the same.

"I-I've dreamt of you, I swear, but–" He shakes his head, unable to look into my eyes as his cheeks burn. He has no idea he just sucked the air out of me, my heart pounding itself into overwhelm. "Sorry, that's so weird to say. I-I meant– I just–" He takes a deep, shaky breath. Then he dares to look back into my eyes. "You feel i-important to me, and I was drawn to you, a-and…" The man bites his lip, hardly able to suppress a smile as mine only grows. "Fuck, I *finally* found you."

An elated laugh spills from me. He's more precious than I imagined, flushing deeper as I cup his cheeks. Erupting into shy, airy giggles, he drops his forehead against mine. Our laughter feels celebratory, brightening the forest around me despite how dark it's grown. The breezy relief between us washes away my fears, a tremendous feeling inside me screaming, *This is exactly where I'm supposed to be.*

In a bed of dry leaves, the truth spills out of me. "You are him. The one I've been waiting for my whole life."

His fresh tears pool as he pulls me in tighter. His thumb brushes my neck again, and I shudder, hardly suppressing a moan. That single touch shoots through me before flourishing in my groin.

My cheeks blaze, stunned by my own reaction to this stranger. I pull away, peeking up at him. Does he have any idea what he's doing to me? Is it perverted to have this much blood pooling between my legs, or is that spot on my neck another G-spot they didn't want to teach us about in Sex Ed? I can't *actually* be turned on for once, can I?

But slow, blissed-out blinks greet me, and an uptick in a delicious, saccharine scent surrounding us makes my mouth water.

"Good job," his deep whisper rumbles, and it's over for me. "If it's too much, we don't have to keep–"

Grabbing fistfuls of his jacket, I drag my cheek across his

chest, exposing my neck to him for more. When he gives it a delicate bite, a burst of heat flashes through my groin.

Oh, my God, I *do* want to get down and dirty in the leaves. This is the first time since–

No, I can't think about what happened. I want to enjoy this, now that I'm finally feeling this way.

He redirects my mind easily, adjusting his embrace to give me a full-body squeeze. Pleasure tingles up my spine. His all-encompassing touch feels so good that I grind into his lap without a second thought. He shifts one hand to my hips, pressing me deeper into him with every tingling caress of my neck.

"Oh, Goddess, you're so much more gorgeous than I imagined." His deep voice breaks with desire. "I want you, I–"

I run my nose along his neck, returning the favor, but the man gasps. By the end of my touch, he's shuddering, burying his expression in my shoulder.

"Holy fuck. N-no one has *ever–*"

My heart sinks. "Was that bad? Should I stop?"

"No. Fuck, no." He cuddles me closer, but by the way he's hiding his face, I'm certain he meant he's only been on the giving end of whatever this golden spot on my neck is, and God, it's good.

"Do you like it?" I ask.

After an adorable pause filled with slow strokes of my back, he nods into my shoulder.

He wants it. Craves it, maybe.

"Then I'll be gentle, okay? You deserve affection too." My words raise his shoulders. But they also tilt his neck, bearing his pulsing jugular for more affection.

By the second time I run my nose along it, he gives what sounds like a low purr. I gasp at how beautiful he sounds, but when my breath traces his neck, it's like a piece of him snaps.

He dives back in to caress my neck. Except it's not his nose that greets me; it's his hot, wet tongue. My breath restarts, my core flexing with each lick like we're fucking. It widens my knees and tightens my grip on his back for more.

I have no idea why this feels so strong, but it's the first time

I've verged on climaxing with a man in years, and we're still wearing clothes.

His hot breath thrums against my neck with the next lick. But this time, his love bite starts off a little too hard.

I cry out, and he jumps back like a scared animal.

"Sorr– sorry! I thought y-y–" He winces, shaking his head. When he speaks again, he enunciates every syllable with painful precision. "I thought you wanted me to…"

My insides somersault as I stare at the man, his worried eyes locked on mine as I grip my nibbled neck. His stare is honest, revealing a tender innocence that doesn't match the sexual prowess I just felt.

I have no idea who he is, but one thing is undeniable: I want him. With every piece of my soul.

But that terrifies me. "Who are you?"

He swallows hard. "N-Noah…"

That's all he has to say?

He crawls closer on all fours. His cinched eyebrows tug at my heartstrings. "How'd you get here? Omegas aren't safe out here all alone. You can't shift?"

What is he even talking about?

Noah's hand draws near, and I flinch. He freezes, but the urge that drew me to him in the first place begs me to let him in. As I reach for his hand, he meets me halfway, tracing a soft line down my neck.

Whatever he's doing to my neck makes me feel things I've never felt with a man in my life. My hips squirm, itching for me to strip bare and roll over for him.

I don't even care that I moan in front of him. "Why does that make me feel so good?"

Noah jerks back. "Why? Oh, *no*…"

It takes everything in me to fight the primal need to love on him, but his expression sobers me; despite being the bulkiest man I've ever seen, Noah shrinks by the second.

So does my heart. "What's wrong? Do you not feel the same about me?"

"No, Goddess, of course I do. We're mates."

Mates. The word feels like an endless field of rosebuds popping open in my chest. The word I've been searching for all along - why nothing ever felt right no matter how many dates I went on.

"Do you mean... Soulmates?"

"No. I mean mates." Noah's hopeful eyes falter, and it burns down to my bones. "But you're not another wolf, are you?"

Confusion drowns my joy. "Wolf? You're not making sense…"

Noah reaches for me again, and I hug his hand to my chest, desperate to understand.

"Oh, Goddess… This is so hard." The shivering pain in Noah's voice churns my insides.

"I'm not what you're expecting, am I? You don't want me?"

Before Noah can respond, a glint of eyes appears behind him. I scream as the same massive, brown wolf lunges for us, sinking its teeth into Noah's back.

4

My eyes squint shut as Noah crashes toward me, but the impact I brace for never arrives. When I open my eyes, shock zaps my system.

Noah pins the hulking wolf to the ground by the neck with one bare hand. His clothes burst, the fabric streaking over his expanding body in rippling ribbons until they shred under pressure with a loud *snap*. But beneath his clothes isn't the skin I expect. His body morphs into a new, inhuman form. Fur. Claws. A dark snout as long as my entire body.

An enormous black wolf emerges from Noah, snarling at the cowering wolf beneath him.

Reality bends, and I'm reeling with it. But I don't have time to. The brown wolf snaps their jaws, ready to tear into Noah the second his black, towering form meets it face to face.

And I have an opening to run.

But no matter how terrified and confused I am, everything in me screams to protect Noah.

As the wolves tumble, I scramble across the forest floor, searching for a large enough rock. When Noah pins the strange wolf to the ground again, I throw with all my might.

The rock hits the brown wolf square in the head, and Noah's ears shoot upright in surprise.

Then he looks at me. Golden, piercing eyes spike my heart down to my knees.

But Noah can't stare for long. His attacker squirms to run away, whimpering louder by the second. Noah isn't letting up. Hot, furious drool drips from his fangs as he lifts his lips. The

black wolf's low, rumbling snarl morphs the brown wolf's cries from whimpers to yipes.

I can feel Noah's anger - his thirst for revenge shakes in my own chest. And I get why; maybe the brown wolf would've hurt us, given a chance. But from what I know about wolves, they don't attack without reason. I probably encroached on their territory, maybe even their den with newborn spring pups, and now they're pissed and trying to shoo us away.

Regardless, Noah's dominance has triumphed by miles - no blood necessary. And after the losses I've experienced, I don't want to witness anyone else die.

My voice comes out shaking and squeaky. "Noah, it's over! Let them go!"

Noah pauses, glancing between me and the animal beneath his massive paws, each paw three times larger than my head. With one final warning snarl, Noah releases the wolf.

Well, relatively. He chases it until it scrambles into the forest with its tail tucked.

Noah gives one final, irritated huff through his massive black snout before turning around and padding toward me. He makes the trees feel like twigs in not just size but presence, every insect and animal softening into silence within a wide radius of his shimmering coat.

Fresh adrenaline stings my nerves. Even if Noah saved my life, a truck-sized wolf approaching sends red alerts to my system. I withdraw a step, and Noah freezes.

"Oh, God. You're…"

He slinks back, his ears tucking in embarrassment.

"I'm sorry! It's just– You're so big, and I'm small to begin with, and–" I have to crane my neck to look at him, leaning so far that my shaky legs drop me onto my butt with a grunt.

Noah's ears pop up in concern.

Before I can stand, the massive black wolf circles me, huffing hot air all over my body with his huge nose.

"Noah! What–?!" I giggle at his ticklish nose without meaning to, only cutting my laugh short with gasping, anxious breaths.

He stops at my hands, bloody from falling earlier. My nerves buzz throughout my palms as he gives them the softest lick he can manage. This has to be a dream, right? Noah's big, golden eyes peek at me before his tongue moves to my bloody knees. As I stare into them, I can't help but feel he's putting care into every lick.

When he's done, his massive head moves in. But I flinch. Seeing him this close, he could swallow me whole.

Noah pauses a few inches from my nose, analyzing my tense shoulders. My heart burns from how hard it pounds.

This day makes no sense whatsoever, but that doesn't stop Noah from being gorgeous. Layer upon layer of thick black fur frames golden eyes, his pitch-black nose blending with his snout. I want to memorize every strand of fur. Become one with them.

But Noah awaits my next move. His sweet, puppy-like stare kneads my heart muscles into action, protective instincts welling in me as he flashes the white beneath his irises.

I can't help myself; I sink my hands into the fluffy fur on top of his head.

He's softer than I expected. Goosebumps erupt across my entire body, begging to immerse more and more of my skin into Noah's downy fluff.

But that's not the best part; Noah's eyelids droop in bliss as I stroke him. My heart twirls.

As if he notices, his eyes laze open. They gaze deep into mine as I shift to scratching his cheeks. He looks so serious that my hands freeze.

Nudging his cheek against my palm, Noah easily brushes my hand from him.

My stomach drops. Was it rude to pet him without his permission?

"Sorry, did I–?"

I'm stunned as Noah nuzzles my palm back open until I hold it out for him. Noah's eyes glint with a reflective glow in the moonlight as he tilts his head, pressing the bridge of his snout into my palm. As he shuts his eyes, trusting me to touch him, my heart swells with emotion I didn't expect. I think this is as vulnerable for him as it is for me.

But this isn't close enough for Noah. My skin erupts in tingles as his warm, silky fur smushes against my forehead - his bowed head meeting mine. For a moment, all I can hear is his deep, gentle breath, coursing through his snout against the bridge of my nose.

I've been lonely for so long, but within minutes of meeting Noah, I feel valued. Just like Jenny said.

Whether I like it or not, tears stream. Noah's bright eyes pop open, breaking our intimate bubble. He nuzzles my cheeks until his wet nose douses me much worse than my eyes.

I break into shy laughter. "Sorry, I don't know what came over me. I'm okay."

But Noah doesn't buy it. After staring deep into my eyes, he whines. Wrapping his chin over my shoulder, Noah tucks me against his furry chest with a powerful scoot, and I give a small, surprised yelp. But once I'm enveloped in his scent, my shoulders drop.

He's so warm and fluffy. I'm wrapped in the biggest hug I've ever felt - comfort seeping through my ribcage until it spreads to every bone. I can't admit how badly I needed this.

Hiding my face in his dense fur, I shed silent tears. This is the first time I've let myself cry around a stranger in years. I thought I'd be more scared to be vulnerable, but he's so gentle that I relax in his warmth.

As my muscles soften against him, Noah lets out a soft, purring growl, tucking me closer. I close my eyes, soaking in his comfort as a wave of fresh emotion floods my soul. He's so sweet that I want to thank him, but I'm not sure how.

"You're so soft. And so warm. And you smell so good. It's nice." My cheeks burn the second I blurt out every compliment I can think of, forgetting to thank him in the first place. "And thank you! For protecting me. I feel much calmer, thanks to you."

Deep, thumping vibrations erupt from the ground, pulsing through my feet. A sharp spike of worry pierces through me, and I whip my head around - until I spot the source behind Noah.

"Oh, my God, are you wagging your enormous tail?" I giggle, and his tail thumps harder, kicking leaves in every direction.

When Noah snuffles my side with huffing, ticklish breaths, I let out a surprised squeal of laughter. But he nudges me toward his back, dipping a rippling, dense shoulder to my eye level.

"Do you… want me to get on your back?"

Noah looks me in the eyes with shy, tucked-back ears, and my heart flutters with adoration. Then he glances all around, the concern for our safety in his flickering focus.

He's right; safety is temporary out here. But I don't know how safe Noah is for me, either. I barely know him. Stranded in the forest like this, who knows where he could take me?

But my gut wants to trust him. Is that irrational?

The thought of rejecting those sweet eyes makes my chest ache, and I still want to know what Noah meant earlier. Why he looked upset to discover me, yet never left my side.

Oh, and why he's a wolf.

Yes, I've lost it. With how comforting Noah feels, I'd rather believe that shapeshifting humans exist than say this day is a new version of my recurring dream.

I scramble onto his broad back with an embarrassing grunt, not wanting to pull his silky black fur. Noah nudges me the rest of the way with his wet nose bumping my butt.

But once I'm 10 feet off the ground, I grip fistfuls of his coat. "Oh, my God! This is higher than I thought!"

Noah spins, attempting to look at me on his back, and I burst into laughter. He seems to like this, breaking into a smiling pant.

Oh, my heart. I want to squeeze him.

So I do, stretching my tiny arms across only half his back. I can feel his butt wiggling behind me from his happy tail, and I laugh. "For a big, tough wolf, you're actually super adora–"

I fall silent as Noah's fur stands on edge. His paws rigidify against the forest floor. Listening in, I can hear it too–distant, soft crunching in the leaves. Footsteps.

Noah's ribcage expands beneath my legs with a heightened breath. His tension ripples through me, leaving me quivering.

Without waiting another moment, Noah takes off. I cling on for dear life.

With his nose huffing against the forest floor, Noah finds a scent and breaks into an even deeper sprint.

"Noah, where are…?" I trail off, recognizing the mossy landmark tree I always pass when taking the long way home. "Wait, are you taking me home?"

Wind rushes my ears as we fly, forcing me to bury my nose into Noah's dense fur to keep my eyes from watering. His thick paws beat the earth, spraying dirt in every direction as we bound through the forest. It feels like I could fall off if I don't squeeze him with my entire body, jostling in this direction and that as leaves blur past my peripheral vision.

We've traveled at least a mile within minutes with how fast Noah claws across the forest floor. Noah's slinking figure slows, and I dare to look up.

My parents' old cottage rests in our land's small clearing, freshly trimmed roses lining the pathway to the chipped wooden stairs. Like always, my eyes catch on the half-painted number "1" on the weathered, baby blue siding, the only house Westfield developers had to number for miles.

"No way! You did bring me home!" My laughter makes Noah taller. "You're amazing!"

Noah's pant widens as he approaches my house, wagging his tail again. Circling my front porch with expert weaves through the roses, Noah kneels to the ground, helping me safely step off.

At least, I try to. I stumble on shaking legs from all the adrenaline, catching myself on poor Noah with his massive snout against my belly.

Hugging his snout, I'm face to face with him again. The urge gluing me to him bursts inside my chest once more, forcing me to suck in a shaky breath. When I look into his golden eyes, I can't convince myself to stop hoping he might be different from the rest.

This has to be a dream. All I've felt for years in my real life is hurt or fear.

Wait, what am I saying? He's a *wolf!*

As if I've tempted fate, I'm crushed to see Noah scurry into the woods the second I'm upright. His black fur blends into the night's blanketing darkness, and my heart snaps.

No matter how scared, confused, and exhausted I am, my words come out as a desperate scream. "Wait! Come back!"

5

I hold my breath, aching for a response. When Noah peeks from behind a tree, my eyes have to zip down to his human height.

He changed back.

There's no way this is real life. And if this isn't real, I might as well follow my heart.

Noah fidgets behind the tree, clearly uncomfortable. I can practically see his wolf ears slinked back to his head, but all that's left of his black fur is his dark, artfully messy hair and scruffy jawline.

His deep voice surprises me with how delicate it is. "Sorry, I– I had to shift, and…"

When he steps out a bit more, a flash of his bare, golden thigh catches my eye. My heart rate kicks up for a different reason, and Noah must notice, clearing his throat.

"I-I… I accidentally ripped my clothes."

"Oh! You're not leaving?"

"No… W-well, unless you want me to." His heart-crushing puppy dog eyes still appear in human form.

I bite back a smile. Is this the same wolf from earlier that made our attacker crumble into a shivering ball? He's so shy. He reminds me of my little preschooler students on their first day. And after teaching for three years now, I know the shy ones always end up being the silliest.

I dart up the porch steps. "Hang on, I'll find you something to wear."

Rushing through my front door, I quiver through every exhale. None of this feels real, but my body says otherwise – my hands and knees sting from falling, my feet kill, and my chest burns from leftover life-threatening stress. A part of me hopes my pain is proof this isn't a dream. I want Noah to be real.

Rifling through my drawers for the largest clothing I can find, covering Noah's bottom half seems trickiest. Poor Noah might have to squeeze in no matter what. Even in his human form, he's twice my size in width and a head taller.

I never let strangers touch my late father's clothing, but the gym shorts Dad gave me over twenty years ago have the least sentimental value. They don't even smell like him anymore. I bet Dad wouldn't approve of me lending these to a man I like, though.

I laugh, imagining Dad's stern worry-face that used to scare everyone but me. "Sorry, Dad."

Darting back down the hall, a part of me is terrified to open the front door and find Noah gone. If I want to protect my heart, I'll have to accept that possibility. It's true - he could leave, anytime. Of all people, I should understand that.

After taking a deep breath, I swing open the door.

Noah's head perks up from behind the side of my house, and I try to hide my relief.

"Here you go."

Noah takes the clothes with one massive hand. His grip encompasses clothes that took two palms for me to hold. It makes me realize how small I am compared to him, let alone when he unfurls my oversized shirt and it looks like children's clothing.

"Um, sorry, I can–"

"T-thanks for this," he says simultaneously.

We stare in silence. I expect him to return my clothes, but when Noah disappears beyond my cottage's siding, I don't know if he understood I was offering to find something else, or if I should speak up a second time.

Words escape me as he sidesteps past the cottage's cover and I catch an expanded glance at his thigh. No, not his thigh. That's his ass, Aliya. My heartbeat ticks into the roof of my mouth.

He slips the shorts over one foot, cussing and disappearing behind the cottage. All at once, I realize I'm gawking at this poor stranger changing and I avert my eyes.

I need to get a hold of myself. Why am I so drawn to him?

My heart pounds into my ears, unsure if Noah caught me. But stepping into view, Noah gives me a soft smile. Then my eyes catch on his built chest - threatening to burst from my tight shirt.

I gasp. "Oh, gosh, I'm sorry–"

"No, it's perfect. Thank you."

It's not perfect, and we both know it. But with a delicate touch on my back, Noah guides me onto my porch. I follow with more curiosity than concern; I was already hoping he'd join me inside anyway. But when I open my front door, Noah stops at the threshold.

"There's… Something I didn't get to say yet." He won't meet my eyes, staring at my muddy teaching sneakers as he shuffles before my doorway. "You asked if I was rejecting y-you?"

"Oh. Yes." My speeding heartbeat threatens to implode.

Noah shakes his head, struggling to steady his breath. "I-I'm not. And I wasn't. I'd never–" Noah swallows hard. "I know I'm not good with words, b-but I have a lot to say, and…"

He's anxious. I want to comfort him like he comforted me.

Running my fingertips down his arm, I give Noah a reassuring smile. "It's okay, Noah. You're doing great."

Noah opens his arms for a hug. I'm lightheaded from my anxious heartbeat, but I step closer to his chest anyway. He doesn't waste a second before embracing me, cuddling his head against mine.

"Thank you." Noah boops my neck with his nose, and my heart soars. "I'm just worried I'm scaring you more. You haven't stopped shaking."

He's right – my teeth are chattering with nerves.

"Maybe we can continue this tomorrow, after you've rested?" Noah asks.

He pulls away to give me space, but my heart screams not to let him go, even an inch.

Okay, heart. I think it's time I listen.

I rush back into his chest, throwing my arms around him. "Please, don't go. Stay with me tonight."

Noah exhales. "Oh, thank the Goddess."

He wraps bulky arms around me, pressing my forehead to his thumping heart. I can't believe this. His heartbeat says this is just as beautifully overwhelming for him, but I don't get the sense it's for the possibility of sex. Noah strokes my hair until my breathing slows.

Trauma roadblocks my freedom to trust, so I'm not used to experiencing instant attraction. But pressing against Noah stirs sensations I can't deny.

I shift my feet, trying to stifle the flash of heat pulsing through my groin. But the second I do so, Noah's eyes zip to mine. They're heavy-lidded, and I can guess he feels similarly by the bulge emerging against my stomach.

I would've had sex with Noah in the forest, right then and there. I think he would've too. But his eyes aren't hunting for sex as we gaze at each other. They're relishing in me.

His wide thumbpad moves from stroking my hair to petting my cheek, pausing beside my lips. His cheeks burn bright red, but his stoic expression tells me he wants me. Especially as his eyes dart to my lips.

My lips part on their own, desperate to taste his. And I want him to know it.

Noah sucks in a surprised breath as my hand raises toward his neck. I wait for him to pull away, but he's motionless, waiting despite his heart pounding against my ear.

But his eyes widen. "Wait."

I freeze. "Did you not like it before?"

"N-no, I… I did." He can't bear to hold eye contact. "But I have to know if you realize what you're doing so I know this is what you want."

My lungs tense. Did I break some sort of wolf code?

His golden cheeks awash in red as he stares at my neck. I'm itching for him to touch me there, but he points to his neck instead.

"This is a scent gland." His fingertips trail just behind his jugular vein. Goosebumps erupt down my chest just watching him, but they double when I'm hit with a fresh wave of his sweet, delectable scent. My limbs loosen, allowing him to hold even more of my weight against his chest.

Wait, his scent *meant* to soothe me, didn't it?

I'm still reeling with delicious relaxation when Noah says something I don't expect.

"It feels good because… B-because mates bite each other there, leaving a scarred mark to seal their bond." His voice softens until he's barely audible. But I heard him, latching onto every word.

As the gravity of that scent gland sinks in, my body ignites with an even deeper hunger to touch that place on his neck.

"So when I touch there, that tells you I want to feel bonded with you?" I whisper.

He bites his lips, nervous eyes glancing between mine. "Yes. But marking with a bite is a bit deeper than *feeling* bonded. Mate bonds are tangible. You'll feel me, I'll feel you. Kind of like sewing our souls together. B-but - um - for life."

I've never made lifetime commitments to anyone.

But the urge in me screams, *This is what I've always wanted.*

If I went back in time and sat beside myself in Jenny's office a couple hours ago, I'd never believe I'd fall for someone tonight. But me, considering committing myself to Noah, for life? Something *has* to be wrong with me.

But I have to be dreaming anyway, right? What if - just this time - I let myself chase my deepest desires? Follow them, instead of pushing them away to make others happy?

I lift my hand again, awaiting Noah's permission to touch that luscious gland. His breath picks up, but as he stares into my eyes, he lifts the corner of his jaw. My heart skips. He's certain about allowing me to do this. Bonding with me.

I trace a gentle line down the sensitive gland. Staring at him, I hope he can feel it. How risky it is to free my heart.

Noah's eyelashes flutter in delight, which gives *me* butterflies. My cheek rises against his chest as he draws a slow, heavy inhale, indulging in every second of my touch. But before the third time I stroke him there, he moves in.

Noah's hand scoops behind my neck, pulling me into a deep kiss. The lungful I have to suck in to stay upright makes me almost as dizzy as his lips - my stomach catapulted into my throat. A flurry of electricity shoots from his warm palm behind my head to my toes. I grip fistfuls of his stretched shirt, and Noah tilts his head to kiss me deeper, his lips' full weight close to bursting my

heart. A small moan escapes me, and Noah pulls back to look me in the eyes.

His pupils are huge, and his cheeks are flushed. What do I look like right now? I'm so turned on that I probably wouldn't recognize myself.

But I want Noah. My *mate*.

I lean in to kiss him again, and Noah cuddles me tighter, squeezing our bodies flush as he kisses me back. My hips press against his thigh on instinct, eager for pressure, and Noah rasps through a tight breath.

He snaps back. His eyes are wilder than his hair, tracing my body in his arms. "Y-you smell too good. We have to go inside."

"Wait, what–?"

Noah pulls me inside after him, dropping his broad back against the creaky cottage door to close it. I struggle to catch my breath from pure overwhelm, gazing into the eyes of the most beautiful man I've ever met as my lips buzz from his phantom touch.

But Noah doesn't seem to want to continue kissing, drawing me to his chest much gentler this time.

"You still seem nervous," he says.

It's true. I haven't been this intimate with a stranger. With how much my college peers acted like hookups were the expected norm at 19, I feel like I seem immature to never have experienced a hookup at 29. Really, I'm scared of being hurt again if I sleep with someone on day one.

But should I be even more vulnerable with Noah and tell him that?

"I'm sorry, I'm just a bit cautious." My stomach churns, but the concern in Noah's eyes makes me whisper the truth. "About being hurt again. And it's nothing about you, it's just– When you see a pattern in life, it's dangerous not to pay attention. At least, that's what I've learned. A-and I didn't know if we'd…"

I glance toward my bedroom, swallowing hard.

Noah's breath is just as short as mine, his sharp eyes zipping back to me after catching on the bra I left on the hallway floor. "Don't apologize. You're my mate. I don't want to do anything you're not interested in."

My heart twinges. "I *am* interested, I'm just anxious."

Noah is silent for a moment. "I'm anxious too."

I feel like he wants to tell me more.

I guide him to my couch by the hand. Three steps in, I trip over my scrapbooking mess from the night before, ready to meet my doom as the coffee table's glass top inches closer by the millisecond. But Noah tucks me to his side like it's the easiest thing he's done all night, righting me on my feet with one arm. I flush, but then I see his shy, flustered glance and my embarrassment washes away.

He's so damn cute. I'm dying to reassure him.

"Is there something we're doing that's making you anxious?"

Already sitting, Noah gazes up at me as I say those words. It has a heavy effect on him, his face reddening by the second.

A smile peeks from his stoic lips. "I want to tell you more, but please, feel free to sit with me."

He's right. I'm hesitating, unsure how close he'll want me to sit beside him and awkwardly hovering my butt over the cushions. I'm relieved to see his amused smile and break into giggles.

When his arm wraps around me from behind, tucking me into his side, I burst into laughter, huddling closer. Noah squeezes me tight, and I welcome his embrace as I lay against his chest.

His poor heart is still pounding. At least I'm not alone.

Noah clears his throat. "It's just... Wolves are all instinct, but I know humans need longer to feel comfortable with bonding for life. And I want to respect your boundaries. You were raised as a human, right?"

The way he phrased that is weird...

Peeking at my furrowed expression, Noah softens. "That's part of what I wanted to tell you. Wolves don't always like humans - too many hunters. My initial reaction wasn't about rejecting you. I was afraid that my pack - everyone I care about - wouldn't accept my mate. I hate that I'll be putting you through that, just by my position, and–" Noah's jaw twitches. "Well, it'll probably be a fight. If you'd eventually like to be with me, I'll welcome you into my life, no matter what they think."

My heart scrambles until I'm dizzy. But I haven't felt this

elated in years. Whatever expression I'm making, Noah smiles the sweetest smile.

"D-do you have any questions, sweet Omega?"

"Yes. But my name's Aliya, not Omega."

Noah's head drops to his lap, burying his face in his palm before I can see his full smile. "Sorry… A-Aliya."

My whispered name makes me suck in a deep breath. Noah pauses, having to catch his own.

When I don't say anything, he speaks even softer. "I-I just registered you as my Omega the second we met, but I'm sorry, I shouldn't have called you that without even asking your name - what a fail." He groans, and I can't help but giggle. Soon enough, we're laughing together. "I-it's just, you smell really sweet. Like the sweetest Omega alive, but you're also sweet, as in kindhearted, so I just thought…"

That's how he perceives me? I don't know what an Omega means to him since I only know some people used to claim it's the lowest wolf pack rank, but the way Noah says it makes me feel like it means something beautiful. If wolf hearing is a thing, Noah can hear my hammering heart.

But when he doesn't come back out from his makeshift hiding place, I lift the edge of his palm with my pointer finger. "You really are a shy wolf. My… what did you call yourself? My Alpha?"

Noah slams his palm shut again, curling lower with a groan. "Fuck, you're so cute. I don't know what to do."

I burst out laughing. The sound breaks Noah's red face free from his palm, but an eagerness in his stare steals my breath. I'm bombarded with a hug, his head rubbing into my shoulder until I laugh even harder.

"Is this because I called you my Alpha?"

"Y-yes. I never thought someone would call me that."

"Never? But I thought that meant you were my pack leader, so to speak. Aren't Alphas the dominant wolf?"

Noah was already shaking his head "no" before I finished talking. "Not always. Traditional wolves act like it's a hard-wired wolf sex based on reproductive organs - that wolves with balls are dominant Alphas and wolves with a uterus are submissive Omegas."

My stomach churns. Wolves sound as sexist as humans.

But Noah, an Alpha likely steeped in patriarchal belief systems since birth, rolls his eyes. "I've met plenty of wolves, and trust me, it's way more complex. It's more like our inner wolf's personality trait, except our personalities boost the smell we give off. I mainly give off Alpha pheromones, meaning I'm more impulsive and protective about everything I care about. There are also Betas with blended pheromones. They tend to be resilient mediators. But you smell more like an Omega, most likely making you more calculated and aware of the whole picture. Thoughtful, warm, and comforting, by instinct."

I'm surprised by how much this prompted Noah to speak. Not only speak, but also speak from his heart. I can hear it in his steadied voice.

But Noah's brows pinch, his stare dropping to his knees. "Some people want to call Omegas docile, but I think that's unfair. I think they're forced to be scared of Alphas to survive, and unfortunately, a lot of Alphas want to keep it that way. So no, I'm *not* your leader. That's not what this is."

I understand what he means about Alphas forcing Omegas into survival mode. Human men like Steven used the same concepts against me, a human woman.

But today feels different. Noah isn't telling me what he thinks I want to hear to win over my trust; he knows nothing of my history, and his thoughts on Omegas were unprompted. He could've easily said yes, he's the dominant one, and I'm required to submit to him in the wolf world. But he told me the truth – many Alphas assume dominance over Omegas, and he's aware of our implied power imbalance. He's been actively combatting that imbalance since we met, even when I knew nothing about it.

Trust unlocks a new chamber in my heart. One I never thought I'd let a man see.

"Are wolves just as homophobic as humans too?" I mutter.

My eyes widen. I didn't think that one through before blurting it out. What if he has no idea what I mean?

But Noah breathes out an airy chuckle. "Now you sound like me. It's hard to say, though. Our pack seems more open compared to what I've heard about most human societies, but there's still a social expectation for Alphas and Omegas to be mated." He glances at me warily. "B-but I– I never pictured myself as an Omega's Alpha. Just *someone's* Alpha."

I can't contain my smile. "Now you sound like me too. I'm bisexual."

His shoulders loosen, allowing him to sink deeper into my couch like I just offloaded a boulder from his arms.

My heart stings at how relieved he seems. I can only imagine he's had years of painful misunderstandings around disclosing his sexuality, just like me.

I huddle in closer, hoping it soothes his heart. "So you're my Alpha, as in *my* Alpha mate? You never thought you'd find your mate?"

"Not after e-*everyone* else I grew up with found their mates, and I'm already 31. Especially not a mate anywhere close to–" He dares to peek at me for a mere second. "To someone *gorgeous*, like you."

The second he says it, I know he means more than my body. I've never felt such a rush of adoring yet soothing emotions, every atom of me whispering, *You're safe. He's safe.*

I grip his hand, whispering raw truths before I hide them away again. "Noah, how much I want you scares me. After the life experiences I've had, it's hard for me to open up. But something about you makes me want to be vulnerable… With my shy Alpha."

Noah's sweet, flustered stare flips my heart.

"But I'm not used to these feelings," I blurt out. "To the point where it's safer to believe you'll hurt me. Because then, I won't be disappointed if you use your power to take advantage of me too. If you walk out that door when you're done with me, knowing it'll leave me behind with nothing."

Noah lets out a pained breath, stroking my cheek.

I can't believe I just said all that. Even weirder, that was surprisingly easy to confess. Noah is fully listening, focused on every word with furrowed eyebrows.

"You don't have to trust me yet," he says. "I'm here now, either way. You're safe."

Tears slip down Noah's thumb on my cheek. But my smile bursts across my face just the same.

I feel it. I don't understand how it's possible, but I feel it, nonetheless. I feel safe.

Noah kisses my forehead before drawing me lower on the couch to lie beside him. "Let's j-just hold each other for tonight."

"I'd like that."

Snuggling into his chest, I squeeze him closer just to feel him squeezing back. With every pulse of his heartbeat against my forehead, every slow expansion of his ribs beneath my arms, I relax.

His scent washes over me as he plants a soft kiss on my neck, sending electricity through me. This time, his kiss there doesn't feel sexual. I feel loved.

Curling up with my arms hugged to my chest, I allow Noah to cocoon me. His warm, sweet scent lulls me to sleep.

The next morning, I wake up to find Noah nowhere in sight.

6

At first, I wonder if any of it was real, flushing with embarrassment as I replay the way I acted. The irrational, impulsive things I confessed.

But the clothes I'm squeezing to my chest are proof; my oversized shirt is stretched a size further.

Noah *did* wear this. I draw the shirt to my nose, struggling to slow my breath enough to inhale the fabric's scent.

It smells like him. Sweet, but leafy from all that running we did through the forest.

Noah is real.

Which means everything I did was real.

Oh, God. I don't understand how assertive I became, taking charge of my desires. Why I felt so strongly for a stranger. No, why I *still* feel strongly.

My gut churns as heat pulses in my groin - an ache for touch that hasn't gone away since last night. It dawns on me that it wasn't just a spur-of-the-moment fling; I would've had sex with a stranger last night. I almost did.

That's the most vulnerable I've been with my body since Steven hurt me.

But after how much I told Noah it would hurt me if he left after I opened up, he still left. He's *gone.*

Sobs rip from my throat, startling me with their intensity. Anxiety and heartbreak burn throughout my limbs as I hunt around my parents' living room for any other trace of him. Scrambling around the couch, I throw flowery couch cushions, chunky knitted blankets, and well-loved, sauce-stained pillows to the floor in search of something, *anything*. But Noah left no visible trace beyond the clothes he borrowed. Not even his number.

Does this mean he left, never expecting to come back?

I whimper through tight breaths, feeling ridiculous for everything I believed and did last night. I took a risk in accepting this love-at-first-sight thing, and one of my worst possible outcomes came from it. It fucking kills. I wobble, gripping my heart as it aches with every beat.

I'm so hot that the room spins, threatening to topple me over. It burns. *Everything* burns. I strip my clothes in a fit of discomfort, afraid I'll pass out if I don't lower my temperature fast. But as I stand shaking in my living room in my bra and panties, I only burn hotter, doubling over in pain as it wreaks havoc in my guts.

I feel sick enough to die. Am I losing it? It's starting to feel dangerous to be alone. What if I pass out and hit my head?

I call Jenny without questioning it.

Until the dial tone rings. What the hell am I going to tell her? That I got lost, met a man I almost fucked in the leaves, and brought him home? That I thought the dream *came true?*

She answers on the second ring, and I bite my thumb, knowing I have no time left to think.

"Hello, my dear! How's it going?"

"It's– Well, it *was* going well–"

Jenny loses her singsong cheeriness. "Are you safe? You don't sound okay at all."

I struggle to breathe deep enough to speak. "I'm safe. I'm just feeling really sick, and I'm panicking."

"Okay, let's talk through this. Are you resting comfortably?"

"No…"

"Let's start with that. Why don't you grab some water and a blanket to help yourself relax."

I grip Noah's borrowed clothes on instinct, curling up with them on the couch. "Okay. I already have water."

"Okay, great! So what are you thinking about that's bringing up some panic?"

I take a deep, shuddering breath. Inadvertently, I inhale a wave of Noah's scent, and that single whiff stops me from shaking.

He's important; even my body knows it. If I'm honest about

Noah, Jenny might never believe me. But I don't want to lie to her either.

"I met a man last night," I mutter. The silence on the other line sends my breath into a sprint. "I thought it was something real. Even deeper than my dream. But I woke up and he–" My tears choke me out. "H-he was gone."

"Oh, honey... Did he hurt you or coerce you?" Jenny's aching voice inspires fresh tears.

"No. I'm just hurt emotionally, now that he's not here."

"Is that why you're feeling sick?"

"No, I– Well, it could be from stress, but I think I have a bad fever. It's making me dizzy."

I'm too embarrassed to tell her that I'm also horny as hell.

Which is really why this fever feels worse. Every time I think of Noah, another wave of heat hits my body. I'm so sexually frustrated that it hurts - my hips squirming on the couch with pounding pain deep enough to make me nauseous. But I feel way too sick to do anything about it. Even more ridiculous, my body screams to let Noah - *only* Noah - do something about it. But what if he's gone, forever? I whimper, crying even harder.

"What about Amy?" Jenny asks. "Could she come check on you?"

"Yes, I could call her."

"Great! Let's have you do that, and then text me what happens."

"Thank you, Jenny."

"Keep me updated. Promise?"

"I promise." Even though I have no way of explaining this to her.

Before I can land myself in ruminating hell, I call my best friend.

Amy's familiar pep softens my breath. "Hey, girl! What's up so early on a Saturday?! You're usually dead asleep if I try to call!"

"Hi, Amy."

"Whoa, are you okay?" Her voice darkens. "Do I need to come over there and kick someone's ass?"

I smile through tears, inhaling a deep breath of Noah's scent. "I'm sorry to ruin your anniversary weekend. I'm just not feeling well."

"Oh no, like how?"

I need to tell someone about Noah, or I'm going to lose it. Thankfully, Amy has seen me lose it before.

"A., I met someone. Someone I thought was my soulmate." My sobs hitch, warping into bawling. "But now all he left was the clothes he borrowed, and they smell so good, but…"

"Wait, hold up. You had sex with him?!"

"No! But I wanted to! Can you believe that, Amy?"

"I mean, no, to be honest." Amy's shock only makes me cry harder.

"And it's super embarrassing, but I feel *horrible* now that we didn't have sex. I've never felt like this."

Amy falls silent. It's so out of character that it heightens my nerves. Then I hear her clunky hiking boots dash across her wooden floor. "Horrible like how, babe? Sexually frustrated?"

"Yeah… But not in a normal way. It hurts so badly that I feel like I'll *die* if he never comes back." I slap my forehead with a groan. "Oh, God. That's the most toxically attached thing I've ever said!"

Amy doesn't respond for a good ten seconds. Did I just make a fool of myself?

Concern lowers Amy's voice when she finally speaks. "Hun, do you happen to have a fever? Like the worst fever of your life?"

"I think so… Why?"

She pauses for a long time. I grip my phone hard enough to dent my fingers with its edge.

When Amy speaks again, her voice is gentle and even. "I might know what's going on with you, but I have to come over and see it for myself. I'm leaving right now."

"Really? God, thank you. I feel really sick and scared, Amy. I don't know what I'll do if he never comes back."

"Don't move. Kira and I will be there in a heartbeat, okay?"

I burst into another bout of sobbing as I hang up, guilt crushing my chest for putting my problems on someone else. I can't believe I got myself into this mess. Why couldn't I just have a simple crush? This whole "mate" thing sounds ridiculous.

But I believe it - he's my mate. I can't get myself to not believe it. It's making me so sick.

7

Amy shows up faster than she ever has, pounding on my door within 10 minutes. "Hey, babe! We're here!"

But I swear I heard her at home, and it takes 30 minutes by car to get here. How is that even possible?

"Come in," I say.

Amy and Kira rush into the cottage, their eyes widening at the state of my search's destructive mess before finally finding me in it - shaking in pounding pain as I rise from the couch.

With silky, shoulder-length red hair framing her round cheeks, Amy looks beautiful even as her eyebrows warp in sorrow. But she still gives me the wide smile I've known and loved my whole life. "Hey, girl! Not doing too well, huh?"

"Hey, were you already on this side of town? How did you...?"

I trail off, stunned by the sudden, wide-eyed expression in Amy and Kira's faces as they close the door.

Kira tenses, her short, baby blue hair fading at the roots - probably after having pool sex with Amy all night. I cringe at the thought, desperate for some pool sex of my own.

Kira scrunches her nose. "Fuck, Amy. Those pheromones."

"I know. I recognize it from someone who does perimeter runs, but I have no idea who. He must be pretty powerful. Do you think–?"

Amy eyes Kira warily, but my jaw drops. Am I delirious, or are they talking about Noah?

"We're safe. That's not it." Kira grits her teeth. "It's a different... *intoxicating* smell."

Amy grips Kira's arm. "Oh, shit. Are you going to be okay?"

"Yes, but I'm dead serious when I say I had no idea about her."

Now they're both staring at me.

Amy swallows hard. "I... I can't believe this either, so…"

I grip Noah's shirt to my chest. "B-believe what? You're freaking me out."

Amy steadies my dizzy body, helping me lay back down. "I'm sorry, A., it's just… I don't know how this fever thing hasn't happened before for you."

Kira keeps her distance with a wide circle through my kitchen. Her voice is oddly rigid. "I'll get her some cool washcloths."

Amy smiles. "Thanks, babe."

After making me drink water, Amy tests my temperature with her hand against my forehead. My head spins. Hugging the shirt Noah wore to my chest, I take a deep breath of the fabric, aching for his presence.

Heat swells in my core. My untouched arousal rises until my stomach gurgles in pain. I try my best to hide it, but I have to squeeze my knees together, arching my back in discomfort.

Amy holds my hand, pressing my cold water glass against my cheek. "I know you're uncomfortable, babe. I'm so sorry your guy isn't here. It hurts a lot without him, doesn't it?"

What the hell? For how confusing this is, Amy isn't asking enough questions.

"Amy, what's wrong with me? What do you know?"

Amy groans, rubbing her head. "Thank God I can tell you all about it in a minute! You're so damn perceptive, and I love you for it, but it's really difficult too, you know? Your guy better not try to hide anything from you. It'll never work."

I whimper, realizing by "my guy," Amy means Noah. "If he even comes back…"

"Oh, he's coming back. Believe me."

I grip the couch. "What?! How do you know?"

"His scent is everywhere. I'm surprised he left today at all, but this tells me he must've had to run for a huge reason."

God, I hope she's right, but not if that means something bad happened to him to make him leave.

"Wait, you can smell him too?"

Amy stares for a moment, sorting out my hair. "You're pretty deep into this fever thing you've got going here, A. I want to explain some things to you before it fully hits, so pay close attention, okay?"

Sweat drips down my temple as I squirm again, my heartbeat pulsing between my legs. "It's going to get *worse?*"

"I'm so sorry, but yes. I'll be here the whole way through, though."

"Amy, you're starting to freak me out. I don't feel like any of this is real."

Taking my hand, Amy clears her throat. "Does the word 'mate' mean anything to you?"

I recoil where I lay, uncomfortable by the rising urge in my core strengthening at the word "mate" alone. "You're scaring me, Amy."

"I know you better than that. You know exactly what I'm saying, you just haven't processed it enough yet to admit it."

I swallow hard, feeling painfully called out. But a part of me is dying to hear more. For this to be real.

Amy strokes my hand. "I love you, okay? I just want you to know the truth."

I nod, my desperation to hear more winning over anything else. "I love you too."

Whatever the truth is, it makes Amy take a deep, shaky breath. "Do you remember that trip your dad would take every month? He'd go hunting for something special to cook?"

"Yes."

"Do you happen to know which day he'd go?"

I think about it, long and hard...

But the words "long" and "hard" remind me of something else. Dammit, I need to focus!

"I don't know. My dad's trips never really lined up on the same day of the week or month, I guess."

"That's because it was on a full moon. Your dad was a werewolf, hun."

As if this is a rational explanation, Amy gazes into my eyes for a response.

"Well, wait, that's what I'd tell a human, but it's not exactly right. He was a Lycan. And he had to go wolf out somewhere else.

But Lycans don't spiral out of control like fictional werewolves, so it's not the way you're probably thinking. It was for a cultural ceremony we hold every Full Moon, and..." Amy trails off, frantically searching my expression. "Sorry. I'm getting ahead of myself."

I gape at Amy, unsure whether this is some cruel joke.

But I didn't tell her about the wolves from yesterday... at all.

"Amy, what are you talking about? Werewolves - well, Lycans - don't exist... Do they?" I swallow hard, well aware of the shapeshifting man I met last night.

No, last night couldn't have been real. This has to be a long, continuous dream.

Amy raises her eyebrows. "So you *didn't* see any wolves last night? You didn't find your fated mate, and he didn't tell or show you he could shapeshift into a wolf?"

"I... I didn't say that. It's like you said - I just can't believe it. Especially because—" My body stings with how hard my blood surges. "Why wouldn't my parents tell me something that huge? And if my dad was a Lycan, and he was as giant as those wolves I saw, who could've been strong enough to take him from us, Amy?"

Amy's eyebrows arch, reflecting my sorrow, and I have to fight back fresh sobs. "Aliya, I'm *so* sorry, truly. It wasn't fair."

I angrily swipe at my tears. "Are you trying to say you're not human either?"

"Nope, I'm not. Neither is Kira."

My gut burns. With how much has lined up in the past 24 hours, I'm starting to believe her. To believe everything.

But to believe is to accept I've been kept in the dark my entire life.

With one look at Amy, my crying warps into hot anger. We're supposed to be the two A's, sharing everything and more than our first initials.

My voice heightens despite warping into gutted tears. "What else are you hiding from me, then? I thought we didn't keep big secrets."

Amy shuffles in her seat, her eyes widening in panic. "I know, which is why before this goes any further, let me make this clear:

I *never* wanted to keep this from you. If I didn't think it was for your safety, I'd say 'fuck it' and tell you anyway." Her tight grip on my hand tells me she's serious. "And the same went for your parents. If they knew this would happen to you, your parents would've told you. I know it. They didn't expect to die either. But your dad was killed by hunters."

"I know that…"

"But you don't know everything. He wasn't out hunting like you think he was, getting shot by mistake."

I'm ready to freak out. "What do you mean he wasn't out hunting?! You didn't think to tell me how my own father died?"

"It's not like that, Aliya! You know the truth, just not the wolfy stuff!" She huffs in panic, and I sit back, stifling my rage.

I want to believe her, but how can I?

"A., please, listen. Human curiosity is too deadly to tempt, and I'd never want to put you in danger." Amy shakes her head with bulging eyes, reading the doubt on my face. "All those hunters saw was a huge wolf on the run, and rather than staying curious, they stole him from us. 'Curious' humans made a split-second, permanent decision that changed *everything*."

She swallows hard at my angry, pathetic whimper. I don't know who I'm mad at anymore. Life, maybe.

Amy softens her tone, unable to keep looking me in the eyes. "This is exactly why wolves keep it a secret, even from your best friend. It was your parents' choice while they were alive, but after your dad died, I was so terrified you could die from either side's fear and prejudice that I realized why they did it. That could've been *me*. Fuck, that could've been *you*, getting shot by proxy." Amy grips her head, her voice shaking. "I've had nightmares of you getting stripped away from me for our differences, A., even when we were kids. I'm lucky I got to be by your side at all."

I feel sick. When Dad died, nothing added up. He could spot birds from distances I could never, follow any invisible trail in the forest to get us home, and hear a thousand times better than me. How could he not notice a hunter nearby and warn them that he was also hunting so he wouldn't get shot? Killed.

But if he was a Lycan - shifted into a wolf, like Noah - it

51

makes more sense why someone shot him. He was just another beast to display on their wall.

Or was that really all it was?

Fuck, I sound irrational again. Jenny, Amy, and Kira were gentle about it after Mom died, but no one believed me when I thought Dad was murdered on purpose, chalking my theories up to grief. Absolutely *no one* will believe it this time, now that I know he was a wolf being literally hunted.

But it just doesn't feel right.

Although, I do believe Amy's wide, petrified stare. Even if her explanation sounds like an irrational, imaginary tale, it's *her* truth.

"You smell too much like a human for Lycans to not see you as a serious threat to their safety. I have no idea what they could do to you, and there was no reason to risk it and find out." Amy winces as tears brim. "But I should've given you a choice somehow. I'm so sorry, Aliya. I fucked up. You don't have to forgive me, but please know I just wanted to keep you alive and by my side."

I never understood why my parents appeared so torn the first day I clung to Amy's side after school, but it's sinking in now. She was a wolf. A ticking bomb if she spilled the truth.

But she's always been the only friend who understood my heart. Why even back then, the disapproval in my parents' eyes gutted me, lapsing me into horrific, ear-piercing wails when I thought they'd never let me see her again.

They let me have her, and I never let go.

But neither did Amy. She kept this a secret: choosing to stay by my side too.

"I couldn't risk losing you, even if there was only a chance," Amy whispers.

I grip Amy's hand to pull her closer, part of me still afraid to lose her. "I'm still hurt, but I love you."

Amy dissolves into tears. "I love you too."

We huddle together, a mess of soft sniffles as my overwhelming body heat boils us both. After a silent minute, Amy pulls back, testing my forehead with worry straining her eyes.

Tears scrape my throat when I try to speak. "Did my mom die thinking he was shot by mistake too?"

"No, but... Your poor mom..." Amy's voice shakes as much as

mine. "You've always been right by saying she died of heartbreak. It's unlivable to lose a mate. Wolves are tied down to the soul."

I swallow hard, graphic memories of Mom's rapid decline searing my heart. "I've always thought it was like my dad's death took her soul with him."

"See? You're so damn smart, girl. You knew this stuff all along, just in different words." Amy squeezes my hand as I finally let myself crumble.

"But does that mean my mom...? Was she also a... Lycan?"

"No, she was a human. But she was your dad's fated mate. It's so rare that the wolves didn't accept her at first. Or maybe they never truly did. I can only assume your parents lived outside of pack territory due to speciesism."

My eyes widen, a glimpse of last night flashing past my eyes. "Just like Noah said might happen..."

Amy's eyes bulge. "Did you just say *Noah?*"

"Yes? He's– um... The guy I'm hoping comes back. My... Alpha."

Amy gapes, sending a fresh wave of numbing anxiety down my limbs. "Oh, girl... Noah's not just *your* Alpha. He's *the* Alpha."

My heart leaps into my throat. "What do you mean?"

"I knew whoever dumped his scent all over this place was powerful, but no wonder I couldn't recognize him; he's swamped with pack problems and supposedly super shy, so it's rare to catch a glimpse of him. I've never met him up close. He's the Greenfield territory's pack leader. *My* pack leader. Kira's pack leader..." Amy throws her head back, letting out a dramatic sigh. "Thank the Goddess! If he's your mate, this changes everything. You'll be safe if you're with our top Alpha."

My eyes widen with Amy's every word. Amy winces, giving me a moment to process, but I can't get over what she just said.

"He really *was* the pack leader? He told me Alphas weren't necessarily leaders, so it wasn't what this was between us..."

Amy breaks into a soft smile. "Oh, that's Alpha Noah, alright. He wanted you to know he sees you as his equal when, historically, Alphas like to believe they're destined for dominance, even over mates. It's a bit patriarchal if you ask me."

Just before I freak out at the thought of Noah domineering like Steven, Amy smirks.

"Not your Alpha, though. He's pretty outspoken in hating Alpha domination, actually."

My heart flips. Everything Amy is saying rings true to Noah's words. "But it sounds like he still happened to be the pack leader?"

"He's *strong*. No one here can dethrone him, so he's the natural leader. But I think it's a Greenfield family thing to be powerful as hell." Amy's smile fades. "Noah took over the pack after his dad passed... Ritchie Greenfield."

I jolt upright, struggling to contain my rapid breath as my heart shatters.

My dad and Ritchie Greenfield were shot on that hunting trip, side-by-side. Noah had to experience this grief too?

But our dads were best friends, as tight-knit as Amy and me. "How the hell did I never meet Noah before?"

"All we knew was that you were a hybrid, but you never shifted into a wolf, so we had to protect you from both the pack and human hunters." Amy rubs my arm as I groan, my head spinning. "We figured you were mostly human. Maybe entirely human. But after what I'm seeing right now... I think we were wrong."

As Amy says those words, it finally sinks in - the piece of this story that isn't adding up.

I already suspect the answer, but with how impossible it sounds, I ask the question anyway to be sure.

"Me... What about me?"

My heart pounds as Amy searches my eyes. "A., why do you think I decided to tell you this today? When before this, I couldn't tell you, only because–"

"You thought I was human." I shudder, the truth exploding from my chest - just like the moment I knew Noah was my mate.

My mind flashes through my entire life. That feeling something was always wrong with me, but I never knew what. All those moments my human authority figures berated me for being too loud. Too unruly. Too unladylike.

Until I became quiet. Shy.

Domesticated.

"Amy, oh, my God... I'm a wolf."

Brushing my messy hair from my face, Amy looks me straight in the eyes. "I think you're more Lycan than anything. And you're in heat."

My rapid breath turns into stressed whimpers, unsure of what she means. "Like... a cat?"

"More like a wolf." Amy grins. "But cats are similar. You'll be craving to mate with Noah, and it might be uncomfortable for a while."

I gasp through panic. "A *while*? What about my kids? I can't teach preschool like this." But heat is all I can focus on, my body boiling to the point of delirium. "I don't know how I'll survive this, Amy."

She grounds me with a sharp stare. "Listen to me closely, okay? Lycans can shapeshift, but only into their wolf. Our wolves are stable, individual beings - like alternate versions of ourselves with fairly strong opinions and personalities. Do you feel your wolf yet?"

"I don't know. How can I tell?"

"My wolf feels like another side of me. A wild, unfiltered side that's all gut instinct."

In a rapid replay of my life - how much I stifled myself as a child and still continue to - I wonder if any wild, unfiltered side of me still exists.

"Amy, what if I killed her?"

She giggles, giving me a soft smile. "Trust me, she's there. I smell her, and she's absolutely an Omega in heat. But she'll be strong enough to dramatically alter your behavior, and I don't know how you'll feel about that."

I whimper, gripping my arms. "Not good, obviously."

Amy smooths my hair, staring deep into my eyes with such worried eyebrows that I wish I could massage them back into tranquility.

"You have to keep listening closely, Aliya. Your wolf will want Noah to mark you - biting your neck to seal your mate connection."

The urge pounds deeper. My nails dig into my thighs, imagining Noah's teeth piercing my neck in vivid detail.

"He told me about that, and I... I can't get enough of it."

"Hey, stay with me." Amy redirects my focus, hardening her tone. "Knowing you, you'll need more time for a lifetime commitment. Do post-heat you a favor - do *not* let him mark you today."

My heart throbs, torn on what to do. When I had a clearer head yesterday, I wanted to trade marks with Noah. But now I'm stressed as hell. Amy's right - this could've been my silly heart talking all along, ignoring what's truly right for me. My heart and brain will have to battle this one out, and I won't win either way.

Amy frowns at my obvious disappointment. "Come here, girl. Your braid got all undone from last night. Let's get you more comfortable, okay?"

I weep, unable to hold still as Amy unravels my hair, spreading it like a fountain of cool silk across my overheated back. "Amy, you really think he's coming back?"

"I do. I have a lot to say to him for not being here, though." As her fingertips brush my shoulder in reassurance, Amy gasps. "Oh, my God, your skin is practically on fire! This isn't good." She turns over her shoulder and bellows. "Kira, where'd you disappear to with those washcloths?!"

As Kira peeks into the room, my focus switches from the throbbing ache in my core to Kira's penetrating stare. Her breath is rapid. Distressed. She doesn't look happy, and she's staring straight at us, ready to pounce.

I instinctually dive behind my best friend, but Kira doesn't seem to like that. One glance at her clenched jaw sends me scrambling across the living room floor, backing into the brick fireplace. The frigid red bricks against my boiling skin startle a tiny yelp out of me, but it's better than whatever Kira has in mind.

"Oh, my God! What's wrong?!" Amy's focus tracks my stare, zipping to Kira in the entryway.

Soaked washcloths trickle from Kira's arms as she seems to forget she's holding them.

Amy freezes. "Holy shit– Kira?! What's gotten into you?"

My heartbeat skyrockets as Kira edges between wolf and human, her nostrils flaring and voice deepening as her eyes flicker into an even darker brown. "It smells like someone needs a good fuck in this house."

Amy chucks a pillow at her. "You adorable, annoying Alpha! Are you seriously going to cheat on me with my best friend over some pheromones?!"

Kira gives a low growl, dropping the remaining washcloths onto the floor with a wet slap as she approaches Amy. "Don't be ridiculous. I want *you*."

Kira scoops Amy's hair off her neck, hugging her from behind to lick that same sensitive gland. The breathy way Amy gasps spikes a thrill through me.

My insides ache for Noah to do the same thing. I shed a few extra tears.

Kira growls against Amy's neck. "I want to strip you bare, Beta. Then I want to kiss you between your legs until you come against that coffee table."

Amy's voice clouds with desire. "Well, shit. This is objectively a bad situation... But that also sounds kinda good to my wolf."

I wedge myself deeper into the fireplace. "Amy, is she going to hurt me?"

Amy snaps out of her haze with a gasp. "Oh, no, babe. I know you can smell that Alpha musk, and it's probably driving your instincts wild. But it looks like she's only got eyes for me. I've got it under control..." Amy's half-hearted smile can hardly hide her arousal. Then she gasps. "*Kira!* I'm still talking. You need to wait." Kira removes her hands from Amy's bra with a frustrated huff. After a grounding breath, Amy lowers her voice. "I don't know how to control *two* Alphas slipping into a hormonal rut, so let's hope Noah has more self-control than my horny Alph–"

Amy is cut off by Kira's sultry kiss. Amy's eyes shift with need, clinging to her wife's arms. This only encourages Kira. She deepens their kiss, a heavy touch climbing Amy's body until she reaches Amy's neck. Amy's voice erupts with bleating, desperate breaths. "Oh, Goddess, *Kira...*"

They're not helping. Whether it's right or not, my eyes lock on the two wolves nuzzling. I feel every touch of their skin as if it's Noah. His hands on my breasts, caressing my nipples. His grip latching onto my thighs, wrapping my legs around him. I swallow hard, rubbing my legs together on instinct with soaking wet underwear.

But here I am, all alone. Heat stabs me over and over again, burying pain down to my bones. My tears turn into heaving sobs.

"It hurts! I'm on fire, Amy!"

"Oh, shit, Aliya. I'm so sorry! I didn't mean to–" Amy reaches for my hand, and Kira snarls at her. "*Excuse* me!?"

I huddle deeper into my fireplace, silencing my tears out of fear. Kira slinks back too, her eyes locked on Amy as she curls into herself from being scolded.

"That's right, Alpha. Get your gorgeous ass outside so we can fuck in the woods."

Before I can blink, Kira sprints for the door, and Amy bites back an amused laugh.

Until Kira flings open the door, crashing face-first into a wide torso.

8

A hulking figure blocks the morning sunlight, having to duck beneath my old cottage's short doorway to enter.

"Why the fuck is there another Alpha in here?" Noah's chest puffs, donning an identical black Sherpa jacket to the one he shredded yesterday.

I grip the arched brick at my side, peeking around the fireplace's edge. "Noah!"

He doesn't hear my quiet, pained cry, his focus on the Alpha cowering in my doorway. "If you don't get her out of here, I'll drag her out. She better not have hurt my mate."

Amy gasps, scrambling to shove Kira out the door. "I've got it under control, Alpha! She's leaving with some *serious* motivation, trust me."

None of what they're saying makes sense to my fever brain. All I know is that I need to soothe Noah just as much as I need him.

I try to run for him, but my sick legs only get me so far before I'm tangled in my living room's messy floor. Noah's glare softens into sorrow when I crash to the ground, grunting in pain. He drops the grocery bag and huge comforter blanket he's carrying, diving for me.

"Aliya!"

Hearing my name on his lips changes its meaning, sweetening my heart into overwhelm.

He plucks the hair from my eyes. "Why were you in the fireplace?"

I swallow hard, taking a few seconds longer to answer his question from how captivating his lips are. "I was scared."

"Oh, my poor mate…" His eyebrows warp as his cool hand on my forehead tests my temperature. "How did it get this bad already?"

Amy slams the door behind her, locking Kira out. "The real question is where *you've* been, Alpha? She thought you stood her up! What if it killed her?!"

Noah whimpers as he nuzzles my neck, sending intoxicating waves of tingles down my body. "You didn't see the note on your bed that I went to get food and blankets for you?"

"O-oh, I didn't look there…"

Amy growls. "You didn't leave it here, where she'd wake up? She's half-gone already, if not more, and not thinking clearly."

Noah shrinks. "I thought she'd want to nest in her bedroom. I-it came on so fast, and I didn't want to wake her and make her feel worse. I'm so sorry."

"She didn't even know she was a wolf, Alpha. I didn't either, and I'm her best friend."

I can't stop crying, squirming against Noah as he finally holds me. "Help me!"

Noah hugs me to him, wrapping me in a thick duvet that smells like he yanked it straight off his bed. I grab fistfuls of it, squeezing it to my chest. The second his scent envelops me, I gasp in relief.

Noah strokes my cheek. "Good job. Follow your instincts. What else are they saying you need?"

My fever chills have stopped now that I'm immersed in his bedding, but it's not enough to quell my aching core. Maybe I need more of Noah.

I rub my whole body in his scent, climbing into his lap and clinging on with all fours.

But that's not right either.

"I don't know what I'm doing! Something still feels wrong—"

Noah's fingertips skate down my neck, brushing the hair from it, and I freeze. My heart beats so fast that I gasp for air, gripping Noah's fluffy Sherpa collar to pull him closer.

"O-oh. You like that?" He whispers.

When he plants slow, soft kisses on my neck's golden spot, the pain dissolves piece by piece from the source of his touch.

"Noah... *Noah*, Oh, my God. Don't stop."

As the pain fades, I'm more than soothed; I moan in Noah's arms, every inch of my body alighting with pleasure. He kisses my neck harder, his fingers digging into the roots of my hair as he tugs me tight against his lap. I'm wetter by the second, each kiss sending a pulsing wave of delight to my groin.

"Oh, God, *yes*, Noah."

At the sound of my breathy voice, Noah's kisses revert to rough licks. I shiver from head to toe, but something in me screams that this is what I want. What I *need*.

My moans revert to heavier, desirous groans, my hips wriggling. Noah growls as he licks me the heaviest yet.

"Noah! Do *not* mark her!" Amy shouts, startling us.

Noah pulls back, his chest heaving. "Shit, I... I even took five rut suppressants."

Amy gasps. "*Five?!* Alpha, are you trying to die? What the hell are we going to do without you?"

Noah groans, scrubbing his forehead. "They weren't working! I feel like such an out-of-control asshole."

Amy's tone softens, but she ravenously chews her nails like she always does when she's anxious. "You're not an asshole. You just met your mate, and now her pheromones are exploding, begging you to mate with her. It's a lot, even for me as a Beta. Will you be okay while I go help my Alpha?"

Noah sighs, tracing his thoughts as his eyes roam my parents' flowery couch. "Yes... Yes, I'll be fine."

"Do we have to stop?" I ask.

I hadn't noticed I started crying again until I heard my shaking voice.

Noah's irritation dissipates the second we meet eyes. "No, I'm going to help you feel better. I'm not leaving your side again." He kisses my cheek, and I whimper for more. "But first, you're going to eat something. Do you want me to carry you to bed?"

"Yes. Please."

Noah reaches for the brown paper grocery bag he dropped with one hand, lifting me with the other.

"Use a condom!" Amy calls after us.

Noah glowers. "Thanks for the sex ed."

Amy laughs. "I'll come back to check if you did, Alpha! Tell your wolf that!"

I cling to him as he carries me down the hall to my bedroom, my entire body shaking. As Noah eases me onto my unmade bed, it kills me to let go of him.

Until he drops his grocery bag, fetching a colossal chocolate donut out of a second, smaller paper bag. The donut is almost as big as my head, dripping beautiful, sugary rainbow sprinkles everywhere.

Before Noah sets the donut onto a napkin, I throw myself across the bed - placing the donut at perfect face height - and chomp off an enormous bite. Sugar erupts into my mouth, enveloping my aching muscles in bliss. Grabbing Noah's wrist, I slam the rest into my mouth until his empty palm meets my lips.

For the first time ever, I hear Noah's full belly laugh. It's soft and airy - a hint of the shy sweetness I keep discovering beneath his stoicism.

"I guess I chose the right heat food." He grins, showing off gleaming incisors. My stare locks onto them, wanting them to nip my neck while his touch devours the rest of me.

I try to tell him how goddamn incredible his laugh is, but my cheeks are stuffed. "Hmph hm hmph hmph!"

Noah laughs shyly again, draping his comforter around my bare shoulders. For some reason, this infuriates me.

Noah winces. "Fuck. That was a mistake."

That's not how that blanket needs to sit!

I want to tell Noah this, but I'm still chewing. I fumble with his blanket like it's a rogue snake, struggling to figure out how to soothe the irritation in my gut. The feeling is familiar; it's exactly like a compulsion, but too strong of one to resist - eight out of ten on the SUDS scale. It takes every pillow I own, cramming them in every direction until they're just right. When I find the perfect combination, I wedge myself beneath the comforter, out of breath.

I swallow the last of the donut.

As I soak up Noah's sweet smile above me, heat explodes in my core. "You're beautiful, Noah."

With flushing cheeks, Noah's eyes soften into an expression I can't place - somewhere between happy and sad.

"Why don't you call me your Omega anymore?" I ask this the second I think of it.

"O-oh, um, I can... M-my sweet Omega."

Noah's eyebrows raise even higher as I grip my blankets to my chest, unable to contain my smile.

But my irritation flares again when I see my hands ruining the blankets, all by myself. My eyes water. "I made the bed nice for us. Why are you over there?"

His eyes widen. "I-I didn't want to mess up your nest. Again."

With piled blankets encompassing me, that word fits a terrifying amount. "My nest... I... I made a nest."

As we lock eyes, the meaning of all this pain and frustration becomes clear. I don't just want Noah to mark me after having wild, heavy sex with me. I want him to get me *pregnant*. Need him to.

The heat in my core explodes, screaming that I've found the answer to relief. At the same time, it sobers me a little from my heat haze.

This is so unfair. I've always wanted a baby, and I want Noah more than I've wanted anyone. My stare drops to his erection, bulging through his tight black jeans; he wants me too. But even though this is everything I want - a special connection, genuine desire, and someone who wants me back - I'm still scared if I let myself go, opening up my body to him alongside my heart, he could hurt me worse than anyone has.

I cry whether I want to or not, hating the way it makes Noah's smile fade. Noah cups my cheeks in his hands, his wide eyes dissolving into fear with mine.

I grip his hands back. "I hate how I'm like this! Why can't I just be normal?"

"W-what do you mean? You're just in heat. It's okay to need to nest."

"I want you so badly, but I'm still so scared. Why can't I just be okay with having sex with you? I want to have a baby with you..."

Noah's eyebrows shoot straight up. He pulls back, keeping a safe distance between us. "A baby? No, no, no. This is just the heat talking. We just met, and what you said yesterday makes me think you need to take it slow. You mentioned you wanted to have sex yesterday too, so that's as far as I'll allow us to go. But I'm *not* getting you pregnant today, no matter what you say in heat."

I warp into heavier tears, and Noah's face sinks into guilt.

"Fuck. I-I'm sorry, that came out way too harsh–"

"No, I said it all wrong. Having a baby isn't the problem," I blubber. "Why am I so messed up?! Why can't I just move on? I do want to have sex with you. Beyond that, I've always wanted to marry a soulmate, and eventually, have a baby. How can we get there someday if I can't even open up?" I can't bear to keep looking at Noah's terrified, wide eyes. "All I can think about is how hurt I'd be if I lost it all. But that's so infuriating! Why can't I just live, now that I finally feel safe enough to survive again?"

"Oh, Goddess..." Noah scrambles onto the bed. He squeezes me to his chest, holding strong against my returned chills. "I don't know what happened to you, but whatever it was, it's bad enough to overpower a wolf's heat. That fucking breaks me." His voice quivers. "I've never seen this in my life. Someone or something hurt you, and hurt you badly. I *refuse* to blame you for that."

He's taking me so seriously, shaking with anger like I was inside for years after what my ex did to me. He *believes* me, and I didn't even give him details.

"Noah..."

His voice speeds into a frustrated pant. "I'll never force you into sex or even dating me. I don't own you. Fuck anyone who made you think that was normal! If you're not ready, you're not ready."

I gape in awe at his fury, loving anger in a man for the first time. Relief floods my core, but grief for the past also wracks my system as I tug him deeper into my bed. This is how it could've been, all along?

Noah's body is rigid when he first lays down, hesitant as I rub myself over him from head to toe.

My internal filter officially breaks. "After what he did, I didn't think a partner like you existed in this world."

Noah lets out the most honest whimper I've heard from him yet, rolling me into the tightest hug. I grip his back furiously, gasping through tears.

I didn't give Noah details, but I did it. I told him something I rarely tell. Pride loosens my breath.

As Noah hugs my head to his chest, his voice comes out hoarse and quiet. "I want to protect you so badly. But I didn't show up soon enough. I'm so sorry I wasn't there to stop whatever happened."

I squeeze my eyes shut, a smile breaking through my tears. "You're here now."

When I try to meet his eyes again, Noah is too shy to look at first. Then I see why. His teal eyes have turned greener than ever now that they're lined with red.

He's crying for me. *With* me.

My soul splits at the seams, bursting with affection. For the first time since my parents' deaths and rejecting my abusive ex, my heart fully opens. I want to trust Noah. With my heart, my body, and my mind. Even if it takes me years.

And to start, I want to kiss him. Hard.

Throwing one leg over his hip, I'm surprised by how easily he lets me roll him onto his back to straddle him.

Shit. The sight of him under me - my bare thighs gripping his waist - erupts heat from me again.

Running my hands up his chest, I'm elated as he sucks in a shuddering breath. His gentle palms land on my back as I lean over him. My post-braid wavy hair pools around his serious stare, shrouding us in our own secret den. As I lean into his lips, his touch on my back grows stronger - hot and urgent caresses that flutter my heart. Kissing me long and slow, Noah sends my pulsing heat into a frenzy as one hand slides up to my neck, the other to my hips.

I tilt my pelvis forward on his lap, eager for pressure, and Noah sucks in a tight breath. He flexes against me in response, startling a gasp from me as a shockwave of desire echoes through my groin.

I forgot I was practically naked. I can feel the heat from his shaft so clearly, warming the thin, soaked core of my panties.

Laying my body against his, I immerse my fingers in his thick hair before kissing him hard. Noah leans into my embrace, squeezing me tighter against him. He eases his lips against mine over and over, filling me with butterflies until I let out a soft moan, unable to hold still.

He pulls back. "Are you feeling okay with this?"

"No, Noah. The heat is hitting me stronger than ever."

"So is this t-too much?"

"No. It's not enough."

Noah sucks in a desirous breath as I kiss him again, rubbing my clit against the hot bulge in his pants. His hands slide down my back to aid my movements, but they hesitate just before they reach my hips. I slip his warm hands under my lacy waistband, placing them on my ass.

He squeezes both bare cheeks as I roll my hips. My heavy rub stimulates a soft growl from Noah. I pull back this time, my heart pounding as I stare deep into his vibrant teal eyes.

"I can't take it anymore. I want you."

"L-like how?"

I lean over him, giving his hard cock the heaviest rub yet with my hips, his jeans rough against my inner thighs. Noah gasps against my lips, brushing them with his hot breath as his hips automatically buck into me.

"Whatever you'll give me, Noah. I want it all."

Noah's eye color shifts from teal to bright green, his grip tightening on my ass. "Don't say that. My wolf is begging for yours, but he's too instinctual. There's plenty he'd want to do that feels way too early for us."

I know what he means. The urge in my core heightens, ignoring logic until it spouts declarations I'd never speak aloud. "I want him. If he wants me to please him, I will. If he wants to fuck me silly, that's what I want too. I want my shy Alpha."

Noah rolls me onto my back before I can blink, and I gladly welcome his heavy body on top of me. His cheeks are hot red, his stare more serious than ever.

"*I'm* shy... But my wolf isn't shy about how he feels about you."

My heart flips. I hear the beast behind his words, a low growl that wasn't there before. With one hand on either side of my head, Noah bends to press a slow kiss against my lips.

"There's something you've got wrong about this, Omega."

Each time Noah kisses me, his lips are more thorough, stirring my heart as if it's receiving a loving massage.

"This isn't about what *I* want. This is about my wolf pleasuring the heat out of yours."

I grip his jacket tighter, my breath heightening just before he gives me a soft tease with his hips. Heat saturates me. The need to mate with Noah - and only Noah - pushes out a soft moan.

Noah freezes, his Adam's apple bobbing as he swallows the sound of my pleasure. His eyes search my face, growing hungrier by the second.

I'm starving too. Except "the urge" I keep feeling in my gut isn't a feeling anymore. It's the vulgar, bold side of me I've always suppressed.

She's me. My wolf.

The second I recognize her, she takes the lead, making way for thoughts I've never deemed acceptable. She relishes each fleeting second without fear of consequences; all that exists is here and now.

And she's not shy about Noah either.

I give him a teasing smile. "Your wolf isn't shy when it comes to me, Alpha? I might have to see it to believe it."

Noah's sweet scent bursts from him, his chest heaving. His scent screams one thing: he wants me. It pushes another trickle of fluid into my drenched panties. My eyelashes flutter as Noah scoops my head in one palm, nuzzling my neck.

"You're not hearing me yet. My wolf doesn't want to 'fuck' you, sweet Omega." Noah's tongue leaves a slow, heavy trail of wetness along my neck, hardening my nipples with excitement. "He wants to *make love* to you until your wolf screams for her Alpha."

I involuntarily moan as he nips my neck, rubbing his bulge against my clit. He's rock-hard.

But that's not what's torturing me the most. It's his gentle, deep voice, still soft and reserved despite his dirty words. They feel like sultry secrets, spoken just for me.

My knees raise and open for him. Noah lets out a heavy huff

as he grinds into me, increasing the pressure. And my wolf wants him *now*.

His hum is more of a deep growl as I smash my lips against his, sitting up to pop off my bra. Noah pulls back, capturing every millisecond of my bra straps sliding off my shoulders, revealing hard nipples.

Taking in not only my breasts, but all of me - open and exposed for him - Noah flushes. "I can't believe you're my mate."

I bite my lower lip. "Is that a bad thing?"

"No, it's... No, what? Fuck, I can't think." Noah swallows hard, hesitating on whether to touch or only look.

Placing his hands over my breasts for him, I lean back, keeping his knees beneath my hips. Gentle fingers splay across my breasts, each digit brushing over my nipples one by one. I shudder, squeezing his hips between my thighs.

Noah's jaw tightens. "Fuck."

I press his palms against me, urging him to squeeze. Despite his rapid breath, his movements are slow and massaging, running over my nipples as he kneads them rather than the painful squeezes I've had from exes.

Memories threaten to take over, dragging me into the past by the hair, but Noah's slow, thorough massage recaptures my attention, cradling me in the present. Within seconds, I'm here, and I'm coated in bliss.

I hum, grinding against his lap, and Noah's chest heaves. Noah leans over me, slipping my nipple into his mouth as he teases the other. His soft, suckling pressure makes my hips rock with his tongue, the slick muscle flicking my nipple. When he sucks the other side, the rush of cold air on my wet nipple makes my hips squirm.

I can't take it. My skin flushes all over, craving more of him.

Hooking my ankles behind Noah's hips, I urge him closer until I can pop open his pants before he bursts from them. Noah exhales in relief as I free his heavy cock from his boxers, only to find him dripping like me.

Oh, God. He's *thick*.

Flushing bright red, Noah studies my reaction. But my wolf is impatient. I yank on his pants, struggling to pull them past his muscular ass. He easily slips them to his knees before stripping his jacket and shirt.

As I gaze at his wide chest and plump, flexing cock above me, the rising heat burns throughout my body again.

"I-I think it might take some work to get you to fit in me," I blurt out. "But I want you to."

When Noah speaks, his voice is deeper and rougher than ever, washing my spine in chills. "Oh, *fuck*. So much for suppressants. I'm grabbing a condom before I slip into a rut and can't see straight."

After Noah snatches a box from the grocery bag, my eyes widen as he fetches a condom wide enough to encase my garden's juiciest cucumbers. Just as he places it on his tip, I interrupt to roll it on for him, sparing a moment to massage his shaft from base to tip.

Noah nuzzles my neck more frantically than ever, eager fingers sending tingles up my inner thigh. His warm hand stops just before my groin, and I squirm in frustration.

He purrs at the sight. "What if I used my hands first, Omega? Prepared you for more?"

I suck in a tight breath, gripping his hand with a nod. Noah slides his hand higher and higher until big fingers caress my wet core through my underwear. My back arches at this tiny touch alone, each gentle stroke that much stronger just because it's Noah's.

Blush creeps down my bare chest. Before I can overthink, my wolf spills the truth of my desires. "Please do."

9

Noah eases me onto my back with a heavy kiss. His fingers slip down my abdomen, fluttering my heart as they brush past the edge of my thin panties.

Panic strikes, but I can't identify why. Out of fear that I'm about to have a flashback, I grab his wrist. Noah freezes. When he removes his hand, my gut aches with regret.

"Do you want to stop?" He tilts back to check my expression, but I dive for his neck, hiding my cheeks.

"I don't want to stop, but I... I didn't shave," I whisper. "I'm sorry."

Hot tears prick my eyes, igniting a memory of this exact position - crying beneath a man in bed. How many times was Steven disgusted by my hair? By all of my body's imperfections?

Noah hugs me close. "Why are you sorry? Please, don't shame yourself over some hair. It's there to protect you."

My heart hammers. He's right, but I never thought about it like that. I always just dealt with stinging razor burn and excessive UTIs, figuring it was just part of life - or my fault somehow.

But as my shame fades, a fire takes over me. Noah's still looking at me like I'm the most gorgeous being he's ever touched, his fingertips brushing the top of my pubic hair. With a rapid breath, I dare to slide his hand further, staring at him for his reaction. My heart burns from pounding so hard, but Noah's eyes soften with lust. I urge him even further, but he pauses, immersing his fingers in my hair.

At first, my heart threatens to explode. But then Noah gives my pubic bone a thorough, massaging scratch, melting the tension in my body.

"Gorgeous." His voice comes out rougher than I expected, desire slipping through the cracks.

I let out an uncontainable whimper, diving for his lips. But Noah doesn't just kiss me. Feverish lips devour mine, stealing what's left of my breath. My hips twist with delight, his circling pressure on my pubic bone burying into a nerve that craves his attention. But as our tongues collide, Noah's fingers slide past my pubic bone. I suck in a heaving breath against his open mouth.

Tingles flurry up my belly as warm fingers trace my clit in delicate, slow strokes. I haven't had someone touch me like this in so long that it makes my legs jerk in overwhelm despite his gentleness.

"Too much?" He whispers.

"Not too much, please–" I smash my lips against his, desperate for more but nervous with all this attention on me. Noah's fingers slip past my clit to my wet core, circling there until my hips circle with him.

"You smell so fucking *good*." Noah's deep, growling voice makes me flex around his finger as one easily slips in on its own.

"Oh, *God...*" I gasp.

As his finger pulses inside me, I part my lips for him through a heavy kiss. His warm tongue tastes sweet, caressing me with the beat of his finger.

"No, these need to come off." Noah's finger relishes my G-spot, even as his other hand makes quick work of stripping my panties - a hot palm caressing my hip, ass, and thigh in the process.

Once they're fully off, I can see what he means; this is a thousand times better, allowing me to spread my knees as wide as I want while Noah's hand loosens into tender, deeper strokes. My heart races, warning me of an incoming climax. And the only shock I'm feeling is that this is the best sex I've had in my life - with just my mate's *finger*.

But when he introduces a second finger, I suck in a heavy breath.

"Oh! Noah– Ah!"

They glide inside me, sending heavy waves of pleasure straight to my heart. His hands are so big that two fingers together have to be as girthy as my dildo. I raise my hips, eagerly shoving his fingers deeper as they pulse against my inner wall.

Noah lets out a heavy purr as I nuzzle his neck on instinct, only pausing to moan against it.

"Noah, it's so– Oh, my God."

His palm kneads against my clit from the outside as he massages me from the inside, thickening the rising delight in my belly. The pleasure is so intense that fluid gushes onto the sheets with a jerk of my hips.

"You're so wet, Omega," Noah whispers.

But I'm not just wet; he's making me squirt. No man has ever made me do that. Only my own hands, caring about my pleasure when there's nothing else to focus on.

All I can do is moan, my fingernails digging into his back as his fingers pulse faster.

"Noah! You're going to make me come–"

With a deep purr, Noah licks my breast with his full tongue. He sucks my nipple as his fingers flex into a sprint.

The heat gathers in my gut, my moans weak and rapid with every breath as his touch consumes my senses. I grip the back of his head, burying my face into his neck.

"Ah! Please, don't stop–"

My knees fall slack, giving him easy access. Noah takes full advantage with relentless, tapping pressure against my inner walls, but when my hips work themselves over his fingers, Noah sees straight through my need to be penetrated at the edge of my orgasm. He takes me to the edge with slick, slapping thrusts of his hand - his palm contacting my clit until my pelvis fills with a fluttering, sweet ache. For the first time since I moved back home, my blissful moans fill the room. I arch my back high off the bed, my core muscles gripping his fingers. Fluid bursts from me as I come.

His hand slows as my body loosens, dropping against the mattress as I struggle to catch my breath.

Coming down from my high, I blink off my disbelief. I just had sex with a man, and instead of wincing in pain or crying quietly in the bathroom afterward...

I want *more*.

10

The heat isn't better at all. It's worse than ever, burning my eyes.

And Noah is rubbing his lusty scent all over my chest and neck until I'm lightheaded.

"Fuck. I want you," he says.

Each breath is still a moan as I flex around Noah's fingers, desperate for deeper pressure. The heat becomes so unbearable that I find it hard to breathe.

Pulling back, Noah searches my grimacing face. "What's wrong?"

"Noah, the heat is worse. Help me."

I reach between us to rub his covered tip over my pussy until Noah's chest heaves with each breath.

But he stops my hand. "Something else is wrong. I can smell it."

He's right. My heart is racing so hard that it thrums through my ears. But as I squirm beneath Noah, I know it's my wolf, jerking around to free herself from my mental reins.

"Are you still scared? We don't have to do this," Noah says. And he means it.

But my wolf screams to let her pounce on him. It's just a matter of me letting go of control.

Noah strokes my cheek, willingly pulling away despite how heavily aroused he is, and I feel safer than ever.

I swallow hard, my voice shaking. "All my life, I've been fighting against my wolf. But you're bringing her back out. I think I'm ready to stop resisting her... And she wants to make love to her mate more than anything."

Noah flushes. "O-oh. Are you sure?"

I slip his tip against me again, teasing us both. "I'm more than just sure. I want your wolf to show me how badly he wants mine. Make me feel like a wolf, Alpha."

Noah's chest rises faster with each breath, his eyes sweeping my bare body. Then the essence behind his eyes shifts, irises reverting to that glowing, golden yellow I saw on his wolf.

Noah was right; his wolf isn't shy about me. He looks me dead in the eyes, his pheromones suddenly so strong that I wriggle beneath him, vivid images of what he might want to do to me alighting my spine with pleasure.

When Noah places his hands beside my shoulders, blocking the light from the window with his broad stature, his cock falls flush with my pussy. My heartbeat pulses into my groin.

Leaning a breath away from my throat, Noah's voice comes out as a low purr. "You want to feel like a wolf? Follow your instincts with me, Omega."

As his fingers slip between my legs, he nuzzles against my neck.

I shudder, leftover pleasure reigniting from his teasing on that delicate scent gland. Sparks zip back and forth through my torso as my neck and groin share their enjoyment in his touch. Then, as instructed, I follow my instincts.

Wrapping my hands behind Noah's head, I urge him close enough to give his neck a heavy lick. My toes curl as Noah's hungry scent burns my nose, his fingers slipping faster until I'm revved up again.

Noah scoops up my hips, coating his shaft's length in my fluid with a delighted purr. I squeeze his hips with my thighs, pulling him closer. He happily indulges in my request, digging in with a hearty rub.

An honest purr erupts from me, just like Noah's, and I freeze in shock.

Noah's golden eyes widen, a sly smile creeping across his lips. "Tell me, Omega. Do you want it from the front, just like this?"

Leaning in, Noah tickles my scent gland with his whisper until I whimper. "Or from behind… like a wolf?"

I gasp through desperate breaths, gripping the sheets at the mere thought of him pounding into me from behind. But I don't know what to say. A woman calling the shots was never an option with Steven.

My wolf speaks for me. "F-from behind, Alpha."

One second, I'm facing Noah. The next, I'm on my hands and knees. His sheer power thrills me - not because he's strong, but because it proves his gentleness is intentional. Warm hands steady my lower back, the back of my thighs falling flush against his. Noah places my hands over my headboard, allowing me to hang over it in a stretch.

But he doesn't shove himself into me right away like I'd expect from every other man I've had sex with. Running his fingers up the length of my back, Noah gives me a soft, sweeping scratch. Goosebumps erupt across my bare body, hardening my nipples. I let out a delighted moan, rubbing myself back against his hot, flexing erection.

Noah settles his torso against my back. His breath brushes my ear as he kisses the base of my neck. While one arm hooks around the front of my hips, keeping me snug against his grinding pelvis, the other slides past my belly, teasing my clit. It's so swollen with arousal that instead of the sensation dulling from Noah's previous attention, sparks of pleasure make my hips jerk back into him. I twist to grip his hair, smashing my mouth against his.

Noah purrs - a happy growl vibrating through my back like he adores teasing me beyond my limits. When I let out a desperate whimper, he flexes against me. That little flex gives me a taste of the pressure he'll introduce, tempting me to beg for it.

"Please, please, hurry. I want you."

"Listen closely, Omega." Noah presses a hard kiss into my cheek, teasing me faster until my hips squirm. "Most asshole Alphas submit to no one. But I'm *your* Alpha. The second you say the word, I'd happily roll over for you like a cowering dog." Noah nips my neck, rousing the deepest ache in my groin yet. "If you want to stop, we stop. If you want more, we do more. Just say the word. No begging necessary."

I shiver as he traces a line between my breasts, to my clit, and back again. This man has prepared me for sex more thoroughly than I ever have, leaving me dripping. Between his teasing and his attention to what I like - even repeatedly calling me "Omega" just because I asked him to - I'm melting beneath him. But his willingness to submit to me turns me on more than anything, my core flexing on its own ever since.

He liked it when I called him my Alpha too, right?

Raising my hips, I position myself for him to enter me. "I want more, Alpha."

Noah spreads one hand across my lower back, steadying me as he prods my entrance. "Breathe for me. Relax everything."

I let out a slow, shaky breath, softening my eager muscles. Just as my wound shoulders loosen, Noah glides into me the tiniest amount.

A shockwave of pleasure blasts up my spine. I want to gasp, but I can't find the air, my jaw hanging in eye-fluttering bliss.

"Is it okay?"

"*More*," I breathe, unable to say a single extra syllable.

Noah delicately pulls back before entering me again, pushing an inch farther this time. When he slips past my pelvic opening, a wave of pleasure swells my heart like a balloon.

"Oh! Ah!"

Noah freezes. "Does it hurt?"

"No, it's–" I arch my back through a moan as I reach for his hips, tugging him deeper.

He's so thick that fluid drips from me, every millimeter of my insides met by delicious pressure with no spare room. Easing out in one deep breath, Noah leans back in with the next to keep filling me, pushing himself the furthest he has yet - until he bumps against my cervix with nowhere left to go. Pleasure ricochets down my arms and legs, coating my skin in shivers. The sensual gasp that escapes my lips is unheard of, heightening each minuscule movement with its novelty.

My eyes widen as it happens again and again, each gentle press of his tip into my cervix massaging shudders down my body; I think he found my new favorite spot. He settles into a gentle rhythm, sensing my comfort by my heavy, delighted moans. The thick pressure he's applying builds – each thrust the deepest internal massage I've ever felt despite how careful he's being with me.

My voice comes out wispy and unfamiliar. "Oh, God, Noah, I might come already…"

"Tell me, wolf…" Noah gives a low purr, kissing that golden spot on my neck until I cry out. "Do you want it slower, faster, harder, or deeper?"

I swallow hard, my knuckles turning white against my pale wooden headboard. Forget choosing the position before sex, I've never made a request like this *during* sex, let alone been asked.

But I whisper the truth. "Deeper."

With no further questions, Noah thrusts into me as deep as he can - slow, luxurious pulses making me grip the headboard for dear life as pleasure wracks my entire body.

"Oh, I–" My jaw drops in bliss.

Gripping my lower back, Noah guides himself into me with heaving breaths, emphasizing his movements with my wispy moans. My legs shake, relishing in the pressure he pounds into me. I can't escape from the heavy, stroking sensation as he fills me over and over again. Fluid escapes down my legs, Noah tongue-fucking my neck until my chest aches with every thrust. It urges him to move faster, my old bed frame creaking in distress. Within seconds, I writhe on the edge.

Noah's roughened voice comes out in a sedated growl. "You feel so fucking *good*, reacting to me like that–"

My eyelids flutter as I flex around him, squirming as I come. Noah's fingers dig into my hips as he teases out my orgasm like he craves it. The sensation lasts with every lick of my neck, carrying my moans throughout the room.

As my heart throbs in delight and my limbs fall slack, Noah's frustrated breath has turned into a pant.

"Fuck. I want to mark you."

My body readily welcomes him, the pleasure restarting with every thrust as my wolf grows eager for his mark. Each hot press of his tongue feels as indulgent as his thick cock, enticing me to expose more and more of my neck to him.

I moan. "More–"

Noah licks harder than ever, the rough back of his tongue spiking pleasure into my groin. He scoops my neck into one palm, pressing me against his tongue. Heat explodes from my neck, bucking my hips back for him until I'm the one thrusting him inside me.

I can't believe it. I'm having heavy sex, and loving every second of it.

But a little voice in me speaks up: something else is off about this.

Noah groans. "Fuck! I can't bite you, but I want to so badly…"

I snap out of my heat haze to find Noah's eyes wild and glossy, his incisors extended into fangs that drip saliva onto my shoulder. "Noah! No!"

He freezes, but that's not what I want either. I grab the nearest pillow with shaky hands, slapping it over my dripping neck.

"Okay. Go ahead and bite."

With a frustrated growl, Noah restarts his hips. But when I jut back impatiently, he thrusts into my wet core so heavily that his hips clap against my ass. He's growing so thick that I can hardly take how stimulating it is, my nails burying into his thigh. As he sinks his teeth into the pillow, I gasp at the euphoric rush that bursts through my body from his bite, even though all I can feel is dense pressure sinking through the fabric.

Noah bucks into me as he comes, holding my ass flush to his pelvis as he empties himself against my cervix. Despite the condom, I suddenly feel so ridiculously stuffed that my belly flutters with an explosion of butterflies.

It makes me moan all over again, warmth billowing up my chest from how deep this extra pressure massages my cervix. "Noah! Oh, my *God!*"

He moans against my writhing body, his teeth still clamped into the pillow and muffling his voice. I don't know how, but I can feel that he suddenly can't pull in and out of me anymore. But I'm so delighted by the heaviness against my cervix that I rock my hips against him with a whine.

With a deep, warning growl, Noah sends shivers across my body. Then I register the sound - this is his "stop."

I halt in place. Noah softly nudges himself against my newly discovered favorite spot, keeping our hips cinched tight.

"Oh! God, *yes*– It's so–"

He rocks against me harder, rubbing me from the inside until my moans heighten into cries. When he slips his hand down my abdomen, teasing my clit with rapid circles, the growl vibrating through my neck is what sends me over the edge.

As I come again, I'm so full that my muscles can't squeeze him, packed to the brim. But Noah seems to feel it, shuddering with delight as he rubs his hands across my breasts and belly in soothing gratitude.

After we fall still - my moans reverting to whimpers - Noah's jaws release my neck. He's breathless, bright red, and spitting out feathers when we finally meet eyes.

"I-I'm sorry... I... I knotted you."

My cheeks flush. "What? Does that mean you got me pregnant?"

"N-no!" He ducks his head, suddenly shier than I've ever seen him. "B-but my body tried to, filling you so that nothing would spill out... Even though we're using a condom and–" Noah flushes darker, hiding his face behind frazzled hair. "Basically, we're stuck together like this for a while, because I... It felt so good that I... grew."

11

After Noah pleasured the heat out of me, I'm tied to him. Literally.

Noah clears his throat, afraid of my reaction. His flexing abdomen rocks my body, our organs fused so tightly that I shiver whenever he takes a deep breath.

He genuinely must've grown inside me. It's unusual, but I'm too high on Noah's touch to care.

This moment is a celebration. I allowed a man inside me again, and I feel *good*. Happy, but coated in a lazy bliss.

And I can't stop smiling. "I do feel pretty full."

Noah drops his head against my shoulder with a shaky sigh. "I'm sorry. I hope it doesn't hurt."

"No, it actually felt ridiculously good."

I don't usually admit my pleasure aloud, but it's worth it today; my heart explodes with affection for Noah's blushing cheeks, a slow smile creeping onto his hiding face.

I bite back an excited giggle, not wanting to embarrass him. "Which part... *grew*, exactly? Like, it got longer, or...?"

Noah clears his throat, pausing before muttering, "W-wider. We're - um - literally knotted together."

This is the opposite of Noah's horny wolf that I just let screw me to heaven and back - shy, teal irises glued to my pierced pillow despite how closely he huddles into me for affection. I chew on the inside of my cheek, stifling my adoration.

"I-I didn't know I could knot," he says. "You're the first, so I... I don't know how long it will take to stop swelling. I'm sorry."

My heart flips. Does he mean I'm the first one he's felt good enough with to knot?

I urge his lips closer, kissing him softly. Butterflies fill my stomach as he flexes inside me. We both softly moan.

"Don't be sorry. This was a first for both of us. I've never asked someone to do so much for me during sex. I feel so free," I say.

He buries his nose into my neck with a giddy smile, his hot cheeks coating me in shivers. But his shy nuzzling isn't sexual, sending fuzzy warmth into my heart.

"How's the heat?" He asks.

"A thousand times better. My body feels so relaxed." I break into a giggle at his rising, delighted shoulders. "But you seem like you have some energy left."

Noah wraps his arms around my waist, squeezing me tight to his chest as he grows quieter. "My wolf is happy."

I giggle, and I can feel Noah smile against my neck.

As we settle into a relaxed flop against the mattress, Noah weighs me into the cotton sheets. I return his nuzzling affections, rubbing our noses together.

He pauses to give my swollen lips a gentle kiss. "Tell me about something you love."

My heart throbs, delighted by the heaviness of his body draped over me and the earnestness in his exhausted voice.

"I want to know everything about you," he whispers.

I don't know why, but my eyes water.

But I'm also smiling. "God, how are you so adorable, Noah? I love it."

His worried eyes soften into a bashful glint.

"You wanted me to tell you about something I love?" I ask. He nods, peeking up at me curiously. My breath shortens, taken by this soft side of him. "I-it's a little silly..."

Noah rumbles out a disagreeing hum, cuddling against my cheek. "Tell me anyway."

I flush, unable to hold back a smile. "I love... feeling needed. I love nurturing people around me, making them feel loved or wanted. My favorite part of my job is coming home covered in tears, snot, or grubby finger smudges. I like to believe it means my little preschoolers know I'm a safe person."

Noah grins. "You teach preschool, sweet Omega?"

"I do. It's hard work, but they make me smile every day."

"That's– Ugh, Goddess, I still can't believe you're my mate." He smashes his nose into my cheek. "We just met, but I can already picture you being the sweetest teacher."

With each of Noah's doting whispers, I flush just as soon as my last blush fades. "Well, I try. I like to create a class that feels like their second home."

Noah's eyes dance between mine, his full attention on me. He gives me another massaging squeeze. "My sweet Omega."

I laugh, pressing myself back into him in return. "Why do I feel like your tail would be wagging right now in wolf form?"

"It so is." He chuckles, pressing a soft kiss on my neck. My heart flips.

I want to know more about him too.

"Noah?"

"Hmm?"

"Who's your most important person?"

Noah hums, kissing my shoulder. "That's a tough one. My whole pack is important to me. I wouldn't be able to function without my top Beta, Yasmine. She's technically my badass second-in-command, but she's really my best friend and always has been. But there's also my mom, the current Luna. She holds us together, and she's an Omega who takes no shit. But if I'm honest, my little sister, Rainn, is always my most special wolf. She's a sweet Omega too - so warm to everyone she meets and always smiling. Maybe her." He gazes into my eyes, running a wave of comfort down my sides with his palms. "You're also now on my top favorite wolf list."

So Noah has an entire community behind him, and it's seemingly close-knit. That's something I've always wanted.

My heart pounds even before I ask my next question. "Am I part of your pack now?"

Noah smiles, stroking my hair back to kiss my bare neck again in wave after wave of buzzing pleasure. "I want you to be, but it's not up to me to decide."

My stomach sinks. "Even though I'm part Lycan, you still think your pack will reject me?"

83

"Oh, my poor Omega. I didn't mean that. I meant that it's *your* decision and yours alone. I've already decided I'm fighting for you if anyone has something to say about it."

I furrow my brows, unsure about something in his words. "Noah, how big is your pack?"

He drops his head. "About twenty thousand wolves…"

I have to fight to hold back a gasp. He's way more influential than I think he'd ever like to admit, chewing his lip and avoiding eye contact. But now I know what sounded off. "So why does it matter if one new wolf joins? Is it just because I'm your mate and you're their head Alpha?"

Noah sighs. "I didn't want to pressure you with anything, but they're expecting my mate to be the next Luna."

"The next Luna…" I rack my brain, struggling to understand what that has to do with his pack accepting me. "Didn't you call your mom that?"

"Yes. She was my dad's Luna - the usual pack position for the top Alpha's mate. They led the pack together."

My stomach drops.

Noah's scent sweetens, washing calmness over me. "I don't expect you to want to become my Luna. I don't live by tradition, even though half the pack resents me for it."

I stay silent - despite my wolf begging me to speak up. She wants to be Luna so badly. But besides barely understanding what "Luna" means, do I have what it takes to lead twenty thousand wolves? I *just* learned I'm part Lycan.

Noah whines as he kisses my neck, likely smelling my distress.

But before I can speak, my front door slams. I jump, tightening my abdomen in panic. Without knowing why I'm so startled, Noah soothes me with a steady squeeze.

"It's just your friend," he whispers.

"My–?"

"Taming my Alpha took longer than I expected!" Amy shouts. "You better be unmarked and using protection!"

Amy stomps down the hall, making headway.

And we're butt-naked and still knotted.

12

My voice cracks. "Amy, don't come in!"

"Oh, I'm *definitely* coming in now," Amy says. "Can I? I want to make sure the heat isn't clouding your judgment, and I promised to protect you."

"Shit," I whisper, inspiring Noah's eyebrows to raise. "Fine," I shout. "But just give me a second to–"

By the time I pinch the thin sheets beyond Noah's muscular thighs, Amy arrives.

She stops in the doorway, squeezing her eyes shut. "Oh, Goddess, Alpha, I never expected to see your ass this close in my lifetime. I mean, I knew what I was getting into today, but–" She gasps, studying us closer. "Wait, why aren't you separating? You look done to me."

I shrink, and Noah hugs me tighter.

"*Leave*, Amy. We just settled her heat."

Amy's protective scent makes Noah's chest puff against my back in defense, and I cower into him.

She storms across the room with a scowl. "Noah Greenfield! I don't care if you're my Alpha. You did *not* knot my best friend five seconds after meeting her! Bro, you probably blasted that condom. What if she's pregnant now?! Fuck, I should've been here to help–"

As Amy approaches, instincts well inside me, spilling out before I can register them.

I catch Amy's hand before she urges Noah off me, giving her a rough growl. "*Stay away* from my mate!"

Amy jerks back. "Holy shit, okay, okay! Sorry!"

"Hey, it's okay. We're okay." Noah licks my neck, each caress loosening my tense shoulders until I expose my full jugular to him. A flash of heat explodes through my chest.

But I whine as Noah exits me, surprised by his sudden absence.

Noah clears his throat. "Thanks, Amy. You helped turn me completely off."

Amy laughs. "It's my job, after all."

My whines warp into cries; panic washes over my wolf now that I'm not fused to Noah. I cling to him, trying to hold on, but Noah is so strong that he easily sits back.

"Hey, I'm still here." Noah positions me on my back to face him. He hovers over me as I quiver through a wave of sadness.

"No, I– I was liking that, and now I–" I can't speak through hiccupping tears.

Noah's expression warps with mine. "Oh, you look *so* sad... I'll go back to holding you, I promise. Just give me a second to clean up."

I fall silent, wide-eyed as Noah pulls off his condom. The tip is full.

To my surprise, my heart sinks; it hasn't broken like my wolf hoped.

I groan, curling over in bed as my abdomen cramps with a heavy, dull ache. I expect the pain to stabilize like period cramps, but as my cheeks flush with heat, it only worsens.

"What's wrong?"

"Noah, you didn't get me pregnant."

His brows arch. "I told you I can't, sweet Omega. Is your heat coming back?"

"It hurts..."

Amy bites her nails. "Another reason why I wanted to be here to help mediate. This is going to be a challenging topic for her to let go of, Alpha. It might prolong her heat."

I let out a heavy sob, unable to agree with Amy aloud no matter how true it is. I've always wanted a baby, but I've been so afraid I'd never find a partner I'd feel safe to raise children with after being hurt so many times. Amy and I even discussed a plan for me to carry a child alone with her and Kira's caregiving support. But

Noah arrived, and so has my wolf. Now that I'm not censoring her, there's nothing she craves more than to finally carry a child.

Noah nuzzles me with soft whines, lying flat against my chest. The pain softens with the pressure of his warm body, but I need more.

I frantically rub my nose against Noah's scent gland, hoping to entice him to stay huddled into me.

But Noah draws my chin toward him to look me in the eyes. His soothing scent slows my pounding heart just enough to breathe deeper.

"You're okay, Omega. You're okay." His whisper is much gentler than I expected, tickling my lips. "I've got you."

Noah squishes me beneath him, sandwiching our naked bodies from head to toe. I sigh in relief.

He hums. "Good job. I know I'm not making you decide anything yet, but I've already made up my mind about you as my mate. I'm not going anywhere. W-well, unless you ask me to."

"Please, stay."

Noah laces his hand into my hair, sending tingles down my spine. When he kisses me, it's so soft and sweet that my shoulders rise in delight. As I lean in to kiss him again, Noah purrs into my mouth. His gentle head hold turns into a full-body cuddle, an arm digging between the mattress and my lower back.

I lift my hips into him, whining for more pressure, and he readily grinds against my clit. Noah's slow kisses shift into a tender makeout, caressing every millimeter of my lips. Wetness seeps from me as I crave for him to lift his hips, knowing he could have leftover seed on his shaft. But he keeps me in place, overwhelming me with fuzzy warmth until I forget all about it.

His movements are so slow and soothing that our sexual teases feel relaxed. Romantic. As Noah lets out a happy purr, the heat spikes, but my stomach has so many butterflies that it softens the cramps.

Amy lobs a condom at Noah's shoulder. We stop to stare at her.

"Sorry. Just doing my job."

Noah glares. "Are you seriously going to watch?"

"Trust me, this isn't what I had planned today either. But with how painfully shy you both usually are, you sound fucking *feral*. Did you both agree on trying for a pregnancy today?"

Noah huffs in annoyance, but he lifts his hips to slip the condom on early, nonetheless. "No, we didn't. You're right."

Amy sighs. "Sheesh, I didn't expect your wolf to be this sassy. Your top Beta has to mediate for you for all sorts of things, right? Am I not up to his standards compared to Yas?"

"No. No one can fucking deal with him. Hence, five suppressants," Noah grumbles.

"Stop being mean to him, both of you. He's adorable." Cramps bring tears to my eyes, leaving me to squirm in Noah's absence.

He drops on top of me, returning me to his snug embrace. "Oh, my poor Omega… Are you in a lot of pain?" Noah winces as I nod, arching off the bed as a sharp ache tenses my back muscles. "Fuck, this is torture," he hisses. "I'm so sorry, gorgeous. Goddess, Amy, what do I do?"

Amy bites her lip. "I guess we'll have to just help her through it for a few days since it's too early to–"

"A few *days?*" As I break into soft weeping, Noah's eyebrows contort into agony with me.

He huddles into me, peppering kisses all over my nose and cheeks. "I'm here, I'm here. Do you want to have more sex? Would that help?"

At the mere thought of him entering me again, my core flutters so heavily that I groan, shifting my hips beneath Noah's weight. But we just had wild sex, and I'm tired and sore.

"What's wrong?" He asks. "If you don't feel up to it, I can give you a cool bath."

"No, it's just– I just don't know how to ask–" I huff, frustrated with myself. "C-can it be gentle?"

Noah's eyebrows soften. "Of course."

He kisses me softly, and I hum in delight. Noah slips his fingers into mine. As we squeeze our palms, diving in for another kiss, I realize holding his hand was exactly what I needed. He might not know it, but some part of his wolf does - I can feel his presence behind Noah's yellowing eyes. My cramps soften, replaced by a flurry of pleasure as my mate rubs himself against me with each kiss.

When Noah tilts his hips to slip his big fingers between my legs, I'm already shivering from his light touch. My core muscles widen on their own, begging to be touched as deep as Noah can reach.

"Goddess, you feel ready for me, but just in case–" Noah glides his fingers in, and I moan against his lips in surprise at how soothing it feels.

Noah's tongue caresses mine as he prods my inner wall with his heavy touch. Each flex of his fingers hits just the right spot to build a mounting ache in my core. When my hips raise for more, already dripping and nearing the edge, Noah takes his chance to slide a pillow beneath my back.

"I'll be as gentle as possible, okay?"

My eyelashes flutter as his tip brushes my entrance, and my wolf speaks through me. "Alpha…"

Lifting my pelvis for him, I grip Noah's hips and slide his thick cock all the way in.

"Ah!" My head drops back with a heavy moan at his introduction, the fullness exaggerated by how swollen he made me earlier.

"Holy *fuck*. So much for taking it slow, feisty Omega." His whisper tickles my neck as he settles into me, pausing to allow my muscles to relax. The second my inner walls stop death-gripping him, Noah slinks in and out of me, pushing deeper with every gentle thrust.

"Ah, Noah– You're too big, I–"

He slows, easing himself deeper with every deep exhale until he brushes against my cervix again. Delight blooms in my groin, making me purr just like Noah.

Noah purrs back, pulling almost all the way out before wedging himself as deep as he can into my swollen pussy and staying there. And fuck, it still feels stupidly good. My body responds by gushing onto the pillow beneath me.

I try to stay focused, but the heavier the pleasure he massages into me, the harder my wolf fights to the surface.

Until she consumes me.

"I want to make my Alpha feel good," she breathes. I rub my

head and breasts across Noah's chest, trying to make him just as overwhelmed by my scent as he made me.

Noah shudders, his cock flexing and disrupting his rhythm, and I purr.

My wolf knows what she wants. When Noah almost marked me, it felt unbearably good. I want him to experience it for himself so he can come as hard as I did.

Gripping Noah by the hair, my wolf licks Noah's neck with my full tongue, laying on as heavy pressure as possible. I'm rewarded by his soft, shy moan and a burst of euphoric scent.

"Oh, fuck. *Mate*." His frantic, yearning voice gives me goosebumps.

In the corner of the room, Amy uncovers her eyes. "Wait, what?! No, no, no, Alpha—"

I don't care what Amy thinks. I lick Noah faster, grinding into his thrust as pleasure bubbles in my core with his rising moans. When Noah tilts his neck for more, locking his arm around my hips to pump into me as heartily as he can, I lick him deeper. Harder.

"*Mate*," I say.

Amy gasps. "What?! No, you're an Omega, Aliya! It shouldn't work like this!"

Noah snarls at Amy, and she drops to the floor, cowering. Then he grips my head against his neck, urging me for more.

I test a small bite, and Noah gasps, bucking into me until I squirm.

He can barely breathe out his words. "Fuck, I don't want to hurt you—"

I know exactly what he means; each thrust is barely restrained, veins bulging on his arms. But to my surprise, my body blooms for him, loose and ready for heavier attention.

"I want more, Alpha. Don't hold back."

His heavy cock slips into me, thicker than I've ever felt it, and I whine in delight. My knees pop to my sides, allowing him to penetrate me as deeply as he wishes. And he really digs in, especially as I cry out against his neck, licking his golden spot harder by the second.

"Alpha!?" Amy frantically paces. "Are you going to let her mark you? Stop her before it's too late!"

"No," he growls. "I want it. I want her. *Please*, Omega–"

My purring turns into yearning whines. Noah's hard grip on my ass smashes my wet pussy into him, hitting my deepest nerve so deliciously that I squirt - gushing enough to soak Noah's hands. We're so lubricated that he's lusciously soft inside me despite how heavy he thrusts, the friction between us heightening my flexing core into hard, satiating squeezes of his body. Noah sounds like he loves it - his wispy moan spiking my heart into my throat. Without a second thought, I latch onto his neck with heavy, suckling pressure.

"No, Aliya! Don't do it!"

I growl at Amy, slamming my hips into Noah as I slurp his neck even harder.

"Shit, you're worse than Kira!" Amy presses herself against the wall, and my wolf finally stops glaring. "Noah, you should know better, asshole! Growl, push her, do *something*. She's going to mark you!"

With heaving exhales, Noah swells inside me until I'm almost unbearably stretched. But his arms squeeze me like he never wants to let go - his desperation for me is so intense that his scent burns my eyes.

His voice is soft and breath heavy. "Omega, I want it! Don't stop–"

With Noah's full consent, my wolf urges me.

Bite! Bite, until you taste iron.

My chest cavity vibrates with my growl's strength. Noah's neck falls slack, exposed and relaxed for me.

At the sight of it, my wolf takes over. I clamp my teeth, sinking into Noah's scent gland as hard as I can.

Hot, sticky fluid spills down my chin, and my senses are overloaded. Noah moans, his scent exploding with pleasure, but I know what he's feeling runs deeper than physical pleasure – and when I say I know how he feels, I *know*. Deep in my soul, I can feel Noah there too.

My eyes haze over, the most beautiful colors I've ever seen rippling past like rainbow ocean waves. But out of all moments to begin feeling another soul beside mine, his orgasm hits me first. It ignites a pleasure I've never experienced, stealing my breath as I feel the reaction from each pulse of our hips twice.

Noah knots me, this time stationing his tip so deep that my moan turns into a wet yell against his neck. I've never had cum in me before, but the second a thick heat floods my core, I know the condom broke. The image of Noah filling me makes me come so hard that I flex even tighter around him, massaging all seed from his shaft. Noah has to force his bucking hips to jam into me and stay there, no room to move without causing pain for either of us from his forming knot. My tongue continues to taste his bloody neck, urging more and more of his scent to wash over me. I quiver, consumed by him.

With each pounding heartbeat, something within me shifts. All I can feel is Noah, his presence surrounding me beyond just our physical bodies. As my heart turns inside out, a rush of unfamiliar thoughts, feelings, and experiences enter my mind, as if I'm merging into someone new. This unfamiliar existence settles into my heart, satiating my soul.

The more I see, the more I recognize that these aren't my experiences at all. They're Noah's. Shy, sweet curiosity. A heavy, pulsing sadness. Agony. The need to protect. To love fiercely enough to keep everyone alive. Everything that was his is becoming mine, just like everything that was mine is becoming his. I welcome it all, desperate to understand every inch of his soul inside me.

Tears slip from my eyes. I hadn't realized I never truly felt it before, but this feels like love.

Noah nuzzles me, dripping his hot tears down my chest. That's when I hear a separate voice in my head.

Mate. My beautiful, gorgeous mate. I love her. I love her, already.

I gasp through sobs. Are these Noah's thoughts?

As our bodies slouch, covered in sweat and blood, I'm startled back into myself by Noah's sudden, elated laugh.

Resonating throughout my mind, his deep, soothing voice sends me into luxurious shivers.

Welcome to the pack, my beautiful Omega.

92

13

My wolf's heat erases from my awareness as I re-enter reality. Amy is crouched on my bedroom floor, gripping her hair and stunned silent. My legs are splayed and shaking, and Noah still heaves over me.

At first, I'm elated. Then I'm embarrassed. I just had the hardest sex I could manage with this man, right in front of my best friend, and spoke like an uncaged animal. But when I see Noah's bloody neck dripping onto my bare breasts, I forget every other worry with a horrified gasp.

"Noah, oh, God! I-I made you bleed!"

He presses my palm against his pounding heart. I'm shocked to realize he's still crying.

And smiling. "This is the best day of my life. I don't mind a little blood."

Goosebumps erupt across my body. The racing heartbeat in my ears slowly links to Noah's pulse thudding against my palm.

We're one.

I feel his happiness - a sugary, soothing warmth filling my core to replace the fire he started when we first met. It dances with my confused, yet hopeful emotions, our unique blend warping into a new emotion by the millisecond.

"Noah, we– What is this?"

He weeps through a smile. "We bonded."

Bonded. That word pulses through me until my heart soars. Bonding describes this novel sensation perfectly, and it's better than anything I've fathomed in my lifetime. I *know* Noah, even though we just met. I know his core self deeper than I've known another soul.

But I can't allow myself the pleasure of happiness when I see a major problem: we didn't agree on this beforehand. Was Noah's consent spurred by a moment of passion, or does he truly want to be bonded to me? Noah's entire life just changed, and it's all my greedy wolf's fault.

I wipe his tears as my heart breaks for him. "Did I upset you? Hurt you? Is this really what you wanted?"

Noah squeezes me to his chest, smushing wet kisses onto my neck. "This is better than anything I've ever wanted."

The crackling emotion in his voice makes me let out a soft sob, but a smile erupts from me beyond my control. Despite this version of reality being completely unbelievable, I can't get over how Noah just experienced every emotion I've ever felt. And he still accepts me.

Not to mention Noah has been through hell also. I couldn't sense the details, just his feelings, but I know he has a thoughtful, deep heart - one that hasn't been taken care of, either. We can understand each other.

This is everything I've ever wanted too. My wolf jumps for joy.

I squish Noah's cheeks and kiss him hard before yipping in pain. "Ow, my lip! What's wrong with my teeth?!"

Noah giggles. "Oh, sweet Omega... Look at your little fangs!" He loops one huge pointer finger around my new fangs, making them feel tiny, and we break into laughter.

But then I gasp. "Wait, are they stuck like this forever?"

"No, they'll go back when your wolf chills out." Noah's grin bursts from him - overjoyed despite the pain he's experienced in life - inspiring fresh tears.

I cry-laugh, soaking in every ounce of Noah's happiness as we smash our foreheads together. My heart has never been so light.

But Amy stands, seething. "What are you going to tell the pack, Alpha?! What happened to not wanting to mark her?"

My smile fades.

But Noah's grin slides into a rebellious smirk. "I didn't mark her. She marked me."

Noah laughs as Amy's eyes grow wide.

"Are you saying… She's the new Alpha?"

My stomach drops. I grip Noah in panic, but he laughs again, nuzzling into me as he speaks through our mental link.

Don't listen to that. That's not how that works, but I'd also never put that duty on you. You're a free wolf until I mark you, and you're not forced to join my pack. You're the only one I'll submit to now, that's all.

I cling tighter to him. *That's all? Noah, you just committed yourself to me, for life!*

He shivers as excitement twirls through our bond, and I know his wolf probably has the zoomies.

I did. And I'm proud of it.

I'm so stuffed with excitement, overwhelm, and endorphins that I could pop. But before I can figure out how to express it in words, I'm surprised by how naturally Noah switches between our mental link and speaking aloud.

"She's not the Alpha. Although, I did let her dominate me, which everyone's going to get a kick out of."

Amy is just as concerned, gripping another fistful of her frazzled hair. "They're going to question your legitimacy as the most dominant wolf now, Alpha!"

"Just because I let my mate mark me?" Noah scoffs. "So fucking what. I'm sick of Alphas acting like they're superior gods. It's just giving them an excuse to abuse Omegas. There's no tolerance for sexism in Greenfield."

He curls me into his chest, whether it's intentional or not. But as he continues, I'm still struggling to keep up with a second person's emotions rippling through my chest. His fierce protectiveness runs so deep that I shudder.

"I'm not ashamed of mating with an Omega, so I don't see the problem if she marks me back," Noah says. "Judging by Aliya's instincts, maybe all Omegas would want to mark their mates, and everyone's gender bullshit is stifling their instincts. They're the ones missing out on the best experience of their lives."

My heart jolts. Not just because Noah just declared bonding with me to be the highlight of his lifetime, but also because it sounds like I seriously did something weird.

"I didn't know it wasn't normal. I'm so s—"

95

"No. Don't apologize. They're the ones who are wrong," Noah says. Then he tenses. "Or, wait... Do you mean you regret marking me?"

"Of course not! I wanted to, from the second you explained it. If not now, then someday."

Noah's shoulders soften. "Then that's all that matters. You're my mate, and now I can proudly show off your mark to prove it."

Amy looks more stunned than I am. "Noah, no one has come close to dethroning you, but this might be pushing it. You're *that* serious about my best friend?"

I stroke his wide back, letting out a whine.

Noah kisses away my worries. "I am."

After a long silence, Amy's voice comes out choppy and quiet. "I love that. For both of you."

My heart has done fifty flips, but now I can't contain myself. I want so badly to be Noah's lifelong mate. Maybe even his Luna. But now that my heat is clearing, all my old fears resurface with my logical mind - intrusive thoughts escaping from my lips before I can parse through them.

"What if one day, you don't want me? What if you realize I'm not the one, or you regret being marked?"

Noah shakes his head, dismissing it without needing a moment's thought. "I trust my wolf. I've never felt like I've found my mate before I met you, and everything in me says you're the one. If I'm wrong, then that's just a risk I'm willing to take."

I have to admit, that makes my heart feel invincible. It pounds into my throat, soaking in the pressure of my mate's bare body as he stares me in the eyes. He looks so sure of me. And honestly, I'm sure of him.

Which is why I hate watching my mate bleed.

I don't know why, but I lean in and lick Noah's bleeding wound. Cringing at how that might've hurt, I prepare to apologize, but I'm too stunned to speak as my saliva stops Noah's seeping blood; his raw wound holes shrink into fresh, dark pink skin before my eyes.

"What the hell? I stopped you from bleeding."

Noah chuckles, kissing my temple. "You really are a wolf. Thanks, sweet Omega."

Holy shit. Now that I think about it, my palms and knees are healed after Noah licked them last night.

Noah is still knotted in me, his body vibrating mine with excitement. I'm dying to feel the same way, but with yet another discovery to add to my mental pile, healing saliva feels a bit too surreal. Overwhelm sinks my stomach into the mattress.

But I don't have time to ruminate; Amy perks up at the same time as Noah. Their eyes zip to the bedroom door, and I hold my breath. When my front door slams yet again, I jump.

"W-who's there?!" I call out.

Noah's scent soothes me despite my nerves. "It's all good. Just Yasmine."

As my new guest speeds down the hall, I instinctually cover my bare breasts. "Just your second-in-command?! You're inside me, and I'm naked!"

Noah's raising eyebrows seem to realize all at once what position we're stuck in. He rushes to hook the bedsheets over my splayed knees just in time for Yasmine to enter.

Her artfully messy ponytail spills over her shoulders with a disapproving shake of her head. "Goddammit, Noah. You really did let her mark you."

Noah huffs, his smile fading. "You got a problem with her, Beta? Nice first impression on my mate."

The Beta sinks into herself, glancing at me with sleek, dark eyes set into her olive skin. "Sorry, you're right. That was rude. Let me start over."

I'm awed at the woman in front of me. Why hasn't Noah already mated someone like her? Just her essence is grand, proud shoulders squaring off to face me over wide, gorgeous hips. She plasters on a smile that I know steals hearts, her lips arched in a perfect bow. But then I spot them - four sharp fangs peeking beneath her lips. Does that mean she's showing her wolf side? *Always?*

"Hi, I'm Yasmine - 99% of Noah's brain cells."

While I can't stop staring at her exposed fangs, Noah chuckles, shaking his head.

Yasmine's eyes bulge, and she nudges Amy. "Did our Alpha just laugh?"

Noah groans, burying his face into my neck. I can't help but giggle, stroking the back of his head.

Shy Alpha, I mindlink.

Noah's smile widens against my neck. He flexes into me, filling my belly with fizzing excitement.

Yasmine blinks a few times. "Well, shit. I've never seen my best friend so happy."

Amy wipes her tears, smiling as she shakes her head. "I haven't seen my best friend this happy either. Not since we were kids."

Yasmine clasps her hands with one loud clap, and I jump in Noah's thick arms. "Alright, Alpha. When your dick stops being dramatic, we've gotta get home. The wolves can sense you're mated with a stranger, and they're freaking out."

Noah frowns. "My mate's in heat. They can wait a couple days."

"I actually feel better now," I say. When everyone stops to stare at me, I cup my hands around Noah's ear, my cheeks flushing bright red. "I think you really did break that condom. My wolf is satisfied."

Noah's eyes pop wide open, and within seconds, he's stressed enough to be able to pull out. I bite my lips, unsure what to say as he stares at the broken condom, rolled to the base of his shaft. My abdomen stirs, still heavy despite Noah's absence, and I know why: he unloaded every drop he could into me, right against my cervix too.

This is mainly my wolf's fault. I feel a little guilty, even if a pregnancy is also what I want, deep down.

Noah's voice is quiet but firm. "Amy and Yas, I don't want to keep having an audience."

The two Betas scurry out faster than I expect, and a part of me sighs in relief. But Noah still doesn't look into my eyes, lacing his arms beneath my shoulders to lift me.

I gasp. "Noah, it's all going to spill–"

He wipes me clean with his blanket as his sperm seeps out of me, not seeming to care that he's dirtying his bedding. "Are you in pain?"

I give a nervous giggle. "Not a bad kind. Just satisfyingly sore." Oh, and my uterus is cramping, dragging his seed deeper. With how grooved Noah's forehead is with worry, I keep that to myself.

Noah only half-heartedly smiles, offering to carry me to the bathroom with open arms. I fit snugly against his chest as he lifts me, but I'm too concerned to enjoy it.

He's thinking way too hard. As Noah closes the door behind us, I can't stop looking at his sad eyes, the worry in my heart more nauseating by the second.

Noah holds me close with a soft whine. "I'm so fucking sorry."

A heartache onslaught tempts me to double over as dread guts me.

Noah finally looks up. "Oh, Goddess, Aliya, I felt that pain through our bond. Are you okay?"

"Noah, do you not want kids? Not even someday?" I swallow back tears. "Please be honest. I need to know as soon as possible."

My heart throbs as Noah aches with sadness through our bond, grasping me into a heavy hug. "That's not it, sweet Omega. I haven't even marked you yet, and you told me you weren't ready to be pregnant. I feel horrible for you."

Hope fills me even though logically, I know I should be worried about a potential pregnancy. We *just* met. I don't know what the hell is wrong with me for trusting him this much - unless this is just a wolf thing.

But I also know I can't keep rejecting my needs anymore. Even if they're illogical, my wolf might kill me for repressing myself for another second. I've hit my limit one too many times, often unsure why I was alive and sentient if I couldn't fulfill a single desire. No wonder I numbed out, nearly erasing my wolf and all my heart's desires with her.

But now I feel *everything*. Through our bond, I let Noah feel what I usually bury deep down – the excitement that even if I don't end up pregnant, at least I'm dating someone who wants to have a baby with me. And the deep, gnawing pain I carry for why that never happened. How Steven held it over my head, using my lifelong dream of becoming a mother to get what he wanted. How I stuck with him embarrassingly long, thinking I was lucky he stuck with someone as worthless as he convinced me I was. I genuinely believed Steven was my only chance, wasting my life for him.

Not just wasting, but tainting. Now his abuse will likely seep into my future kids through me.

"I… I do want a baby someday," I whisper, unable to suppress gushing tears.

Noah whines, pressing a slow kiss into my lips. "Oh, Goddess. If you decide I'm your mate, and the timing is right for your life and career, I'm giving you that baby one day, okay?"

I hide my face in Noah's chest, not wanting him to see my warped crying face.

I'm crying not only from happiness at his compassion, but also stinging tears as the past resurfaces. This is how gentle it could've been?

The losses in my life are too much to bear, and Noah only knows how they felt. He doesn't know the hows or whys. I don't have it in me to speak of them right now. Not about this.

But Noah just strokes my back, allowing me to keep my secrets.

14

Once everyone is certain my heat has settled - for now - I prepare to spend the night at Noah's top Alpha lodge. He thinks I'll be safer there tonight after his pack meeting, but I'm nervous as hell to be around all those wolves who may or may not like me.

After packing an overnight bag, I change into my favorite pleated dress, blue and white stripes lining my frame with little ruffles peeking over my shoulders. Noah grins when he sees me in it, flooding our bond with excitement. I halt in my living room, in pure awe of my ability to feel someone else's affection for me. He *adores* me.

Noah holds my hand until we stop on my porch, sharing one last kiss before Noah disappears into the woods to shift. When his massive black wolf returns, ears alert and tail wagging, my heartbeat restarts.

I still can't believe how beautiful you are, I mindlink.

Alertness flashes through Noah's eyes. My skin shivers. His ears shoot straight up and his paws splay, but that's the last clear look I get. He bounds over faster than I can brace myself or dodge, so I cringe with a laughing scream.

Noah skims past me, doubling back to scamper to my side with a disrupting, skidding halt and forcing Yasmine to sprint from flying mud. Noah spits his clothes into the dirt before licking me from hip to neck, and I squeal.

"Noah, don't! I just got cleaned up!"

He huffs against me, sniffing me all over. His tail makes so much wind that it ruins Amy's hair.

Yasmine can't stop shaking her head. "Honestly, what the hell. You turned into a goddamn puppy, Greenfield."

Noah doesn't seem to care, nuzzling my neck until he finds just the right spot to light my spine with pleasure.

"Alpha, no!" Amy snaps. "Don't reactivate her heat!"

Noah shrinks. His shy glance darts between Amy and me before giving me one last, sneaky lick. I burst out laughing, burying my fingers into his fluffy cheek fur.

But Yasmine drags me away by the hand. "Alright, let's head out before Noah gets any other ideas."

Noah's wolf circles the three of us, keeping guard as I walk on foot with Amy and Yasmine. I had no idea I lived in a territorial warzone - unclaimed land between Noah's territory and Westview, the neighboring town. Otherwise, random wolves wouldn't have been after what Noah called my "lusty Omega scent," calling out to Noah to mate. It's good he found me when he did. Now I can't wait to pass into Noah's territory, more like a safe haven.

But as we walk, I spiral down a mental road I haven't allowed myself on since my heat cleared. I'm scared to think of what I don't know. Was Amy right in that Ritchie's pack was never able to accept Mom, and that's why my parents lived outside of pack territory, or was it for other reasons I don't understand?

Noah's hulking wolf shoots me a subtle glance. Concern riddles his beautiful golden eyes, but I give him a placating smile. I'm not ready to talk about my parents' hidden past, let alone play a guessing game on what they must've been thinking. Pain seeps through the base of my heart, no matter how hard I shove it down.

At the border, a boxy, off-roading, black SUV waits for us. Noah disappears behind another tree to shift and change back into his clothes. I'm itching to follow him, but Amy and Yasmine hang back, so I stick to Amy's side, unsure what else to do. The second Noah reappears, reaching for my hand, the Betas spring into action, as does the driver.

I assume this means they wait for the pack leader's call on when to do everything, right? I'm missing basic social cues. It's so natural to them that they don't think to explain.

Now that I can hear him out loud again, Noah's rumbling, soft voice gives me chills. "Thanks for picking us up, Dave."

The scruffy driver grins, his wavy hair and thick beard just as dark as Noah's. "Welcome back, Alpha. And welcome home, new pack member."

Goosebumps erupt across my arms. This is it. I'll belong in a community soon. Not just any community, but a pack. *Noah's* pack.

But I still have no idea how to act. They're wolves, but not all-wolf, right? Does that mean they sniff each other or something in greeting?

Dave is staring. No, *everyone* is.

So I put on my brightest smile. "It's so nice to meet you, Dave! Thank you so much for driving all the way outside Greenfield. I know my parents' old cottage is far."

Dave's wide eyes zip between me and Noah before finally landing on Noah's fresh, crimson bite mark. "Holy f–"

The bulky wolf tackles me into a hug, and I gasp. But whoever he is to Noah, I can feel his excitement for us in his heavy grip.

"No wonder he looks so fucking happy! I was wondering what was wrong with him." Dave laughs, but my stomach flip-flops at what Noah must've seemed like before we met with how everyone's acting. Was he as depressed as I was? "It's so nice to meet you, future Luna!"

I try to brave a smile as I'm face-to-face with Dave again, but my heart lurches at those words. Future Luna?

My wolf, however, perks right up. *Future Luna!*

Dave tackles Noah with a similar hug. "I'm so happy for you, cuz. Your own Luna, damn."

Judging by Noah's smiling, squinty eyes, he couldn't be happier. As the men break apart, Noah brushes his mark, hugging me to his side with rosy cheeks. "Aliya, this is my cousin, Dave. And let's not pressure her with the Luna title just yet, man."

"Oh, shit. Sorry, that *is* a lot of pressure."

My chest clenches. "No, wait, I actually–"

I cut myself off, gasping at what I almost said. What am I doing? I can't claim I want to be Luna. I don't even know what it fully means to fulfill that role.

But what I already blurted spoke volumes. Noah tightens his grip on my side, unable to contain his rising eyebrows. Everyone is waiting for me to finish my tactless declaration.

"Oops, I guess that one slipped out." I giggle anxiously, inching closer to Noah. "I don't mind being called the future Luna, really."

"Y-you don't mind it?" Noah mutters.

"Okay, I guess it would be more accurate to say that I like the sound of it."

Noah stands straighter. Hope peeks through our bond even though he's trying his best to stay neutral. *You don't have to do anything you're uncomfortable with or cater to anyone's expectations. They'll answer to us. Not because they have to, but because that's how they show their love to their pack leaders.*

They'll answer to both *of us? How? I'm not your Luna. Yet.*

Noah's pheromones erupt with affection, and my heart leaps. But when everyone else is hit with a wall of his doting scent, they gape at us.

"Um… Noah?" I bite back a giggle, but no matter who stares as we have our internal conversation, Noah can't stop beaming.

Yasmine clasps our shoulders with muscled palms, forcing us toward the car. "Alright, everyone's getting in, stat! No neck touching in there, I mean it!"

Noah laughs, opening the car door for me. His adoring stare sizzles through our bond. "I guess Yas is right. Let's get to this pack meeting before an Elder bites my head off."

My stomach drops, sensing the seriousness beneath Noah's sly smile. The thought of him getting hurt because of me, even socially, makes me want to cry.

But Noah helps me into the car, scooting in beside me. His bulky shoulders smush me into Amy, so he wraps his arm around me to fit me against his side. It relaxes me a little, but not enough. I'm so anxious that I'm nauseous. My wolf gloats at possibly being the next Luna, but I was lost at *introductions*. There's no way this will work.

Noah interrupts my thoughts, leaning in with the softest whisper I can imagine from his deep voice. "Are you okay?"

"I'm okay, considering everything."

"Good to hear."

I slump, wishing I shared the full truth with my mate.

Noah takes a deep breath, squeezing me closer. *If you ever want to share anything private, no matter where I am or what I'm doing, you can tell me through mindlink.*

I bite back a smile, peeking at Noah. He's beaming as if I haven't been making a fool of myself since we met. I lean my head against his chest, inhaling his sweet scent as he hugs me closer.

To be honest, Noah, I don't want to disappoint you or your pack. But there's a high chance I will.

Noah takes my hand with a soft squeeze. *Not possible.*

But I know nothing about pack rules. That doesn't give me the best odds.

Just be yourself. I'll let you know anything important, but you're in a position where you don't have to know any rules. His mischievous excitement rises in our bond. *You've already marked the one wolf there is to impress.*

My cheeks flush, and Noah's giddiness stirs faster.

So much for being shy. Don't excite my wolf, Alpha.

Sorry. I'm just excited to introduce you to the pack.

His sweet smile makes me smile so hard that my cheeks ache. *I'm excited too.*

Despite my nerves, I'm ready to conquer everything that's thrown at me with Noah by my side.

Until we pull up to where the pack holds official meetings - a set of buildings deep in the Greenfield Forest. Unlike the sprawling, wooden cabins of Greenfield's cozy Lycan town, the Community Center buildings are made of dark brick and cast stone, perfect for the mountainous climate. Canopies blanket them in cool leaves, acting as a second roof. Just the sight of them feels important. Sacred. But in nuanced ways I can't imagine, never given the chance.

A wave of thoughts barrels down on me like an avalanche – did Mom ever feel like this? When Dad introduced her to the pack, was he oblivious to what it's like to be an outsider because he's always belonged somewhere? Did she ever get used to it? Was she accepted eventually, or was she completely ignored by them?

Maybe Amy or Noah's relatives know more about what

happened back then, but I'll never know how Mom felt in her words.

Yasmine and Dave mutter in the front seat, their profiles lined with the sunset's pink glow.

Noah steps out of the car the second we park. Everyone piles out after him in a rush, but then they stand there, waiting for us like there's no true hurry. They peek inside the car, looking at me expectantly like I'm holding the reins.

I bite back a smile. It's not just Noah - they *all* act like big puppies.

Noah takes my hands, helping me from the SUV on my wobbly legs. "Are you okay?"

"I'm ready for this. Just shaking off the nerves."

"Just nerves?" He furrows his brows. "Well, let me know if you feel a little off. I was worried you might feel worse from being on pack territory. I thought your mark would introduce you to the pack bond, but if you couldn't hear Yas' ridiculous mindlink just now, you might not be fully admitted into the pack without my mark."

As I breathe the open air, I swallow hard through my gut's sudden churning. "Okay, maybe I feel it a bit."

Noah wraps me into his chest, shielding me from everything but his scent. Releasing a huge sigh, I grip Noah's jacket and bury my forehead into his wide sternum.

"There you go. Take a deep breath," Noah whispers. "I've got you the whole way through. No one can hurt you."

I hone in on Noah's pulsing heartbeat against my forehead. He feels just as anxious as I am, but I can also sense his elation. His wolf is probably rooting for this to go well, just like mine. I want to get through this for both our precious wolves.

As I soak in Noah's scent, his pheromones act as a soothing blanket. But Noah's steady demeanor could calm anyone, mate or not. I love that about him.

"Okay, I feel much better now. I can do this." I smile. But as we approach our friends, I lower into a whisper. "But what did Yasmine mindlink us?"

Yasmine sputters into belly laughter. "He probably called me obnoxious or something, didn't he? I said—"

Noah groans. "Yas, don't–"

"I *said*, he better help you out of the car before I come swoop you off your feet first. It sure got him moving."

Noah releases an aggrieved sigh, and Yasmine cackles. When Amy and I meet wide eyes, Amy snorts back her laughter.

"You're lucky I love you, Beta," Noah grumbles, turning his back to Yasmine.

But the words send a shock through me - not in jealousy, but from hearing "I love you" on his lips for the first time. Noah seems to have noticed; he won't meet my eyes, tucking his chin to his chest despite his hand clasping mine harder with nerves. Amy and I share a subtle, knowing glance, biting our lips shut when Amy's wink almost makes me giggle.

We head up the stone steps, our mini pack of Beta wolves in tow. My heart hammers, feeling more important than I've ever felt in my life. I've never enjoyed too many eyes on me, but because *this* attention symbolizes love for mine and Noah's bond, I'm changing my mind. Maybe I can handle becoming Luna someday.

But within twenty minutes of stepping into the pack meeting room, I'm gripping the pleats of my dress. Pheromones stain the air, making my teeth chatter. Angry elders shout at Noah, and Noah's advisors shout back. All because of me.

I already can't handle this.

15

Cowering behind Noah's arm, I cringe at every raging Alpha in Greenfield Pack's meeting room. It was going okay - until everyone saw my mark on Noah's neck.

On top of terrifying me, they're stomping on my heart. Bonding was such a happy moment for Noah and me, but now we're getting yelled at for it. If this meeting sours our relationship in any way, it'll sever part of my soul.

"I have no fucking clue what's happening," Amy whispers. "These are only the top Elders, and no one's here from Noah's generation of advisors except Yasmine. I thought pack meetings were more of an equal debate, not putting our Alpha on blast."

Regardless of how these pack meetings usually look, the three top Elders have no problem scolding Noah at the top of their lungs as if they're filling in for Noah's late father.

There's Elder Alpha Aaron, late Alpha Ritchie's head of security. To either side of Elder Alpha Aaron, there's Elder Alpha Frank, a trusted friend of Noah's grandparents, and Elder Beta Terence, Noah's great uncle-in-law.

Despite Noah entrusting his pack to the Elders, Noah holds me behind him like he's protecting me, and I need him to. These wolves emanate deadly scents, forcing me to shake where I stand. Yasmine has me walled off beside Noah, and Amy's hands on my shoulders reassure me she's protecting my back, but no matter their protection, my instincts scream to run.

"You're the most disrespectful Alpha we've seen!" Elder Aaron bellows, his white comb-over quivering with rage. "This isn't the only atrocity you've committed. If your father was alive, I'd scold him for how poorly he raised you."

Noah crosses his arms. "Well, he's not alive, is he?"

Across the table, Elder Frank rubs his temples, unable to keep his eyes on Noah without flexing his jaw. "Look at you, gloating. Real lives are at stake, and you're flouncing around as if it affects no one else."

"Of course this affects everyone else. I just don't see the problem with it."

Elder Aaron scoffs. "You don't see a problem?! Our pack will be in danger the second other packs hear our top Alpha submitted himself to an *Omega*."

Elder Terence clears his throat. The Beta's smooth voice softens the tension. "Are you questioning Alpha Noah's ability to protect our pack, Elder Aaron?"

"W-well, I…" The Elder Alpha trails off, his breath catching at something in Noah's stare.

"You, what? Are you done speaking your mind?"

All eyes are on Noah, and I can't help but shrink. Noah, on the other hand, feels like a solid pillar in a room of otherwise chaotic energy. I have no idea how he's remaining calm. I'd lose my shit or bawl if anyone talked to me like this.

But Noah's dark laugh consumes the room, silencing it. We wait for him to speak, not even my bond hinting at his true intentions.

Then his sorrow hits me, threatening to bring me to my knees. But rather than crumbling beneath it, Noah's back straightens.

"That's the last time I want to hear any of you talking shit about my mate."

No one speaks, let alone takes a breath.

"You say Omegas are weak, but now you claim they have the power to destroy our entire pack by mating with us? Which is it?"

The Elders shuffle in their seats, struggling to look at Noah longer than a millisecond.

"Who gave birth to most of us here? Who are you mated with? You don't have Omega children or grandchildren?" Noah scoffs. "I hope they never have to hear you talking about them like spoiled fucking meat."

The room remains silent. Noah doesn't move a muscle, allowing his words to echo through our minds.

An icy sheen coats Noah's gentle voice. "You wouldn't be alive without Omegas, just like we can't function without Alphas and Betas, and you know it. Have some fucking respect, or I'll have none for you."

My breath is shaky, but my soul is on fire. I can't count how many times I've wished for just *one* person to stand up against my ex. His misogyny sounded a lot like this Omega-hating rhetoric. Thanks to Steven, the last thing I expected was for a man to defend my wolf sex this fiercely.

But Noah is infuriated, losing grasp on his usual cool.

I loosen my fearful grip on Noah's arm, sliding my hand into his. Noah's shoulders drop, and he looks to me for reassurance.

I'm beaming. *You're a true leader, my shy Alpha.*

He softly smiles. *Thank you.*

There's something I'd like to say to the Elders, although I'm not sure they'll listen. I peek at them, and Noah squeezes my hand.

You can speak. They're listening.

I grip Noah's hand tighter. But when I clear my throat, everyone's attention zips to me, and I flinch.

Shit, now what? I'm used to speaking up for myself, over and over again, only to be shut down in the end. But now they're listening. No, not just listening - patiently *waiting*. All I can do is speak through my shaking voice.

"I know I'm biased, but I'm already so impressed by the Greenfield Pack. The best example of a strong society is the health of their most vulnerable. And with how I was welcomed–" I drop my stare, softening my voice in fear of their response. "W-well, with how I was treated before I entered this room, I felt safe as an Omega, and as a woman. I teach preschool, and I'd sleep better if I knew my students had the same caring leadership running their communities."

The last of Noah's tense features soften, and I break into a smile.

Thank you, sweet Omega.

My hands are shaking, but I'm impressed by the room's airy,

sweet scent. It's shocking, actually - these powerful men listened to what I had to say. I guess I *can* make an impact here.

With a deep breath, Noah turns back to the Elders. "You can't win a challenge against me for Alpha, and neither can anyone from neighboring packs. If they do challenge us because I'm marked, it's my responsibility to deal with them. We're going to be just fine. I'll make sure of it."

"So you'd like to think," Elder Aaron mutters. Concern creases his cheeks in a frown.

Noah shrugs him off, and I bite back a smile.

But Elder Terence leans in, studying my face. "What's your last name, dear, if you don't mind me asking? You look familiar, but I can't place how."

I have to wipe my sweaty palms on the back of my skirt. "You might've known my father. It's—" I pause, taken aback by Noah's spike in concern through our bond - strong enough to sear my veins. "What's wrong?"

Noah stays silent. He tilts his head, listening with all his focus. "Does no one else hear that?"

Yasmine tenses. "Hear what?"

"There's a little wolf linking me - four to six, maybe."

As fast as he mutters those words, Noah speeds from the room, and so does everyone else. I scurry after them, struggling to keep up with Noah's tall legs.

"What's the kid saying?" Yasmine shouts after him.

"He's a little Omega, calling for help. I think he's trapped somewhere nearby, but I don't know why he called me instead of his parent—"

"Alpha!" A little voice cries.

We whip our heads around, searching for the screaming voice's source. His muffled, strained cries sound familiar.

When it registers why, my heart drops. "Oh, God, Noah. He's stuck inside something, I know it."

16

The wolves break into action, sniffing at their eye level, but I know how young kids behave. Where might I want to squish into and hide?

I crouch, examining the crawl space beneath the building, peeking between tree roots, and shining my phone flashlight into the spaces between boulders for any small entrances. Noah spots me and sniffs lower. Soon, everyone else drops to the ground with us.

Then Amy gasps. We whip our heads to her in unison, rigid with focus.

Only Amy's bottom half peeks from behind a nearby shed, stooped over the surrounding thicket. Amy parts tall weeds obscuring her view, the frond tips brushing her dirt-stained knees.

We rush over to look at the ground with her, unsure what we'll find. As we approach, my eyes catch on her tight grip on the shed, her tense knuckles as pale as her cheeks.

"Hang on! We're here to help, okay? Don't move!" She says.

My stomach crawls into my throat when I see the wriggling little boy, wedged at least seven feet into a narrow hole in the ground with his arm pinned behind his back. Except he looks like he could be buried any second: mini dirt waterfalls pool past his shoulders with every jerking movement. The hole must've been created by a burrowing animal, blanketed by long grasses to create a perfect safe haven - unless you want to be found. Rescued.

Noah grips his hair, looking to the sky for answers, and I know why: that hole is way too small for any Alpha or Beta to fit.

"My wolf could dig him out?" He rasps.

"No, it might sink in and collapse on him," Yasmine whispers.
Calm washes over me. "I might be able to fit."

Noah grips my shoulder, his eyes wide. I prepare myself for his
incoming disagreement, but Elder Aaron steps in first.

"Luna, no. We don't want both of you stuck."

I dismiss this concern with a shake of my head. That little
Omega wolf is bawling and absolutely terrified. It physically
hurts my heart to do nothing.

I try not to show my decision on my face, but Noah gasps as
I lurch forward.

"No!" He shouts.

But I don't waste another second. I brace myself on the hole's
edge, sticking my head in as far as I can. My fingertips stretch to
their limits, straining to touch the little one, but the whimpering
boy remains beyond my grasp. Even if I could barely reach him,
he's wedged so tightly that he needs small hands to wriggle him
out - something I've had to do one too many times on our school
playground's obnoxious, covered slide. I have no choice but to
crawl in after him.

With arms outstretched, I slip into the cool earth, trying my
best not to kick too much dirt onto the boy.

He shrieks. "It's dark!"

I keep my voice light and even. "It is, huh? But I'm right here
with you, see?"

I brush dirt off his cheek with what little light creeps past my
hips. Inching closer, I finally squeeze close enough to touch his
shoulders.

A hand grabs my ankle. It takes everything in me not to yelp
in surprise.

Feisty, feisty Omega. You're about to give me a heart attack.

*Noah, he's jammed against a wall of rocky mud. If you pull us out
now, it could break his little arm.*

Fuck. What should we do?

Just give me a minute. I have an idea. I take a deep breath,
imagining sending the boy a soothing scent - just like Noah does
for me.

He immediately stops crying, peering up at me with big tears
in his eyes.

My chest aches, but I smile. "What's your name, sweetheart?"

"Colin," he coughs, straining against the rock.

"Nice to meet you, Colin! My name's Aliya, and I'm right here with you, okay?" When I softly squeeze his shoulder, he grasps my hand with his free arm, hugging it to his chest. "There you go. I'm here. Hey, you learned the Forest Song in preschool, didn't you?"

"Yeah." His lip wobbles, but his focus locks on my eyes. I make sure to steady them for him.

"Let's sing it together, okay? By the time we're all done singing, we'll be outside."

"Okay."

Then I sing. "I'm in the forest, look at all the trees!"

The little boy reaches for me with his free hand to gesture to the "trees," and my heartbeat skips; he remembers the dance moves from preschool.

"Look at all this dirt around, even on my knees." He grunts through his lyrics, trying to show me his knees, and I smile.

"You've almost got it! Show me your knees!" While I hold his free hand, I lightly tug him to lean against the wall on his side. As he bends his knees, wriggling to show me them, he stoops just enough to yank his pinned arm free. I let out a delighted laugh. "Good job!"

Then I continue to sing. "Look at all the little birds, blowing in the breeze."

After flinging his arms up to fly like a bird, Colin links his hands behind my neck, his breath jagged. "Look at all the laughing wolves, chasing all the leaves."

"Jumping through the flowers, I think I might sneeze!" I grasp his torso beneath his armpits the best I can, wriggling his chest left and right until he slips free, allowing me to lift him enough to latch one arm behind his lower back.

His voice shakes, fear revealing itself through his death grip on my skin. "Take me to the forest, take me there, please!"

Tucking my head over him to ensure he can't hit his head, I triple-check my hold on him and let out a slow breath. *Okay, Noah. Your turn.*

With Noah's grip on my ankles, we're lifted by the Alpha. As

Yasmine predicted, dirt spills around us, forcing me to hold my breath as poor Colin coughs. Noah yanks faster, anxiety spiking our bond. I open my eyes just in time to watch the hole collapsing around us, threatening to swallow Colin's ankles. Multiple wolves help hoist the boy from the ground after me, allowing my strained muscles to relax when Colin finally touches solid ground.

Noah sets me on my knees, dropping into the brush with me to kiss my dirty cheeks. "Fuck. Fuck, fuck, fuck, I fucking hated that—"

But before Noah can finish cussing his brains out, Colin darts for me. He crashes against my chest, grips me with all four limbs, and bawls.

My heart tears as every instinct in my body yearns to soothe him. I gather him into my arms, tethering him to the earth with a soft squeeze. "You did it, buddy! You made it!"

His chin quivers as he rubs his head against my shoulder, immersing himself in my scent. "Luna…"

My eyes water on their own. I tuck his head under my chin as I rock him. "I know, it was really scary, wasn't it? It's all over now, okay? We have you."

Noah wraps his arms around us, his protective scent loosening my tense muscles. The boy stops crying.

"Your mom is on her way, little Omega." Noah's deep voice softens for Colin in a way that stirs a deep nerve in my tender heart. "Is she linking you?"

"Yeah." Colin wipes his eyes, a shaky smile returning.

I can't relax until he's finally reunited with his mom. The poor woman breaks into tears like she almost died, herself. As we sit in the brush, watching her vigorously scrub and lick the dirt from his body, I lean into Noah, closing my eyes. "Thank God. I was terrified he'd wedge himself even deeper before I could get him out."

He sighs. "You scared the shit out of me. But I loved it."

I laugh. "I'm sorry."

"Don't be. You're clearly a fucking badass, so I better get used to it."

I giggle until another voice appears above us.

"Alpha, Luna."

My eyes pop open, revealing Elder Alpha Aaron towering over us. Realization dawns on me all at once; everyone is calling me "Luna."

17

Elder Alpha Aaron wrings his hands, struggling to look Noah in the eyes for more than a second or two. "I sincerely apologize for my words earlier. I can't say I understand the lifestyle choices you've both made, but–"

Noah huffs out a subtle growl, and the Elder winces.

"That was a poor choice of words. What I mean to say is that this is all new to me. But you are our trustworthy Alpha and Luna, nonetheless – that much is clear." Aaron smiles at me in particular, and my heart flips. "I have high hopes for you, future Luna. You have our protection for life, but maybe you won't need it. I have a feeling you'll be our most resilient Luna to date."

I'm stunned silent as Noah kisses my head - a subtle signal of agreement that sends my head spinning.

But there's no time to question it. Wolves flock to the commotion outside the pack meeting center, flooding Noah with attention. As my mate is pulled away from me to support his pack, I'm left all alone, uncertain where I fit in. If there's even space for me.

Amy catches my eye, giving me a sad smile as she approaches. "You okay?"

I huddle closer, softening to a whisper. "A., what does it mean to be Luna? I don't understand. Am I just supposed to be Noah's glorified housewife? A princess to tote around for looks? Or am I going to have to do what Noah does and get yelled at by Elders all day?"

Amy snorts. "Okay, if you were in another pack, I'd have to

agree with the glorified housewife thing. But Greenfield is different."

She links our arms, walking me to a quieter spot. The forest welcomes us with a cool breeze, laced with humidity to suggest the incoming rain. But Greenfield wouldn't be green without rain, so we slip on our waterproof jackets by the time the light sprinkling shifts into a soft shower. We settle between a circle of thin, tall trees, spring flowers budding with bursts of color in every corner of the clearing despite the gray sky.

Amy lets out a heaving sigh. "Do you remember when we'd sneak away into the forest to play house, and I'd always ask you to be the mom?"

I grin. "Yeah. I figured you just liked having an excuse to call another girl your wife."

Amy laughs, smacking my arm. "Well, that's a fair point. But do you remember what else I used to say about your maternal side?"

My cheeks flush. I do remember, but I didn't think Amy did. I loved what she said so much that I've secretly held onto her words for decades.

Amy smiles, tucking stray hairs behind my ear. "I told you how if there was ever a job to give a whole city pure mom-love, you'd be the best at it in the world."

I bite my lips, trying not to cry.

She laces her soft fingers with mine. "Oh, babe. I said that because that's exactly what being a Luna is. From the day we met, you reminded me of a little Luna."

I let out a soft sob, but I'm smiling. "That could be my *job?* Just loving the pack?"

"Yeah, A." Amy sighs, beaming with absolute adoration. "Only if you want it. Noah won't pressure you, but I know he thinks the same as me. He didn't even have to know you your whole life to figure it out."

I hug Amy as hard as I can, blinking the tears from my eyes. "Amy, I need to know everything there is about becoming the next Luna. Can you teach me what you know?"

She laughs. "Of course I can!"

"You really think I could do it? This isn't just getting my hopes up and getting myself into another mess?"

Amy pulls back to look me in the eyes. Her smile widens. "Look at you. Most people would run away screaming at this idea, but you're glowing. This means the world to you, doesn't it? That says 'Luna,' right there."

I chuckle through tears, dropping my flushed stare. "I literally work at a preschool because of how much I loved that idea you planted in my head."

"Oh, girl. Now I'm crying too."

I laugh, diving back in to hold her. "If that's all true, being Luna is my dream job. And I want to do it right."

"I know you can. You just dove into a hole after a stranger's kid - in a skirt! You've got the stuff, girl." She laughs, squeezing me hard before pulling back to face me. "But you won't do it alone. We'll all help you."

Hope fills my heart for the future. Between meeting Noah and his pack, I'm growing into hope's warm, curious sensation, allowing it to exist without fear it'll be stripped from me.

But Amy's smile wavers. "The only problem is…"

My heart deflates.

Amy grabs me by the shoulders. "This is going to be difficult to hear, okay? But don't let go of this dream! It'll happen, I know it."

"Just tell me, Amy. What's the catch?"

"We also have to teach you how to be a wolf first, before *anyone* finds out you've never shifted before."

"I've never shifted… You mean into a wolf?"

Amy nods, her frazzled stare at my reaction only bolstering my anxiety.

I've felt my wolf all this time, but shifting - my body jerking, growing hair, and spawning a massive wolf ten times my size - hadn't crossed my mind as a possibility for me. Or anyone, for that matter, until I met Noah.

But I don't think I'll *ever* be comfortable with shifting. It's perfect intrusive thought fodder.

My stomach sinks. "Is it really that bad that I haven't shifted before?"

"Not exactly, it's just…" Amy looks around, stepping closer to whisper. "Remember how I said they don't take kindly to humans here? Someone shot your father, the top Beta, and Ritchie, their last Alpha. Wolves don't need guns to kill. As far as Greenfield Pack is concerned, humans are responsible for killing their beloved pack leaders five years ago."

My stomach rolls, making me hunch over. I can hardly even whisper my words. "Oh, God, Amy… Wouldn't that make Noah hate humans?"

"He told the pack he only hates recreational hunters, and he doesn't believe in hating an entire species for the actions of a few. But you have to wonder…"

I grip her arm. "But he still accepted me, without a second thought? Mated with me, then showed off my mark?"

Amy wipes my tears. "He did, babe. I think he's serious about you, to say the least."

No wonder Noah has kept me close ever since we got here. Our relationship sounds like a way bigger taboo than my mark.

But something doesn't add up. "Wait, I am a wolf, though."

"You are. At least, mostly. But the fact that you never had your heat until meeting Noah and also never shifted is highly… unheard of."

"Even for other part-wolves like me?"

Amy winces. "I can't say I'm well-educated on hybrid wolves, unfortunately…"

"No one else has been some type of hybrid before?"

"They have, but not in this pack. And especially not mated to the Alpha. If I'm being honest, I've never heard about any Alphas mated to hybrids."

I have to take a deep breath, feeling lightheaded.

Which is when Noah's mindlink interrupts my thoughts. *Are you okay? I know you're talking to Amy in private, but I feel something off, and I'm concerned.*

My heart lifts just enough for hope to re-enter. *I'm okay, thanks. We're just talking about something heavy. I'll be back in a minute.*

Take your time. Let me know if you need anything.

I smile, wiping away my tears. Gripping Amy's hands, I've

never felt more afraid yet certain about what I want. "I guess *someone* has to be the first hybrid Luna. Why not me?"

Amy breaks into a huge grin, tackling me with a hug. "I love you. You're such a badass."

"I love you, too, Amy. I don't know where I'd be without you."

"You don't have to know, because I'm not planning on going anywhere. We'll get it all worked out, okay?"

"Okay..."

But everywhere I look, wolves display their affection with hugs, nuzzling, and laced hands throughout their casual conversations, and there isn't a second of questioning their demeanor or social cues. But here I am, relishing in the fact that I let a man touch me for the first time in five years without panicking. I've never felt more behind.

18

Amy and I find Noah still crowded by eager wolves. The only indication he's there is his head - poking just a bit higher than everyone else's. As wolves trickle away, one woman stays by Noah's side, animated and giggling.

Noah passes me a subtle glance. The young woman follows his gaze, revealing sharp, glittering brown eyes set above stark cheekbones. When she spots me, she grasps Noah's arm to whisper, and his feet shuffle nervously.

I've never been the jealous type, but now there's even less reason to be; our bond reveals Noah's innermost emotions. When he looks at this woman, he feels adoring and protective, but his affection for her is in a separate category altogether from the romantic attraction he feels for me. She peeks at me again, nudging Noah harder, and that's when I feel it – soft, fluttering gushes of affection I witnessed from the moment I marked him. Noah touches his mark as he blushes, and I smile no matter how heavy my heart still feels; she must've mentioned me to Noah.

I stride over, hoping to meet this bright young woman. "Hello, I'm back!"

"Hi!" The woman beams. She raises her eyebrows at Noah, nodding toward me to urge him to introduce us. I giggle when Noah only shuffles his feet again, intense shyness erupting from our bond. The woman scowls. "Noah!"

He scowls back. "I-I know, I know."

It surprises me at first - a snappy youthfulness to Noah's demeanor that I've never seen from him. But Noah reaches for my hand, and I gladly take it.

"Sweet Omega, this is my little sister, Rainn."

I gasp, looking at Rainn with fresh eyes. Thick, silky brown hair frames her cut jawline, glowing, copper skin radiates warmth from her pink cheeks, and the same piercing eye shape encompasses her gaze. I have to laugh - I didn't see their stark resemblance sooner thanks to Noah's stoic resting face, whereas Rainn is a ball of vibrant energy.

I open my arms, dying to hug her. "Oh, my gosh, hi! It's so good to meet you!"

Rainn gives me the tightest squeeze she can, only pulling away to take another look at me.

Noah beams at Rainn as she breaks into a full-faced grin, opening her palms for me to grasp. When I take them, she lifts my hands to her nose to give them a good sniff.

I gasp. "O-oh! Uh–"

"Wow, you smell so nice! So woodsy and sweet!"

My smile wavers by the second. How the hell do I respond to that? Am I supposed to sniff her too?

I'm not ready for sniffing, so I give a polite laugh and blurt out an automatic response. "You too!" Rainn's eyebrows lift just as I remember she last told me I smell woodsy and sweet, and I haven't even smelled her. "Um - from here!"

Noah bites his lips, suppressing laughter. He wraps his sturdy arm around my waist, and my heart flutters.

"Rainn, we'll be seeing you soon to hang out for longer, but I've gotta get my mate home."

"Wait, has she met Mom yet?"

Noah puts a protective hand on my shoulder, urging me in another direction. Multiple wolves walk with us, and the unspoken pressure on Noah hangs over me. He's clearly trying to gain some personal space, but wolves circle him constantly.

Noah lowers his voice. "Not yet. But she will."

"Hmm... Okay..." Rainn fiddles with her purse strap. "Maybe you both should... Take a look around first..."

My stomach sinks. Did I do something weird already?

But Noah squeezes me closer, enveloping me in his protective scent. Rainn raises her eyebrows with a teasing smile, unphased by his deepening scowl.

"I know what you're thinking, Rainn. I'm not ashamed of my mark," Noah grumbles.

"I didn't say anything about the mark!" Rainn gasps, yanking on her brother's arm. Then she smirks at me. "That mark is pretty metal, though. You've got guts, Omega. I like you already."

My shoulders soften in relief. "Thanks."

Noah lets out a soft, clear laugh. I melt into its sound, holding his hand tighter.

"My mate *is* pretty metal. Especially beneath the surface," he says.

Rainn winks. "Then you two sound like a perfect match. Have fun!" With a giggle at our reddened cheeks, Rainn turns to the lingering wolves and bellows far louder than I expect from such a petite body. "Who's ready for dinner?"

She lets out another bright laugh when she's swarmed with attention. Rainn gives Noah one last smile, softening his eyes into genuine warmth, and I realize she announced that just to relieve him for the night. The second she disappears behind a crowd of hungry wolves, Noah releases a heavy breath.

"She's a sweetheart, and so damn cute," I say.

"Y-yeah? You like her?"

I giggle at Noah's hopeful smile, nuzzling into his arm. "I do, my shy Alpha. Hopefully I can get a chance to talk to her longer soon. As well as your mom."

He drops my stare. "Soon."

Oh, great. Something's up with him and his mom.

Noah seems as drained as I am as we drive a winding forest road to his home, huddled in Dave's back seats. I can't tell if it's just an assumption of mine or if there's a hint of sadness in our bond.

I nuzzle my forehead into Noah's chest. *How are you feeling?*

Noah's abdomen softens beneath my palm. *Tired. I'm sure you're exhausted though, with all you've been through.*

When he holds my head against his chest to kiss it, our bond lightens.

But I don't think he gave me the full truth. Noah strikes me as an extremely private wolf, so I'll have to check in when we're alone.

The sun disappears beneath the horizon, the sky's soft purple glow fading into indigo by the time we pull up in front of Noah's home. His cabin is more of a lodge. Rich wooden panels line the sizeable structure in a cherry warmth against the cool night sky. We're so secluded from the neighboring town that there are even more stars here than at my parents' old cabin, glittering across the sky like a gentle nightlight.

"This is *beautiful*, Noah."

He dips his head with a smile - back to his shy self - but he doesn't seem to have anything to say.

Okay, I'm worried now.

I'm mesmerized by Noah's scent the second we walk through the door, tension releasing from my body. But Noah solely focuses on me.

I pick at my thumbnail. "Are you oka—"

Noah drops my overnight bag, rushing to hug me to his chest. "I'm sorry."

"What? Why?"

Noah doesn't respond, but his heart drums against my ear. His stress pheromones put me on edge, crawling over my skin as they only magnify.

When I spot the source of his sadness in our bond, panic strikes - it's not a little upset, something is *seriously* wrong. What do I do?

19

Guiding Noah to a frigid metal barstool at his kitchen island, I give his shoulders a grounding squeeze. "Relax here for a second for me. Where are your cups?"

I search for a glass to fill with water, opening every cabinet with no luck. But Noah ditches his barstool, reattaching to me with a hug from behind.

Okay, he's seriously freaking out.

I try to nuzzle against his head on my shoulder, but his breath is still ragged. He might be too panicked to respond to my scent, but I'm not sure I'm even doing this scent thing right. I feel childish and inexperienced. But whatever Noah is experiencing needs immediate attention - whether it's wolfy attention or simply the best I can manage.

Dragging Noah by the hand into his living room, I swerve to the worn leather couch the second I see it; the faded dye on the sectional's long end tells me it's Noah's favorite spot. The cushions dip further beneath my weight than I expect, welcoming my body with a soft hug like it was broken in just for me.

But Noah doesn't sit with me, breaking away to pace across the living room rug. His breathing is rapid, and my heart pounds with each flex of his lungs.

I grip the couch cushions beneath my thighs, straining to keep myself calm for him. "Noah, talk to me. Don't hold it in."

"I'm just s-sorry," he gasps.

"There's nothing to be sorry for."

"No, I'm fucking everything up. I could've gotten you pregnant, I'm forcing you to meet all these cruel Elders who scared you on purpose, you're still new to this, and I'm–" Noah drops off, facing the wall so that his back is to me.

"You're what?"

"I'm not sure I can protect you from everything. What if I can't?"

My shoulders loosen. Now *this* is a fear I know how to handle. Uncertainty really does kill.

But if I reassure him now - with an "of course you will" or "it'll all be fine" - it'll be a lie. We *can't* know what will happen in the future. I don't know if it'll be fine, or if he'll be able to protect me. If I'll be able to protect myself.

It's terrifying to do, but giving up control over the unknown actually gave me my life back.

Instead of reassuring Noah, I state the truth. "Maybe you can protect me, or maybe you can't. That doesn't mean we can't get through it - figure it all out once we get there. And either way, it's my job to protect myself. I've made it this far on my own, and it's my responsibility at the end of the day to do what's best for me."

Noah's voice shakes as he finally meets my eyes. "But you haven't been okay in the past. You've been hurt a lot. I can feel it." He works his lip between his teeth, struggling to say his next words. "W-what if I accidentally hurt you someday?"

Pain spikes my core at the ache in his voice. This is it. What he's actually afraid of. And I can completely relate.

"You know, I've felt that fear around people I care about too. But like you said earlier, being with you is a risk I'm willing to take."

He bites his lips, sad eyes searching my face for answers.

So I continue. "I also know people get hurt in all relationships. It just happens. It's something I have to go to therapy to accept too. And I'm sure you know that already, having to lead all these wolves. No one will ever be 100% happy, no matter what you do."

Noah nods, his breath slowing. I hold out a hand for him, hoping he'll join me now.

He doesn't take it. "I still don't want to hurt you more."

"I know. I don't want to hurt you either. But what if I do someday, even by mistake?"

"I-I'd... Hope we can work it out."

Giving Noah a soft smile, I nod. "If it were the other way around, I'd hope so too."

Noah touches his mark absent-mindedly, and relief flows through our bond. But it's not enough for him to return to my side.

I soften my voice, unable to stop my heart from burning for him. "Is there something you need? I want to support you."

"I-I don't know. You're already so nice to me, and I'm being ridiculous."

"You're not. I get it. I really do." We lock eyes. I grip the couch even tighter, knowing what I have to say. "To be honest, I'm a fearful person. I don't want to be, but most people and things scare me. Which is why I'm pretty amazed by our bond already. I don't know how, but I'm not afraid of you, Noah."

My breath is rapid, but Noah's tension takes a rapid nosedive, leveling into a gentle hum.

"I think we're more similar than I realized," I say. "Believe me, I get what you're saying."

After Noah's glossy irises flit over my face, his wound eyebrows loosen. "I believe you."

He leans forward to approach me, but he stops himself.

My heart sinks. I don't think he's only afraid of hurting others. I think he's just like me; it's terrifying to know you could hurt anyone after you've been severely hurt.

I swallow hard, trying to sink into my instincts. What should we do, wolf?

An idea pops into my awareness, and I give Noah a soft, sad smile. His eyebrows raise in confusion.

"Noah, I have a bit of a personal question."

"Okay…"

"I know you're an influential, tough Alpha, and that probably makes it hard to be the one comforted." I take a deep breath, worried my next suggestion might pressure him. But with how eager my wolf becomes to soothe her Alpha, I know I have to try. "Has anyone ever held or comforted you before while you're hurting?"

He drops his head, rubbing his forehead.

Oh, shit. He's trying not to cry.

Noah simply shakes his head, "no." As in no, he's never been held. It guts me.

But with those big hands shaking in front of me, I melt for them. "Come here, my shy Alpha."

He doesn't show me his face beneath a curtain of his hair, but he takes my hand, sinking into the cushions beside me. Noah automatically tucks me into his chest, but I pull back, gripping his shoulders to pull him to me instead.

For the first time, he doesn't seem to know how to fit against me.

"It's okay. No one else is here." I scoot back on the sectional couch's long end - wide enough to double as a bed. Then I pat the open space between my legs. "Come lay right here with me."

He obliges, scooting closer until his legs dangle off the edge. I bite back a smile; Noah makes his huge sectional look like a toddler bed.

We have a silent battle; I have to urge him to stop tensing to keep himself from crushing me, helping him adjust his position until his head finally rests on my chest. His breath is rapid but quiet, uncertainty flooding our bond. I lace my fingers into the back of his shaved hair, hooking my arm across his wide back to squeeze him against me.

Kissing the top of his head, I stroke the long, tousled strands beneath my lips. My wolf is so happy that she spins, nipping at her tail.

Noah's abdomen tightens against my thigh, but he doesn't try to escape. He's letting himself be held.

My heart must be throbbing against his ear, but I can feel how badly he needs this. I hope he takes it in.

Lowering my voice, I nuzzle into his sweet scent. "I'm sorry you can understand. I wish you weren't hurt so badly too."

Noah curls into himself, digging his arms behind my back to squeeze me hard. He holds his breath, and my heart rate increases. Is he too uncomfortable? Maybe this wasn't a good idea.

But then Noah's shoulders shake us both. He lets out a soft sob. The fragile, crackling sound stabs deep into my heart.

I hug his head, cuddling him with my whole body. "I know

you've got me, but I've got you too, okay? You don't have to be alone anymore."

Noah holds his breath again, so I rub his back, and he lets out another whimper.

"Good job," I whisper. "Keep letting yourself feel it. You're doing so well, gorgeous."

I close my eyes, riding Noah's emotions with him as I breathe out my own heartache. It tears me apart to hear him softly crying, but it's also such a relief he's letting himself go with me. Offloading his heavy heart. I hold him through it, allowing him to cry for minutes upon minutes.

By the time Noah stills - his arms drooping behind my back - his heavy body lulls me to sleep with him.

20

When I stir in the middle of the night, I'm somewhere new. My half-asleep brain sends panic signals through me, popping me upright in an unfamiliar bed. How could I miss something this huge? Did I learn nothing from–?

Noah rises from a dead sleep beside me, placing his hand on my abdomen with his eyes still closed. Sleep roughens his voice. "You're okay, Omega. I've got you."

Tension drops from my body, flopping me back against the pillows. As my breath slows, my mate's scent floods my nostrils, and I know exactly where I am.

Despite the darkness, Noah's room glows with diffused, crystal-blue moonlight spilling in from massive windows. The panes are just tall enough to reveal the top of the pitch-black forest's silhouette.

Noah keeps his space tidier than I imagined, only a stray sock flopped underneath his stocky relic of a wooden vanity. But beside it, his closet is propped open, revealing an odd pattern.

I blink a few times, struggling to grasp what I see in the dim light until the black and white blobs morph into real objects: Noah has at least two copies of every shirt, jacket, and pants, planting an instant vision in my mind of his wolf leaping from his human form without warning and tearing his clothes into incomprehensible bits.

I sputter out a sleepy giggle, glancing over at him. He's already peeking up at me with bleary eyes. But what startles me is the moonlight reflecting in them like a true wolf; I've been sleeping in a nocturnal beast's den.

Yet every millimeter of me feels safe. He even moved my body, and something within my flighty nervous system knew I could trust him enough to stay asleep. I bite my lip, peeking into his eyes with an uncontainable smile.

Noah groans. "No, stop. That's too cute."

I laugh, plucking his tousled hair from his eyes. "What–?"

With the opening my raised arm gives him, Noah takes his chance to tangle our limbs, cramming his face into my pillow beside my neck with a purr. It feels so good that I don't even question my desires, rolling onto my side to bury myself deeper into him.

He adjusts for me, curling me into his chest until no side of me feels untouched by his heavy warmth. Comfort washes down my spine, and I let out a sleepy purr. Noah shifts to encompass more of me, scooping the back of my head in one palm.

Once I lie still for a while, slipping back into sleep, Noah softens his voice into the gentlest whisper.

"I adore you already."

Butterflies erupt in my stomach.

I rub my leg between his. "Noah…"

"Sorry. Stay asleep."

I drop my head back, reaching for his face. When I press my lazy, relaxed lips against his, he sighs, cuddling me tighter.

As my lips part, Noah kisses me long and slow, his scent flourishing with longing. The second our tongues meet with soft, slick pressure, my groin flexes with desire. I wiggle my body into him, craving to get closer even if it's physically impossible. He seems to feel the same, massaging my back with heavy, rolling pressure. His touch compresses my abdomen against his, and I moan into his mouth.

That's when I realize I'm still in my favorite dress. I urge Noah's hands beneath my skirt, kissing him through a satisfied purr as he grips my bare thighs. But when he can't roam any higher beneath the fitted bodice, he strips me of my uncomfortable clothes, cool air shocking my skin compared to his hot chest.

With Noah hovering over me, I hook my legs around his thighs, teasing his flexing cock until he hugs my hips tight. Noah grinds into me through my underwear, alighting my clit with tingling pressure. I work his tongue, gripping his hair.

Noah can't stop purring. *You're beautiful, Omega. I don't know what to do with myself.*

Keep going. You feel so good.

Noah's pleasure slips through our bond, pulling a moan from my lips. Noah grips my ass at the sound of my enjoyment, rocking himself against me faster and heavier.

The more I grasp his back, urging him closer, the deeper he bounces my ass into the mattress. Soon, I moan with every breath, unable to keep kissing him. When he gives my lip a soft nip, my knees fall slack, opening myself wide to him.

Grinding into me faster and faster, Noah rubs his hot shaft over my soaked underwear until my back arches.

"Noah!"

As he kisses me hard, his thumb strokes my neck with the pulse of his hips, amplifying each rub of my clit. My feet hug his hips into me as my knees squirm. Noah huffs as he dry-fucks me faster, my core bursting with pleasure as I come in a writhing, moaning mess of limbs.

Noah continues to kiss me, rocking against me until I settle into a mushy heap. Heat trickles through my chest as I hum through residual delight.

But when Noah releases my lips with a wince, I look down. He's so hard that his boxers look like they could rip open.

"Poor Alpha," I whisper, my wolf slurring my speech with leftover lust.

Slipping my thumbs into his waistband, I stretch it up and over his wet tip. Noah gasps in relief.

"Bring your hips up here, gorgeous."

He obeys me, lifting his hips, and I meet his leaking tip with a soft kiss. Noah shudders, gripping the headboard as I stroke him. When I lean in to lick the wet drop escaping his tip, Noah gasps, bumping his cock against my swollen lips with an eager flex.

It's even bulkier than I remembered, but with how relaxed he just made me, my throat is as loose and ready as it'll ever be. I stroke him with slower, deeper pressure as I slip my lips over his tip.

Oh, God. This is actually way too big - stretching my jaw to its limits if I want to keep my teeth off him. I soften my jaw muscles, opening my throat as wide as I can, but the second he hits my soft palate, I cough.

Noah jerks back. "No– I don't like feeling like I'll choke you."

My eyes widen at the thought, but my wolf stirs with excitement. "Is licking okay?"

Noah releases a desperate, pleading whimper, scrubbing his face before nodding behind his palm's protection.

I guess I'll just have to work with my tongue.

Noah's chest heaves as I massage his tip with my fingers. But when I bend to lick his shaft from base to tip, his breaths shift into gasps. I stroke him faster - my tongue leaving no section of his cock dry - and his purring turns into helpless whimpers.

"Oh, *Goddess*–"

My wolf gloats at how responsive he is to me - maybe too responsive. Each desperate breath sounds like I better speed things up before he can't take it any longer. I spit into my palm, using both hands to rub him until he thrusts into my grip.

"Fuck, you're going to kill me, feisty Omega–"

Squeezing against his rough thrusts, I flick the tip of his cock with my tongue, hardly able to chase him. Within seconds, he comes across my lips and chest - hot spurts of warmth slipping between my breasts. Warmth pools in my belly, delight filling me as his pleasure trickles through our bond, and I had the luxury of being the source.

I hope he feels it. How hard I've already fallen for him.

Noah's eyelids flutter as I gaze up at him, out of breath and licking him from my lips.

"Holy *fuck*," he wheezes.

Reaching over his nightstand for a tissue, Noah gently wipes me clean. His delicate touch over my breasts and lips makes me shiver. I'm struggling to grasp how sweet he is, wrapping my arms behind his neck as I indulge in his soft, grateful kisses. I nuzzle our noses, closing my eyes as he presses our foreheads together.

Without a single word, we ease back into each other's arms, agreeing to weave our limbs together.

I'm shocked at how instinctual I can let myself be around him.

Especially if this is our comfort level while it's still new. One of these days, we'll meld into a powerhouse unit. I can feel it in every satiated, blissed-out muscle.

Noah gingerly kisses my scent gland, sending shivers to my toes - a silent confirmation of our bond. I grasp his hair, nuzzling my mark on his neck, and he squirms with pleasure against me, huddling in deeper. All night, we tangle ourselves together in the deepest cuddle I've ever felt.

When I wake up beside my mate, I'm stuffed to the brim with comfort and affection. Noah's exhausted face is pressed against mine, his breath brushing my lips in his sleep.

I've never met someone who matched my craving for non-stop, full-body cuddles all night. It must be a wolf thing. I try not to laugh - recognizing our limbs as a literal dog-pile - but my giddiness rises in our bond anyway.

Noah snuggles harder into me, rubbing his nose against mine as he stirs. After pressing a kiss into his sleepy, full lips, I vibrate with excitement along with my wolf that I'll get to talk to him soon. Be with him for yet another day.

Noah chuckles himself awake, his limp hand lightly stroking my back. "Cute. So cute."

"Good morning, Alpha."

He frowns. "No, I don't want it to be morning."

I smile. "Well, unfortunately–"

Noah rolls on top of me, squeezing me with his massive arms until I let out a shout-laugh.

"Hey!"

"Please, no," he grumbles. "I want to hold you longer."

I burst into giggles, but then I jump when my phone alarm goes off on the nightstand, rattling Noah's lamp. Noah just groans.

After shutting off my alarm, I suck in a horrified breath at the numerous missed calls and texts since I met Noah.

Noah sighs. "Ugh, no... I'm going to have to let you go, aren't I?"

I laugh, even through my panic. "Oh, my God, Noah. I forgot to tell my therapist I was okay!"

Noah moans his response into the pillow.

"I'm sorry, I have to call her back."

"Okay," he says, lifting his chin just enough to breathe. "Can I hold you while you call her, or do you need space?"

I giggle, re-dialing my therapist as fast as I can. "Keep crushing me all you want, Alpha. I'll make it quick."

But as it rings, I realize I'm squashed beneath a man in his bed, and I might want to be with him - forever. The last Jenny heard, I lost all faith that anything this powerful could happen.

Not only that - I now believe I'm a freaking *wolf.* I can't tell Jenny that!

I hate lying to her. How the hell am I going to explain what happened the past few days?

My heart races into my throat, just in time for Jenny to pick up the phone.

21

"There you are!" Jenny's voice chimes through the speaker. "How are you feeling? I've been debating whether or not to do a wellness check."

My heart drops. "I'm so sorry, Jenny! I had a fever, and I... It's all been a blur!"

"I saw your texts about that, and they didn't make much sense. What happened, exactly?"

I suck in a horrified breath, putting my phone on speaker as I whip open her text messages. "Holy—"

Noah peeks over his shoulder as I scroll through several typo-ridden texts that autocorrect couldn't save.

Me (8:32 AM): I thouhght he was th one
Me (8:33 AM): Whyf he leave
Me (9:05 AM): Amys helpinf but I want Noah ti luck ny bwck

My cheeks burn hot, and my heart pounds against Noah's chest. He pats my head, struggling not to laugh, but I'm screaming internally.

"Jenny, I'm so sorry. I genuinely don't remember these fever texts! Amy was there to help me with my high fever, and I was—well, delirious."

"I figured as much, and I'm so glad you had Amy come to help you. But how are you feeling now?"

"I feel... good, actually."

There's a long pause, followed by Jenny's audible excitement. "Oh, *really?*"

Oh, God. It's depressing that my therapist is this shocked that I feel good.

"What about this Noah guy you met? You're over him already?" She asks.

That thought feels so wrong that I tense in Noah's arms. "No," I say, a little too strongly. I soften my voice, panic-spouting my words. "I mean, no, it didn't turn out how I thought. He left a note that he stepped out for supplies to help with my fever, but I was so busy being anxious that I didn't see it. Then he helped Amy take care of me."

Jenny laughs, and my heart feels a bit lighter. At least I've covered the gist of what happened.

"Oh, goodness. So you're still talking to him, I assume?"

Noah holds his breath, smiling against my ear, and I bite my lips.

"Um, yes. We're still talking."

I can practically see Jenny's mischievous smile through her heightening voice. "Oh? Why do I sense something more here?"

I giggle, gripping Noah's shoulder. "Probably because we're doing a lot more than just *talking*."

Jenny gasps before letting out a rambunctious laugh.

Noah's breath picks up the pace, eagerness buzzing through our bond.

"Okay, *what?!* I need to hear this before our next session Friday, or I'll be curious all week!" Jenny laughs, lowering her voice. "Did you have sex with him?"

Noah's chest stiffens as I grip him tighter.

His wolf ears will hear anything and everything, but it feels too nerve-wracking to loudly announce, so I take my phone off speaker and cup my hand around my mouth to whisper. "Jenny, I had the best sex of my life. Not even just one time."

She gasps. "What?! That's amazing!"

"And I was the one who initiated! I felt safe with him, and so comfortable, and it was just–" I catch my breath, unable to stop smiling. "Everything about it was so good."

Noah's cock twitches to life against my leg, and I suck in a yearning breath.

"Oh, my God! I'm so proud of you!" Jenny says.

I giggle, knowing she understands the true depth of this accomplishment. My stinging, watery eyes conflict with the rising heat in my groin - my body reacting to Noah's eager scent. I rub my thigh against Noah's erection to tease him, and he shuffles against me.

"He asked for your consent?"

"Multiple times."

"As he should! It wasn't painful this time at all?"

Noah freezes, and his emotions dip in concern.

But I can't stop smiling. "No, it didn't hurt. I couldn't believe that either. It felt amazing, the whole time."

"Aww, honey, I'm so happy for you! You've come so far."

Caressing my back in a massaging cuddle, Noah kisses my shoulder silently. His hands stop on my hips, and although he pauses, the silent suggestion that he's ready to give me more anytime is enough for wetness to seep into my underwear.

"It sounds like you went outside your comfort zone, and had a great time while you were at it," Jenny says.

"I really did. Well, I'm *still* having a great time."

"Oh? Are you saying you're planning on seeing each other again?"

Forget just my cheeks, my whole body flushes. "I'm - um - actually in his bed right now."

Jenny cackles so loud I have to lower my phone volume, and I laugh with her.

"I actually plan on seeing him for a long time. I can't believe it, but I feel like he's an important person in my life. I-" I swallow my words, nerves pounding through my arteries. "I really like him, Jenny."

I'm talking to Jenny, but that was for Noah. He nuzzles into my neck, stirring my wolf into giddy shivers.

"Aww, honey, I'm just so happy for you."

I swallow hard, dread creeping through my excitement. It's so familiar to me that I don't stop the compulsion in time, the insidious creature worming through my brain and out my mouth beyond my control.

"Y-you don't think I'm being irrational or moving too fast, do you?" I ask.

Jenny breathes, and my heart kicks up in worry. Noah holds perfectly still.

He's probably confused. He doesn't know how damaging even an innocent question can be. How "just one" will lead to just one *more*. And one more. Until I'm buried beneath a pile of fearful behaviors I hate, struggling to navigate even the simplest tasks.

Jenny's steady voice snaps me back into focus. "I'm a little torn as to if I should give you reassurance or not; that sounds like a compulsion."

Oops. Noah's wolf ears heard that, but does he know what Jenny means by a compulsion? "Okay," I say. "Or, well, I know. I didn't mean to. I hope it's not disappointing, or—"

I wince - there goes another tiny one. There's a brief pause. Jenny is being careful not to reassure my anxieties into cycling more, just like I had to do with Noah last night.

"I-I mean, I caught that one after it slipped out too," I say.

Jenny's smile shines through her voice. "It happens that way sometimes, doesn't it? And Aliya, I have to say it's the first time I've heard you so sure about how you feel with someone."

I smile. "Yeah. I'd have to agree with that."

"Do you feel like it aligns with your values to pursue this relationship?"

I hug Noah closer, rubbing my forehead against his neck, and he shivers. "Yes. Absolutely."

"If your gut says you want to be close, then keep acknowledging your fears and do what you'd be doing if those fears weren't there. I know you'll get there. Keep following your instincts, just like you've been practicing."

My heart throbs against Noah's chest as he turns his head, meeting my eyes. I flush as he strokes my cheek, beaming at me.

As we hang up, my gut twists with anticipation for Noah's thoughts. Before I called, I didn't think about how Noah would hear everything, but he's the one who brought out my wolf - the true, unfiltered side of me I've always hidden away. It's so easy to be my genuine self around him that it felt natural to let him hear. I just hope he was okay with everything I said.

But as Noah lifts his chest to hover over me, his grin widens, and my worries wash away.

Noah dips to kiss me, his shoulders flexing above his outstretched arms like a prowling lion. I slide my palms up them, caressing all the way up his neck. With my fingers tracing gentle circles over the golden spot I marked, Noah purrs into my mouth.

I immerse my fingers into his hair, spreading my legs for him, and Noah lowers himself flush against me.

But then he freezes, his lips still pressed to mine. It looks like he heard something.

After a tense silence, Noah growls.

I mindlink him with our lips still locked. *What is it?*

Noah sighs, kissing me deeper. *My mom wants to meet you. She's telling me off for not wanting her to.*

I break our kiss, my heart sinking. "What's so bad about meeting me?"

Noah sits up off me, his shoulders deflating. "I'm sorry. I didn't mean it like that. She's just–" He sighs, scraping his fingers through his bedhead until it's captivatingly messy. "She's not very warm. I don't want you to have to be around that just yet."

Dropping my stare, I hug my chest, hiding my boring, old bra. "Is it because I was raised as a human?"

Noah scratches the back of his neck, dropping his head. "Well, unfortunately, she's speciesist, so yes, that's part of it. We fight about it constantly." My heart pounds, but Noah meets my eyes with a shy smile. "I also just want to keep you to myself a bit longer. Without the stress of outside input."

I try to smile, but I feel too sick from his words.

Noah deflates. His shaky fingers sort out my tangled hair this time. "I-I'm sorry. This is part of what I meant last night. I hate putting you through this."

I need to get my head straight. This is Noah. Unless he says otherwise, he's not embarrassed by me like my ex. He's concerned for me like my mate.

Grasping his hand to my chest, I look into his eyes. "Noah, I'm your mate, and I want to be. There will always be something

143

to compromise on or share the load with during a long-term relationship. If this is what comes with ours, that's okay."

My heart throbs faster, debating on whether or not to share the rest of what I want to say. The full truth. But Noah gazes at me with such hope and relief that I can't help myself.

"There's something else." I give his knuckles a kiss, waiting for a response. He's frozen, but wrapped up in my every breath - teal eyes tracing my stare with full trust.

And just like when I discussed it with Amy, I know this is exactly what I want.

"Noah, I want to be your Luna."

He sucks in a sharp breath, and I flush down my neck.

"I know that's a lot to say and that I'm clueless, but my wolf is certain, and I'm certain about you, and—" I trail off in a sputtering, red-cheeked mess, but I'm too afraid of what's behind Noah's eager stare to hear it just yet, so I prattle on. "I'm sure all sorts of uncomfortable situations will happen often as Luna. I want you to see that you can trust me to handle it."

After a heavy swallow, Noah's voice comes out soft and steady. "It's not you I don't trust. I don't want anyone to be hurtful to you. Especially not my own mother."

"How she treats me is up to her, and not about our relationship. As long as you and I treat each other with kindness, I'll be happy."

Noah grasps my hand, lacing his fingers through mine. But when I finally look at him, I'm surprised to find he's not smiling. "I just don't want to put you in situations I know will suck if there's still a chance I could do anything about it."

I give him a playful smile. "Sounds like you're still taking on this protection thing all by yourself."

He leans over me, kissing my cheek. "It's in my instincts to protect you, sweet Omega. I care about you too much to not follow them."

His deep whisper makes me shiver. My core aches with desire, and I chase Noah's lips before he pulls away. He settles in to kiss me, heavy, longing drags of our lips curling my toes off the bed.

But after kneading his lips a few times, I can tell he's distracted.

"Is she still linking you?"

He sighs, sweet puppy-dog eyes dropping to my collarbone. "Y-yeah…"

"How bad will she react to me, honestly?"

Noah groans, scrubbing his forehead on my stomach. It tickles so much that I burst into giggles. He pops back up with a smile.

"I don't know." His smile fades. "I haven't been able to predict her behavior since my dad died."

My throat tightens. "I'm so sorry. My mom changed when my dad died too. But she died of heartbreak only a month later."

Noah drops his forehead against mine. Grief flows from both sides of our bond.

"That sounds horrifyingly painful to go through, one after another," Noah says.

I nod, cupping his face to hold him to me.

Noah cups my cheek back, toying with my bottom lip with his thumb. "I think my mom would've died too, but instead, she just became someone else. My dad wouldn't recognize his mate."

Noah's darkening voice tingles my spine. I sit up, and we break apart, facing each other in our underwear as if we've known each other our whole lives.

"Like… her personality changed?"

"Her personality, her attitude towards life, her care for others… It's all gone. She just kept her hatred."

I shrink. "That makes her sound cruel."

He shrugs. His nonchalant attitude strikes me as a bad sign. A cover-up.

I feel like she hurt Noah. Badly.

"I don't think I've met another Luna like her. Or another Omega, for that matter." Noah kisses me, but as he slips off the bed, my heart still pounds. He grabs a fresh set of clothes, shooting me a soft smile from his dresser. "Hey, it's okay. Let me talk her down today. Then we can meet her together next weekend."

As Noah heads for the shower, I grip his duvet to my chest. A flash of hot anger stirs my wolf into action, pulling me from Noah's warm bed to shake off my sweating palms.

There's no way I'm letting Noah take any abuse in my stead. If she's cruel to him in front of me, I'll give her a piece of my mind.

But let's hope it doesn't come to that. I'm going to try to make the best impression I can.

With a fire in my gut, I whip up a quick breakfast by the time Noah meets me in his kitchen, the longest strand of his wet hair outlining his cheekbone. His eyes widen as I slide a plate of eggs and grilled veggies toward him.

"This is for before you head out for the day."

"I-I don't expect you to wait on me."

"It's breakfast for both of us. But also as thanks, for such a good night's sleep - and then some."

With my wink, Noah flushes a deep red, sitting at the kitchen island with a subtle smile. I notice him eyeing the vegetables warily, but he quickly shovels them into his mouth once he has a taste.

I add more of everything to his plate. "Let's invite your mom to lunch today."

Noah's fork freezes in the air, mid-bite.

"We can invite Rainn too - take some tension off the situation by making it a whole family thing. And if your mom hates me, she hates me. I'm still your mate. She'll have to accept it on her own. I'm not letting you face this alone, either. Don't underestimate your feisty Omega."

Noah's eyes are laced with fear, but my words turn his expression into mush. "Okay. I'll link them both."

22

By the time we're sitting across from Rainn and the Greenfield Pack Luna for lunch in the Forest Café, my stomach knots hard enough to evaporate my appetite.

Lilian's golden-brown skin glistens beneath the cafe's gentle lighting, but her angular eyes are just as set and hardened as Noah's, if not more. Her graying hair winds into a tight bun behind her head, youth still gracing her full lips and lean cheeks. I've tried to keep my eyes off the white scar streaking the left side of her forehead, slipping past the right side of her nose and just beneath her eye, but it's difficult to make eye contact without my gaze catching on it. Guilt permeates my lungs when she notices me staring, but Lilian carries on as if it's expected, not sparing me a second glance.

Introductions went okay, but not even Rainn's lighthearted chatter can take my mind off Lilian's set jaw. I'm getting the sense she's talking to Noah privately through mindlink, which means I feel like the odd one out. Embarrassment and hurt simmer in my gut. I know Noah feels awful about it; his stormy eyes shoot me pained glances every minute or less.

But I want to learn from Lilian about becoming Luna, and get on her good side while I'm at it.

As the waiter takes Lilian's order, Rainn cups her hand over my ear. "Mom likes it when people ask specific questions. She'd never admit it, but she's a bit shy without a little boost."

My rising headache softens. I touch Rainn's arm with a smile, leaning in to whisper. "You're an angel."

Rainn's grin brightens until it scrunches her nose at the top.

When Lilian turns back to me, I straighten. "Luna, I'd love to hear about something you admire most about the Greenfield Pack. I've been so curious how it's been for you as an Omega here over the years."

Lilian lowers her fork, settling in with her stare. At least I think that's a stare, not a glare. "Greenfield is highly admirable. I remember wondering the same thing as an outsider Omega and being pleasantly surprised."

I don't appreciate being called an outsider, but I smile anyway. "I can see why. The pack you and Noah are holding together makes me feel at home. Thank you, Luna."

Lilian nods. "My mate left our pack in incredible shape for Noah to inherit. I personally believe we didn't have to change much, but Noah is never satisfied with tradition."

My heart sinks. Did she have to phrase it like that? On top of slamming Noah's belief system, she gave him basically no credit.

But Rainn folds her hands under her chin, grinning at Noah. "And Noah's advocacy work really took it the extra mile. We're really living up to the Greenfield name, wouldn't you say, Mom?" She nudges Lilian softly, and I bite back a laugh - the two of them suddenly looking like a Maltese puppy poking a mountain lion with her nose.

Noah scoots closer, but his voice still comes out so soft that I have to lean in as he speaks. "I-I forgot to mention my grandma was the first Greenfield Alpha."

"Your *grandma?*" I gasp. "Wait, that must've been decades ago. Wasn't a woman leading a pack pretty untraditional?"

Noah grins wide enough to show off his sharp incisors. "Absolutely."

I follow his eyesight to Rainn's proud smile. But when Lilian looks up from her water glass, Noah drops his head to shake out his tousled hair - or to avoid his mom's glare. She rolls her eyes.

But Rainn pays her no mind. "Grandma would be so proud. Her son and his son already left a vital mark on the world."

"Your dad certainly did," Lilian mutters.

I can't take this anymore.

"It seems like they've *all* been incredible Alphas," I blurt out.

The resulting silence raises my shoulders.

When Noah peeks over with a stifled grin, I lighten my tone. "I'm sorry I wasn't here to see Alpha Ritchie's leadership. But in meeting your son, I have no doubt his dad was an outstanding top Alpha."

Lilian quirks one eyebrow. "Well, you don't really know Noah yet. You've only marked him."

Rainn gasps.

But Noah's gentle voice sharpens. "Mom."

Oh, no. With how defensive Noah already feels, my wolf is boiling.

I grip Noah's hand beneath the table. "I did mark him. And after waiting my whole life to find my mate, I'm excited to get to know him more every day."

Lilian drops her stare, shaking her head as she sips her water.

Rainn puts her arm around my shoulders in a gentle squeeze. "I'm excited for you both too."

I try to give her a reassuring smile, but it's a wimpy excuse of one - only lifting one cheek.

The waiter arrives with our order, including a full plate of meat for Noah. I shrink into myself; I probably shouldn't have fed a wolf mostly vegetables this morning. He's so sweet to have eaten it anyway.

But Lilian is right. I have so much more to learn about Noah.

Noah slips his hand from mine to rub my back. My tense shoulders soften.

His gentle voice is even quieter than usual, lowering our conversation into a hum. "Mom, I was hoping you could tell us more about what it's like to be Luna."

"So she can strip me of my title?" Lilian snaps, intending to silence us, but Noah doesn't miss a beat.

"You mean like you did when you mated with Dad? That's how it usually works, yes."

Noah's stoic stare is icier than usual, leaving no room for questions. Not even Rainn gives her room to budge, meeting her with a rare straight face.

Lilian falls silent, turning to her food.

I feel too sick to keep eating. I don't even know what to ask, this time.

149

"It's a lot of work, being Luna," Lilian mutters. She says nothing more.

I try not to visibly dissolve, wishing I could hide beneath the table.

But Lilian clears her throat. "However, it's manageable for the right person, considering much of it just requires some compassion for those who need it."

Okay, I can work with this. I give her my preschool teacher smile. "That's wonderful. Thank you for sharing that, Luna."

She nods, shoving more food into her mouth without meeting my stare. I bite back a smile; with her flushed cheeks and short, fleeting glances, I recognize a little bit of Noah in her now.

"Luna, I'm curious, when you say those who need it, which pack members are you referring to? Do you feel like certain groups need more support lately?"

She softens her glare, still gluing her focus to her plate. "The Rogues. Noah is like his father, seeing the majority who suffer over the few who create chaos. I'm grateful for our family's long-term values in that."

Rainn glances over my head at Noah, her voice soft and sincere. "Me too. You still have no idea how much you help the pups I meet."

Noah's tense jaw finally loosens, allowing a sweet smile to shine through his eyes. "I-I'm glad. They have the best teacher, so they should be happier during the day, at least."

Rainn laughs. "Oh, stop. You're too sweet to me."

I gasp. "Rainn, you're a teacher too?!"

Rainn's chest lifts. "I am - Greenfield's Forest School daycare teacher! I was so excited to hear that we had that in common!"

I peek at Noah, surprised by my shy mate. "You didn't tell me Rainn was a teacher!"

Rainn laughs. "Because I'm not his mate. Once you get Noah talking about something he *adores*, he'll never stop."

My heart flips.

Noah sighs, his focus buried into his plate over burning cheeks, but he's still grinning. "Never?"

Rainn grips his shoulder over the back of my chair to give him a playful shake. "No, never!"

I can't stop smiling as the two siblings beam at each other, Noah rising into a playful giggle that lifts my heart.

But Lilian isn't smiling. "My heart genuinely aches for those Rogue pups. Your Alpha is right; they're lucky to have you as their role model, Rainn."

Rainn bites her lip, but she's smiling softer than I've seen all day, her eyes glassy with emotion.

From what I've gathered, Rogues are Lycans outcast from a pack. They have a bad reputation in most places. But I had to find that out through Amy and Kira; Noah never says a single disparaging word about Rogues. In his eyes, they're displaced refugees. Abuse survivors, stuck without resources to move like I was – if my parents didn't die and leave me everything they ever owned.

I clear my throat, not expecting to get as choked up as I am. "I'm so grateful for your family's compassion in that too, Luna. You have no idea." But she must have some idea of how much I really mean it, holding my stare a fraction longer with a surprising burst of warmth.

Lilian fiddles with a meat scrap, passing it back and forth across her plate. "But I believe you initially asked about my personal opinion, yes? About who needs a bit more compassion?" She only meets my eyes for a split second - just long enough to see me nod before zipping back to her plate. "I have to admit I have an extra special place in my heart for those who have lost a loved one. A mate." Lilian chews on her lip. "Well, if they survive. There's only a few survivors every decade."

Noah's overwhelm spikes. I grip his hand harder, attempting to stabilize us both, but I'm shocked too. Lilian is offering this information herself, and it's deeply personal. Not only to Lilian, Rainn, and Noah but to my parents too.

She swirls the meat scrap around her plate faster, her voice quieting into a delicate purr. "Maybe I've become more jaded with age, but being Luna didn't feel like a job when I was Noah's age. And certain tasks still don't feel like work, so I hang onto those moments. Let them carry me through the rest."

"I love that. What types of tasks?"

"Even before we lost Ritchie, Noah was our rainbow baby

after his sister's loss, so I understood grief on a level many can't without experience."

I clench my jaw, stifling the sharp pain in my chest. So they lost Noah's older sister during pregnancy? I have a million questions and heartaches, but I wouldn't dare interrupt Lilian.

Her voice rings with confidence, no matter how quiet. "I visit grieving wolves and check in with them, ensuring they feel supported. We have a network of wolves bringing grieving pack members daily meals and comforts."

My heart pounds. "I wish I had a community like that when I lost my parents."

She places her hand over mine, her comforting scent washing over me. "Now you do."

With loosening shoulders, I smile away the threat of tears. "Thank you, Luna."

"You're welcome, my dear."

Lilian gives me an honest, shy smile, and the atmosphere in the whole restaurant lifts. I finally feel safe enough to take another bite, feeling Noah's wolf relax with mine.

But then Noah stiffens. I look up to find Lilian glaring at him. He won't even look at her.

Turning to Lilian, Rainn's whisper is surprisingly sharp. "We're eating."

But Lilian doesn't even look at her daughter, locking her focus onto her rigid son.

After a fiery silence, Lilian shakes her head with a scoff. "Oh, enough of this. If you won't even talk, why are you here? Look at how uncomfortable you've made your poor mate."

"Mom, don't drag her into this."

"I'm doing this for her sake! Especially since she's a sweet girl, and I'm unhappy with you for a reason."

Noah slinks into himself, and my heart breaks into a sprint.

"What are you even talking about, Mom?" Rainn rubs my arm, her protective, nurturing pheromones flooding my nose.

Lilian leans toward me. "I do think you're a kind wolf, Aliya, but I'm not sure anyone is cut out to deal with my eldest. This pack is doomed without my mate."

I can't help it - I'm furious. I grip my napkin, focusing as hard as I can on keeping my voice neutral. "I'm sure things are different when any leadership changes, and I know it must've been horrific for your family. But I don't appreciate how you're talking about Noah. I'm not 'dealing with' your son. I'm his *mate*."

"And a pity it is for you."

Noah's chest puffs, and I wrap my arm around his bicep. Through the shared pain in our bond, Lilian's words sting me too.

But Lilian grips the table, ready to dig further. "He's quiet. Guarded. So inflexible with his personal opinions about traditions to the point where he's always clashing with respectable wolves. A bad name for Alphas everywhere."

Noah scoffs, but I speak my mind before anyone else has a chance to talk over me.

"Because he cares about the pack. Like you do."

"No one would know it. Hardly says a word. You didn't see *me* stop talking when I was traumatized."

Is Lilian implying that Noah stopped talking after a traumatic event? That's not her information to share. I'm so shocked by her callousness that I can only stare; my thoughts whir too fast to form words out of them. Rainn's wide eyes only sting my heart harder - the disappointing reality settling in.

Panic shoots through our bond. Noah jerks upright, bumping his thighs into the table and spilling my water glass all over me. He catches it, but it's too late to keep me from being drenched, ice cubes toppling out after the frigid drink douses my thighs.

Noah gasps. "I-I'm s-sorry!"

I quickly soak most of the water with Noah's napkin. "It's okay! It just was an accident–"

Guilt seeps into our bond as he dries my wet lap, his face bright red. Then he turns to leave like his life depends on it.

Lilian scoffs. "You're blowing me off, again? I forgot to mention he always leaves when it's convenient for him. How can you lead when–"

It's my turn to stand, glaring at Lilian. "Oh, he can leave whenever he wants to. But *I'm* not done talking to you."

Noah freezes in the doorway. His breath is jagged as he glances between Lilian and me.

"I don't see the point. I know you don't understand why yet, but he's not healthy. I'm just trying to warn you," Lilian says.

Rainn is crying now, shuddering through hot tears. "Seriously, Mom? This isn't what I came for."

My stomach burns. Rainn is right. Lilian isn't rubbing Noah's trauma in his face for another second. No wonder Noah keeps his thoughts to himself.

I'm so angry that my voice shakes. "It's obvious you're bringing up something personal without his permission."

"Something personal?" Lilian laughs. "You're his mate, aren't you? Or did you just bite him like a clueless pup?"

Her words burn, prompting Noah's figure to tense in the distance. But after everything Noah promised me, I can't let this go.

"Maybe I am clueless. But I sure as hell don't own my mate." I blink away the dizziness of my racing breath.

I know this game. She's distracting me. Flinging personal insults until I forget myself and say something I don't mean.

But this game is familiar. And I hate how familiar it feels for Noah.

I straighten my back, circling back to the actual problem at hand. "Trauma changes the brain. I can't believe you're acting like he changed on *purpose*." My spine alights with electricity as my wolf speaks through me, warping my voice into a growl. "I'll never be embarrassed by my mate experiencing trauma. I'm only embarrassed for you that you've held that against your own son."

Lilian rises. Her infuriated pheromones shrink me. "You think I don't care about Noah? Look at my face. I've protected him my whole life, and I have scars to prove it."

"That doesn't give you an excuse to be cruel now!"

"Come back to me when your mate dies and your big, tough Alpha son wasn't there to do anything about it."

I shudder as Noah's emotions darken past anything I've felt in our bond. Noah bolts from the building, slipping from my sight.

23

Rainn's lips warp through heavy tears. "I can't believe you."

She storms out after her big brother. But where Noah disappeared, Rainn takes a sharp turn, dashing past the windows down our side of the restaurant. Her shoulders shake as she trudges home with heavy stomps of her black boots.

When I turn around, Lilian looks like she aged ten years: cheekbones hollow and eyebrows contorted in sorrow.

I want to charge after Noah, but what Lilian said was personal. "I wasn't there either! Did I kill my dad too by not going with him to lunch that day?"

Lilian's eyes bulge. "Wait, what?"

"Ritchie and my dad were shot by a *hunter*, not Noah!" I suppress furious tears, my breath hitching. "Are you trying to kill Noah next? Because that's all you're doing by blaming him for it!"

"You're Takahiro's daughter?" Lilian's eyes widen in horror, but I don't stop to give her another thought.

I'm already sweating as I sprint out the door, Noah's pain rippling through our bond and burning my heart. He's fast, and he could be anywhere. Where would a wolf escape to?

Outside the restaurant, I veer for the forest. My chest clenches painfully tight; he's nowhere to be seen. I try what I've seen Noah and other wolves do - sniffing the air for clues - but I still can't trace scents like they can. Lilian's words echo in my mind - I really am an outsider.

But I care about Noah, and he needs someone, outsider or not. *Where did you go?* I mindlink Noah.

Even as I sprint deep into the forest's mass of trees, Noah doesn't respond.

That's right, Lilian mentioned Noah shuts down around whatever this trauma is. He probably doesn't mindlink either. But I'm sure he could still hear me, right?

Noah, I'd never dream of blaming you for this! I'm so, so sorry you had to hear those awful words.

A sudden tugging in my chest urges me to follow it.

Mate, he mindlinks. Except it's more of a feeling than the word itself, a concept I've never had to notice within my own thoughts until they joined with someone else's. Noah must be 100% wolf brain right now.

I chase the tugging sensation toward him, so focused on him that I don't notice the roots beneath me until I smack straight into the dirt. The impact steals the air in my burning lungs, freezing my diaphragm in place. After a few grueling seconds, I can cough my lungs back into working.

God, I'm such a mess. Always tripping and falling, even at work - making a fool of myself in front of important people who already think I'm incompetent just because I'm an anxious, young woman. I stumble back to my feet with a wince. Noah's mood only darkens, so I break into a sprint.

I know my opinion might not seem significant compared to your mom's awful judgment. But I just met you, and you're already so important to me. You're—

I forget everything I'm trying to say when I spot a wolf in the distance.

Now that my wolf has surfaced more than ever, my internal alarm rings from the stranger wolf's posture alone. The thready heartbeat pumping through my ears sinks into background noise as my senses hone in on the wolf.

After hunching into the bushes, my muscles freeze still.

Noah, there's another wolf.

The tug I feel in our bond surges with Noah's urgency, but I'm too afraid to move. Scents become so overpowering that I envision them as colors, whispering through the forest like smoke.

This wolf must think I'm an outsider, unmarked by Noah's scent that would verify my place in the pack. Running isn't an option; I know better than to do what I did last time and make this wolf chase me. But if Noah isn't nearby, this wolf is close enough to attack, no matter how quickly Noah finds me.

Hunkering into myself to appear smaller, I back away as slowly as I can with my eyes locked on the wolf. With every step I retreat, the wolf takes one forward.

After three steps, they exit the shadows. I stiffen, absorbing every second of their brown fur shining red in the sunlight. It's not the first time I've seen a wolf with a brown coat before, but I also don't know how common they are among Lycans.

But a little voice in the back of my mind won't leave me alone: is this the same wolf that attacked Noah the day we met? No, it can't be, right?

My stomach sinks. Either way, they mirror my movements, recognizing me as a threat. The more I retreat, the more this wolf will want to corner me. Maybe I should act like I belong here. Claim my space.

I freeze in place, standing my ground. Remaining as still as possible, I soften my breath.

The quieter I stay, the more my senses heighten. Every brush of leaves sounds like skittering bugs across my skin, bristling the tiny hairs across my body. There are so many scents at once that my head throbs with each heartbeat until I'm nauseous. My wolf stirs more than I've ever felt her, my eyesight warping as she demands control.

Oh, God. I feel weird.

Noah, something is wrong with me.

My gut flip-flops with every pounding heartbeat as the feeling only gets worse.

The tingling starts in my fingers. I raise my hands and find my nails stretching and sharpening. I resist the urge to shriek, shaking out my fingers and shoving my wolf down, down, down.

Is this what shifting feels like? No, I don't like this. I don't feel like myself.

But then the wolf in the distance moves. Slow, creeping paws lift one by one, easing back into the forest ground cover without a single sound.

Until the wolf startles: something draws their attention deeper into the forest. Their eyes widen, locking onto whatever they find. When they sprint away for their life, I follow their gaze, my teeth chattering with fear.

A black wolf stalks through the forest. His entrance silences every bird, bug, and squirrel in the vicinity.

My heart drops when I see my mate. He carries his massive form more menacing than ever, hanging his head low with rolling shoulders. But I can feel him aching - his tense, frothing snarl is a fearful cover-up.

"Noah," I whisper. His ears twitch, halting him in place.

I run to him, scrambling over tree roots as his ears slink back. As I throw my arms around his snout, he catches my full weight, closing his eyes to my touch.

Our bond sparks with a shred of comfort. But when Noah lets out a soft, pained whine, I feel sick.

"I'm so sorry," I say.

Noah's huff blasts my legs with hot air. Then *I'm* in the air, laying on his snout.

"Noah!?"

My yelp becomes a laugh as Noah's limp tail gives a soft wag. When he places me back on my feet, he nudges my hand to get me to follow him.

Guiding me through the forest, Noah pads alongside me with rotating ears, capturing every minor sound. To my ears, it's remained silent since he appeared.

But that was freaky earlier. I felt so threatened that everything was so much louder. Was that adrenaline, or was that really my wolf?

Noah side-eyes me, and I give him a sad smile. When he side-eyes me again only five seconds later, trying to pretend like he's not staring, I laugh.

He tilts his head like a perplexed puppy, his big ears perking up, and I laugh harder.

"You're so cute, Noah."

His ears slink back, but the giddiness in our bond tells me he's pleased to be seen no matter how shy he feels. But as we continue to walk in silence, his ears droop all the way down again.

He's still hurting. I want him to know why I'd never blame

him like his mom does; it doesn't even make sense, considering what I was told about Ritchie's death.

"Noah, I know our situations aren't exactly the same, but I used to find a way to blame myself for their deaths too. Until I realized it just didn't make sense. I didn't pull the trigger, so…"

Noah's paws slow, his chin lowering in alarm as he stands straighter.

I study his hulking wolf, struggling to figure out what I said to make him look so confused. Then I suck in a horrified breath.

Noah doesn't know who my father is. If Amy didn't tell me, I wouldn't have known who Noah's dad was either. I've only called my parents "Mom and Dad," and every photo I own of them is tucked away from when it was too raw to see them smiling on the walls.

Noah's wolf stare makes my heart race more than usual, but it's even worse when he's so intent on my next words. If I don't explain this in a sensitive way, he might blame himself for my dad's death too.

"Our dads were close. Which I knew, but I never knew Ritchie had a son, or that he was a Lycan." I swallow, bracing myself for what I'm about to say. "My dad was shot and killed too. Otherwise, I wouldn't want to act like I understood how you feel."

Noah's ears stiffen higher than I've ever seen them. My heart rate spikes.

I grip my arm, afraid I haven't said enough. "I can explain better once we get to where we're supposed to be going. I'm a little anxious out here after almost getting attacked."

He nuzzles my palm in reassurance before guiding me between two massive boulders. Once we dip to greet the other side of the rock formations, the trees grow tighter and thicker, blanketing the hilly forest for miles like evergreen snow.

I hike in antsy silence, replicating Noah's footsteps. Everywhere else is overgrown and wild, but he's left a small trail in the ground. I wonder how often he visits.

The trees part, revealing one of three forest rivers. I'm mesmerized by the river's serenity in this section.

"Noah, this entire place is so gorgeous."

I turn back to where he last was to realize I've lost sight of him

- which feels impossible, considering he's massive. Just before I call out his name, his sulking, black head pops out from between a small inlet of rock, patiently waiting for me. I round the inlet to find a wide, dark den, tucked into the hillside.

I gasp. Is this a pack den? No, it's too empty.

A gust of wind scoops out a familiar wash of scent to greet me: a sweet, contemplative smell that sends goosebumps from my neck to my thighs. This is *Noah's* den, and his rising nervousness tells me this is a deeply personal gesture.

24

Noah peeks at me with only his eyes, keeping his head bowed. *This is my den. No one else is allowed.* His tail softly wags as his eyes dart to the ground and back to me. *Except for the little wolves. I can't seem to get mad at them.*

My heart pounds as I trace the rocky entrance's cool surface with my eyes alone, unsure if I should enter.

But Noah sits on his haunches, thumping his tail softly on the ground. *When I said no one else is allowed in, I meant besides you and me, sweet Omega. This is yours now, too.*

"Noah, this is…" My eyes water, although I can't place why. As I take my first step inside, my spine alights with warmth despite the chilled, damp air. "It smells like you. I love it."

Noah stands, his tail wagging harder. He does a few circles before slinking to the ground, leaving an obvious space for me against him.

But I can't bring myself to sit. How am I going to tell him about my dad?

Noah whines, easing back to his feet. As he nudges my cheek, my fingers disappear into his fluffy head.

Talk to me. I can handle it, he mindlinks.

I swallow hard, wanting to believe him, but I know this will be a painful conversation, no matter what. For both of us.

But Noah nudges me again. His vibrant, golden irises are piercingly serious, and I know I have to share the truth eventually.

"I realized we're not on the same page about our dads' deaths, and I don't even have all the information," I say.

Delicately nuzzling me, Noah slinks around me with soft whines. His earnest cries make my eyes sting hot.

It sounds like you know more than I realized too, he mindlinks. *How did your dad pass?*

I shiver, terrified of this conversation. Noah misunderstands my quivering as being cold and huddles closer.

"Noah, I'm so sorry you understand this pain so well. Amy told me my dad was in your pack, which I had no idea existed. Not only that, but..." I grip my dress. "She explained they were more than just best friends. My dad was also Alpha Ritchie's Beta, which is why they hunted together and passed away on the job. That a hunter mistook them as targets... supposedly."

His huge wolf eyes gaze deep into mine.

"I don't know how you and I never met. My dad was Takahiro Matsuoka."

Our bond ripples and shifts, aching so badly that I wince. Noah tenses, pulling back from me, and my stomach flips. I jump to my feet as if he's tearing my heart out with him.

"A-are you leaving me?"

He freezes, his snout puffing dirt around me with his heaving breath. *N–no. Please don't keep thinking that about me.*

Guilt stabs my gut. He's right; I keep assuming the worst based on past relationships. But I also get the feeling Noah runs away to cope.

I'm not leaving you, he mindlinks. *But I don't know how to live with the guilt.*

"What do you mean? You're not listening to your mom, are you?"

He slinks back, and I automatically chase him. He freezes again. *She's right. I should've been there. I'm so sorry. We never met because Takahiro never wanted you to live like us – fight for our lives like us, get shot like us... I should've seen it coming and protected you from having to lose him too. Goddess, I wasn't there to protect you in so many ways now.*

His massive wolf suddenly looks so small, curled into himself with one raised paw against his cheek - almost like he's hiding from me.

I don't know why, but I wanted to stay home that day on our usual perimeter check, and Takahiro went in my place. Fuck, I'm so sorry, I'm so sorry...

I stumble forward, grasping Noah's fur. It feels like if I don't cling on, he could disappear. "You mean I could've lost my mate that day too? I would've truly been alone, forever?"

He whines even louder, bowing his head.

"I wasn't there either, Noah. I took a pass on our weekly lunch date, so he left to see Ritchie early."

Noah's whine morphs into a soft howl that makes my entire body shiver. The second he does it, I burst into tears. He crawls on massive paws. One big black paw pad scoops me against his chest before Noah drapes his head over me.

I'm sorry. Even if I don't deserve someone as sweet as you, I want to be your mate. Please don't think otherwise. I don't want to leave you.

"Please don't, especially not because of this. I'd never blame you for someone else's shot."

I know you wouldn't, sweet Omega. But I'll blame myself for not being there, forever.

As he wraps himself tighter around me, Noah tucks me against his ultra-soft belly. His heavy heartbeat thumps against my head. Immersed in his fur, it's pitch black. Safe.

I let myself cry with him. He gets it. How horrific their deaths will feel for the rest of our lives.

Maybe Lilian was right. Noah is hurting worse than it seems, and it's taking a toll on his health. But I can't say I'm as cheery or healthy as I want to be either. Like Noah, I want to be his mate, regardless. Even before our bond, something within me felt connected to him, down to my soul. I want to get to know him, however long it takes for us to open up.

I run my hands through Noah's fur, scratching his chest until his breathing slows. As my hands reach where I marked his neck, Noah's muscles loosen and our bond flourishes with warmth. He cuddles me closer, sending waves of pleasure through me with his pleased scent. Despite my tears, I smile at the love filling my core.

That's right. We have each other now.

"Thank you, Noah."

How could you thank me for this?

"I didn't even know how my dad really died until I realized I was a wolf. All that time, I could only theorize it wasn't an accident... Which made a lot of people think I'd lost it. But now that I know it happened during a perimeter run, it comforts me to think he was already choosing to risk his life for this beautiful pack. Whether his death was an accident or not, he died doing what he wanted." I bite back fresh tears, smiling through it. "And if that means his death spared your life, then he protected my future home with you in this pack too."

Noah gingerly licks the tears from my cheeks, tugging at my heartstrings until I release a satisfied sigh.

But he doesn't say much else. We sit in silence for a while until he gives me a soft neck lick. I gasp at its cool, pleasing shock.

Over time, I'll tell you everything I know about your dad. He was special to all of us too, Noah mindlinks.

My heart twists with relief, knowing my dad had a community behind him. But with how much I was excluded from this pack when I needed it most, I'm ashamed to feel a sinking bitterness.

I'm sure Noah can sense it seeping through our bond, but his golden wolf eyes remain stoic. He nudges my stomach with his big nose, and his huffing breath startles me into squealing laughter no matter my mood.

His tail wags, brightening my laughter even more. *Come on, it's your turn. I want to reassure you now too.*

"But you're hurting."

I'm fine now, thanks to you. Wolves move on quickly, and I'm ready to stop thinking about this if you're not upset with me.

"Of course I'm not. None of this is your fault... Or mine, if I'm honest."

Well, good. If you want to share, I want to listen. His curious, tilted head relaxes me, especially with how deeply Lilian shattered his heart.

But I bite my lips, not knowing where to start after the past few days. "I guess I'm a bit stressed about joining the pack."

Don't be. We induct new pack members every full moon in an official welcoming ceremony. So before the next full moon in two weeks, we just have to get your wolf ready. Which will apparently be easier than I thought, feisty Omega.

"Wait, what? How do you know?"

You already almost shifted on your own earlier. I could feel it.

My heart flips. "That's what that was?!"

Noah nuzzles into me, and our bond buzzes with his giddy excitement. But I'm still stressed after how out-of-control shifting felt, especially if it can't be avoided.

I'll help you learn to release your wolf on your terms. Then you can take your first pack run with us. Excitement fills me with every word Noah speaks. He wags his tail again, flopping over on his side. *I also just want to play with your wolf so badly.*

I laugh, laying on my side so we're face-to-face. As I pretend to paw at him with my human hands, Noah pants with a happy smile. That sweet face mends my sore heart.

"What else do I need to do if I want to become Luna someday?"

His panting increases - giant paws carefully bumping me despite his desperation to play. I burst out laughing.

Nothing. You're perfect as is.

"Nothing in the world is perfect. Believe me, I'd know."

Fair enough. Then as long as we can work with your wolf, I'll show you the ropes. Otherwise, just keep being your sweet Omega self.

"And if I'm pregnant? How would you feel?"

Noah's warm, fluffy paws fall still, resting on my sides. His hesitation makes my gut churn.

Is this where things finally come crashing down? Just like I'm used to?

I know Noah says otherwise, but with everything I've been through, I feel like it's naive to trust anything this good. We're bound to have a blowout eventually, aren't we?

Noah studies me intently. I swallow hard, nervously combing his fur.

"I-it's not too late for me to take the morning-after pill. Maybe I should, just so there's less uncertainty," I say.

Noah's left ear flicks back. *It doesn't work well on Lycans - along with most other medications. Our metabolism is too high.*

"Well, that explains my whole life."

You probably need higher doses of everything like me, but since you're part human, I don't know how much higher. I'd be worried about either under- or overdosing you and giving you complications.

"But I'm also supposed to start my period in the next few days. I'm not sure I could get pregnant in the first place. Or does going into heat mean I could?"

Not necessarily. It's also possible to have a spur-of-the-moment, hormonal heat if your mate riles you up.

I bite back my smile. "Oh. Well, I was pretty... *excited* by you."

Noah's tail thwacks the ground again, fluttering my heart. *Sweet Omega, I'm not meaning to avoid your question about possibly being pregnant. I'm just having a hard time figuring out what I'm missing. I thought we cleared it up already.*

My heart drops. "Oh, God. I guess I *am* obsessing about this and didn't realize... but... um..."

I don't know what to say. How to explain, or if I need to. There's no indication that Noah understood what Jenny meant earlier about my disorder.

That's not all that scares me. I worked tirelessly with Jenny for years, some days sleeping off exhaustion from retraining my brain to function in daily life. And before I progressed in my treatment this year, I really couldn't function. Everything terrified me, leading me down a path where I was afraid I'd destroy everyone around me or destroy myself. Jenny explained I'll likely have minor setbacks for the rest of my life, but I never want to be back in that mental space.

Either way, I'll have to tell Jenny I'm relapsing from multiple triggers in a row - accidentally letting compulsions slip through and worsening their intensity.

Hey, it's okay. You don't have to explain yourself. Noah boops my cheek with his giant, wet nose, soaking half my face. *I just don't like to plan too far ahead anymore. My life has derailed too many times.*

I deflate, still drying my face with my sleeve. "I know exactly what you mean."

But I already know we'll figure it out if the time comes, even if I don't know how just yet. I'll support you if you're pregnant, no matter what you want to do about it.

I mentioned it first, yet I'm so flustered that I can't speak. Noah means every damn word; our bond adds transparency to our conversations that I've never had with another partner.

I need to work on this in therapy. He's completely smitten, and I'm not used to it. I don't want to keep accusing him based on other people's behavior. With Noah, I finally might be able to enjoy myself. To keep feeling this freedom. I don't want to ruin that.

My heart flutters, feeling more and more whole the longer he gazes at me. I hold Noah's snout steady before leaning in to kiss his wet, huffing nose. Noah's tail hits the ground so hard that my whole body vibrates.

Suddenly, I'm body-slammed with hundreds of pounds of excited fluff.

My mate. His wolf play-growls, and I burst into squealing laughter.

"Noah?! Don't crush your mate before you mark her!"

He gives an excited yip, licking the back of my head until my hair is in shambles.

By the time I can escape him, his eyes are wild and I'm breathless with laughter.

Ugh, fuck. I want to shift so I can kiss you, but I left my clothes in my tree hole, and I don't trust us naked.

I giggle. "You have a *tree hole?* That sounds…"

He pants, nudging me to my feet. *This is exactly why I can't be naked. Don't excite your mate even more. I have a territory negotiation dinner I can't be late for.*

Noah burrows his head into my belly until I'm smushed against his side, failing to escape his ticklish attack with breathless laughter. He wags his tail so hard that his butt wiggles. *Let me take you to my tree, then I can kiss you before you go home.*

I climb on, taking the chance to hug him with my whole body.

Noah gives a happy growl as he slinks from the cave, weaving into his forest.

When Noah shifts out of his wolf form beside his tree hole, his teal eyes lock on mine. I bite my lips, struggling to stop staring at his gorgeous, copper skin, stripped bare and glistening beneath the orange sunset.

Noah huffs, having to turn his back as our bond tingles with desire. All he can slip on are his boxers before he whips back around, tackles me in a huge hug, and kisses me against the tree. I flush from my core to my ears.

His lips are feverish and serious, his hands caressing me with so much cuddling pressure that I sigh in delight. After his kisses grow soft, losing their desperation, I'm left dazed and smiling. But Noah remains serious.

"Sweet Omega…" His voice is gentle, making me want to stifle my flustered breath just to hear him out loud again. "Thank you. Thank you so much."

I trace his stare, soaking in his sincerity.

When I lean in to kiss him, I brush his mark with my fingertips - like he keeps doing to that golden spot on my neck. I think I'm finally getting it. It's an "I adore you" without the pressure of explaining how or why.

Noah sucks in a heavy breath, hugging me as tight as he can as his eyebrows melt into tender emotion. We gaze into each other's eyes, the tips of our noses touching as we breathe each other in.

Then he groans. "No, I can't. I can't let you go for the night."

"I don't want to go either, but I have to teach tomorrow," I say. "Maybe I could sleep over some nights and leave early for work?"

He perks up. "Y-yeah? Will you?"

"As long as you'll stay at my place sometimes too."

Noah kisses me through his smile, his warm lips making me ache for more. "Of course I will. I'm still dying to hold you."

"I want to hold you again too, Alpha."

He flushes, his head dipping with a soft smile.

Melancholy fills me. "I'll… keep the door unlocked for you. Just in case."

"Then I'll… try not to mindlink you too much."

I smile. "Please do."

Noah laughs, and it's the last I see of him for the night.

As soon as Amy turns onto the forest road home, I'm struggling not to cry in her passenger's seat. I bottle it all, angrily shoving everything into my gut.

It's not only from missing him. I'm questioning everything,

intrusive thoughts souring my insides with petty, brutal questions about my reality. *What if he's faking it? What if this is just new relationship energy? What if this the best it'll ever feel, and it'll only get worse from here?*

Maybe, I tell myself. It's possible, but I can't know for certain. That finally settles me into my chair.

But I'm still annoyed at myself. How can I be so pessimistic when I have a chance at everything I've ever wanted? Why can't I accept it's real and be happy?

Amy grabs my hand as she drives, keeping her eyes on the winding road. "A., you seem on edge. Are you about to have a panic attack? Or did you have a flashback? Or something else?"

"I feel like I'm doing something horribly wrong. What if this is unhealthy?

"Wait, what's unhealthy?"

"How I feel about him. I shouldn't be this attached, especially not this early. It's a recipe for disaster. But if it doesn't work out or I back out now, I'll be so crushed that I'd regret letting him go forever."

"Aliya, take a deep breath with me, okay?"

I shake my head no. "It's not going to help."

"Then what if I told you I felt the exact same way about Kira when we first met? Do you remember my freakout?"

That's right - Amy wallowed on my apartment floor when they had to spend their first day apart. "Yeah. That was worrisome too, to be honest."

Amy laughs, nudging me playfully. "You brat. You want to know why it's so hard?"

"Why?"

"You're *mates,* not human partners. This isn't like any relationship you've ever had because nothing else is like it." She strokes my hand, but I'm not convinced. "Werewolves bond at the soul level. You'll feel torn apart when you're not together because you *are* being torn apart. It's painful as hell."

"Oh, God. I'll feel like this forever? Whenever we separate, even for one night?"

Amy sighs. "You'll get used to it. Your bond is still fresh, so your instincts will want to nest with him nonstop. Just get through this early stage, then we'll worry about the next part, okay?"

I exhale, feeling slightly better. "Okay. But you'll call me out if I'm being irrational and don't realize it?"

She shrugs. "Maybe I will, maybe I won't."

"Ha ha. Very funny." I relax into her passenger's seat, smiling at how well my best friend knows me - enough to know reassurance only makes my compulsions worsen. Especially since she was there through the worst of them.

Before I can ruminate over how I'll ever explain my disorder to Noah from the beginning, I close my eyes, finding comfort in my best friend's hand.

25

After spending days by Noah's side, I stand in my doorway alone tonight, reeling at how strange it feels to come home to an empty cottage. I thought I'd be used to it from now on, even if I snuggled up with a new partner for a few nights, but the longer I stand in the silence, the more my gut aches, hunching me over.

While Mom was quiet and guarded, she had a playful side that would make Dad laugh his weirdest, most contagious laughs, which I was convinced were the definition of a "guffaw." Dad was tender with his words, careful to choose what he wanted to say so he could heal your heart in a single sentence. On the worst days, Mom would swoop in during Dad's sage advice with steady hugs to top it all off - only before watching our favorite comfort movies with a big bowl of popcorn, just the three of us.

Between missing my parents and my newfound mate, I bite back searing tears. Rushing to the bathroom, I bury my head beneath the showerhead before my emotions spill over and reveal too much.

After showering off dirt and wolf slobber, I find a few of Noah's shirts in the bag he left. My shoulders soften as I smash my face into one of them. God, yes. It all smells like him.

Immersed in his scent from both his shirt and where his head rested on my pillow, I'm soothed enough to sleep. But I still toss and turn all night, aching for Noah.

By the time my alarm goes off at 5 AM, I'm unbearably frustrated. I don't want to wake Noah by linking him, but I already miss him enough for my wolf to pace frantically in our bond - like she can't stop searching for him, in fear he'll never return.

But in my heart, I know I'm scared of more than him "not returning." I'm scared he'll return to me as something else entirely, taking off a mask to reveal he's someone who loves to twist my wildest dreams into my greatest nightmares.

Maybe he will, maybe he won't. Either way, I'm looking forward to seeing Noah again more than anything. Hopefully this school day will go by quickly, and Noah and I can train my wolf to shift.

But I'm excited to see my kids today too. My hands make deft work of braiding my hair - protecting it from grabby hands - and throwing on breathable clothing I can run around in.

After a quick breakfast, I head out the door with an unsteady heart. I still feel ridiculous for wanting Noah's attention so badly. Maybe it's more extreme after being lonely for so long.

An unfamiliar rock catches my eye on my porch, startling me into pausing on the first step. Beneath the rock, there's a note.

Out of reflex from the past few days, I sniff it. Then I burst out laughing at myself. I really am a wolf.

This totally smells like Noah, though. I try to stifle my overbearing excitement as I unfurl the note.

I didn't want to wake you but I couldn't stop thinking about you and went on an early perimeter run. Link me when you're headed to work and I'll walk with you.

I find myself with a goofily huge grin on my face and groan. Okay, fine. I give up. I'm hopelessly into Noah.

I mindlink him, my massive smile still glued to my face. *Good morning, my shy Alpha. What gives you the right to be so adorable?*

Our bond flutters with warmth from Noah's end, and I giggle. *God, I missed you so fucking badly,* he mindlinks.

I missed you too. Please hurry back to me.

Believe me, I'm on my way. But don't wait for me – I'll meet you on your route so you're not late for work. Which path do you take into town?

Sweet Alpha, thinking of my needs.

The second I link him this gentle tease, I hold his letter to my chest, laughing at how flustered we both are through our bond. Noah can't bear to speak, too overwhelmed with shy excitement, and I laugh out loud on my porch to myself.

I always take the road that passes Ms. Jensen's farm, I mindlink. *The one with the cows, horses, and the vineyard. Have you seen it?*

Sure have. Plenty of times.

Wait… Is she a wolf too?

Sure is. See you soon, sweet Omega.

I rush down my porch, overcome by excitement. I didn't think I'd get to see Noah before work. I want to kiss him, first thing.

By the time I speed-walk out of my section of the forest, I have to slow to catch my breath. Wait, we didn't choose where we'll meet on the path. Can he still track me while I'm walking so fast? I'm already a quarter mile from Ms. Jensen's farm.

I jump as the bush to my right gives a violent shake. The animal inside scratches through the dirt until–

A chicken bursts through the bushes, flapping her golden-brown feathers. I scream, my back slamming against the nearest tree, which makes her scream too.

I grip my chest, struggling to catch my breath. "Oh, my God, where did you come from, baby? Are you one of Mrs. Jensen's girls? Terry? Nancy, maybe?" She pecks at some worms in the dirt. "…No? Well, Little Miss Jensen, I don't think you're supposed to be out h–"

Little Miss Jensen has had enough. With a violent flap of her wings and claws outstretched, she charges at me, revealing her dinosaur ancestry. And I reveal my own survival tactics passed down for generations, jumping higher than I knew was possible with my knees tucked and voice screeching throughout the forest until I'm sure someone a mile away must hear me. Then I sprint.

I don't stop until her clucks have faded. Gathering my wits is painful once I realize I've dragged myself all the way to Mrs. Jensen's farm. I almost wish no one really was nearby on the off chance they saw what just happened – I'd never want to show my face in Greenfield again. But as I dust off my clothes and bite back my embarrassment, a sharp movement catches the corner of my eye.

This time I'm too scared to run. This creature was silent. Eyeing me.

I shriek when it moves.

"S-shit, sorry–" I'm met by Noah's apologetic, wide eyes, emerging from the bushes beside the cows. My shoulders droop in relief.

But as Mrs. Jensen's brown cow peeks from behind a bale of hay to give Noah a wary moo, I can't help but laugh. "How'd a wolf get in the cow pen?"

He flushes, dropping my stare with a grin. "I had to put my clothes back on somewhere private."

Maybe it's the thrill of seeing him again, or the relief of finding my mate in the bushes instead of another threat, but my imagination is on fire. Arousal courses through me as I picture Noah shifting in the bushes, his bare body caressed by the morning sun. Noah's clearly aware of it, his jaw clenching.

His eyes widen as I charge at him with a wide smile. Fresh facial scruff scrapes my fingertips as I throw myself into his arms, smashing our lips together with my full weight. Noah catches me, but he doesn't stop there. Squeezing me closer by the waist, he leans to gain a fuller reach of my lips. My lips part on their own, itching to taste him.

Noah's tongue slips against mine without hesitation, and a fiery spark of lust grinds my hips into him. He grunts softly into my open mouth, kissing me harder as he grips my hips for more. I pat the space behind myself without looking, feeling for a mass of cool leaves. Once I'm sure we'll land somewhere soft, I yank him by the jacket collar with me, toppling into the bushes.

Noah sucks in a surprised breath, easily catching me, but my giggling is cut off by a fierce kiss.

Blood pools between my legs, heating my whole face with it, but as Noah's kisses deepen, a tangible heartbeat forms in my core. Each pulse sends another wave of pleasure to my groin, soaking my panties.

He must be able to smell it; with a deep inhale, Noah groans, tearing himself away from my lips with red cheeks. "Feisty Omega, you're killing me. We have to stop here, or else you'll really be late."

I flush, the chill morning air no longer noticeable in the slightest as Noah's bulging pants nudge my belly. "Then we better hurry and separate before my wolf jumps you again."

Noah chuckles, taking my hand. We brush ourselves off with sneaky glances and shared giggles before heading on our way.

I hug Noah's arm on the path to town, shocked by my behavior as reality sinks in.

I can't remember the last time I threw myself at someone like that - diving for Noah's lips as if I'm sure he wanted me there as badly as I wanted to burrow into him. I've been all instinct since meeting Noah. But I guess my instincts were right; he enjoyed it as much as I did, still adjusting his pants as we walk. My cheeks burn, struggling to absorb that this gorgeous man existed in Greenfield this whole time.

"Are you okay?" He peeks at me. His lips are still bright red and swollen.

I giggle. "Yes. I'm just having a shy Omega moment."

Noah chuckles, kissing the top of my head. "Don't think I didn't want to continue. I've been dying to feel you next to me, ever since we said goodbye last night." After an abrupt pause, Noah sucks in a tight breath. "N-not in a sexual way. Well, I guess sexually would be nice too, but, um… I care about you, romantically and emotionally, and–"

I giggle, rubbing his arm. "I feel the same. It was hard to sleep without you. But I don't mean to pressure you either. I understand you're busy and can't visit all the way out here every night."

"I can make time for you." His soft but bold declaration flutters my heart. "And I did actually try to visit late last night, but I figured you needed some space."

"What? What made you think that?"

Noah shrugs. "Your door was locked. Which is perfectly fine. I want to respect your boundaries–"

Panic grips my chest, tightening my hold on his arm. "No, wait. I thought it was unlocked, like I told you I would leave it for you. Are you sure?"

He furrows his brows, not quite understanding my sudden fear. "Yeah, I'm sure... Why? What's wrong?"

My gut sinks lower and lower as I trace back my steps last night. It never sunk in, but it happened: the silent war between my compulsions and what I actually wanted. Stopping at the door, locking it without thought. Realizing it's locked and unlocking it while cooking dinner. The quiet, gnawing burn in the back of my mind, guiding me back to the door. Locking it. Unlocking. Locking again. Growling at the lock, tearing it back open, and demanding it stays that way. Giving up, falling asleep unsure if I really did lock it or not before bed.

But fuck, apparently I did. I'm relapsing worse than I realized, and I wouldn't have even noticed unless Noah pointed it out.

Fear pins me to Noah's side, just as we cross the border between Greenfield and Westview. And of course, Noah spirals into concern with me, our bond giving everything away. Confusion etches into his forehead, followed by a deep worry when I don't continue walking.

I'm not prepared to tell Noah I have OCD.

Door locking was one compulsion Jenny and I worked on forever ago. I had hundreds of other compulsions to sort through, but we tackled this one first; I couldn't stand how I used to waste hours on fucking *doorknobs* every night.

But it wasn't just the front door. I'd repeatedly lock my front, back, and side doors - waiting for just the right click. I'd close all the other doors without locks, and hang bells on the main doors in case someone opened them. Ever since my ex broke in and...

We're stopped where the farmland meets the river, the town waiting across the bridge. Noah pulls me closer, his eyes only on me despite the gorgeous scenery. "Hey, you okay?"

"Yeah, I'm okay..."

He raises one eyebrow at my obvious lie, and I laugh in embarrassment.

Noah has no idea about any of this, and I know he'd be understanding... If I took the time to explain. And pushed past the fear of him thinking less of me for my disorder.

But I don't know how much I want to share just yet. How far I want to let him in.

176

Those teal, gentle eyes pull the truth out of me anyway. "Sometimes I'll feel a deep, unavoidable urge to do things out of fear, even if I know they're not logical," I mutter. He's still listening, and it's out there now, so I continue. "I've worked in therapy to feel better and stop doing these things, but sometimes it creeps back on its own."

He takes a moment to digest this, readjusting his grip on my hands. "W-what do you mean? What types of things?"

"Things like the lock. I used to be afraid someone would come in if I didn't lock it correctly, but I'd lock it repeatedly until it felt 'right.' It was excessive, to say the least."

Noah's expression remains stoic, but I know he's distressed beneath the surface. My throat tightens.

But then he asks, "If that was in the past, what's making you afraid again now?"

My stomach flips. "Oh. I don't know."

"Is it what we talked about? With my dad?"

"No. Absolutely not." I pull him closer, ensuring he knows I'm serious. "It's not you, Noah. Please don't think that. I think I'm torn because I'm happier than I've been in years when I'm with you. At the same time, I'm stressed from all this change, even though it's what I've always wanted. And sometimes even good stress makes me feel like I have to do… *things*. To try to cope, or hang on to control. Like re-locking the door without realizing it."

"O-oh…"

Maybe I made a mistake. Or shared too much. Or confused him. Or–

"I-is it–?" Noah shakes his head to stop himself.

But I step closer, touching his chest. "Is it, what? You can ask."

"Is it… From trauma?"

"Part of it, yeah. I've always done a few of these things, but it got really bad after my parents died." My voice shrinks as I speak. "And then… Something else happened. At my cabin. Something that makes me want to lock the doors, even if no one knows where I live."

Noah's expression darkens. Our bond sparks with concern.

And deep, boiling anger.

I grab his hand, unable to meet those gorgeous eyes.

177

But he holds tight, grounding me to the earth. "Is there any way I can help you feel less afraid of that happening again?"

At first, I'm overcome with affection that he'd think to ask.

But he's staring, waiting for an answer.

Whirring through possibilities, no solution seems to stick except eventually having Noah there for the most extreme Prolonged Exposure session for my PTSD yet: having a male figure enter my home, unannounced, and with no further explanation. Noah would be the first man I'd trust to help me with an exposure this deep, knowing he'd never actually hurt me. Eventually, my brain would realize that not everyone who walks through my door is entering to hurt me.

But God, I don't even know how to categorize that type of exposure. Would it also include Exposure and Response Prevention, considering I've developed OCD compulsions around locks? I'd need Jenny's guidance on juggling triggers from both disorders at once, the mere idea sending my head spinning.

I'm not ready for that yet, even with Jenny's help. If I give Noah a key in the meantime, it won't stop a potential severe PTSD flashback when Noah enters on his own. I can't imagine how terrifying that would be for him - coming home to me shaking and crying like I'm dying over something so seemingly simple. Relying on the key would also give OCD another excuse to lock the door, intensifying its power over me.

But is this really about keys and locks, or am I avoiding the past again?

I groan, dropping my jumbled head. "I-I don't know, I'm confusing myself. I've never had anyone to help with this besides Amy, and it's… complicated. I don't want to accidentally make things worse, so I'll have to ask my therapist what to do."

Noah pulls me closer, stroking my hand with his thumb. "Okay. Please let me know. I want to help."

His soft voice fills me with enough warmth to want to cry, but it's too early in the morning for that.

So I wrap my arms around his waist, nuzzling into his chest. "I like this, though. Can we just stay like this the whole day? I don't want to go to work."

It's an obvious breach of subject, but Noah chuckles, cuddling me back. "Me neither. I wish I could hold you all day, trust me."

But I have to go to work. So I do - hours zipping by in a chaotic haze.

After two toddler meltdowns and a full day of soothing a scared three-year-old who wouldn't let go of my pants leg, I'm exhausted by the time the last preschooler is picked up by their grown-up.

I can't stop thinking about what I told Noah about my disorder. At least he responded better than my ex, *but what if…?*

I stop myself there, recognizing that "what if" thought pattern early this time.

Fuck. I'm scared shitless. I never want to feel like this is taking over my life again. I don't want to relapse. I can't. I'd never want anyone else with OCD to feel ashamed, but it's always been adept at making me feel like an exception. The one who ruins everything.

I'm so embarrassed that I have to tell Noah about this at all. That it could ruin his peace.

No matter how much I don't want to, I call Jenny without dwelling further. Might as well get a jump-start on making myself uncomfortable on purpose. Show my disorder who's the boss.

But when Jenny hears my recount of multiple compulsions I've noticed, she has news I don't want to hear. "How about we start seeing each other twice a week again for a bit? Catch this early, and get you in a better place?"

"I should be fine, though, shouldn't I? What if I'm just being ridiculous, and I–"

I cut myself off, realizing I'm criticizing myself for needing support and using words like "should" again. It petrifies me.

But Jenny's voice remains steady. "You're going to get there, I know it. You can do hard things."

"I know. I can do hard things."

I schedule an emergency appointment with Jenny for tomorrow, knowing it's for my best interest. But as I hang up, I burst into tears on the playground bench.

I hate this. I'm living a nightmare I can't escape. Why is it always when I'm finally happy that things implode again? I turn my back to the school windows, hoping no co-workers see me upset.

A hint of sadness creeps through our bond. One that's not coming from my gushing pool of it.

Sweet Omega, where are you?

26

My heart lurches at Noah's mindlink, threatening to overturn my stomach. If I tell him where I am, Noah will want to comfort me in person, but I'm terrified of putting this on him.

But deep down, I want to let him in. I know I do, and every time I have so far, it's been worth it.

I decide to mindlink him, but fear grips my chest, strangling my breath.

Come on, future Luna. You can do hard things.

I slow my breath with a steady, whistling exhale. *I'm at school.*

Noah responds before my next inhale. *I can be there in 15 minutes. Is that okay?*

I chew my bottom lip, another batch of tears gushing from me. Maybe I don't have to go through this relapse alone either?

If you can, I'd like that, I mindlink. *I need your support right now.*

Our bond aches with Noah's concern, and my anxiety skyrockets. But just before I dissolve into panic, I'm shocked to feel a wave of Noah's immense relief.

I'd love to support you. Thank you so much for telling me.

I grip the hem of my shirt. *Are you sure you have enough time for this?*

Sweet Omega, you have no idea what it's like to hear I can do anything at all to support you, he mindlinks. *Maybe you haven't realized it, but the past few days, you've saved me time and time again. I know you think I'm taking on too much by wanting to protect you in return, but it's actually doing me a favor. I–it makes me feel... like I matter. That I can make a positive difference to the ones I care about most. Which is why the other day, when you held me...*

He can't bear to continue, but his whirring, touched emotions say enough. I'm teary-eyed again.

It sounds like providing emotional security is his love language, so my comfort meant a lot to him. I guess I really shouldn't worry about bothering him by letting him in.

Okay, Noah. Please, come here.

I'll be there as soon as I can. Do you have everything you need from work? I can take you straight home, if you'd like.

I swipe my tears away, and my lip quivers through a smile. *Not yet. I have to stop crying before going back inside in front of my coworkers.*

Then stay right there. We can grab your things after we sit together for a bit.

After talking to Noah, things are looking a little less dark. But the longer I wait, the more time I have to think.

And I don't know, maybe this isn't a good idea. He'll want an explanation. Everything I could say would still make me fall short.

What if... I'm ruining his life by making him deal with me?

Anxiety burns through my chest like hot acid.

What if I feel like this forever?

This makes my tears return, followed by the worst sickening feeling in my stomach yet - enough to make me panic-search for the nearest trash can, just in case.

I've got you, Noah mindlinks. *Even though I'm not there physically yet, I'm still with you.*

I hug my own shoulders, trying to get a grip on myself. I can't let him see me like this. No matter how much I want to trust him, I don't want anyone to think I'm weak again. Reveal the gap in my heart for him to strike.

But the second Noah parks a slick black SUV in the preschool's drop-off zone, my mind hones in on one thought only: *mate.*

I'm still crying, but as we meet eyes, the way Noah's shy glance warms at the sight of me makes me smile through the tears.

Joining me on the bench, Noah doesn't ask for an explanation. He doesn't even say a word. He simply kisses my forehead, hugging me tight.

It's just a hug, but my heart swirls. With his warm chest

catching my tears, his firm touch on my back, and his soft breath against my neck, I close my eyes, allowing myself to sink into him.

By the time we gather my things from my classroom, I'm so grounded in the present moment that I can take slow, even breaths.

Noah drives me home to my parents' old cottage, curling against me on the flowery couch. Every second is so comfortable with him that I haven't even realized something until I glance at the clock; we've been holding each other in silence for two full *hours*.

Noah senses me gazing at his beautiful profile and meets my eyes. I comb my fingers through his hair, sorting the strays from his teal eyes.

With a pounding heart, I allow myself to feel every bit of his eyes on me. He eases towards me in the absolute slightest, just enough to spur me into drawing a bit closer too. Breathing his air, my focus glides over every dark eyelash, heavy brow, and golden iris fleck between the soft blues and greens, absorbing all I can of him. Each blink we share is slow and heavy, just as intimate as the soft brush of his fingers in my hair.

I'm overcome by tingles, indulging in every minimal touch. Just Noah's presence feels monumental. When we close the gap between us, his lips press against me so slowly that endorphins flood my heart.

It feels like I'm breathing in his affections, soaking in every millisecond as I inhale, exhale. Nothing else matters but here and now.

This is the most intimate I've been with him yet, and it's just a gentle kiss.

But it's not just a kiss. I feel his acceptance washing over every ounce of my body.

My eyebrows arch with emotion, and Noah punctuates the end of his kiss with heavier pressure. As he pulls away, I drop my chin, regretting ruining the moment with my sudden tears.

But Noah takes my hands, dropping to his knees in front of me. "Let's forget about everything else for a while."

I gape at my mate, unsure what he means by forgetting about "everything."

"What?" I whisper.

"Forget all the pressure to train your wolf. Forget joining the pack on a deadline. Forget becoming Luna immediately. We can get to those things, one by one... But right now? *This* is all I really want. Just you."

I bite my lips, unable to prevent myself from crying anymore. Noah brushes tears from my cheeks, his eyebrows furrowing.

"I went about this all wrong," he says. "You were thrown into all this with your wolf, and there's all this pressure with the pack–"

"But I want this pressure. I want all of it, especially if it means I'll have you as my mate."

"I know, and I believe you. I feel that in our bond."

My breath heightens, searching for my worst fears in his stoic expression. "But what? You think I can't handle it?"

With a small squeeze of my hands, he softens his voice. "I know you can. In just a few days, you've handled more than I ever would've expected from my mate. And everything we've already been through in this short time–" My heart twists as his voice cracks with emotion. "...Has already meant the fucking world to me. No one has stood up for me like you did since–"

Noah cuts himself off, shaking his head with an embarrassed, weepy smile. Our emotions amplify each other, stacking until we're bleary-eyed and overwhelmed. I let out a sob at the deep ache in Noah's heart, wiping his tears away. But despite his flushed cheeks, Noah doesn't drop my stare.

"I haven't had anyone this close to me, maybe ever, Aliya, and I get the feeling you haven't either."

My heart flips at the serene way he says my name, gliding over every letter like he's savoring it. "I haven't. It's all new, but that's not a bad thing." I trace his palm with my thumbs, and his grip softens.

"When I look at you, I see someone powerful. More than you've probably been given credit for."

After genuinely believing I came off as weak - especially to an Alpha leading a pack of twenty thousand Lycans - I'm so surprised that I'm speechless.

An ache tenses Noah's worried stare. "But also in the sense that I see someone who's been strong for too long. Way too long."

I chew on my lip, desperately staving off a deep cry. But as Noah strokes my head, it slips out - a whimpering gasp for air as my walls collapse.

He catches my tears with his thumb. "Before you, no one told me this either, but you don't have to be strong with me, okay? I'll never think less of you for it."

His words drag me out to sea like a riptide, carrying me to a new depth of connection I've never shared with anyone. Slipping my arms around his neck, I whimper through tears as I ease our salty lips together.

Noah leans into my touch, encompassing as much of me as his arms can hold. His kiss consumes my focus, strengthening my core into taking another breath. And another. Soon, we're kissing tenderly and slowly, our tongues tracing every ounce of affection we have for each other until my heart wildly thumps through the endorphins squeezing it.

But Noah gently pulls back. "I don't want you to push yourself for me. I want to form our bond in a way that feels good for both of us, which means we can take as long as we need."

I suck back tears as I nuzzle into his neck, embarrassed by my swollen features. "I don't want to make you wait."

"I'm not waiting. Nothing about holding you in my arms right now is waiting." Noah hugs me to his chest until I'm snug in his lap with no gaps between us.

Neither of us plan on separating an inch. Noah dips his head to look into my eyes, and I rest my head on his shoulder to meet him halfway.

"We grew up in different cultures, so maybe that's where this is coming from. But when I say you're my mate, I mean for life. I know it's different for humans, and I'm okay to take it slow." Noah plants a delicate kiss on my cheek. "B-but I let you mark me because... all my instincts point to you. There's no doubt in my heart." I grip him tighter, absorbing every shy, soft-spoken affection - his heart laced into every syllable. "But for now, I'm just getting to know my mate, and I'm happy with that. It's the best experience of my life."

Oh, God, I *love* him.

Overwhelmed by my love surfacing, I kiss his mark as softly as I can, hoping he can feel it. Noah lets out a helpless sound, burying his head into my shoulder.

"I feel that connection with you too, Noah. I really do. That's what terrifies me. What if I ruin the best relationship I could ever have?"

"What if *I* ruin it between us?" He asks. "What if we both do?"

I swallow hard, tracing his eyes. Everything in me says that's impossible.

As long as I don't let my fears get in the way.

"If this only lasts a month, a year, or twenty years, would you still want to be here with me, right now?" Noah's question sounds rhetorical, but as we cling to each other, I know it's not. I know if I told him I don't want to be close to him - that I changed my mind, or that this is too risky for my heart to withstand - he'd walk away, just for me.

But that's not what I want. My heart has no problems showing itself when it comes to Noah. Around him, I'm allowing my heart to finally show up on the outside. And he's holding it like the scarred recluse it is.

I'd do the exact same for him. Based on what he just told me, maybe I'm supporting his heart already, and I just don't realize the depths of my importance.

"You're right," I say. "No matter how long it lasts, this is where I want to be. I've waited my whole life for you. I knew it was you, the second I saw you in the forest." I grip him closer, losing all care about how ridiculous I might sound. "I used to see you in my dreams."

His breath halts. When it returns, it's shallow and rapid, his pupils dilating. "W-what do you mean?"

"It's kind of funny, actually. The dream ruined my dating life. No matter who I met or how open-minded I was, nothing could compare to my literal dream guy." I laugh at myself, and Noah breaks into a soft smile.

But his focused stare lets me know he wants to hear every word I have left to share. Nuzzling the tips of our swollen noses, I close my eyes before I can second-guess myself.

"I'd have this dream where I'd be walking through the forest, looking for someone. Someone I didn't know."

Noah's grip tightens with a surge of his emotions, and my eyes snap open.

His wolf stirs with interest - strong enough to be felt as an individual presence in our bond. But beneath that, in the depths of our connection, love stirs too. It's so woven between us that I can't make out its source. Either way, it sets my cheeks ablaze.

"Y-you'd find them?" He whispers. "The one you were looking for?"

"Yes. Well, no, not just 'them.' I'd find *you*, Noah. The man in my dreams looked just like you." My voice is airy, my heart throbbing in my throat.

I can't believe I'm telling him this. But with Noah's yearning scent, I can't stop the words.

"The second I saw you in that dream, I'd know you, but I didn't know you yet." I kiss him, and he whines against my mouth. The raw sound of it makes me gasp. "I'd know we were connected, down to the soul, and you'd know it too. We'd kiss, our bodies touching all over. It'd feel so powerful that we'd end up on the forest floor, and—"

I suck in a breathy gasp: Noah's hot tongue caresses from my collarbone to jawline. Pleasure slithers up my spine until it pops like a firework at the source of his tongue.

I grip his hair, kissing his mark until every muscle in his stomach flexes against mine to raise his hips. "Then it was like we went feral, in the leaves. It wasn't just 'sex,' but it wasn't just 'making love' either. It was so intense that I'd say we'd 'fuck' in the leaves, but it was more like…"

"We'd *mate*." His low, pleasure-roughened voice halts my breath. "We'd mate in the leaves."

27

My whole body quivers at his words, melting into his arms as his teeth scrape against my neck. But his teasing, near-mark doesn't feel lusty like it did while I was in heat. Our bond is exploding with our emotions, and he's so… enamored. Like everything about our bond is precious to him too.

But it's not just our bond. *I* feel special.

Noah rubs his head all over me, his breath frantic between whimpers. "I can't believe this, Omega. We're more than just fated mates."

My heart skips as I cling to his words. "What do you mean?"

"Our connection is deeper than that, meaning we've been mates for many lifetimes. Prophetic dreams are a sign from the Moon Goddess to mate a soul you already know. I've never met another mated pair who had that, so I thought it was a fairytale." He shakes his head in disbelief, holding my cheeks in his palms like he can't believe I'm in his arms.

I feel its truth, but I don't understand the full meaning behind the fiery spark forming in Noah's eyes. "How do you know?"

"I'd have that same dream," he whispers.

"What? The same exact…?"

"Yes. The exact same dream, for *years*." His firm confirmation ignites my skin with fiery goosebumps, our bond fizzling with it. As Noah's wild, half-shifted eyes meet mine, I feel his honesty. No matter how unbelievable, he's telling the truth. "At first, I struggled with envisioning you so clearly in the dream. You were so vividly an Omega woman, but I wanted to keep my mind open about who my mate could be since I'd be happy no matter your gender–"

I gasp. "Same here! I worried I was counting a potential partner out by overfocusing on a specific image of one."

Noah shakes his head in disbelief. "You get me so well. That's how you felt in the dream too. The second I'd see you by that rock, I'd look into your eyes and feel understood. Every lonely day I waited to find you would become worth it. I couldn't deny you were the one fated to me."

Noah looks just as perplexed as I am, but even more taken by me than I've seen him yet - an irresistible softness in his eyes that can only be described as love.

I smash my lips into his with a whine. As the gravity of this revelation strikes me, my heartbeat pounds faster than I can handle.

Noah breaks away with a heaving chest. "You saw it happen the same way, right? No matter how submissive your pheromones seemed, you wouldn't care if I was an Alpha. You'd take a dominant position over me in a heartbeat–"

My eyes widen. As my ravenous grip tightens around his back, Noah growls, sinking another sedating lick into that golden spot on my neck. Pleasure swarms my core, quivering my legs at his sides.

He's right. I'm such an obnoxious bottom that I never understood that part of my dream at all - topping my dream guy with confident slips of my hips over his shuddering torso. Jenny always thought I just wanted more autonomy in my sexual relationships after what happened to me; I wasn't "allowed" to be on top for years. But now that I know I marked Noah first...

Seeing the recognition in my eyes, Noah draws me in for an even deeper kiss. My lips part as my hips seek pressure in his lap, just like the day we met.

"Yes, Noah, just like this." My words come out more like breaths, prompting Noah to purr against my lips. "I'd strip you bare and mount you, your hands all over me."

Noah's body rolls against mine, moving in tandem like every cell in my body is communicating with his: my arms raise to massage his scalp, his arms lower to my hips: I lean back, he leans in: I grind, he flexes. But then he huffs against my neck, urging my legs around his waist. My groin clenches, aching for him.

"Show me," he says.

I'm suddenly in the air, lifted in his arms.

But as Noah sets me on my feet, my pulsing, wet core makes it almost impossible to stand. He holds me steady, frantically nuzzling my head to immerse me in more of his scent.

"Show me how you saw it happen. In the forest."

Holy shit. Is he about to recreate the dream with me?

My legs wobble like we've already begun mating. "I want you so badly that I can't walk. Can you carry me there?"

Noah huffs through a sexual frustration I can smell, his fiery scent stinging my eyes. His hands slip behind my thighs. As he bends to scoop me up, he can't resist giving my neck a hearty lick.

"*Oh*, my–" My knees dip with pleasure, threatening to give. The second I wrap my thighs around his waist, Noah ducks out the back door.

He dashes into my backyard, immersing us into the forest within seconds. I nuzzle into his neck, instincts welling in me. "Noah, I need to get down here."

He sets me on my feet, checking my expression with furrowed brows.

But as I grip his arms, my wolf howls to act already. "I don't understand, but I need to do something."

"Do it. Follow your instincts."

It feels nonsensical and weird, but I do the first thing my wolf demands - nudging Noah through the towering trees. I smush my side against his until we move as one, circling each other in a doting dance. When that's not enough, I rub my chest, shoulders, and head along his torso.

I sigh as Noah joins me, mimicking my motions.

Noah purrs through his erupting smile. "O-oh, yes. You're right. We were missing this."

Ripples of loving warmth shudder through me as Noah exaggerates his movements, eager hands trailing my sides to encourage me.

Within seconds of his body all over mine, I'm purring with

him. "I don't know why this feels so much better, but I love it, Noah."

His breath shudders. "You're courting me like a wolf. It's so sweet, I can hardly stand it," Noah breathes into my lips. "Keep following your instincts. Let me meet your wolf."

As our lips lock, I'm flooded with a sugary warmth, mixing with lust to make me moan into Noah's mouth. He backs me against the nearest tree, rolling his hips into me with a growl. The sound sets my system on high alert, intensifying the pressure of his cock nudging my clit.

I hadn't realized how much I repressed my wolf until Noah coaxed her back out to play today. Noah's touch roams over every corner of me, his hands and lips massaging pleasure everywhere he explores. I can't stop whining. Just his grinding hips bring me to the edge, but Noah's deep growl against my neck makes me squirm.

Between kisses, a gray mass catches my eye over Noah's shoulder. I stop Noah with a hand on his stomach. Noah backs up, shoulders raised in alarm.

But I can't stop staring at the vision behind him. "That's the rock," I whisper.

Mossy, overgrown patches blanket this massive boulder, sheltered beneath the canopy shade, but Noah and I are immersed in the light of the fading sunset over the horizon. It peeks between trees, leafy shadows dancing over Noah's broad chest as he catches his breath. We're still hand-in-hand, not daring to separate, but this is it. The rock where we met in my dream. *Our* dream.

And it was right behind my parents' cottage all along.

28

I never dared to travel into this thicket. It wasn't Steven holding me back this time, but my parents' belief that I'd get myself killed if I wandered too far.

A part of me always knew I was different - subpar in a way I could never pick out. Mom and Dad knew to protect me from stranger Lycans, but all my child self concluded was that I wasn't good enough. I became my own oppressor. Mistakes were unacceptable, and no matter how well I thought I accomplished something, I always had to work harder, or else I'd ruin it. By default, I was wrong.

Which made me dangerous. I saw myself as a toxin, parasite, or bomb; what if my incapabilities hurt me, my parents, or my friends? Killed them, even? I'd be a terrible person. But little Aliya would say, *no, I already am that terrible person. It's too late, and one day, everyone will finally notice.*

It wasn't until I met Jenny that I realized behind every compulsion, I was fighting to reach a different fantastical day: the day I was *finally* perfect.

But I'm not perfect. I'm a shaking, anxious mess, staring at who I'm pretty sure is the love of my life in a forest I was never allowed to travel alone. Not just by my loved ones, but by me. I trapped my wolf too.

My lip wobbles, but Noah scoops me into his embrace, catching my heart before it falls. He courts me with tender precision, starting with a gentle drag of his nose over my jawline.

"I can't believe I'm finally here with you." Noah's whisper shakes like it escaped his lips without his permission. This moment stirs his side of our bond just as deeply, drawing up heavy emotions that I can't begin to understand.

I'm not alone.

And the last threads of my wolf's leash are snapping.

Noah nudges my body with his wide form until I'm breathless with the affection fluttering in my chest. My nails grip onto Noah's back, needing more of him. I didn't intend for the effect it creates; Noah's eyes flicker between green and a saturated yellow. His wolf is begging to be set free too.

Noah drags his forehead over mine, hardly able to catch his breath. He leads us back a few steps until I'm pressed against the boulder, icing my back while Noah's body engulfs my front in delicious warmth.

I slump against the rock. Here with Noah, I'm tucked away from past danger, losing myself in our kiss. Noah's hot mouth seeks every angle of my lips, meeting them time and time again until my jaw is slack with bliss. Tasting his sweet tongue, I massage his scalp for more. Delight stiffens my nipples until they ache.

But we came here for a reason. We pause, gasping an inch from each other's noses.

"Your wolf led us here," Noah whispers. "I can sense her so strongly, even without marking you."

My stomach flips. "I can't believe this is really happening. But you feel too good - I can't bear to separate us to reenact the rest of it."

"Then I will." He rushes a few steps back, and my wolf whines for him. But the second I can see him from head to toe, I gape.

Noah shakes with need, his chest heaving, eyes heavy-lidded and locked on mine, and pants straining over his shaft.

Oh, God. Just like Noah, this real moment is a thousand times more beautiful than my dream. In our bond, it's clear Noah wants me, but not just my body. He wants all of me, even though he's sensed my dark side.

I'm tired of being afraid. I want to let my heart rule, no matter how ridiculous it sounds. If I really do love someone this early into a relationship for the first time in my life, I want to let it happen. More than declaring it, I want to live it. To feel every second.

Noah is frozen as he takes me in, but his wolf pants for me. Barely holding back.

"Follow your instincts too," I say. "Let's set our wolves free together. Let go, as far as we can."

With a stunted breath, Noah unleashes his gaze across my body. A piercing thrill beats through my veins as I watch his self-control slip.

As he rushes for me, I'm surprised by the softness of his fingers trailing my sides, slipping beneath my shirt. It makes my voice come out raspy and desperate against his scruffy cheek. His wide palms soothe me as I strip his chest bare, desperate to feel him skin-to-skin. But by the time I've removed my shirt, Noah has dropped to his knees.

He courts me differently this time, dragging his cold nose down my belly. I gasp, immersing my fingers in his thick black hair. Splayed hands massage my thighs until they part in delight. Then his nose dips between my legs.

My heart bursts into an anxious sprint as he caresses me with his nose, inhaling my scent, but his reassuring pheromones unwind me.

I remember this from the dream too - before I understood we were wolves. It makes much more sense now.

When he makes up his mind about me, he gives me a heavy lick through my jeans. The pressure spreads over a wider area from the fabric's thickness, soothing my aching core. My head drops and my knees dip as my pheromones explode.

"Mate." He purrs, licking my clit through the fabric so roughly that I dip my hips against his tongue for more.

"Oh, God, Noah..."

He'll make me come in a mere minute if he continues. In my dream, I'd always stop him here so I didn't have to wake up yet. But I can sense his wolf so clearly today, his intentions set and focused.

Don't stop me this time, he mindlinks, pausing only to kiss my clit until my hips jerk again. *Let me prepare your body to mate.*

I shudder as his words douse my groin with wet heat. I almost forgot he remembers the dream too.

"Oh, God, it's so intense, Noah..."

He purrs in satisfaction against my clit. His wolf nudges mine into action until I wriggle against his lips.

"Do you want me to stop?"

I grip his shoulders, barely able to speak between heaving breaths. "No. Don't stop."

As Noah falls into a licking trance, I grip the rock behind me. My shaking legs pulse open beside his cheeks. He grips my waistband but pauses there, unable to pop my pants button between heaving flicks of his tongue. I know he can feel how soaked I am through my jeans, but now his saliva seeps through, warming my core.

Noah frantically tugs my pants beneath my ass, exposing my panties to his huffing breath between my legs. My thighs quiver, and until he licks me mid-sentence, I hadn't realized I was crying out for him.

"Alph– ah! Ah!"

His growl buzzes through my clit, sending a throbbing ache through my core until I nearly burst. I melt down the rock. My hips buck as he holds them steady - rocking with me as his tongue laps up the wetness that dripped down my thighs. His shoulders ripple above me as he scoots between my knees, carrying my hips in his massive arms as he works me.

The rising pressure in my core is undeniable now that he's made it happen multiple times; my back even arches in preparation. "Alpha, you're going to make me squi–"

His lips latch to my clit through the thin fabric, switching between sucking and slipping his tongue between my legs. A rush of fluid spills from me, dripping down my cheeks into Noah's palms. Hard rock scrapes my hands as I cling to the boulder, my hips squirming through his tingling growls.

Don't hold back for me. I'll just have to make you come again later, he mindlinks - his rapid tongue far too occupied to speak.

Noah's fingertips caress my abdomen, but his head dips, chasing my hips when he's not lifting them for me. As tingles devour my senses, I grip Noah's hair as I come, sinking Noah's tongue into me through my soaked panties.

He licks me softly through aftershocks until the sensation is

195

too strong, my legs jerking. I pull my hips away, breathless as his focus zips to my face.

My heart flips. Noah's stare is raw and vulnerable, hazy from fully submitting himself to my pleasure. His wet lips are redder than his cheeks. At some point, he pulled his heavy cock free from his pants; it flexes with urgency beneath me.

But as his scent and emotions wash over me through our bond in waves, I'm stunned by his fondness for me.

"You're so beautiful, Noah," I breathe.

He massages my legs and sides, rubbing his head against my belly with blushing shyness. My heart burns with affection for him as I stroke his hair, aching to hold him.

Meeting him on my knees, I nuzzle over his cheeks with his head in my palms.

Holding him like this, I can't deny it any longer; I was scared I was hazy with lust and jumping to conclusions earlier, but now that Noah took the edge off, I know I'm in love with him.

29

We share soft, slow kisses despite the fire between us. My shoulders droop as Noah's hands trace my neck; his longing scent draws out mine through his fingertips.

Pressing my abdomen against Noah's, I hum in delight as he gingerly unhooks my bra. His fingers send waves of pleasure down my arms as he guides the straps from my shoulders. The cool forest air sends shivers down my body, but with Noah's sturdy arms circling me, I'm twice as warm.

With his tongue slipping into my mouth, I kiss him back with my full being, itching to get closer. Slipping his pants off his hips, I hurriedly grind against his cock. Noah growls, his embrace so luscious and all-consuming that I purr.

But then Noah's frustration slips through his desire, and my heart aches for him. I want to take the edge off for him too.

I coat his neck in kisses, stopping to lick his mark. Noah gasps against my ear, suddenly hugging my hips to frantically slide his shaft against my abdomen.

"You're okay, gorgeous. I've got you." I lick his mark harder, ensuring it's just as wet and sensitive as his dripping tip in my fingers. "Let me help you."

Noah huffs, his hips bucking on their own through my fist. My fingernails trace his chest, leaving a goosebump trail in their wake. Noah shudders as my head dips. With each kiss I place on his tip, he pulses into my hand, dripping down my fingers.

Purring for him, I slip my lips over his tip to taste him. Noah's hands skate across my back as he can hardly hold himself back; a soft, shaky moan escapes his lips. By the third time my lips slide over his tip, he gives out a weighty gasp, thrusting himself a little further.

Good job, Alpha. Show me how you'll mate me.

Noah whimpers at my linked words, stroking my hair with desperate hands. I'm getting so aroused again. His pleasure travels back into me through our bond, and I want to see how far I can take it. If I can get myself to the edge, just by pleasing Noah.

Softening my jaw with every suckle, I prepare myself to take more of him this time. I spread my tongue over the underside of his shaft, giving his tip a gentle, sucking pressure in the process. Desire blooms in my core as our bond explodes with delight, my wolf urging me to ease him into my throat. But just like last time, I choke on his thick shaft the second it brushes my soft palate.

Noah juts back with a gasp. "Don't go so deep."

I hum against his tip with an idea, and Noah's legs shake. *So is this okay?*

Chasing his hips, I suck on his bulging tip, swirling my tongue around it until Noah's moans turn into whimpers.

"F-fuck - yes!"

My spine shivers as his hands travel to the sensitive spot on my neck, tracing pleading circles to mimic my touch. "Mm," I hum, licking faster.

"O-Omega—"

I moan against his cock, pumping the rest of the shaft with both hands, but my voice is cut off by the sudden flood of cum in my throat. Doing my best to swallow as he empties himself in bursts, my hips squirm as Noah crumbles over me.

As I struggle to catch my breath, my groin pulses - desperate to trade places with my mouth. Noah lifts my chin, still shuddering as he wipes my lips clean with his big thumb.

"Oh, fuck," he rasps. "Oh, my sweet Omega…"

But I'm not done with him. I slide my hands up his chest, urging him onto his back. Noah wants to caress me back, but I want this moment to be about him. I gather his hands off my abdomen, taking a second to just stare at him with our fingers locked.

Noah is breathless beneath me. His cheeks are bright red and scent just as urgent. Despite being the top Alpha of all Greenfield

Alphas, he's happily splayed on his back for me. As I straddle him, his breath catches - leftover cum dripping onto his abdomen from his tip.

The condom's edge peeks from Noah's pocket, so I grab it before he can put it on. With a hammering heart, I spit into the tip, lubricating it for his pleasure - something I've never tried before. My face flushes deep red as Noah watches, wide-eyed. But as I glide it over him, he flexes into my hands, already ready for more. His chest shudders as I massage my spit over his tip in slow circles. Judging by his heavy-lidded eyes, he loves it. My wolf begs me to tease him relentlessly, coating my skin with goosebumps. Since Noah enjoyed it so much a minute ago, I drag my thumbs along the underside of his shaft, kneading it until his lips part and hips lift.

I can't wait another second. I toss my panties off, leaving me bare and shivering without my mate's heater of a body pressed to mine. Warming me with his hands, Noah rubs my thighs and back until I'm on fire. My shaking legs drop my wet core over him in a sudden release of tense muscle.

Straddling his hips, I swallow hard. This is it. This is where I top my Alpha mate, just like in the dream.

He's still catching his breath - fluttering eyelashes taking in every inch of my body above him with soft moans. I weave my fingers into his, coating him with fluid as I drag my wet pussy along his cock. Noah squirms, rolling his head through the leaves as he indulges in my touch.

I can't get enough of his reaction. Letting out a soft growl, I surprise myself with how wolflike I sound. It breaks my stride, slowing my hips to a stop over him as Noah's eyes water.

My voice shakes when I see his threatened tears. "Shit, sorry, I got ahead of myself. Are you okay?"

Noah gasps, cradling my head as if he's stopping it from spinning. "Sweet Omega, I just– I can't believe how gorgeous you are. Not just your body, but how you're letting yourself go despite everything you've been through. You are so fucking courageous that I'm–" His teal eyes are surrounded by so much red that they appear green, making mine water with them. "I love... seeing your wolf run free. Keep going."

My heart flips. I lay myself over him to kiss him hard. Is it just me, or was he about to say he loves me? I don't know how to contain myself.

With a newfound depth to my rocking hips, I purr. Noah's hands slide up my ass to my lower back, then all the way up to my neck - holding my head with such tenderness that I open my eyes despite our intensive makeout. Noah's blinks greet me, his body undulating against mine.

"Noah, I–" My throat catches.

Oh, my God. I almost said it. I almost told him I love him.

But he's right. I never expected to be here. To love again, first of all. But to trust this early, trust my heart, despite how horrifically I've been betrayed? I never imagined it would be possible.

I hold his head, beaming at my mate with one thought only. "I love you, Noah."

Noah whimpers, smashing his lips against mine until my heated grinding mixes with moaning cries. He cuddles me against him, rocking me like I'm precious.

"Aliya, I love you. I love you so much."

My bottom lip quivers. Nuzzling Noah in gratitude, I'm hungrier than ever to feel him inside me.

"I want you, right this second," I whisper.

His muscles loosen all at once. Then they tighten twice as hard, squeezing me in his embrace as his lips crash against mine. His flustered scent overwhelms me, stinging my eyes as our heavy makeout morphs into drawn out, passionate cuddling - squeezing every inch of each other's backs.

I sit up, gazing deep into Noah's eyes as I line him up to enter me. Noah's heaving torso tells of the nerves I feel coursing through our bond, but his hands remain stationed on my hips, tracing delicate circles over my hip bones. I ease myself over his tip, watching his expression melt with pleasure. Living it with him.

As I slink lower and lower, I shiver all over with delight. I forgot how thick he was. He's barely in, but I already feel stuffed. His warmth glazes my insides, sprinkling shivers over my body.

As I ride him with soft, delighted moans, massaging his chest beneath me, it comes from a place of worshiping our bond rather than the dominance Noah saw it as in our shared dream.

My thoughts slip out on their own in soft, pleading whispers. "I want to nurture every piece of you, Alpha."

Noah shudders so hard that he flexes inside me. Its palpitating massage tips my head back with a moan. As Noah bucks harder for more of my cries, I rock my hips into him, hitting my deepest pleasure point. My back arches, tightening my core until fluid drips into his bellybutton with my sharp moan.

"Oh, *Noah*–"

I can't remember how to speak as Noah's purring shifts to urgent growling. My body squeezes his swelling shaft, flexing against the mere sound of his primal moans. Noah props himself up to kiss my neck, slamming my ass into him with an eager hand, and that's it for me. Every ounce of control I have over my senses vanishes as my wolf takes over.

With my neck exposed, I cry out with every pulse of Noah's hips, bliss climbing my spine. He caresses my abdomen and breasts, smashing his hips into mine in wet slaps. Noah's tongue grows so heavy that his urgent licking turns into a nip. Its sharp ache makes me clench over him so hard that more fluid spurts from me, and Noah's fingernails dig into my ass with a growl.

He's growing so thick that I can't escape the pleasure - my pussy bearing down with no chance to squeeze him. If he hadn't made me orgasm so hard beforehand, I would've come already. Now it's a slow, rising ache, growing in intensity but never releasing.

Noah hugs my loose, squirming body, helping me to ride him as I cry out to the sky.

He strokes my neck with his fingertips, relieving his tongue's duty so that he can meet my eyes. I shiver as our stares lock. It seems terrifying to stare at him while I'm about to come, but I can do hard things, so…

I pin his gaze with mine, moaning against his lips. "Help me– I can't take it any longer–"

"I've got you, sweet Omega. Do you want it slow and deep again?" Noah rocks into me, adding extra pressure to my cervix at the end of each slow, deep thrust. "Or do you want it hard and fast?" As he speeds into relentless, rapid thrusts, my rising knees tell me what I want.

"H-hard—" I gasp, gripping his chest to mine so we're breathing each other's desperate air. "And fast."

With that, Noah pounds into me, the beat of our colliding bodies echoing through the forest. I take in his every minuscule expression, his eyebrows warping with his emotions as pleasure spills from my throat.

As his love blooms heavier than ever while staring into my eyes, I smash my hips over him, each deliciously heavy thrust heightening my moans. Another wave of fluid spurts from me just before I come, my "oh"s and "ah"s mixing into blended whimpers.

Noah speeds even faster, kneading my cervix over and over again with his spongy tip. I squeeze his waist with my thighs, digging my nails into his back and coming hard. My forehead drags against his, the pleasure lasting as he continues to mate me with his whole body - slow-rolling waves, thrusting through each leftover shred of my orgasm until it extends into a lasting, blissful ache.

Noah hasn't stopped staring into my eyes. I haven't stopped staring back.

Holy shit, I just willingly let Noah witness my pleasure with no blankets, dim lights, or closed eyes to shield me.

I feel free. Powerful.

But Noah's grip becomes desperate; his panting beats against my neck until he can't resist sucking it.

"Ah!" I cry out, my swollen pussy gripping him with a vice until we have no choice but to slow. "That still feels so good—"

"Oh, Goddess, I want you," Noah breathes. "I want your pups. I want everything with you."

My wolf claws at Noah's back through me with a whine. "Take it. Take it, please."

"Fuck, but I want to mark you." He growls, scraping my neck with his teeth as his rock-hard cock swells until it stretches me to my limit.

"Ah! Mark me, Alpha!"

He's still hesitating. He might think I'm saying it in the heat of the moment.

"I want you for life, Noah," I say. "If I didn't experience it firsthand, I would've mocked myself for falling this quickly, but it's true. I love you. I want you with all of me. So please, mark me."

As Noah pulls back to gaze into my eyes, his tongue leaves a trail of spit hanging from my neck. My spine shivers, enraptured with his feral, craving stare.

I was wrong. Noah wasn't hesitating, he fell silent in a desperate battle to remain in logical control.

But this is Noah's raw instincts staring back - golden, blazing eyes, ready to devour me. His wolf is in complete alignment with his body and mind. Living out this moment with me.

He purrs before smashing his forehead into mine, confirming he's unleashed. As he slowly drags his cock out of me, I gasp at the sudden emptiness in my core.

But Noah rushes behind me, hooking his arms around my hips, and I know what he wants. I gladly widen my knees, raising my ass for him.

"*Mate...*" With his torso pressed to my back, his growl reverberates through my lungs.

"Please, Noah. Mate me."

Leaves crunch in my fists as he re-enters me, stroking my clit to help me stretch over his swollen cock. I moan so loudly that birds flee from neighboring trees, sending a thrill through me. But Noah isn't satisfied with this position yet, hunkering down until his stomach rolls along my back with one deep thrust. He slinks all the way in with how wet I am - fluid dripping from me as I cry out in delight.

But when his fangs brush my neck, I gasp, my nails burrowing into the dirt. An explosion of nerves ricochets through my spine at the mere suggestion of his mark. Noah's heaving pants pour over my neck between licks, igniting the deepest pleasure I've ever felt as he humps me.

I drop my shoulder, baring my neck on instinct. He encourages me to bare myself further, licking faster with every thrust until my toes curl. When his fingers return to my clit, it feels so good that I can't stop my hips from dropping back to meet him halfway. He soothes me with deep, longing touches, dragging his fingers across my breasts and belly until I shiver.

But Noah whines, his tongue suddenly absent from my neck. "I can't bite you. I don't want it to hurt you, Omega."

"It feels good, Alpha! I'm getting close again from it."

Noah growls. His swelling shaft pounds against my cervix so deep that my legs tremble, preparing to come again.

"Don't stop!"

His arms lock around me as his hips jerk into me, instinct driving him to fill my core as he bursts. The resulting fullness is almost too much, its thick heat mixing with his expanding knot.

Noah's fangs sink into my neck.

30

I yelp, a flash of pain zipping through my pierced neck until the sensation morphs into the heaviest orgasm of my life. Noah holds me steady as I smash my hips into him to fuck myself deeper over his knot, undeterred by his groans as my belly flutters in ecstasy. Every hair on my body bristles as pleasure shoots down my neck, meeting the delightful fullness of my groin.

But as our bond evolves, it's clear our initial bond was incomplete. The forest floor shifts into rotating colors, developing into the most beautiful, indescribable colors I've ever seen.

My mind travels to another location. Somewhere only Noah and I can be; the forest where our wolves reside, inside our bond.

Flower fields stretch for miles, creating my new favorite scent: a soft, hyacinth essence blending with Noah's sweet, sugary warmth. Time slows, Noah's presence layering over mine until I can't tell us apart. His wet wolf nose nuzzles me, except I'm not in my human body.

I'm my wolf. Our wolves rub their heads together with satisfied, happy whines. I can feel Noah's wolf form so clearly now - more like a physical piece of me than the whispered ghost I've felt of him in the past. God, he's beyond gorgeous, his black coat shimmering beneath the golden sunlight. But it's those sweet, delighted puppy-dog eyes over my shoulder that gut me. He's so deeply precious to my heart that my wolf nibbles his ear, unable to contain her rising affection.

As my vision clears, Noah's shuddering weight on my back brings me back to Earth. I'm already crying. We communicate purely in whines and body language, gazing at each other with slow, satiated blinks.

Noah unlatches from my neck, softly nursing my wound until the searing ache fizzles into a comforting hum.

My pulse throbs as I feel Noah everywhere - inside and around my body. Merged with my soul. Noah's emotions have never been clearer. He's awestruck by me. Feeling so at peace. He's happy. Not temporarily, but truly; warm, tingling joy buzzes through every cell.

I whimper, cuddling into him deeper as his hands caress my now-bloated abdomen - my uterus unaware that our heavy sex included protection, still cramping in a desperate attempt to welcome his sperm. As Noah soothes my wound with thorough focus, my soul bursts with more love than I can hold. I hope Noah can feel it. Nourish and hold it with me.

Noah whines back, giving me heavy, loving blinks as he gazes into my eyes. He's so gentle with my body, slow, even strokes consuming my skin as I weep against his cheek.

"Thank you, Noah. Thank you."

I can't stop shivering as we remain knotted, each touch we share deepening our newly complete bond. Noah helps my shaky limbs ease us to the ground, draping himself over me like a weighted blanket.

His soft voice is blissfully exhausted, stuffy with fresh tears. "I love you, my sweet Omega. You're even more beautiful now that I can see all of you."

I whimper, hugging his arms around my cramping abdomen. "I love you so much, Alpha."

I've never felt such comfort, melting beneath my mate. As Noah's breath softens against my ear, falling asleep beneath him is an indulgent treat.

Not long after Noah marked me, I'm rudely awoken by a throbbing cramp in my abdomen at least ten times worse than the dull ache from earlier. I groan, trying to stretch through the pain until I realize I can't move.

Noah's breath stirs beside my ear, and I gasp - he's still flopped over me, compressing my lungs. I instinctually cough, but my eyes widen as it makes me clench around his flaccid length.

Noah gasps, lifting off my back. "Oh, sweet Omega, I'm so sorry. Fuck, I could've crushed you." He brushes my fresh mark, and I jolt. "D-does it hurt?"

My blood is still pounding, flustered from the burst of loving electricity his mark provided from the slightest touch. But now that our bond is complete, my heart aches with Noah's, even though I know I'm perfectly okay.

I kiss his fingertips before drawing them to my abdomen. "My stomach hurts more than anything else."

Noah's eyes track my touch. But when they hone in on our connected hips, his gasp startles me.

"What? What's wrong?"

As he slips out from inside me, it's surprisingly slick. "Oh, sweet Omega... I'm so sorry..."

I blink a few times, unsure if my eyes are still blurry or if Noah's legs are stained pink. "Oh, my God, are you okay? What happened to your–?"

Reality hits me, and my hand flies up over my mouth. Noah winces, sad eyes meeting mine as I flush red-hot with embarrassment.

Oh, my God. He mated me so hard that my period started a few days early.

I groan, covering my red face. "S-sorry, I-I made a huge mess..."

Noah whines, curling around me. "Please don't apologize. I'm so sorry I couldn't give you the baby you wanted."

I blink through embarrassment, peeking from beneath my arms to find his worried stare. He must've been thinking about the day our condom broke more than I realized.

Despite how much I want a baby, I giggle. "My sweet, shy Alpha."

He melts beneath my caress on his cheek, nuzzling my palm. My heart soars with him, experiencing how much every touch of mine makes his heart bloom with delight.

"I can't believe this, but I'm okay," I say.

"R-really?" He strokes my cramping belly, his sad puppy eyes gnawing at my heartstrings.

"Yes, gorgeous. Now that we're bonded, I feel so secure with you that I'm at peace with where we are. We can have a baby when we're ready." My eyes widen. "I-I mean, *if* we're ready, someday."

He doesn't say more, but I'm stunned by Noah's quiet, somber reverence - taking my crushed dreams seriously. It awakens a piece of me I've never met before: the unconditionally loved Omega.

I let her exist, growing larger with every inhale of Noah's doting scent.

Noah carries me home, drawing a bath. But as he joins me in the water, licking the sweat off my body until I'm craving him again, a deep sense of permanence settles into my soul. He's here. He's staying.

Noah fucks me slowly in the sloshing water, kissing every inch of my lips as I let my wolf run free. Loving every second with her mate.

31

In a flash of fur, Amy shoves me into the grass with her massive paw, taunting me. I struggle to my feet, out of breath from trying to keep up with a wolf. Well, another wolf. I'm a wolf too, dammit.

At least I should be.

As my nails buzz and stretch into claws with my irritation, I growl, desperate to fight Amy back. She's not even breaking into a pant, and here I am, drenched in sweat.

My eyesight phases into a new set of colors. Sprouting fangs steal an uncomfortable amount of space in my mouth. But the moment a swirling pressure consumes my chest - my wolf attempting to enlarge my ribcage - my breath catches.

Panic shoves her deep inside me, just as Amy rounds another tree, bounding over. Amy bats me, knocking me back into the grass.

My frustration rises, but not toward Amy - toward myself. I grab fistfuls of grass to yank myself upright, urging my shaking muscles to work. But Amy knocks me down yet again.

"Ugh!" I scream, alerting Amy's fluffy ears with a jolt.

This seriously sucks. I can't seem to let my wolf go unless it's in bed with Noah.

But not even Noah has been able to help me shift. Every time I get close, intrusive thoughts hit me like a truck, bending my will.

What if you fail at shifting, and your hybrid body can't handle it? The thoughts creep through my head. *You could die, leaving the*

pack without a Luna. All because of your inability to shift properly,
Noah will be alone, forever. That is, if your death doesn't kill him first.

I let out an angry groan, gripping my head and shaking it
clear - giving into a compulsion to erase my intrusive thoughts
before I can stop myself.

Amy's beautiful, iron-red wolf pants above me, nudging me
with her nose to keep wrestling.

"Ugh, no thanks. I'm done feeling mad at myself for today. My
compulsions are out of control."

Amy whines, sitting on her haunches.

I sigh, stroking her snout. "What if I'll never be able to shift,
Amy?"

Her right ear pulls back in thought. *Yeah, what if? Maybe you*
won't.

I groan, flopping onto my back to catch my breath.

Or maybe you will, and this will soon be a distant memory.

I smile, stroking Amy's soft paw. Now that Greenfield's top
Alpha has swapped blood with me, I'm part of his pack - in terms
of the pack bond, at least. One of the best perks is mindlinking
my best friend. I haven't needed to touch my phone for a week.

"You're right. Maybe I will, maybe I won't. Either way, I never
thought I'd grow up to be regularly butt-naked with you."

Amy shifts back to her human form, her fur morphing into
her silky, shoulder-length hair. "Hey, I'm not complaining. You've
got a nice ass."

"Thanks. You literally have the prettiest boobs."

She giggles, flopping beside me. "Come on, girl. You're the
freaking future Luna. No one will question it if you don't shift at
the welcoming ceremony."

"I'm not officially the future Luna yet either. Noah's mom
hasn't talked to us since I gave her a verbal takedown."

Amy snorts. "She didn't tell anyone you're part human, though.
Isn't that a good sign? She obviously knows."

My stomach curls over itself at the thought.

I feign reaching for my backpack beside Amy, giving up with a
dramatic flop into the grass. Amy cackles, tossing me my clothes.

As I undo my braid, combing the grass from my hair, Amy
shoots me a worried glance.

Ugh. I'm ready to shift the focus off me. "Sometimes, I still can't believe I never knew you were going through all this on the side. Especially in secret."

"Trust me, I nearly let it slip a million times. You just had no idea it was a possibility - of course you wouldn't guess this existed."

I sigh. That's exactly how I spent 29 years not truly knowing myself.

Amy fiddles with a piece of grass. "Not to mention I was out of control back then. I used to clash with my wolf's desires too, and it'd make me lash out. My first shift was right before winter break, when we were 10." She winces, suddenly avoiding my eyes. "I still feel bad about that fight we had, A."

The second I realize which childhood fight she's talking about, I burst out laughing.

"When you called me a bitch for the first time?" I laugh even harder as her eyes widen. "So it was only your wolf who thought I was a bitch?"

Amy playfully nudges my shoulder with a groan, throwing her head back. "Stop it! I know, I know! I was losing my shit, okay?"

"I can't believe you still feel bad about that! We were just kids."

"It was the worst fight we ever had, girl! What if I lost you because I let my wolf hormones ruin everything?"

I grasp Amy's hand on impulse, biting her finger.

She gasps, growl-laughing at me. "What the hell?!"

"There. Now we're even."

"Girl, you really are a damn wolf - a feral one, at that. Get out of my sight." She pushes me down before I can chase after her, and I yank her back into the grass with a tackle. That's about all we have energy for, groaning in each other's arms in the grass with weary limbs.

We gather our things, trekking out of the forest full of smiles and laughter like we've had for each other our whole lives.

But as I approach Noah's cabin for the night, my stomach churns at the waxing gibbous moon - nearly full and shining bright against the baby blue sky.

Shit, I only have a few days left to practice before the next welcoming ceremony. I'm not sure what's holding me back from wolfing out beyond my intrusive thoughts, but I don't want to disappoint Noah.

When my shirt catches on a nearby branch, I hear a sharp *rip*. My focus zips to the massive tree that has me in its clutches. I can't pull my shirt off its branch. All I have to do is untangle it, but this is too familiar. I just keep tugging. Afraid someone will find me stuck here - catch me all alone in the forest.

This perfect combination of sights, smells, and urgency flips my brain on itself like an hourglass, catapulting me back in time.

I fall through my memories until they're not memories anymore. They're now.

32

"Disappoint me? Sweetheart, why would you even think that?" Mom's agonized expression only worsens the tears pouring down my four-year-old cheeks.

I grip her shirt, rippling the bright, primary-colored pattern between my fingertips, but that's not right either. I smooth it down, crushed by guilt for ruining yet another thing. "Mommy, I'm sorry."

"Oh, my poor girl," Mom whispers, squeezing me tight to her chest. "I'm not mad, I just got scared to find you all tied up on a branch like that. You're not supposed to go into the forest without Mommy. It's too dangerous."

Her arms are so big, encompassing my whole torso, but they're not enough to repair my heart.

I don't understand. How could they lie to me like this? Mom hates when I wander too far into the backyard, but today, she's soothing my guilty tears. Why can't they stick with one story, telling me what they really think about me? They hurt my feelings, but they love me too. It makes no sense.

I'm so scared I'm missing something big. That the answer is out there, and I'm too small to see it over everyone's heads. Are my parents good, or are they bad? Do they love me, or do they secretly hate me? I don't know what's right.

I'm four, but then I'm twenty-four, sobbing even though no one will answer my pleas for help. I don't know what's right.

Now I'm eight.

I got in trouble at school today. My heart hammers so hard that it hurts to breathe, but I'm afraid to show it. I don't want to hurt Mom and Dad more than I already have to, coming home with this ugly, neon-red slip in my hands.

I can already tell Mom hasn't checked her voicemail; she's waiting at the bus stop in her work clothes with a cheery smile. I'm about to erase that smile, and it makes me want to throw up.

I wring my hands, unable to walk down the bus aisle. But when the bus driver turns to glare, I scurry past the rows as fast as I can.

As I step off the bus on shaky legs, the first thing Mom sees are the tears crusted to my brown, summer-tanned cheeks.

Then she sees my scraped-up knees. I try to hide them with my skirt, forgetting it's tattered too.

Mom gasps, flipping my heart. "Aliya, what happened?!"

"I– I fell," I mumble.

"What?" Mom guides me by the shoulder down the path home, too worried to wave goodbye to the bus driver. "Sweetheart, you have to stop falling like this. Did someone push you? One of those boys?"

I shake my head no, my chin gluing itself to my chest.

But Mom stops walking. I have no choice but to stop with her.

"Aliya, tell me the truth. Are you sure one of those boys didn't push you?"

I readjust my clammy grip on my skirt, swallowing hard. But the force of Mom's suggestion wins over my fear of telling her. The truth spills from my mouth as my eyes squeeze shut.

"I climbed a tree," I mutter. "I got– I got–"

"You got, what?"

I can't read the tone of her voice. My eyes snap open as wide as they can be, staring up at her for answers.

She eases the red slip of paper from my hands, knowing when I get like this, I can't bear to speak at all. As she reads the details, I want to curl up, blending into the dirt. I don't have to be reading it with her to remember what it says; I already memorized the whole thing through my tears the past two hours in the principal's office while Dad was too busy to pick me up.

To the parents of: <u>*Aliya Matsuoka*</u>
Your child has received: <u>*1 day of limited recess*</u>
For the following reasons: <u>*The yard duty found Aliya climbing*</u>
<u>*a tree in her skirt. Her behavior encouraged other students to*</u>
<u>*climb after her. When she was told to get down, she fell and*</u>
<u>*scraped her knees. Her behavior was not age-appropriate, and if*</u>
<u>*she'd like to wear skirts, she needs to follow the school dress*</u>
<u>*code and wear shorts beneath them.*</u>

Mom's face says it all, dissolving from pity to something dark. Wait, is she mad at *me?* A small part of me hoped she'd understand. I just wanted to run free like the boys do. Be just as adventurous as them. Maybe Mom would get me, see that difference in how we're raised and hate it too?

It doesn't seem to be the case. Mom doesn't say anything, but I can feel her anger. It spices up the air between us, raising my shoulders the whole way home. I want to crawl back onto the bus, allowing it to drive me off somewhere deep in the forest so Mom and Dad don't have to deal with me anymore.

Then she says what I never want to hear. "How could you do something like that, Aliya? This is so unlike you."

I blubber into silent tears, even though I thought they had all dried up.

Mom's right. I'm always too "unladylike." I forgot that when I climb trees, the whole world looks under my dress.

When Dad gets home, I want to beg Mom not to tell him; it looks like he had such a bad day at work that I'm scared he lost his job. But he didn't lose his job, and Mom tells him anyway.

He scrubs his face, looking even more tired. I wish I could wash the worry off his forehead, but I'm the one who put it there.

"What did your teacher think about this behavior?" Dad says. "You need to be on your best behavior to get into Westfield schools. You're not going to Greenfield after the shit I had to witness today."

"Takahiro!?" Mom gasps.

"Sorry," Dad hisses, scrubbing his forehead. "Today has been

215

a nightmare. We're definitely getting her some shorts, An. I can't imagine if one of her teachers—"

Dad chokes on his words, wincing like he's hurting. He hangs his head in his hands, and Mom rushes me to my room. Once I'm all alone there, I shrink into the bottom cubby of my closet beside my mud boots, spiraling into heavier tears.

Mom and Dad aren't usually strict, but they change around what other people think. But aren't strangers the people they warn me about? Why should I care about them?

Amy doesn't seem bothered by my actions. She's mad like I am inside: why did I get a suspension when those boys didn't?

But Mom and Dad don't agree with Amy. Sometimes, they share the same, scared look. They think they're hiding it from me. But I only see them do that when I do something weird.

Something unfixable is wrong with me, and I can't figure it out.

I'm 14.

I'm a prime, subservient example of a well-behaved young woman. I smile hiding my teeth, stifling my laugh to a breathy, polite giggle. I keep a calculated, one-foot space between everyone I know unless they give me express permission to enter their invisible bubble. I cross my legs when I sit, even when I wear jeans.

If I disobey any of these rules, I have to heighten them somehow - make up for my wrongdoings.

But other people don't seem to care about rules as much as me. A classmate looks at my legs in Algebra I, reaching his hand into his pants. I pretend not to notice, hiding the discomfort in my shoulders and racing heart with a neutral, focused stare at the whiteboard. He's a guy, right? A teenage boy. He can't help but be tempted when he looks at me.

And I don't have room to complain. If I'm not careful, a freak like me will fuck something up beyond repair. Destroy the world with me in it. I should be lucky anyone looks at me like this.

I zip through ages so fast that I can't keep up. My dearest friends and newfound college independence loosen two decades' worth of rules. I kiss Amy on the lips over a dare, and realize girls' lips attract me too. We meet Kira, and I'm too happy for Amy to be bitter that I know our friendship will never be just-us-two again.

Then I see his bright, convincing smile across campus. That blonde hair blaring even brighter in the sun.

Steven is 21.

I'm 19.

Steven knows what he's doing. He's always on time, and I want to be too. I want to run track like him - a natural, graceful beauty on the field that leaves everyone drooling in his wake - but I'm a klutz. For some reason, he still chooses to look at me. I feel special.

His rules are simple. Familiar.

Men have uncontrollable, vital needs. Needs that need to be met, especially by women. Women are naturally gifted at comfort, and men are designed to protect women - including from themselves.

As a woman, if I withhold affection from a man, I'm disrespectful. If I withhold sex, I'm torturous. Abusive, even. Men can't control their urges, shouldn't I know that?

I do know that. I'm 23 and no stranger to sex.

So why am I having a heaving, desperate anxiety attack in the bathroom, lying to my boyfriend that I'm getting myself cleaned up before he can have me? Shouldn't Steven be the one upset by my neglect?

I'm so scared of what's happening to me. Steven cares so much about me, ensuring he always knows where I am, who I'm with, and when I'll come home. He doesn't like when anyone looks at me, not even Amy - we kissed once, after all. He's the jealous type, but like he says, that's the strongest type of love.

But my love for him is waning instead of growing the closer we become - and the more sex he needs. Am I a cruel, heartless bitch? Aren't I supposed to revel in the glory of his dick? Even if I don't enjoy sex, shouldn't I live to witness his pleasure? Isn't that my purpose?

No matter how closely I follow the rules, my body simply can't.

I can't do it. I can't.

I'm 24.

Dad died eight days ago. After escaping into my childhood

bedroom for a moment alone, I lift my exhausted forehead from my doorframe, squaring out my shoulders to enter the hall. I just finished spoon-feeding Mom, well aware she's lost the will to exist. Nothing I can do will change that. Mom always said her heart would die with Dad's, and I can see it. She hasn't died yet, but the light in her eyes is already gone. I'm living the dark, nauseating last stretch of her life, looming over me even in my dreams.

Dishes clank in the kitchen, and I wince - Steven's here, doing the dishes. He came over to help, so I hate the anger I feel blasting through my chest for potentially waking my mom, tightening my already sore jaw.

As I enter the living room, Steven's sturdy back steels me. He's familiar, and I'm losing two out of four people closest to me. I need his old stability. The Steven I met who settled my shoulders.

Burrowing me into his embrace, Steven runs his hands down my back until they land on my waist. I expect words of comfort. Crave it.

But Steven chuckles, drawing me in for a kiss. When he pulls away, he stops by my ear, detailing how he wants me to pleasure him tonight.

As he draws back, I gape at him. Can he even see me? I'm drooping like a tattered, overused piece of cloth, ready to shred with the slightest tug in the wrong direction.

He's smiling, but I finally see it; there's no playfulness behind his eyes. Those desires were a command.

I jolt away, and Steven's mask breaks. The sun in his hair snuffs out, darkening his expression until he's unrecognizable. I back away on instinct, the back of my legs bumping into the coffee table, but it only makes Steven angrier. Rage, disgust, and desperation cloud his eyes, knowing he's about to lose everything he trained in me. I can feel him clinging to my soul, squeezing it tight.

But he squeezed one too many times. The wild animal in me - everything wrong about me - breaks from her shackles, shattering the rules Steven built as she leaps.

I act in ways I never have. Wild, unrestrained, impolite ways. I tear at my hair, screaming despite knowing Mom is - well, *was* -

asleep. Steven grasps at the air to catch me, claiming he wants to soothe me, but I rip myself away. Smack his hands off me. I don't recognize my voice anymore. Shrill, pleading screeches, begging Steven, God, and no one in particular to give me one moment to breathe. Can't everyone see I'm suffocating?

All Steven can see is that I've lost my mind over "one little comment" rather than the mountain he buried my soul under. When he calls me crazy, that unfamiliar woman screams in my voice.

"Get the fuck out! I never want to see you again!"

He storms from my parents' cottage, slamming the door behind him. I collapse onto the floor, gripping my aching chest as I sob. I believe it's finally over.

It wasn't.

33

"Aliya!"

Someone grabs my shoulder, and I scream.

I'm zapped back into my awareness by their hands, panting like I've been jogging. I don't know where I am.

No, wait. I'm 29. I'm in Greenfield Forest, somewhere near Noah's cabin.

Noah holds my cheeks, his eyes wider than ever. "It's me– Just me. I-I'm sorry, I didn't know how you'd like to be pulled out of it, but…"

He's talking, but my memories are restarting. I didn't finish the worst part. I shake my head as if it could clear it away, but Noah releases a blast of his protective scent.

"Hey, listen," he says, softening his voice despite my desperate whimpers. "Look at me, and tell me where we are."

Oh, maybe I'm dissociating. I try really hard to look all around us. But I'm seeing an overlay of two worlds, too distracted by the one that feels like it's about to kill me.

"Never mind," Noah says. "You do some type of exposure therapy with Jenny, right? Was it Prolonged Exposure? This is a flashback. Let's walk through it instead of fighting it back. Tell me what you're noticing."

This gets my attention. "Y-you know what Prolonged Exposure therapy is?"

As I look into his eyes, Noah's shoulders fall in relief. "There you are. Good job–"

"Noah, you have PTSD this badly too?" My lip wobbles, but

it's only then that I realize my eyes are already gushing tears. "Enough to do PE?"

Noah's eyebrows warp with mine, an agonized laugh escaping his throat. "Oh, my sweet, gorgeous– How could you be crying for me while you're hurting this much? Goddess, my sweet, sweet Omega."

I'm tempted to smile through my tears as his big thumbpads sweep over my wet cheeks. "You don't understand what I mean yet– This has to be real because my brain would never imagine something this good."

Noah's eyebrows quirk up. "That my brain is fucked?"

I sputter out a laugh. "No!" My mate erupts into giggles with me, settling his forehead against mine. "I just never thought my future partner would get it," I mutter.

After a few short, held breaths, Noah speaks even quieter than me. "I didn't either."

As our emotions ramp up side-by-side, a barrier within me breaks open.

"It took two years of bi-weekly sessions with Jenny to be able to function enough to work. It got so bad, I couldn't leave my parents' house." My voice is shaking, but Noah rubs my back, spurring me on. "With how anxious I was growing up, by the time I was an adult, I felt like anything I could do next could not only ruin my life again, but everyone else's. Then PTSD would say, 'Yeah, and here's how the whole world could hurt you too.' And even though I've worked so hard, it's still something I'll have to manage every day for the rest of my life. I was so afraid that'd be a deal breaker for someone."

Noah nods more and more the more I talk. Could he really be understanding this?

He clears his throat. "Is it a dealbreaker for you?"

My heart flips; everything negative I just spouted could apply to him too. "N-no, I– I'd never think those things about anyone else, I–"

Noah kisses my cheek, "Hey, hey, it's okay. I know that's not what you meant. I just want you to know you always have a choice."

I gape at him. Noah believes we're entwined by the Moon

Goddess, Herself. What he just said sounds like he's even willing to defy fate for me, even if that means breaking his heart.

Throwing myself into his chest, I can't hold him tight enough. "I chose you, and I'd choose you again, over and over, exactly as you are."

Noah's heartbeat hammers against my ear as he curls over me - our bond ignites with a desperate need to be entangled. But when I hear soft, hitching sniffles, I'm afraid my heart will tear.

We spend over an hour recovering in the forest until we're bleary with exhaustion, half asleep on the forest floor.

But when the fading sunset makes me shiver despite Noah's ever-present body heat, he sits up, tracing my side until my heavy eyes open. "You feeling okay now?"

I break into a smile. "Good enough to fall asleep in the forest without being scared in the slightest, thanks to you."

Noah ducks his head, hiding his flustered smile. As I sort out his hair, his low, rumbling voice sinks deep into my belly, warming me up from the inside. "Let's go home and take a nice shower."

The pain of missing each other all day dissolves beneath the hot water. Pressing our bodies together, we breathe in each other's scents as we stroke each other's backs. Noah smells like leafy, forest groundcover. And like stress.

Squirting body wash into my palm, I rub it between both hands before slathering his broad shoulders. Bubbles slip down his chest, escaping through the incave of his wide sternum. Noah's breath heightens as my thumbs smooth over his nipples until they harden. As I move to his back, drawing a deep purr from him, Noah huddles into me until our wet bodies suction together.

My heart rate jumps at how hard I've suddenly made him. But Noah doesn't act on it. His emotions are finally clear of stress in our bond, so I gladly continue onto his lower back. As I concentrate on a knotted muscle, dripping bubbles fizzle against my chest, Noah's cuddle keeping me snug against him.

Soon, my soapy massage makes every single one of Noah's wound muscles roll loosely beneath my hands. His purrs become consistent and soft, mimicking my circling, deep pressure on his back. He drapes himself over me in full relaxation, allowing me to hold some of his weight.

My stomach flutters at how much he trusts my touch.

"Thank you." Noah's whisper is rough with drowsy bliss.

His arms slink tighter around me, squeezing every inch of my frontside against his warm skin. Trailing my mark, Noah kisses my jawline as he rubs my back. I purr in delight, nuzzling into his chest.

After rinsing off, Noah grabs my shampoo with one arm to return the favor, keeping me cuddled to him with the other. Tingles dance down my shoulders as he scrubs my roots, his gentleness never ceasing to be surprising.

"Tell me about your day," he says.

I bite back a smile. "Before or during the major flashback in the woods?"

Noah softly chuckles. "Either. Both."

I hum, unable to open my eyes as I droop against his chest. But the more I think about my morning, the more my heart hurts. Noah sighs in sympathy.

"That same little girl..." I mutter.

"Your three-year-old student?"

"Yes. Today she didn't just cling to my leg, she also begged me to hold her. Not just a hug, but full-on carry her." I groan, leaning into Noah's deeper pressure on my tense right shoulder. "But I'm not allowed to, which I understand, but she doesn't. If she's not held enough at home, I can't stand making it worse, Noah."

"I know. I can feel it."

"At least I'm allowed to hug her when she asks, but it's never enough. Something is seriously wrong, but there's no time to figure it out. My other students need my time and attention too."

"Did you smell anything that could tell you what's wrong?"

I shudder into Noah's smooth comb-through of my hair with conditioner. "That's very wolf-like of you, Alpha. But I can't say I make a habit of smelling my students."

He chuckles, leaning over me to kiss my wet forehead. I drop my head back, standing on my toes to kiss him on the lips instead.

His wet lips soothe me with each gliding slip across mine,

giving me their undivided attention in slow motion. When I pull away, there's a fire in my core. Noah pauses to trace my eyes, taking a deep breath of my rampant pheromones.

He kisses me softly again as if he doesn't smell my desire. "You don't have to smell her directly. Just breathe deeper around her than you normally would. She might smell like stress or anxiety all day, but there could be a certain activity or time where it's worse."

Noah's eyelids droop shut as I comb his wet hair back with my nails.

"You're so damn smart. I'll try that tomorrow."

He breaks into a tiny smile, dropping his head.

I giggle. "Tell me about your day now, gorgeous. Before your mate scared the shit out of you with her flashback."

Noah's hands slide from my back to my hips, pressing me tighter against him. I sharply inhale.

He exhales roughly, dragging his head along mine until I cling to him even tighter. "It might be triggering," he mutters.

My heart flips. "Tell me anyway. I want to be there for you, no matter what it is."

Noah gives me a heavy squeeze, grumbling into my shoulder. "Okay. I guess I hate to say it too, but I can't pretend it's not happening. Long story short, a Rogue Alpha hurt his rejected Rogue Omega so badly that she couldn't shift back."

My hands halt into an anxious grip on his biceps. "What? She was stuck in her wolf form?"

Noah smooths my clingy, wet hair from my cheeks, kissing me a few times. "Don't worry, Omega. You'll never have to get stuck like that forever. She'll shift back once she feels safe."

As usual, Noah knew where my mind went; shifting already feels out of control without the risk of being trapped in my wolf form forever. But staring into those patient eyes, I trust Noah. I bite my lip, scratching soft circles on Noah's back until he shudders.

Then he slumps against me. "But that meant I had to drag her to the pack doctor by the scruff like a giant pup. No one else could do it."

"Oh, my God, Noah…"

225

He sighs, kissing my shoulder. "I'm fine, compared to her. I just keep thinking the same thing I always do when I see someone treated so horribly; I don't get how someone could hurt anyone like that. Willingly."

My heart aches with Noah's, stress creasing his forehead.

"That's horrifying, Noah. I don't understand it either. But I do know these Rogues seeking refuge are lucky to have you, especially since you don't operate that way. They're safe, thanks to you. And I know they can feel it because *I* feel safe here, even though bad things happened in the past."

Noah's serious stare flips my heart. He cups my cheeks, softening his voice. "I love you, sweet Omega."

My smile erupts on its own, inspiring Noah's wolf to court mine in our bond. "I love you too, Alpha."

Leaning in to kiss at the same time, we meld together. Water ripples down our sides, unable to slip between our snug embrace. Kneading his lips, I caress Noah through his hair, across his back, down his shoulders, and along his hips. Noah cuddles me against the wall, his smooth tongue in my mouth toasting my cheeks. His stiff shaft twitches against my belly, but a sudden waft of frustration peeks through his scent.

I'd brush that off as sexual desire, but his frustration seems different. No matter how vividly I can feel his emotions, it's impossible to know what he's thinking.

"What's wrong?" I ask.

Noah's shoulders slump. "Sorry. Nothing's 'wrong,' per se…"

"Well, I can tell something's off, but I don't know what." I bite back my smile, playfully tapping his forehead. "Unfortunately, I'm still a touch away from reading your mind."

Noah laughs, dropping his forehead against mine, but his sweet smile fades as quickly as it arrives. "I'm sorry. I'm trying to control myself. I hate seeming mad since it always scares people."

"Just be yourself around me. If I get scared, I get scared."

He sighs, kneading my back in the slowest, most luxurious massage possible. I melt in his arms.

"But for the record, I'm not scared, not even a little. You're allowed to feel mad," I say.

Noah pecks my mark, sending a shiver-inducing flash of gratitude through me.

But Noah growls beneath his breath. "It's my damn wolf. I just want to enjoy taking it slow with you. This is literally the best shower of my life - just like this. Plus, you've already had a shit day and don't need his nonsense."

I break into a smile. "Oh, I see. He wants sex?"

Noah groans against my neck, hiding his face in my shoulder.

I giggle, hugging him tighter. "What if I want it too? Your sweet self has me extra smitten tonight, Alpha. We can make it slow and romantic, just like this."

"True…" He swallows hard, a tug in our bond urging us to act.

When Noah's eyes phase green, I assume he needs me to take the initiative. Sticking my hand out of the shower, I reach for the condoms in the bathroom vanity. But Noah stops me with a soft touch on my cheek.

"The problem is, I know he'll keep busting those on purpose. Especially because this week, you– um…"

My eyes widen with no idea where he's taking this. "I, what?"

"Well, it's right before the full moon. My instincts get a bit stronger. Or, a lot stronger."

"You're saying you go out of control?"

Noah's eyes darken. "No, no, no. That's a fucked-up excuse for Alphas to disobey consent. What I'm saying is…" Noah's breath shakes. His fingertips skate over my shoulders as he eyes me. "Everything in my body is telling me to get you pregnant… Since I can smell that it's about to be a good time."

My entire face flushes. I'm forced to bite my lips to keep my logical brain in charge. "And it's right before the full moon, of course, making that extra frustrating?"

He nods. His expanding chest compresses mine through our full-body cuddle.

"Then how about we use our hands for a few days until you don't smell it anymore?" I ask.

Noah growls into my mouth, kissing me against the tile with his full body.

I break our kiss with a wet smack of our lips, just to give him a playful smile. "Or - since he submits to only me - I'll stop your wolf before he breaks the condom, and I'll help you with the rest."

"Oh, fuck, don't torture me, Omega. He's going to *ruin* that plan." Noah nips my mark. I automatically whimper for more, and Noah groans. "Okay, my brain is gone. This is your judgment call."

"Then just to be safe…" I trace his lips with my fingertips, aching to feel them again. "I think we should stick with our hands."

My heartbeat pounds into my groin as Noah looks me up and down, ready to devour me. As we crash into each other's lips, Noah's long arm wastes no time in reaching past my ass, slipping along my entrance from behind. I suck in a sharp breath through our kiss as Noah swirls his fingers, teasing my hips to chase after them.

He growls. "Fuck, you're so ready for me."

It's true - something about his tenderness tonight heated me from the inside out. I've only just started stroking him, but Noah's fingers effortlessly slink into me.

I shudder against his chest, and my legs widen for him. His thick fingers align vertically with my pussy, stretching me as if his cock was sliding against my inner walls.

Moaning into his mouth, I break our kiss, dropping my hips for more. "Ah! That's good…"

"Oh, fuck. You want it so badly." Noah strokes into me, slow and deep until I'm liquified, gasping against his lips in soft whimpers. "I've been trying to figure it out every time - which part do you like? The slow pressure, or the depth? It's killing me."

He slows until it's agonizing to wait for his touch to sink into me. But when his fingertips hit the deepest they have yet, I clench over his fingers in delight.

"Ugh, fuck, like that." His voice roughens as his wolf reaches the surface. "You've gotta tell me, feisty Omega. I feel it spike in our bond as I mate you, and I can't stand wondering anymore."

My cheeks burn. But Noah's soothing, gentle kisses make me want more of his touch, no matter how shy I feel. "The– the deep part. That's what I like."

Noah breaks into a soft smile, scooping the back of my head in one hand to kiss me tenderly.

But then his fingers suddenly work me twice as deep, pushing further with every elongated stroke until my eyelashes flutter. "Ah! Oh, *God...*" I gasp.

"Oh, fuck, that's totally what it is. Dammit, I want to be inside you."

I gather my wits, smoothing over the entire length of Noah's shaft. The base already swells, just from watching me.

My voice comes out weak and breathy. "Pretend you're inside me. Convince your wolf."

Matching Noah's movements, I stroke him at the pace his fingers sink into me. It's to my own detriment, my knees a shaking mess.

"Ah! Noah..." I arch my back, lifting my hips to help him reach.

He smashes his lips against mine, flexing his shaft with every stroke of my palms. I rub his tip with one hand while stroking with the other, teasing him until he groans into my mouth.

As his fingers drive into me faster, my knees dip to squeeze him inside me, seeking heavier pressure. He drinks up my voice with his tongue, thrusting into my hands with heavy grunts until he comes over my fingers.

"Mm!" I moan at his heat competing with the warm water, picturing him bursting inside me.

He hugs my waist tight, locking our lips as I writhe over his fingers with desperate cries. When he rubs his thigh against my clit at the same time, I erupt, coming with pleading, breathy gasps.

As we fall still in each other's arms, Noah's heavy-lidded eyes tell me he's still hungry for more. But he shuts off the water, kissing me with sweeping brushes down my back.

Our nightly cuddle ball has become so natural that our bodies meld together the second we hit the mattress. Noah's repetitive, calm breath lulls my eyes into closing, every muscle relaxed from our indulgent shower.

But then Noah's whisper breaks the silence. "I'm sorry, sweet Omega. I forgot to ask how it went sparring with Amy today."

I grumble into his chest, burrowing my nose into his body heat.

He chuckles, stroking my wet hair. His cuddle heightens, rolling over me until I adjust to hug him tighter. "I'll help you tomorrow, okay? You've got this, I know it. If not tomorrow, then someday in the near future."

"But the ceremony this weekend…"

"How about the second you can shift, I'll call an impromptu run? Then you won't be missing out on anything at all."

I sigh, slipping my leg between his to weave ourselves together even more. "You're so sweet to me, Noah. But I want to try to finally get it right tomorrow."

"Okay, feisty Omega. No matter what, I've got you."

As he kisses my head, his loving scent washes away my concerns for the night.

34

My Friday starts back in the classroom, where surrounded by toddlers, things often go from tranquil to chaos in a single breath.

Today is no exception. I plug Andy's nose - blocking his airway so he's forced to breathe from his mouth, and therefore unlatch his teeth from Jenna's arm as she screams bloody murder. My ears crackle with the rising pitch of her screech, Andy's angry, growling grunts peeking through Jenna's scream-pause whenever she takes a heaving breath.

I do *not* have my happy teacher's voice on. "Andy, let go, *now*."

Finally, he's forced to take a gasping breath, dropping Jenna's arm with a trail of spit. I separate the children, and Mrs. Jacobs, the neighboring teacher, rushes to help after hearing the commotion.

But my eyes catch on three-year-old Kelsi, shuddering in the corner instead of her usual attachment to my leg. "Oh, sweetheart…"

She whimpers, too afraid to run to me no matter how much her muscles tense toward me like she wants to. My heart ripples in pain, almost doubling me over. This biting incident won't help her feel safer, and I'm afraid to imagine the consequences.

Andy fumes beside me on the carpet, brimming with hot tears. I have to check on Jenna, but Mrs. Jacobs escorts her away to rinse Jenna's arm in the sink, shooting me a glare.

Great. The older teachers already think I'm young and inexperienced enough. They don't like that I don't believe in traditional punishment, and this incident could support their case.

But I don't see how shaming and isolating Andy will help him understand what he did wrong.

I just don't believe kids are malicious monsters. From how Lilian treats Noah, I bet that's what she believed about him. I felt so much anger in his past when I marked him. But eventually, he gave up. Quieted himself.

My heart aches as Andy whimpers next to me, afraid how I'll react. I want to do what I feel is best, whether or not it's the best method in the world.

Extending my hand to Andy, I steady my voice. "Let's go have a cool-down talk, okay?"

He takes my hand, slouching after me to the quiet reading corner with a weepy, red-faced scowl. Andy plops into a bean bag with a pout. His thick brown hair flops over his eyes, snot dripping from his little button nose. Even when I hand him a tissue to wipe it, he doesn't meet my eyes.

"Can you tell me what you're feeling like inside?"

He still avoids my gaze.

"I know I was playing with Jenna. Did that make you feel angry?"

Andy's brows furrow. "I wanted to play too."

"I would have loved to play with you! What do you think you could say to let me know you want to play?"

He sucks back snot, peeking up at me. "Miss Matsuoka, can I play too?"

I smile. "Yes! You're so right, Andy. Then we could all play together! You, me, Jenna, and our other friends."

His lips warp into a pout. "I wanted to play with *you*, Luna."

My heart flips before breaking into a sprint. I had no idea he was a little wolf. No wonder his first instinct was to bite Jenna.

I neutralize my voice. "Andy, we can't bite our friends. Biting really hurts, and we don't want to hurt our friends."

Andy drops his stare with massive, pooling tears threatening to spill, his lip quivering.

I rub his back, softening my voice. "If you want my attention, you have to tell me what you need, otherwise I won't know what you need. Let's try it. You can say, 'Miss Matsuoka, I need some attention.'"

"Miss Matsuoka…" He fiddles with my long braid, leaning against my shoulder as he blinks a tear down his cheek. "I need some attention."

"Okay, Andy, you need some attention right now? Thank you for telling me." I hug him from the side, and his shoulders finally settle.

But my heart races as I decide to try something I've never tried at school before. Focusing on my wolf's nurturing, soothing urges, I visualize my scent washing over Andy, loosening the anger in his tense shoulders.

He dives for me, burrowing his face into my neck with a whimper. "Luna…"

I hug him tight, my heart spiking at that name. "I'm here for you, Andy. But I'm your teacher, so you have to call me Miss Matsuoka at school, okay?"

"Okay, Miss Matsuoka."

"Let's go apologize for hurting Jenna's arm. We can't bite our friends anymore, okay?"

"But why? The Alpha bit you…" Andy's eyes land on my mark.

My fingers automatically rush to cover it, my cheeks flushing.

Shit. I have no idea if wolves think it's appropriate for kids to talk about marking. Noah healed mine into a faded scar by licking it, allowing me to wear collarless shirts around humans again, but he warned me other wolves would smell his scent embedded into me. We're not just tied spiritually, but physically.

But Andy looks curious, so I answer his question as carefully as I can. "That's because the Alpha is my mate. Have your grown-ups told you about the special type of bites mates give?"

"Yeah. It's a mark."

Oh, thank God. "Okay, then we can't bite our friends like that, right? They're not our mates."

"Yeah... But…"

Wait, wolves *do* bite to play or solve issues. That would be so confusing for a little Lycan in a human school.

As expected, Andy peeks into my eyes for answers.

"We're not with the pack right now either," I say. "We can't bite humans, not even as play."

Andy puts the pieces together with a sage nod, hopping to

his feet as if he's heard that a thousand times. "I'm sorry, Miss Matsuoka."

I chuckle. "Let's go give that sorry to Jenna, okay?"

As Andy grabs my hand, my gut burns. Since I can't tell Jenny about this, I'll have to think this through with Amy or Noah. This changes the teaching game entirely. My teachers sure as hell never understood anything wolfy I did, let alone minor transgressions I made as a curious little one. How many of my instincts got all confused as a toddler, just like this?

Worse than confused, I'm horrifically behind; my preschooler student recognizes I'm another Lycan, knows all about marking, and understands my pack position well enough to contemplate complex social workings around my closeness to the top Alpha. I couldn't even tell Andy was a Lycan when he was in my arms. Before he can smell it on my scent, I stifle the nauseating embarrassment in my gut as I guide him across the classroom. I'm 25 years older than him, one of his designated role models for a major developmental stage in his life, but his Lycan life experience far outweighs mine. Can I really claim I have what it takes to teach a Lycan child?

Andy readily apologizes to Jenna, but my eyes widen at what he says next. "I wanted attention. Next time, I will ask to play."

I cover my smile; my heart whirs as Andy's accomplishment erases the fears from my mind; Andy really took my words in, and applied it without my prompting. Most adults I know aren't even that self-aware. These kids never fail to amaze me. Whether I'm prepared or not, these moments are why I'm here.

When Andy sits in his chair, I stick by Jenna, giving her dripping nose a quick wipe before lowering my voice to speak to her alone. "How's your arm, Jenna?"

"It's okay…"

My heart aches at her quivering pout, and I can tell she's trying to be strong. "Aww, Jenna, it's okay to be upset. That really hurt, huh?"

"Yeah…" She huddles into me for a hug, and I do my best to ignore Mrs. Jacob's glare.

"Do you need a break, or do you want to do circle time with us?"

She shudders through an inhale, but the more she thinks about circle time, the more she smiles. My heart warms. Maybe I'm doing okay in this class after all.

"Circle time," she whispers.

I smile, allowing her to grab my hand before rejoining the class. "Alright, everyone! Come join me for a special circle time on the carpet!"

The preschoolers meander over to the carpet, warily eyeing Andy. Which means Andy doesn't join us, unsure how to reinsert himself.

I glance into the corner to find Kelsi similarly hiding, unbudging from her spot. "You don't want to join us, Kelsi?"

She shrinks from all the eyes on her. I give her time to decide, but when she doesn't move, I give her a reassuring smile.

"That's okay! You and Andy can jump in whenever you're ready, okay?" I turn to the crowd of uncertain eyes. "Let's all take a big, deep breath."

The class follows along, familiar with my deep breathing exercise by now. By the time everyone seems a little more centered, I help them distribute their naptime pillows.

Thankfully, Andy finds his naptime spot with everyone else - except Kelsi. It breaks me to see her scared in class. I hope she still trusts me after today.

But with twenty other eyes on me, I put on a brave face. "Who can show me what their angry face looks like? Here's mine." I soften my wolf growl as much as possible, scrunching up my nose, forehead, and lips.

Thankfully, the class bursts into giggles.

"Where are those angry faces? Let me see them!"

They show me their best angry faces, half-giggling, half-growling.

"Amazing job! Who can tell me what they feel like inside when they get really mad?"

A few kids raise their hands, but by the second hand, everyone shouts answers.

"Hot!" Alex blurts out, her curly bun shaking with enthusiasm.

"My face just goes–" Cory tightens his jaw, giving his little head a muscle-tensed shake.

Jenna gasps through her words, unsure what to do with her thoughts. "Like - like a big balloon, and it just goes– *pop!*"

My eyes widen with Jenna's. "Wow! So you all feel a lot of big feelings when you're angry!" A chorus of little "yeah"s warms my heart. "Sometimes it can be hard to know what to do when you have such big feelings, right? Does anyone know what we *can't* do when we're angry?"

The class shouts even more answers, and I happily ignore my co-worker rolling her eyes.

Until she butts in with a tight scowl. "Biting."

Why is this lady still here like I need babysitting? Her poor kids must be relieved to have her assistant lead her rigid class for a change.

But I nod at her words, ensuring the kids hear my grounded intonation. "You're right, Mrs. Jacobs. Biting is very painful, isn't it? It's not okay to bite, hit, or say mean things to our friends. That hurts! And we don't want to hurt our friends." A focused silence falls over the class. "But it *is* okay to feel angry or mad inside. We all feel mad sometimes. Does anyone have an idea for another way to show our anger?"

The class is so silent that my heart breaks. I guess emotional education at home is still less common for this generation than I hoped.

I smile. "That's okay! Here's my favorite way to let all that anger go. Are you ready?"

There's another chorus of "yeah"s, followed by a curious silence.

Grabbing my clipboard and a red crayon, I furrow my brows as I pretend to write. "Dear diary, I am so mad! Today, I stubbed my toe on the side of the couch. Ugh, who even put that couch there?! Well, diary, it was me who put that couch there."

The class erupts into a fit of giggles, and I have to struggle not to smile. Infusing that energy into cramming my features into an even tighter scrunch, I continue.

"I am so mad at how silly I looked! It happened right in front of my friend, and she laughed at me. Can you believe that? I thought that was so mean. It really hurt my feelings."

The kids are silent now. Concern riddles their sweet faces as they sympathize with me.

I swipe my forehead with a dramatic sigh. "You know what, Diary? Now that I got all that anger out, I feel so much better!"

The entire class gapes, unsure what to think. I'm sure it's because almost none of them can write, wondering how this even applies to them, so I whip my clipboard around. Their eyes widen to find a sloppy page of hot red scribbles over scowling, screaming smiley faces.

The kids burst out laughing, and I break into a smile. "Who wants to take a turn? Let's head to our spots at the tables!"

When they see me heading for the closet with the crayons and paper, the kids scramble to the round tables to draw without any further urging. I can't stop beaming at their enthusiasm.

The room buzzes with shrill, voracious giggles as they try to make each other laugh by imagining the goofiest reasons to be angry. It might seem like they're not taking the exercise seriously, but I know they are. Even the most outlandish stories ace the exercise, detailing legitimate upsets with anger at the root. Although, I'll admit most of them center around poop jokes. I laugh with the kids, encouraging everyone to keep releasing their anger.

But as the class loses their focus to tired giggles, my attention is directed to the commotion in the back of the room.

Kelsi's face crunches so deeply with rage that I freeze at first, unsure she's breathing from her face's darkening shade of red. The kids notice my panicked stare, dimming their voices as they follow my gaze.

My otherwise shut-down student breathes what could be dragon fire. She's jamming her crayon into her paper so hard that she's broken at least four, using nubby remnants to continue scribbling. At first, everyone falls into amazed silence, a whole room of antsy preschoolers miraculously frozen.

But my heart throbs, astounded by the gravity of this moment for this otherwise terrified, silent child.

Any second now, she'll feel the eyes on her. Meanwhile, all the kids look back at me, wondering how they should respond to Kelsi's self-expression.

She's absolutely nailing the exercise, so I clap and cheer. "Yes, Kelsi, yes! You're doing so great!"

The class cheers with me, some kids hopping in excitement. When Kelsi realizes all eyes are on her, she pops up from her desk with wide eyes. I try not to let my worries show, terrified this could set her back even more, but I can't help it. When she locks eyes with me, my stare widens in anticipation. I have no idea what she's thinking.

Kelsi bursts into shrill, squealing laughter, and the whole class joins her. Relief drips from her as students gasp at the beautiful, angry rainbow of colors she smashed across her page, filling the white space ten times more than the average preschool drawing. As compliments flood her, she stares down at her paper. Her grin widens with utmost pride. I'm not sure she's ever been so admired by other kids before, checking between her peers and her angry artwork like she can't believe this moment is real. I have to bite my lip, trying not to cry. It looks like this is exactly what she needed.

I turn to check on Mrs. Jacobs' opinion of us, but she's nowhere in sight.

She has no idea what it took to get here. Why I "took so long" to become a teacher at 26 instead of fresh out of college. She doesn't know I sacrificed myself for someone who sacrificed me, that my world collapsed under the weight of my fears until my dreams of raising and teaching kids were crushed by one inescapable, lurking fear: what if on top of ruining my own life, I ruin their lives too?

The day I was hired at Westview Elementary, I sobbed in Amy's arms. I lost so much before I could gain a single low-paid teaching job, but it was one of the best moments of my life.

As we finish class, my students' squeals of excitement and wide smiles prove why my fight to get here was all worth it. I end the school day with a sore, happy heart - even if I have to file incident reports.

35

The night before the Full Moon Ceremony, I'm all smiles and laughter in Jenny's office.

Jenny smiles with me, her pressed pants accentuating her long, crossed legs. "I know you've had some disappointments lately, but I'm honestly so impressed with your progress! How are you feeling about it?"

I nod, taking a deep breath. "I want to be proud."

"But?"

"But…"

I pause with no idea what to explain. It's so hard to tiptoe around Lycan culture with Jenny. All she knows is that Noah shares a moon cycle-centric spirituality with my father and that Noah is helping me trace my cultural roots. All of which is true.

I stick with the bits of truth I've told her, even if I have to leave out the wolfy details. "There's a cultural event with Noah this weekend - one of the most important ones I'll join. I don't feel fully prepared to participate."

"Does Noah know this?"

"Yes. But he has a lot of influence there, so he thinks I shouldn't have to worry about impressing anyone else." I pick at my nails. "But I want to look good by his side. I *really* want to be involved in this community."

Jenny pauses, studying my sudden tears. "What's this bringing up for you?"

"I guess I just feel left out. A bit of grief. Hurt. But not by Noah, or Amy, or anyone else in my life right now, which is what makes this so hard."

"What do you mean?"

"I can't blame a dead person."

Jenny smirks. "Well, you *can*..."

I sputter out a laugh through my tears. "I could, but I feel bad."

"It sounds like they made you feel bad too."

"Y-yeah."

"And now you're still alive, having to face how that pain actually feels."

I swallow hard, digging down to the truth. "I wish my dad involved me in his culture and spirituality more before he died. I feel like I missed out on a community I could've had to support me this whole time."

Jenny's eyebrows warp in sympathy, but my heart sets into a heavy pound. Dammit, she's going to wonder why my parents left me out again. It's impossible to explain without the wolfy details.

Thankfully, Jenny doesn't mention that again. "Are you worried Noah won't accept you into the community either?"

"No, I know he'll accept me. In all ways. Which is why I want to tell him about my OCD diagnosis too. I just haven't found the right time to bring it up."

Jenny gets a scheming look on her face that makes my heart race. "The 'right' time, huh?"

I laugh. "Ugh, I know. That's totally OCD talking."

"Well, what if I was here to help guide the conversation?"

I grip my jeans. "Like... Next Tuesday or Friday?"

She shrugs. "Or today. Isn't he picking you up after our session?"

Oh, God. *Today?*

Even though I didn't say that out loud, Jenny laughs. "I know that face. Are you waiting to tell him because you're not ready yet, or are you worried it'll hurt him?"

I sigh through a laugh. "You're right, as usual. I'm more worried it'll hurt him. Which sounds like an intrusive thought..."

She smiles. "Then what do you say? Should we call Noah in?"

A momentous feeling wells in my chest. Strong enough to get Noah's attention.

I know you're in therapy so you don't have to respond, but I'm here for you, sweet Omega.

Ugh, I love him.

I nod to Jenny, feeling like it's now or never.

Actually, my shy Alpha, can you join me in therapy? I need to tell you something.

Relief allows me to relax into the couch cushions.

But Noah's emotions heighten into alert. *Are you upset with me? Did I do something wrong or hurt you?*

Oh, God, no! I'm so sorry! My jaw clenches, and Jenny's eyes widen. *This is actually about what I told you once - how I get really afraid of certain things. But I want to explain why.*

I'll be there in five minutes.

I'm left gaping at the immediate resolve in Noah's stance. This felt like an even bigger relief for him. Like he's been waiting for me to let him in. Patiently, at that. I appreciate him so much.

Jenny's head tilts at the whirring emotions flicking across my face. "So... Are you going to call or text him, or...?"

Shit, I forgot I was using mindlink in front of her. It must've looked like I blanked out. I laugh it off, almost dropping my phone before tapping Noah's name on my contacts. "Whoops! Actually contacting him would help, wouldn't it?"

Jenny laughs with me, but I know she's studying me a little closer - a slight pinch tugging her eyebrows together.

After multiple rings, I wonder if Noah will answer at all. Yasmine made a joke the other day about Noah's year-old, unread texts. Maybe he won't even–

"Uh... Hello?"

I flush at his precious, confused voice. Hearing his rich tone through the phone for the first time wipes the tension from my forehead as I break into a beaming smile. "Hi. I know I'm in the middle of therapy, but I wanted to see if you had time to join me?"

Noah chuckles softly into the receiver. *Did Jenny notice your adorable, blank-faced mindlinking too?*

Yes! Play along!

He doesn't skip a beat. "I'd love to join you, sweet Om– *Heart.* Sweetheart."

It's my turn to giggle before saying goodbye to Noah. I awkwardly smile at Jenny. "He's on his way."

Jenny fills the waiting time for Noah, checking in about my

241

Exposure and Response Prevention homework, but I have trouble focusing. When Noah arrives within three minutes instead of five, his text's vibration jolts me in my seat.

Jenny gasps. "Oh, my goodness! Are you okay?"

I sigh, gripping my pounding heart. "I was getting anxious for Noah's text to come in. I guess I just care about him so much that I'm a little frazzled."

"Do you not want to do this today? If you're not feeling ready, we can try again soon."

"No— I'm nervous, but I know I want to do this."

Glancing at Noah's text, I break the tension with a sputtering laugh.

Noah (5:23PM): here.. texting like a human. fingers 2 big

Jenny laughs at my reaction, even without knowing what Noah wrote. "Well, laughter is one way to help with nerves! What did he say?"

I swallow hard, biting back the fear as it chokes out my smile. "He's here."

"Aww, honey... I'm going to be here the whole time, okay? You don't have to do this alone."

"Thank you, Jenny."

We have to listen closely for Noah's quiet entrance into the waiting room, muffled by Jenny's office door. But I already know it's him. His wolf bounds up to mine in our bond, and I smile despite the nerves.

By the time Jenny greets Noah and he awkwardly shuffles his massive frame through her door, Noah cuddles in next to me, studying my face.

I have no idea what to say. "Uh— w-well..."

Noah puts his arm around my shoulders, his scent softening them just as much as his touch. "It's okay. I'm here because I want to know how I can support you."

Already on the verge of tears, I look at Jenny for her reaction.

She mouths, "So sweet," and I couldn't agree more. Gazing into Noah's eyes, I steel myself.

"Remember when you mentioned never wanting to hurt me, even by mistake?" I grip the couch cushion between us, knowing that's an obvious "yes" from Noah. "That's actually what my OCD makes me afraid of the most too. Then PTSD sort of tag-teams with it, trapping me in a fear cycle…" I pinch my palm, unsure what else to do with my nervous energy. "Basically, I have both."

"Oh, my sweet– M-my love." Noah strokes my hair, and I bite back fresh tears.

Emotions swirl across his face - impossible to ignore, even if I couldn't feel them in our bond.

But Noah doesn't say anything else. He hesitates, and it spikes a primal fear of rejection through my bones.

"Do you know what OCD is, or are you confused? What are you thinking?" I ask - a billion other questions itching to follow.

"W-well, I…" He clears his throat. "I wish I did, but I only know a little. I know more about PTSD since I have it too, but–" Noah eyes Jenny warily before dropping his stare. "I-I don't usually talk about that with anyone."

I snuggle in closer, my heart aching for him. "That's okay. There's no pressure to share anything you don't want to."

Jenny nods. "Just knowing you have PTSD, I'm willing to bet you might be able to understand what Aliya experiences better than the average person."

I swallow hard, recovering my shaky breath. Jenny's trying to help me feel safer to share the deeper truth. The part I'm afraid people will judge me for.

Noah scoots closer. "I want to understand."

I drop my head, too overwhelmed to take in this reality. But after a tender silence with two of my favorite people holding space for me, the warmth of Noah's side against mine soothes my heart just enough to continue.

"I get a lot of disruptive, intense thoughts about terrifying scenarios that could happen. About accidentally hurting the ones I love, or getting hurt, myself."

When I don't continue, Noah searches my eyes for more. "You mean intrusive thoughts, right? Is it different for you?"

I hate how much my voice shakes. "What's different is how I respond. Since intrusive thoughts are the opposite of what I want, it makes me so scared I could do something terrible against my will or without realizing it, that I feel a deep, uncontrollable urge to make sure I don't." As soon as it slips out of my mouth, panic grips my heart. "I-I never have before! But my brain gets stuck on it, wanting to prepare me in case my absolute nightmare comes true. Sometimes I even get afraid that thinking about them means I secretly want them, even as they're terrifying me. That's the obsession part of Obsessive-Compulsive Disorder. And the compulsions are what I do to prevent it from coming true."

I pause, peeking into Noah's eyes. But his stoic expression remains focused. Inquisitive, but not judgmental.

"Are you worried what I'll think about that?" He asks.

"Yes, I–" Tears sting my eyes, breaking my voice. "I'm afraid you'll think I actually want to do those things, and that I'm a horrible person."

Noah breaks into a pained smile, and his stare melts with love for me. "Oh, my sweet..." He sighs, stroking my hair. "You willingly hurting someone is unfathomable for me, Aliya. Your heart is so kind, even at the core of it. I feel it every day I'm with you. To me, that fear just shows you care so damn much. More than others probably know."

The future brightens by the second – as usual, with Noah. I can't stop my lip from wobbling. "Thank you."

Noah hugs me tighter, reaching for a tissue for me. I try to laugh off my gushing tears, but Noah remains serious.

"Don't be embarrassed. Please, not with me." His voice is so soft and comforting that my tears warp into small sobs.

But since we're in this for the long haul, there's more I need him to understand. I stare at my fingers as they grip my thighs for dear life. "I know we've talked about how we've both done Prolonged Exposure, but the type of exposure therapy I do with Jenny is mainly ERP - Exposure and Response Prevention. Instead of just sitting with fears during exposures, I have to prevent the response - rituals I'd normally complete to neutralize myself. But if I give into compulsions, it just makes everything worse."

Noah is silent for longer than usual. I can see his mind spinning

- forehead pinched at the center and jaw tight. But before I blurt out explanations, he clears his throat. "So your compulsions are like the locks you mentioned?"

I groan. "Yes, those fucking locks. Or avoiding children altogether because they're impressionable, even though all I've ever wanted is to work with children. Then there are the more subtle mental compulsions like asking a million times if you want kids, checking and rechecking that you're okay or not upset. That I didn't hurt you."

"So… You need more reassurance? In those moments, should I remind you that everything is okay?"

"No, actually. I can't predict the future, so the truth is, my fears might come true, or they might not. I have to sit with the unknown. Accept it. That's what usually helps me heal, in the long term."

Noah bites his lip, his brows furrowing even deeper. "But I have a– a limit, I guess? I don't remember the term. Something about a window?" To my surprise, Noah peeks up at Jenny for an answer.

"The Window of Tolerance?"

"T-thank you." Noah runs his hands through his hair, and his anxiety spikes in our bond. I touch his chest, but that doesn't seem to help. "Y-you know, it's just– It's not always a good idea to keep sitting with it if it gets too strong. What if you're feeling really afraid? I don't want to just sit and wait while you suffer. Wouldn't that just put you under unnecessary stress?"

Now it's my turn to look at Jenny.

She smiles. "For PTSD, yes. For OCD, reassurance-seeking can be a compulsion, which is the real troublemaker. We want to support our loved ones, not OCD. Soothing anxieties or fears might appear to help, but it really just gives the disorder fuel."

"I-I'm not following," Noah says.

She uncrosses her legs, leaning in. Noah leans in with her.

"Let's say you have PTSD from a surgery you barely survived. If our Prolonged Exposure session of reading surgery medical journals became too triggering, causing you to dissociate, I would remind you, 'You're not in surgery right now. You're safe, here in this room.' That's what you might imagine when you think of reassurance, right?"

Noah nods. "Exactly. It feels cruel to just... leave her hanging."

"It might sound cruel, but there's an important nuance here; you're not reassuring Aliya in those moments, you're reassuring her OCD. Using the surgery example, someone with OCD might seek absolute certainty that they also won't trip on the stairs in a freak accident and need brain surgery. But accidents happen, right? If we promise, 'It's okay, that won't happen,' we don't actually know for certain - we all *could* have a deadly fall, anytime we use stairs. That dose of 'reassurance' isn't actual reassurance; it's false promises."

Noah's stress wavers in our bond, sending my body into anxious chills. "But that's not likely. Why can't I just explain why it's probably not going to happen?"

"But it *could*, right? You might logically think these scenarios are unlikely, but OCD doesn't care about likelihood. It targets our greatest fears, and no one wants their worst fears to come true. A possibility is too great a risk. But no matter how many compulsions someone completes, there's never going to be a way of ensuring bad things won't happen. That's how reassurance compulsions are a hidden trap."

Noah rubs my back. His eyebrows are set in heavy concern.

I sigh. "I know, it's a trip, but that's why it took so long for me to realize my OCD wasn't an ally helping me. Compulsions were destroying my life. They do quiet things down for a bit, but OCD will always say, 'Well, what if?' And yeah, what if? I'm not a god, so I don't know, and I can't know. But OCD is a trickster, pretending to keep me safe by piling on compulsions. In the meantime, I just get more and more afraid, constantly increasing the number of compulsions I feel absolutely required to complete to stay safe until I have nothing left of myself." I wipe my sweaty hands on my jeans before burrowing them beneath my legs. "It got to a point where I couldn't do simple, daily tasks without feeling a deep, unavoidable responsibility to make sure I wouldn't die or accidentally hurt anyone else in some freak accident."

Jenny nods. "That's why we want to support our loved ones in accepting uncertainty - reminding them that maybe something bad will happen, or maybe it won't. We don't know, but we'll try our best to figure it out when we get there. That's life, right?"

"Right. If I can accept that everything in life except death is uncertain, I can conquer my fears," I say.

"Fuck, okay. That makes sense, but..." Noah scrubs his forehead, concern riddling his frown. "Shit, I need to wrap my head around this, hang on."

My heart flips. He's so serious about this. Trying his best to understand. I knew he would, but it's different witnessing it in person. I want to shout out Jenny's window, announcing my love for him to the street below us, but I also want to hide under the couch's lavender pillows, feeling a little too witnessed.

But I understand how uncertain Noah feels. I grab his hand, redirecting his focus. "I know, this is probably weird sounding to a protective person, but it's also my responsibility to not ask for false reassurance. I always respond with 'Maybe, or maybe not,' and refocus on the present, but I don't need you to take care of that for me. Just being here with me through my discomfort - like you are right now - is a huge help. What I actually need."

After gazing into my eyes, his worry lines dissolve. Noah grasps my clammy hand, running his thumb over my knuckles. "Okay, if that's what you need, I can do that."

With the arm around my shoulder, he ever-so-subtly traces my mark. The loving, gentle empathy that washes throughout my whole being from his touch makes my eyes water.

"It's okay, love," he whispers. "I can be there. Easily."

I lean in and kiss Noah square on the lips. He sucks in a heavy breath, his hands wrapping behind my head to pull me in deeper. The desire that hits our bond flips my heart a million times over. I grip his jacket for more.

As he gives me a soft, humming purr, I'm shocked into remembering where I am on the planet. I release his lips with a louder smack than intended, placing my hand over his on my waist. "Noah, we're in therapy—"

He jerks away, dropping his head with red cheeks. "Shit. S-sorry."

Jenny and I burst into giggles, and Noah covers his blushing smile.

As Jenny and I walk through everything I want to share with Noah, he gazes deep into my eyes, enthralled with me. Wanting to know everything he can to support me.

The past few years, millions of intrusive thoughts warned me that telling my future partner everything about myself could ruin our relationship. But OCD didn't imagine *this* scenario.

Before Noah, this level of acceptance was too beautiful to fathom. But now it's real. And I'd do the exact same for him.

After the session, we walk through the forest, surrounded by a peaceful hush of rustling leaves. It's raining on and off, soaking Noah's hair and the black denim of his sherpa jacket, but he doesn't seem to care. He can't stop smiling, huddling up to my side as we walk.

I laugh. "What's gotten into you, cutie?"

He pulls me to a stop in the middle of our usual wolf-shifting practice area, taking my hands. "I'm just… *Really* happy you asked me to join you today."

My eyes burn as I feel his emotions digging much deeper than that.

All this time I was worried I'd burden him, but now that I finally told him, I made Noah feel special.

Happy tears spill from me. Noah holds me close in the quiet forest, tracing me with heavy-lidded eyes. I cling to him as we sway together, knowing in my heart that he's the most important person I'll ever meet. Even if I have nothing else but his presence by my side for the rest of my life, I'll feel at peace.

36

The next morning, I have no regrets about spending an intimate night in Noah's arms. Shifting by today was a lost cause, anyway. I'm still terrified to surrender full control to my wolf.

My stomach recoils as I rummage my closet, yanking out options until there's more on the floor than still hanging. The welcoming ceremony is tonight, and even though word spread about Noah being mated, it's my official introduction to the entire pack. I need to look nice, especially since I couldn't get myself to shift in time to run with everyone tonight.

Noah pokes his head into my room, and my shoulders sag.

I'm still in my towel, but he's looking gorgeous in the Full Moon Ceremony clothes I picked out from his collection: embroidered silver thread outlining forests and moon cycles across a black vest. The ornate design is buttoned over a white, billowy-sleeved tunic that contains whispers of his thick arms in its stretched shoulders. The way Noah holds himself is so casual - relaxing into each step like his nimble wolf - that he fits the part of a confident king.

I can't get over how stunning Noah is. He seems so gentle when I look into his eyes, but wearing this, he also emanates power. That's the perfect example of who he is as an Alpha, even if he's not always into tradition.

Taking in my disastrous room, Noah chuckles. "Sweet Omega…"

I flush. "I know what you're going to say, but–"

He raises his eyebrows with a soft smile, and I can't help but smile with him. "Really? Because I was going to say it looks like you were chasing after a squirrel in your closet, little wolf."

I groan through a laugh, dropping my head back. He wraps his arms around my waist from behind, stooping over to kiss me. I drop my weight into him, closing my eyes. His sweet scent soothes me.

He softens his chuckle into a doting hum. "I mean it when I say all you need to bring is yourself. You're incredible, as is."

"But my wolf…"

"We were going to forget the deadlines, weren't we? She'll come out when she feels like it."

I raise my eyebrows. "Well, that's what *you* said, but—"

Noah laughs, nipping my neck. I suck in a sharp gasp as it sends tingles down my arms.

"I know. You worked your ass off to try to get her to come out anyway. But you'll be beautiful tonight no matter what. Not just on the outside."

My heart flutters at his warm smile. Noah kisses me, long and slow, and before I know it, we magnetize to each other until we're chest to chest.

A rush of lust hits our bond as our hips meet. Noah groans.

"Fuck. Okay, let's not let my wolf out just yet." He takes three steps back. "Full moon, and all."

At the thought of potentially letting his wolf have me at the ceremony, my stomach growls with a flash of anxiety.

Noah frowns. "I don't know what Amy told you, but I'm not making you have sex with me at the ceremony. Please don't think that."

I laugh, covering my face. "I know, but be honest with me, Noah. That's normal for the Alpha to do when newly mated, right? In front of everyone?"

Noah softens his voice into a gentle hum as he kisses my hands over my eyes. "It doesn't matter what's normal, gorgeous. I don't give a shit about everyone else's comfort. I care about you, and I'm never having sex with you when you aren't a hundred percent on board. Let's keep it sacred between us - no pressure added."

I nuzzle into his chest, hiding my face. I'm too shy to admit it, but a part of me wants to try mating in front of the pack adults, especially because it sounds terrifying to my human side.

To my wolf, it sounds like announcing my love for Noah to his pack. I love the sound of that. And if I'm honest, the thrill of being seen in Noah's arms excites my wolf too.

While I'm lost in thought, Noah shuffles through my closet. "Here, how about we stick with a much less extreme tradition: the Alpha's mate usually wears white."

I sigh through my smile. "Okay. I can work with that."

Digging through a few items and only growing more frustrated, I give up. But Noah's grip lands on a silvery white, sparkly dress I've never dared to wear, buried in the back of my closet.

"Noah..."

I want to refuse, but the light catches on the silver glint of his embroidered vest as he turns toward me, and my heart skips at the vision it creates: Noah and I, side by side, glimmering in silver beneath the moonlight.

I slip the dress on without a second thought. I forgot how much it complements my body: a low dip in the front and a large slit up my right thigh allows the loose fabric to drape against my curves and spill in a sparkling waterfall over the rest.

"Oh, *fuck*." Noah's voice is so rough with adoration that I can't bear to look at him.

"I-I know it's not exactly me, but Amy made me buy it once she saw it on me, and you should always trust lesbian eyes–"

"Hell, no - not exactly you? I fucking love it on you. You could look incredible in anything, but this looks like–" He clears his throat, his voice faltering with a heavy dose of shyness in our bond. "L-like you came straight from the Moon Goddess to us."

My heart whirrs as I dare to look him in the eyes, startled by how serious he is. What spills out of me next shocks us both.

"I asked about the mating ritual because I– I'm curious."

Noah's eyes widen.

They also shift into a vibrant green.

I nibble my lip. "I just worry, you know, I'd look... weird. Awkward."

My mate's eyebrows raise all the way up. I shuffle my feet in the stark silence, fidgeting with the daring slit in my dress.

Then his irises settle into a yellow glint, deepening his voice. "You think you look *awkward* when we have sex?"

He steps toward me, and I don't move. A part of me wants to challenge him tonight. Drive him wild. Maybe the full moon has its effects on me too.

"I mean, yes. I trip over nothing and bump into doorways, so I can't imagine I'd suddenly be graceful." I drop my head, unable to look in the mirror at us any longer. Now that I've said it, it feels truer than ever, yet I'd hate to hear Noah agree.

But as Noah's body heat wafts over me - laced with a thick, desirous scent - my skin buzzes, awaiting his touch. I blink through the haze, his pheromones absorbing into the depths of my nervous system until my skin is on fire.

Noah lifts my chin, but not toward him; he redirects my focus to the mirror. I hold my breath, terrified of what I'll see.

But as I gaze into Noah's eyes in the mirror, vivid yellow irises stare back.

"Clearly, you haven't seen what I've seen." The half-shifted depth to his voice surges through my chest, but it doesn't stop there. It burrows into my lower belly - a sudden swath of intense arousal cramping my uterus. Noah's eyelids droop as he breathes in my desperate pheromones. "Goddess help me if I think of how fucking good you looked the night before while I'm on my morning perimeter runs."

As his hands slip down my shoulders, my heart hammers through my ears. I grip Noah's loose ceremony sleeves, straining the fabric as his thumb slips beneath my shoulder strap.

My focus flickers between Noah's hands - one on my shoulder and the other warming my abdomen - but I don't dare look into my own eyes in our reflection. The pleasure I feel whenever Noah's hands are on me is too raw. I'm afraid I'll find something to be ashamed of if I catch my expression.

But as Noah's thumb drags my dress strap low enough to bend the cup, my dark nipple pops from beneath the silvery fabric, standing proud with heavy arousal. I can hardly breathe as Noah's big, loving fingers trace it, emphasizing the curve of my breast before circling in closer and closer until he softly flicks the bud. My hips wiggle. A strand of damp hair slips off my shoulder,

caressing the outer edge of my breast with an icy lick. I twist my torso into Noah, gasping for air.

Noah pauses. His hand on my abdomen wraps around my hip, pressing me safely against him as I catch my breath. "Are you okay?"

It takes me a second to gather my wits, burrowing my face into his chest. "Why does this feel so much stronger?"

Noah breaks into a sultry grin. "You like it when I tell you how much your body reacts to me, don't you?"

My heart flips. I never admitted directly that I liked that, but that wasn't a question. Noah is confident in what I like - his wolf's chest puffing with pride in our bond.

"I figured you'd like seeing it even more than hearing about it."

Noah slips my hair behind my back, baring my damp neck to the frigid air. He wastes no time dragging his warm nose down it, his breath rushing down my exposed breast as he breathes in my excitement.

"You do. I smell it." He growls, tightening his grip around my arching back as he nuzzles another burst of pheromones from my neck.

This sequence of events suddenly seems familiar, and I gasp; Noah often breathes me in like this during sex, just before he mates me silly. It's happened enough times that my body gushes in preparation, wet heat pooling between my legs.

He's been scenting me to figure out what I like. My wolf paces, drooling for him. What else does he know about my body that I don't? Does he think I'd not only look okay enough to not be awkward at the ceremony but also love the thrill of it?

I lift my chin, gazing into his eyes. "I do," I mutter. "I do like noticing how my body reacts to you."

37

Rabid eyes flicker between mine. Noah seems to be at a loss for words, but he's certainly not letting go of me - his cock nudging my hip relentlessly through his ceremonial slacks. As he drags his fingertips over my abdomen, the anticipation for his next move sends an icy thrill through my veins.

"Do you want to see what you look like when you feel good?" He whispers.

My heart pounds so hard that it throbs. "I'm worried we don't have enough time before the ceremony."

His embrace loosens. Noah blinks a few times, his silence only breaking once his eyes have shifted back to a tinted green. "Okay. Should we finish getting ready then?"

Wait, did he just register what I said as a "maybe?" He treated it like a "no." God, I want him even more now.

Just before he slips away, I cling to his shirt. "I-I didn't mean 'no.' I meant I'll want to spend too long playing around with you to figure out what we like. I might not want to leave this room for a week."

Noah breaks into a sly smile. Returning me into his embrace, he backs us up until he sits on my bed's wooden footboard. "Guess I'll have to play a little dirty, then. Speed things up."

I sputter out a laugh. "What–?"

He shoves his hand in and out of his pocket faster than I expect, widening my eyes. Then he presses a condom into my hand. "I didn't trust our wolves to not need this tonight."

I erupt into giggles again, but then I yelp; Noah hoists me onto his lap with mischief written all over his fanged smile.

"Noah Greenfield, what are you planning on–?"

His hand slips into my slitted dress. I suck in a desirous gasp, but instead of burrowing between my legs like I expect, Noah skates down the back of my thigh. My skirt falls away, exposing my full leg. I flush when I realize I still haven't put on underwear, catching a glimpse of my bare ass squashed over Noah's thick thighs, and I'm about to see *much* more. My heart bursts into a sprint as Noah lifts my thigh to my chest.

I'm tempted to look away, but Noah's thick forearm replaces his grip, holding my leg upright and allowing his fingers to drag down my pelvis. My eyes widen as he seeks out my core, but I'm not surprised because of what he's about to do – it's how wet I am, glistening in the dim moonlight before I've even received any attention between my legs.

My nails dig into Noah's arm; pressure mounts in my pelvis at the mere thought of his hand finishing his journey. We watch my pussy flex in the mirror, sensitive to his fingertips trailing the outskirts of where I want him, and I've never felt shier.

But I don't want to stop looking. Noah looks just as hungry for me as he smells, and I'm stunned that I'm the one causing this in him. We hold perfectly still as we lock eyes.

Do you want me to keep going? Noah asks.

The second I nod, he indulges in my fluids - two fingers tracing the length of my core as my labia parts for him. All I can do is gape, my cheeks on fire as the tingling pleasure of his touch doubles - no, triples - with the added stimulation of watching his every movement in the mirror. Before I can stop it, Noah's firm, speeding swirls of his fingertips massage a wispy, desperate moan from my lips. I meet my own eyes as it spills from me.

Noah was right - I don't recognize who's staring back, but I can't get enough of her. This woman's shoulders are loose, reddened lips parted with pleasure, and her hand has traveled on its own to Noah's wrist, urging his fingers for more. I don't know if I'd go as far as to say she's confident, but she *is* vulnerable in the most seductive way. I can't even process this alluring, blissful version of myself before Noah sweeps his fingers faster. My chest heaves with each pass over my clit. Slick, slippery sounds fill the room from how hard my core clenches for more.

But what totals me is witnessing Noah's entranced stare in the mirror. Adoration spills from his loosened lips, huffing against my cheek in time with my breath. I can feel his excitement for my pleasure in every pulse of his attention between my legs, working me faster the more my hips rock. My thigh drops to the side, exposing more of myself to both Noah and me in the mirror as I squirm in his lap.

"I– want you–" I gasp. My hips tilt back, attempting to stave off an oncoming orgasm in record time for us, but this new angle just gives Noah's soaked fingers ample room to toy with my swollen clit.

Noah's heavy breath against my shoulder warns me that what I'm feeling in our bond is correct - he's so aroused that he's tempted to nip me. I breathe in soft whimpers, baring my neck. But the second his fangs sting my mark, I grab Noah's arm, stopping him.

We hold perfectly still as I battle through wave after wave of pleasure, straining to keep my quivering thighs frozen. My whole body buzzes, so overcome by our entwined bodies in the mirror that it's almost impossible to hold back my threatened climax. When Noah's questioning stare shifts into concern, all I can do to dissuade his worries is shake my head.

He removes his hands from my legs entirely, holding my hips steady as I breathe. His rising smile captures my focus, spiking a thrilling ache through my chest. "Feisty Omega, are you edging yourself?"

My knees dip, daring me to sit back on the hefty bulge straining against his pants beneath me and succumb to pleasure with him.

But I don't let myself. I take a deep breath, my voice coming out weak and raspy. "I don't want it to end."

Noah's smile dissolves into sudden seriousness. "Can I have that condom back?"

He removes the crumpled thing from my tight fist, ensuring it's still intact. His stare is focused as he opens it, but the fire between us mounts, starting a chain reaction in my clenching core. I grip my knees, breathing through my desire as Noah adjusts himself behind me.

Quick, eager fingers take mere seconds to slip the condom on before reattaching to my hips. We lock eyes in the mirror.

Noah's breath beats down my back. "Are you ready for—"

"Yes," I breathe. My cheeks burn at my bold declaration, but it only makes Noah's eyes burn lighter.

Silence stretches between us as Noah lines himself up beneath my hovering core. My blood pounds, only aiding my arousal, but I can't look away from how raw we look around each other.

Once his tip settles against me, my chest heaves; I'm desperate to drop my hips into him. But I don't want to rush Noah. I'm craving the tension I sense boiling behind his rolling shoulders – waiting for his filter to break. I have to chew on my lip, staving off my impatience as he slips his hands beneath my skirt, sliding it over my ass.

When we meet eyes, I have to grip my chest to keep my heart from jumping out.

Noah's humming voice deepens as his grip tightens over my hip bones. "I love you."

I try to respond, but I can't; the air evacuates my lungs as I watch every millisecond of Noah entering me. With every inch he disappears, my mouth gapes wider and wider, mimicking the generous amount of room he eats up. I'm so ready for him that he slips right past my pelvic opening, pushing a flurry of butterflies up my belly at his deeper entrance. I grip his wrists, choking out a desperate moan. I catch my own stare right as my eyebrows arch – a sharp snap of nerves ricochets through my chest as Noah's tip presses as far as it can reach.

I'm surprised by how fluidly my hips roll back, spurred on by instinct to feel more of him. I hadn't realized I was the one directing us until my hips jumpstart Noah's into action. He hugs my waist, gently brushing his thumb over my lower abdomen like he's thanking me for the heavy pleasure I hear in his hard breath. My swollen lips gape, overwhelming bliss rippling down my legs until my back arches to show off my breasts.

I never realized how beautiful I could look naked - maybe because the only times I've stared at myself haven't been in kindness. But Noah's enraptured stare follows his palms, dragging all over me. Loving me.

I grip Noah's forearms, freezing us in place.

I huff for air even louder this time, struggling to keep my core from squeezing him and taking us over the edge.

Noah growls. "Fuck, Omega. I'm tempted to tease the hell out of you."

I can't bear to hold his burning stare in the mirror. By the time my weak knees can bounce my hips over Noah again, he stops me with a tight grip on my hip.

"No, hang on, I can't–" Noah white-knuckles the bedframe so hard that I get the message, holding perfectly still. He drops his forehead against my back, breathing fast and hard despite our frozen hips. After a solid thirty seconds, his shoulders slump. "I can't knot you, or we'll *really* be late."

I almost made him knot me?

The ache I have for him drips from my desperate whimper. "*Alpha*–"

I don't have to explain that I can't handle edging anymore. The realization crosses Noah's yellowed eyes, and his resulting growl restarts my breath.

Noah gathers the split hem of my dress like his life depends on it. Fisting my skirt in one palm, Noah exposes nearly all of me - only a sliver of fabric clinging around my waist and barely hanging onto one breast. But I don't look away. It's too late to avoid my full, gaping nudity; I'm not just naked on the outside, I'm spilling raw, unfiltered bouts of my pleasure as Noah restarts his thrusts into me. My body quivers beneath his searching stare, a physical tingling following its sweep down my back, over the widest press of my thighs over his lap, and up my throat until he's locked on my face.

What I find in Noah's stare is that no matter how much I forced myself to hide in life, I can't deny I love being witnessed by him. Within seconds, the all-encompassing pressure Noah drives between my legs threatens to take my knees out. Noah hugs my waist hard just in time, sealing my hips to him as I tremble.

"Fuck, hang on–" Noah lifts me from his lap, leaving me startlingly empty. I'm ready to drop to the ground from how weak he's made my legs, but with my panicked gasp, Noah purrs. "I'm not letting you fall, gorgeous. Walk forward a bit."

I try my best to, but Noah has to hold me upright until we're face-to-face with the mirror. I'm already melting to my hands and knees when he meets me there, lining himself up behind me. He teases me with gentle flicks of his shaft, zipping his eyes all over my body as he absorbs my reaction. My core gapes for his return, and Noah growls as it swallows his tip even before we make a true effort to reconnect.

I slam one palm against the mirror - a welcome, cold shock against my overheated body. It's all I can do to keep myself from trembling into a puddle beneath Noah as his shaft slinks back into me, notably more engorged than it was a minute ago. My eyelashes flutter an inch from themselves in the mirror, my breathy moan fogging up half my face's reflection.

As my back arches, thrusting my hips back, I catch a glimpse of my ass bouncing over my shoulder. It feels so dirty and indulgent at the same time that my arms shake, absolutely weak from Noah's pounding motion pressing my breasts into the mirror. The sharp V-shape of his taught abdominal muscles ripple, tensing harder with every thrust met by my core's tight squeezes.

But my body's coping mechanism of dripping onto the carpet isn't enough to combat each heavy reintroduction of his cock, stuffing me with a rising, torturous ache. I'm ready to beg for more: the last of my patience breaking.

Witnessing us in the mirror breaks something in Noah first. He dissolves over me, his torso curled over my back until he wraps his arms around me. With his chest smashed into my back, he moans desperately into my shoulder - jaw dropped and forehead knitted. Edging is no longer possible, the rising pleasure in our bond so intense that I feel it buzzing over my torso until it reaches my face.

As my core squeezes him, sucking out every ounce of delight he'll give me, Noah's voice comes out choppy. "F-fuck, Aliya– I can't–"

He's about to knot me. The thought kickstarts the edge of my orgasm, sending me into drawn-out, pleading gasps. Noah's eyes widen with recognition in the mirror. One hand grips the mirror's edge, creating a sharp crackle beneath his weight, and the other descends my lower abdomen. The second he twirls his fingers over my clit, my body jerks into him, my orgasm pulling a wispy moan from Noah's lips. As he pumps out every ounce of satisfaction in me while I come, my G-spot receives a deep tissue massage from his relentless thickness.

Then Noah's magic on my body happens. I don't just trickle out a rush of fluid like I imagined; his touch makes me squirt hard enough to douse the space between our legs. I suck in desperate air, shocked at my body's reaction in the mirror.

Noah dissolves into frantic whimpers, giving me everything he can until he pulls out in a panic. His drenched cock bounces against my core with every grunt, drowning the condom's clear tip in white.

The sudden weak, tender silence between us steals all thought. We stare at each other in a mess of sweaty, tangled limbs, gripping each other's hands at my waist like a lifeline.

"I think we figured out what we like," I breathe.

Noah sputters out an airy, adorable laugh that sends another wash of loving tingles over my skin.

But Dave honks outside, snapping our heavy-lidded eyes as wide as they can stretch. *Where are you two? Is something wrong?*

Noah's wolf shines through his mischievous grin. "Fuck. We're late to our own ceremony."

All Noah has to say is "late," and I'm scrambling across the carpet on shaky fours to my closet. My legs are so weak that I don't even bother standing to dig through my underwear drawer, shuddering on my knees through echoes of Noah's touch. But as Noah's soft snickering dissolves into full-on giggles behind me, I whip my head around.

He's tripped up on the floor, one leg half-out of his boxers with his ankles hooked like shackles, and absolutely red in the face.

I burst into uncontrollable laughter with him. "Oh, God, let me help you–"

Unable to dash over with my panties roped around my knees, I jerk myself around too quickly and sprawl across the carpet, my arms outstretched as I release a soft "oof." Noah can't breathe – silent laughter stealing his voice entirely as he slaps the floor for mercy. When he finally sucks in oxygen, he releases such a vivid, booming cackle that my entire spirit rises with it into my bedroom's rafters.

"We're a mess," Noah sputters through laughter.

God, that sound is bliss. It's so contagious that I drape myself over him, weak with love for him. For our mess.

Noah shakes his head, capturing me by the waist to tug me into his arms. We share a giggly kiss, but as he cuddles me flat to his overheated chest, his heaving lungs press us even tighter. A deep, satiating ache squeezes my heart, relieved to be back in his arms.

Dave, I'm going to need one more minute to stare at my mate before everyone else falls in love with her too.

Noah's smile widens as I gape at him, unable to trace where this boldness is coming from tonight. But his wolf is there to remind me - zooming around our bond's secret world with pure joy.

By the time we clean ourselves up and rearrange my disastrous sex hair in a presentable fashion, I can't stop biting back my smile at our reflection. What I see in us has forever changed into something beautifully vulnerable. I think Noah feels the same. He freezes behind me in the bathroom mirror, his eyes bright. My grin spills over, creasing the corners of Noah's eyes with his mirrored smile.

It's painful to pry ourselves off each other, but Dave's honking car startles us into action. We race down the hall in a fit of giggles, tied by the hand. With one last kiss on my porch, I anchor myself to Noah's steady form, trusting he'll be there for me tonight.

38

Dave drives us deep into the forest, Noah's SUV rocking over uneven dirt paths. Noah pulls me closer, stabilizing me in the backseat. The moon's delicate glow buzzes over my skin, exciting my knee into bouncing.

As we pass the Greenfield Pack neighborhoods and Noah's cabin, we head deep into the mountains where the forest grows thick with all-consuming trees. In the ceremony space itself, there's a wide clearing, two-hundred-foot-tall trees acting as dark guardians at the perimeter. Everything is a soft shade of blue, dimly lit by the full moon.

I'm already shaking, but we've only stepped out of the car. Thousands of wolves mill about in hushed conversation, a crowd large enough to fill a stadium. I'm dizzy with overwhelm.

A sea of heads turns the second we arrive, lacing the atmosphere with quiet curiosity. I'm not the only new pack member tonight, but with how private Noah and I have been, I get the sense they're curious about me in particular. Maybe even hesitant.

At the same time, serene, welcoming scents surround us, a majority of the pack holding space for its new faces.

Countless eyes track us as we make our way to the ceremonial stage, running my mouth dry.

But I catch a familiar, bright smile at the front of the crowd, framed by silky red hair.

Holy shit, you're wearing the dress! Amy mindlinks.

I bite my lip, unable to contain my gushing smile. *You were right, of course. I feel like a goddamn rockstar beside my rockstar mate.*

You better own it, babe! Huddling against Kira, Amy shoots me a wink. *You look gorgeous beyond words, girl. And not just you. Both of you look incredible, together.*

Amy's mindlinked words expand my ribcage with my rising elation, making Noah turn to me with a gentle smile. I proudly take his hand, and we stride up the stage steps.

With the river flowing behind us and the moonlight brushing Noah's stubbled jawline, time slows into a trance-like state. Noah's voice is soothing and deep, even when he has to project his welcoming speech over a massive crowd.

The Rogue wolves I've met are usually timid and dejected, but Noah takes his time to nip every one of their palms, sealing their blood bond into his pack's family. Many of them weep with joy, their bright smiles warming my heart.

The intention behind Noah's stoicism morphs before me, reemerging as a quiet respect for everyone's emotional state. He meets us where we're at, and he's not putting on a mask of royalty. He's present. A consistent, sturdy pillar, bracing our pack's core.

With each new pack member, a tiny spark of newness buds in my heart, warming a little more space. I hadn't realized how clearly we're all connected until their emotions expand my chest, filling each breath with overwhelming joy. By the last member, I'm weeping. Noah does a double take, pausing the ceremony to dry my eyes. No one rushes him, in the same peaceful, loving trance I am, thanks to his gentle guidance.

He's not what I initially pictured an Alpha to be like. But that's why he's loved.

And targeted, according to Amy. I hate the thought of that more than anything.

"Are you ready to be introduced, my sweet Omega?" Noah strokes my dried cheek.

I lean into his palm, breathing in his sweet scent. It peeks through a blend of everyone else his hands touched tonight.

"I'm in awe of you, Noah. I'm more than ready."

But as I take center stage, my stomach sinks. Whispers flicker among the wolves. The fear of what they could be saying outweighs the kind smiles, threatening to strip away my sense of safety.

Noah's hand on my back grounds me back into the present, allowing me to stand straighter. "It's my honor to introduce my loving mate, daughter of our beloved, late Beta, Takahiro Matsuoka."

At first, there's only silence. One wolf lets out a soft whine, inspiring a rippling reaction of soft whimpers and sad howls for my late father - the pack's last top Beta.

The howls shred my heart in particular; tears blur my eyes on impact. Noah draws me closer, nuzzling my cheeks in front of everyone.

"I'm here, sweet Omega. They're here too."

But I'm extra sensitive to anger after what I've been through. My attention zips through the crowd, sniffing aggression out.

When it dawns on them who my father's mate was, a few wolves shout at one another. I can't make it out, but I don't have to – I hear the dissent in their tone.

Gaping on the stage in front of thousands, I watch my existence divide the pack that was whole just moments ago, fierce defenders on either side. Even with some support, my heart pangs with every hateful cry over my human mother's blood in my veins. I cower behind Noah's back, wishing I could disappear.

Noah reverts into someone more Alpha than he has seemed since we met. He whips off his vest and tunic, his bare, puffing chest daring to shift into his wolf form.

"If you're challenging my mate, you're challenging me." Despite keeping his usual even tone, his voice is booming. Furious.

I've never seen such a massive crowd fall silent in a single breath. All that's left is my rapid breathing, shallow and rocky compared to Noah's deep, hot anger.

As I slip into panic, Noah turns to cup my cheeks. "You're okay, sweet Omega. You're safe. I've got you, and there's nothing anyone can do to change that."

I nod, struggling to slow my breath. But movement catches my eye. A wolf shifts in the distance, prowling at the tree line. They're far behind Noah, but their shoulders shift with intention in every step, revealing us as their target.

I can't speak past the uncontrollable flex of my lungs, but Noah senses my heightened panic. He peppers kisses over my mark, staving off his angry scent even though I can feel him still boiling.

But the prowling wolf charges - a flash of fur whipping through the trees. Pitch-black shadows beneath swollen canopies blur my depth perception, making the wolf impossible to track. All I see are blinking reflections over dark fur, catching in the moonlight like a flashing alarm. Each blip of frigid blue draws nearer, gaining in speed with violent, rippling leaps.

They're coming for us. Coming to rip apart our flesh until we're bloody, unrecognizable shreds of meat.

Fuck, that sounds like PTSD talking. *Is* this fear just PTSD? What if that wolf is just overly excited?

No, they're bristling with rage, claws scraping through the leaves hard enough to hear the dissonant crunching from here. Whether they're furious enough to physically harm us, I have no way of knowing for certain. "Never back a rat into a corner," Dad used to say. The desperation in this wolf's eyes is what scares me.

But what if they're innocent? Noah might kill them if he thinks they'll kill us. What if my panic forces Noah to be responsible for murdering an innocent member of his pack, and he has to live with that stain forever? Be exiled, or killed by angry Lycan families? Wouldn't that make me the ultimate murderer in this?

Fuck, that sounds like OCD talking too.

What do I do? What's the right answer?

I know there isn't one. There never is. I sputter through squeaky breaths, hating every wasted second I've spent indecisive. My eyes are so wide that they ache, uncertainty raging like acid through my veins. But is this *really* OCD talking?

No, this wolf is surging closer. They see me looking at them, yet they stare me dead in the eyes. My skin ices over, battling the burning fire in my limbs that tempts me to scream. This wolf's teeth bare wider with every breath, dripping incisors stringing drool as they open their mouth wider, wider, wider.

Until they're mere feet from us.

Noah is still wrapped up in me, his back vulnerable. It feels like I've been standing here, frozen for minutes, when it's been maybe three seconds. But I can't warn Noah. The charging wolf beelines for his bare skin, nocturnal eyes glistening with killing intent now that they're facing the full moon.

I choke out a panicked yelp - there's no time for anything else.

That's when I finally recognize them. Yellow, burning irises scathe Noah with unfaltering conviction, surrounded by brown fur.

This is that same wolf: the one who attacked Noah the day we met.

But this time, they're not just stalking us to attack. They plan to kill. It rushes in with their scent on the wind, scalding my nervous system with the worst horror imaginable.

I don't have time to think anymore.

But my wolf does.

I'm never letting my loved ones get hurt again!

An explosion of white confetti surrounds me, my dress bursting where I stand. I grunt through a ripping sensation in my chest, my body contorting in ways that shouldn't be possible.

But I don't care about that. My entire focus locks on the charging wolf. My target.

I lunge for their brown fur, baring my teeth.

39

It doesn't matter how surprised the attacker wolf is to see me charging back – I'm too pissed to consider hesitating. Furious at the world that someone would try to take my loved ones away from me again.

I sink my teeth into fur - all twenty fingers and toes digging into the stranger's coat until my nails latch onto skin. The wolf yelps beneath me, but I keep biting. They thrash and spin, trying to tear me off them, but my growls have turned into vicious, angry snarls.

Stay away from my mate!

My mouth is wet and coated in a sticky, iron-tasting film, mixing with tufts of torn-out fur.

But I can't stop. This is what I would've done to that hunter.

When a sharp pinch tightens the skin behind my neck, every inch of my body falls limp in submission. The bleeding wolf beneath me scurries away, leaving me to cower on my back to whoever is above me.

Omega, stop! Noah's wolf eyes stare deep into mine, wide and horrified.

All at once, I realize what I've done.

Panic punches me in the gut. *No! Did I– Did I hurt them? Are they okay? Are they dead–*

Noah clasps my nose and mouth in his giant mouth, and I freeze. *It wasn't like that! Someone attacked me, and you protected me. They're not dead.*

Noah releases me, but my breath picks back up beneath him. I squirm, locking my sight on the tree line.

I scared you! I need to get away before I hurt you—

Noah growls. *No, don't run!*

I halt at his urgency, slinking back into the dirt before holding as still as possible.

His ears droop. *I wasn't scared of you – I stopped you. Not because I thought you'd hurt them, but because of what you told me yesterday. I knew it'd hurt you like this to have to attack another wolf, and I didn't want them to attack you back. I'm so fucking sorry I didn't notice them coming. That I made your fears come true.* Noah whimpers, flooding my heart with his guilt.

He took in everything I had to say yesterday. I try to cup his cheeks, telling him it's okay, but what comes out of my mouth is a shrill whine, and my hands are replaced by puffy white paws, awkwardly prodding Noah's snout.

His ears shoot straight up, his focus zipping over every inch of me.

Holy shit. You're the cutest wolf I've ever seen in my life. His wolf wiggles, his excited tail wracking his whole body. *I don't know what to do with myself, I just have to—*

His massive black wolf bellyflops on top of me, pinning me as he licks the blood off my cheeks and chest. I whimper in response to his stimulating touch, but that only makes him lick harder.

He gives an excited yip. *I love you so much, I could die!*

My head spins, still trying to grasp the situation.

I shifted?!

Noah's tail smacks the ground behind him, a hyper growl escaping his throat. *I want to do everything with you. I love you, I love you.*

Oh, my God. He really is a huge puppy inside his wolf brain. For the first time, my tail wags. It excites me to my bones, sprinkling shivers over my skin.

Noah pants, his eager paws yanking me closer until I'm squashed with no chance to escape. I growl without thinking – an instinctual warning to give me space.

But before I can worry if it offended him, Noah simply pops up and off me, panting and cheery with his tail waving high in the air.

Run with us.

My fur stands on edge. That was a request to the pack, not to me. He means to run with *us*, the new leading pair of the pack.

Run with us.

As wolves shift around me, the skin beneath my fur buzzes - Noah's excited energy clashing with mine. I know exactly what Noah means now; I don't know what to do with all this electricity either.

So I nip at Noah's cheeks, unable to express how much his presence excites me in any other way.

Noah jerks back with wild eyes, spinning in a frantic circle before pouncing beside me in play.

My human side laughs through our bond, but my wolf gives an excited yip.

Chase me! Noah mindlinks. Before I can respond, he bolts into the forest.

I try to stand and chase him, but I've never stood on four legs before. As my limbs splay through the dirt - my chest hitting the ground with a thud - I'm surprised by a wet nose pushing me back to my feet. When I turn around, a regal, snow-colored wolf gazes back with sharp yellow eyes.

Go on, future Luna. You've almost found your wolf legs.

My heart pounds as Lilian holds some of my weight, lifting me onto my paws. I'm so touched that I let out a soft whimper.

Luna, thank you…

Noah doubles back, slamming his paws through the dirt to come to a skidding halt. He looks just as surprised as I am.

Lilian's gorgeous, pearly wolf nudges me again. *Go on, I've got your back. Thank you for protecting the family I have left.*

I whine as not only Lilian helps me stand, but also complete stranger wolves I've never met rush to join her. Wet noses surround me, nudging and supporting me until I take my first wobbling step.

I look up to find Noah's tail softly wagging. He rotates his ears back in sentimental awe. *You're beautiful, Omega. Come to me.*

The desire to run hits me harder than I've ever experienced, pushing me forward, forward, forward. The next steps I take are steadier, my back paws linking in time with the opposite front paws.

Wolves around me mindlink me, hundreds of unfamiliar voices rooting for me.

Luna... Luna... Luna...

They watch me move with happy, tucked ears, licking my cheeks as I gain confidence.

But I can't stop staring at Noah. His emotions pulse with affection I've never felt. Like he's not just in love with me, but starstruck.

Omega, I'm not just saying this: I've never seen such an elegant wolf in my life.

His words urge me to give a small "roo" of a howl, wishing he was closer.

As he approaches, all other wolves pull back, leaving Noah's massive figure to meet me nose to nose. Our noses barely brush, and a sharp, buzzing sensation shoots to my tail. I whine and dip lower, skirting around his front legs to feel more of him against my fur.

He gazes down on me with soft wags, still towering over me despite how much I've grown in my wolf form. Dipping to my height, Noah brushes my side with his coarse black coat. Every slip of our fur sends another wave of endorphins through me, deepening our affection.

As I slowly dance with Noah, my wolf speaks through me.

Alpha, you're so beautiful. I love you.

He circles me again, dragging himself harder against me this time. It inspires me to walk faster, matching his vibrant energy as we feed off each other's joy. Noah gives my cheek a hard nuzzle, flipping my heart. When he stops in front of me, a flash of blue ignites his nocturnal eyes as the full moon hits them.

Without the need for words, his body posture alone tells me his intentions. He bursts into a sprint, and I chase him, breaking into my very first wolf run.

40

I've always been a clumsy mess in my human form. But tonight, I don't care if I trip and fall. Letting go of perfection frees me, allowing me to move further with each racing paw. I bound across the forest, glancing at the wolves around me to analyze their movements.

The more I move, the less I feel like I need to rely on anything but my own paws. Something in my mind clicks into place, like I was made for this. I lean into a sprint, stretching low to the ground until I double in speed. Within seconds, I overtake Noah's pace, gaining on him with every huffing breath through my snout.

Noah's silent paws cut through the forest, thrusting him forward like a low-flying black jet. My shifted eyes allow me to track him, softening the heavy blanket of darkness. But I don't need my vision; my sense of smell creates a constant pull toward what I seek. With every tree I blast past, the wind combs my fur, sending shockwaves of pleasure through me.

Without warning, Noah doubles back faster than I can prepare to dodge. He hardly misses me by half an inch. The thrill it ignites in me propels me faster, especially as Noah rejoins my side.

Before I know it, he guides our pack to the mountain's lookout point, forcing everyone to come to a skidding halt. Below us, the three rivers meet the ocean, cutting through mountainous forests to meet the glittering, moonlit horizon. It's the most breathtaking view I've ever seen, yet my eyes stray from it.

Noah's nose puffs heavy clouds into the frigid air. Silky, onyx fur glistens beneath the Moon Goddess' gaze, softly dancing in the wind. But it's his gorgeous, golden eyes on me that stunt my breath.

Omega, I really am serious. I've never seen a wolf move like you. Run like you. It feels like... He smashes his forehead against mine, giving me an affectionate grunt. *You were made for this. I feel like I'm finally seeing you, and I–*

He steps back. With the sharp silence that falls over the pack, I stop myself from panting. The energy in the pack shifts with us, and I can't place why.

When Noah throws his head back to howl, I don't just shiver; a roaring emotion hits me with his song, the melody transcending words as he pours out his heart.

I think this song is for me.

Wolves all around me join Noah, jolting every hair across my body. Their emotions wash over me, crashing higher and higher within me until I spill over, throwing my head back to howl with them.

Noah's ears rotate with my newfound sound, his soul pulsating with mine. With a deep breath, he resumes his song with twice the vigor, harmonizing with me. Within seconds, the whole pack follows his lead. Except with Noah morphing his song to my note, they're technically following *me*.

I've never heard something like this come out of me. Honestly, I don't think I've ever allowed myself to be this loud. This emotional. This real. The more I merge my heart and emotions with the pack's, the more I can feel every one of them within me.

In my heart, I'm crying. Crying for all the days I lost without this family. Crying for my parents who aren't here to feel it with me. Crying for how much I cherish every second of it, now that I'm here. My wolf expresses that and more, weaving in and out of the voices surrounding me.

By the time Noah falls silent, allowing everyone else to finish the last note of their song, his eyes lock on mine.

I know he feels everything in my heart, but something in them tells me he understands. How desperate my need is to belong.

I draw closer, and he meets me there. His warm snout caresses mine, pushing a whimper from me.

But instead of cuddling me like I crave, Noah pads past me

through the forest, peeking back for me to follow. The rest of the pack trails home, guided by Lilian to finish the ceremonial blessings. I wanted to see how our Luna guided mating rituals, asking the Moon Goddess to bless participants with a deeper bond, or even pregnancy, but that can wait for next month.

Wherever we're going, it feels important. Enough to walk there, rather than run.

Noah's shoulders capture my full attention, rolling and contemplative with every step. When he freezes, I perk up, my senses heightening in alert.

Noah's ears pull back when we meet eyes, his tail wagging. *Cute. So cute.*

Giving me a tender rub with his side as he passes me, Noah points me to the stream, its mouth meeting one of the three rivers.

Look at yourself, Omega. You have to see how beautiful you are.

My heart quivers and skips as I approach the soothing, slow river, itching to use it as a mirror. But when I peek over the riverside, I'm awestruck by more than my own reflection.

Noah's warm presence beside me glistens in the water, my polar opposite in size, color, and posture. I'm stark white, my smooth fur revealing every speck of dirt and leaves cluttering my slender wolf. I'm larger than a wild gray wolf, but I'm still small for a shifted Lycan: not a gargantuan bear like my regal mate. It's so unfamiliar. But at the same time, we look more like ourselves - the souls I feel deep inside our bond. I feel like I can finally see myself. It's enough to make my wolf legs quiver, unable to grasp reality. But here I stand, cold mud sinking between each bare paw pad.

Goddess, I feel that. He huffs, shaking his fur out from head to tail. *You're so clearly... you.*

Whether I want it to or not, my tail wags. It excites us both, inspiring Noah into a playful sneeze.

Tracking Noah's gorgeous, slinking form in the reflection, I whimper in delight as he nuzzles against my cheek. *We're the most beautiful beings I've ever seen, Noah.*

He whines, surging our bond with his love. But then he dips beneath the boulder beside me, disappearing from sight.

My head tilts in shock. When he doesn't return, I slink into cautious steps toward the small opening until I recognize where I am – a narrow cave entrance leading into a cozy nook.

I hadn't realized how much bigger I was; this "narrow" nook is Noah's massive den.

My heart rate spikes as I enter, unsure what Noah has planned here. When I find Noah sitting on his haunches, waiting for me with puppy-dog eyes, my nerves melt away.

My shy Alpha.

He lightly wags his tail, peeking at me with his head bowed - just as shy as when I first visited his den. I drag my nose along his cheeks and neck, relishing in his humming purr.

His warmth soothes me, but there's a hint of sadness in him. Mourning. When we meet eyes, Noah whines.

He guides me into the deepest corner of the cave, flopping against the stone with a grunt.

My paws stutter in place. *Noah, what are we...?*

Cuddle with me. Just cuddle.

Noah's alert ears soften as my tail wags on its own. I circle in front of him, unsure how to fit us together.

Noah's tail lazily thumps against the stone floor. *Just flop on me. Wolves have no personal space.*

So that's why I like molding myself to your body every night?

Noah's breath escapes his lungs in a huff as I plop into the natural opening between his four legs. But Noah's burly body pays it no mind. He curls around me, tucking his chin over my front legs. His overpowering scent is so soothing that every muscle softens. My head naturally drapes over his neck.

Even our wolf bodies fit together, I say. The same ache in his heart surges, and I whine. *What are you thinking about? Is there something wrong?*

Noah whimpers, tucking me in even closer. His pain burrows into my heart.

I know, Noah. I can feel it. Talk to me.

Today was just– He tucks his nose into my fluffy belly, hiding his eyes. *I've never felt anything like this. You're so special to me - more than special. And I'm just so sad. I can't believe I spent so many years of my life without you. Losing all that time to know you. What if we only have a decade or two left, like our parents?*

I whine with him, squishing my snout against his. *That kills me to think about. But I meant it when I said every second with you would be worth it. Even if all we have is tomorrow, this is right where I want to be.*

His slicked-back ears soften, flattening with love. *All I want is to be here with you too. Thank you for finding me, Omega.*

Thank you for waiting for me.

Noah and I huddle in his den. Our collective warmth makes it impossible to keep my eyes open. With soft rain dripping at the entrance, I'm lulled to sleep against Noah's chest.

But when I wake up next, it's with a jolt. Noah is already awake, still in his wolf form. He lifts his head off my side to gaze into my eyes, and I shiver at the icy breeze on my bare skin. Then I gasp; I'm fully naked.

"I shifted back?"

Yes. In your sleep. He tucks me closer, blanketing my bare skin with his warm fur.

I stroke his head, unable to contain my grin; he must've stayed in his wolf form just to keep me from shivering. Noah's ears relax beneath my touch, but it's not enough to erase the tension in his eyes.

You were whimpering just before you woke up. Did you have a bad dream?

I sigh, curling deeper into his fur. "It was about that wolf. The one who attacked you."

Oh, sweet Omega... His ears droop, but then one flicks to the side, stirring his tail into action. *Well, feisty Omega is more like it. You're a powerful wolf, and you haven't even trained before. You made an angry Alpha twice your size escape with his tail between his legs.*

I bite my lip as I smile, indulging in Noah's doting stare.

But a part of me can't let go of my discomfort. "Did you know that wolf? You called him an Alpha."

Not really. It's just easy to smell Omegas, Betas, and Alphas apart after a while.

"Wait a minute— 'Not really' doesn't mean 'no.'"

Noah's right ear rotates back in thought, and I have to giggle. He delicately boops my nose with his, wagging his heavy tail with slow, sleepy thumps.

278

You're right. I can't personally memorize thousands of wolves, but that Alpha has challenged me before. Back before I became the top Alpha.

My heart flips. "And?"

And nothing came of it. This is why I didn't mention it – it might seem like a big deal, but it's actually common. Repeat challengers are especially common. Certain wolves tend to land in a middle zone of dominance, and sometimes I think it must force them to fight more often than me. But fighting against challengers is just part of an Alpha's life. My title will be challenged for as long as I hold it.

I ache at the thought. Especially since Noah was looking straight at me when it happened, pulled away from safety by my panic. "Did I put you in danger?"

No, sweet Omega. This was my fault for turning my back to the crowd and seeming vulnerable. I won't deny it, he was dead serious about that challenge. He probably waited for a chance for weeks.

"*Weeks?* What about before then?"

I put him in his place recently, that's all.

My stomach flips. "But you still don't think he challenged you for a reason?"

Noah grunts in dismissive annoyance, flopping onto his side. *He probably has one. It doesn't matter though. He got his ass kicked by my mate.*

I groan, burying my face into his extra soft belly fur. With slow, deep thumps of his tail, Noah licks my bare back until I burst into laughter, squirming away from him.

But as we settle back into each other to sleep, I can't shake one fear. That wolf seemed too serious for it to be a regular dominance battle. Then again, I'm no expert on wolves. That much is obvious.

That Alpha wanted to *kill* Noah. The thought digs into my stomach, forcing me to curl inwards. Noah is there to cuddle me tighter, but it doesn't help the fact that he could be severely injured if I hadn't shifted. Or dead. Intrusive thoughts trickle in, escalating until one stabs me in the chest in particular - a vivid nightmare of shifting too late, the attacker wolf snapping Noah's neck in two.

Noah licks my cheek, startling a gasp from me.

I can feel your thoughts spinning. It's okay, really. I'll tell you if there's ever any danger.

I nod, sinking into him. "Okay, yes. I trust you, Noah. I just don't trust that wolf."

Noah tilts his head, staring deep into my eyes. *If you're still worried, I'd rather trust your instincts. I'll keep an eye on him.*

"Thank you. That'd make me feel better."

He snuggles into me, letting out a soft sigh.

41

I smell someone else around. Just a head's up, Noah mindlinks.

It's painfully early, but I couldn't be happier to join Noah on his morning perimeter run. We scope the forest's outline, tracing a trail that must've been flattened by his paws a thousand times over. Noah extends his scent around the territory's edge. It's potent enough to burrow into my fur as I fly behind him.

But Noah has been avoiding my eyes. Just to tease him, I bound up to his side with our bundled-up picnic blanket hooked over my bottom fangs.

Noah gives a small "roo," and my ears stick straight up. *No, Goddess, no, why did you have to pick up the picnic bag in your little mouth like that? You look like a happy pup taking her lunch to school. Fuck, I'm about to die.*

As I wiggle through my excitement, Noah blasts ahead of me, leaving me in his leafy aftermath.

I know Noah holds himself back for me. Speed isn't the problem - I've surprised myself with my agility, and Noah's size and power set him apart more than speed. But Noah's true advantage is knowing this forest's ins and outs like it's a map of his own features. Every dip and hill is a steady, unhindered climb for his wise paws, whereas everything for my wolf is dazzling new.

I'm busy ogling his shiny black coat in the morning sunlight when an Alpha wolf bursts through the brush, running alongside us. Except it's not a friendly sprint - he's staring Noah down. I scamper to a halt, but Noah lunges at the Alpha, scaring him away with a swipe of his massive paw.

Fear slams me into the ground, and I tuck my tail as hard as it can press against my belly. Part of me hates myself for cowering instead of having Noah's back, but the surprise attack must hit an old trauma bruise. My heart hammers so hard that my vision blurs, sending me in frantic zig zags as I race for cover. I dive into the bushes, and instinct curls my tail over my black nose. The second I know I'm safe, my focus locks on my mate.

Noah's optical size has grown considerably, his black fur raised on end. It flutters in the wind, carrying his furious scent. He keeps his eyes glued on the stranger wolf in the distance as the Alpha bolts through the field, escaping Greenfield Forest faster than I believed possible.

As soon as the Alpha is gone, I give my coat a hearty shake. I hope Noah was too busy to notice how skittish I was despite my legs still quivering. Our picnic sack is abandoned in the leaves, toppled onto its side after my careful effort to hold it upright. I quickly hook its tied corners back over my bottom jaw.

I've been dying to complete this daily run with Noah for so long. If my annoying, lingering trauma symptoms sour the moment, I don't think I could hide my disappointment.

But as Noah flips one ear back at my approach, glancing at me in his peripherals, he gives an irritated sneeze. *Why they choose to come at me while I'm with my most precious wolf is beyond me. They're not getting soft Noah.*

My tail wags, grateful he's lifting the mood for us. *Are you okay?*

I'm okay as long as you are. He studies me closely. I lower my head on instinct, sensitive to my Alpha's stare.

I'm okay, thanks to you.

In case he's not convinced, I drag myself along his windblown fur, relishing in the icy chill feathered through it.

At my touch, Noah's excitement skyrockets. Before I have time to pant in adoration, his zoomies send him racing for the den. I'm forced to chase him, but I adore it, relishing every second of our combined thrill gracing my bones.

Wait, where are we going? Don't we still have to finish our perimeter run? I ask.

Noah peeks at the sky, then back to me. *We traced a little further than my section for today since you seemed so excited. It's already been an hour.*

My ears flip forward. *An hour?! Are you sure you're not just shortening it for me? I'm okay, really–*

Noah gives a brief howl, sending birds flying through the trees a half mile ahead of us. As a few neighboring howls echo in the distance, Noah's sprint boosts, sending his tongue out sideways. I slink into the ground, stretching my neck and limbs with every leap to catch up with him. *What I'm sure about is that you're fast as fuck. Faster than Yas, even. Look at you - you're living for this.* When he peeks over his shoulder, his fiery eyes send a jolt through me. *It's been that long because you're a natural, Omega.*

I'm so shocked that I lose my stride, slowing to a regular run. Noah adapts like it's nothing for him. After a quick, pouncing circle around me, he yips in excitement at my frazzled stare and bolts on ahead.

Could I really be a natural at something? Is that what this feeling is? Air flows through my outstretched paws, lifting my heart up with it.

But I can't relish in too much happiness; a twinge of unease stations itself at the base of Noah's emotions. Noah tries his best to bound through the forest with his usual spritely mayhem, but he can't hide the subtle droop in his ears.

His paws slow at the riverside, guiding us through the riverbed flora without crushing any of the early summer flowers. Noah peeks at me, allowing me to pass first.

I know that look, I mindlink. But I humor him anyway, ducking my head into his den. He boops my butt with his big nose on the way into the cave, and I whip around to give him a playful nip. Noah dodges it, as usual, prancing just out of my reach until I give up, shifting back.

I laugh. "You're the biggest, most adorable goofball I've ever seen."

He puffs his chest, standing with pride as he moves to block the cave entrance for my naked body. I can't stop giggling as I rummage through our picnic blanket. My blue and white floral crop top is only slightly wet from my wolf's drool, taking most of the hit for my long A-line black skirt.

By the time Noah slips on loose, gray sweatpants and a black t-shirt, we can't stop smiling at nothing and everything, thrilled to just be here together. We spread our green, fleece picnic blanket over the cool stones only to huddle on one little corner of it. I take a deep, blissful lungful of Noah's leafy scent, melting into his arms.

As we discuss the upcoming week, updates on Rainn, Amy, and Yasmine, and what we'll cook for dinner tonight, Noah eventually fades into silence, preferring to listen. Our silences have a warm comfort to them, but today, subtle tension traces Noah's brows.

It pains my heart to think he's hurting in silence, especially when his smile stops reaching his eyes.

"What's wrong?" I blurt out.

When he doesn't answer right away, I sit up properly, tucking my feet beneath me. Just when the tension becomes too much to bear, Noah glances at me with heavy concern.

"Y-you don't have to worry I'll snap at you."

My eyebrows raise. I didn't expect him to say anything near this, shocking my brain into taking a moment to process.

Noah rubs his temples with one wide hand. "Fuck, that came out weird. I'm sorry, it's just–"

I drop my stare to the blanket fibers beneath my knees with a stinging heart. It sounds like he's made some assumptions about my past relationships, but he's not wrong. Could he tell what I was really asking? That my check-ins are out of habit, preparing myself for one of Steven's old "moods" whenever he showed the slightest hint of upset?

Before I can spiral into my own assumptions, Noah rubs my arm.

"I'm sorry, Aliya. I just felt you get so fucking scared when I snapped at that asshole today on our run, and I felt *so* bad–" Noah cuts himself off as my shoulders soften.

"My observant Alpha. You've been worried this whole time that *you* scared me?"

Noah nods, and I bite my lip to contain my affection. I sort out his shift-flustered hair. My gentle, sweeping touch loosens his tense torso.

"To be honest, I've seen you looking over your shoulders too. Or losing focus on conversations when you hear a sound - someone accidentally dropping something and startling your wolf into threat mode. And I think–" I hesitate, softening my voice. "I think we're coming from the same place."

Noah tucks my hair behind my ear, uncovering my face. The ache my words created in our bond amplifies as we meet eyes, but it also prompts us to smile.

"Paranoia's a dick."

I laugh. "Tell me about it."

"But it's trying to protect us," Noah mutters.

I glance back up at him. He's analyzing his thumbnail, softly scratching at the edges. When he feels me staring, he peeks over - rapid eyes flicking over my features.

He must know I can feel him thinking hard, assumedly about the source of my PTSD. But he doesn't have anything else to say.

He is listening, however.

"Sometimes, I feel like I'm being watched," I say. Noah stiffens, alarm creasing his forehead. "But I think it's just PTSD talking."

Noah relaxes back onto his elbow, but his eyebrows remain knitted. His whirring emotions consume my focus, too conflicting to pick apart.

"What else have you been thinking? I feel like there's more," I say.

Noah shakes his head. "It's way too sensitive of a question. I know I'll butcher what I actually want to ask."

I shrug. "Maybe it will come out weird. Maybe it won't."

Noah gives me a sad smile, and I drop onto my side to face him eye-to-eye. He kisses my forehead before leaning his head against mine. "Then, I guess I want to say something before I ask." He takes a deep, shaky breath. "I don't need to know any details. Take care of yourself first, okay?"

I nod, but my heart is racing. I want to be able to tell Noah everything, but the second he said that, dread hit my core. Maybe I'm not ready.

"I-I just–" Noah scratches at his thumbnail again. "I feel like I need to know: where is he? Do you feel like– You don't think there's a chance he'll come back?"

My heart drops. Somehow, Noah sniffed out my deepest fear, setting my nerves ablaze. I burrow into his chest on instinct, struggling to retain my composure.

Noah's distinct Alpha musk floods the cave, forcing me to blink through its stinging intensity. He growls. "Okay, I definitely need to know. You don't have to tell me anything but his name."

I pop upright. "You're not going to kill him, are you?"

Noah frowns. "Unfortunately, no."

I erupt into a startled laugh. "Noah!"

He gives me a half smile, hanging his head. "I just want you to feel safe, and that involves making sure he's not in the pack. Do you know if he's a Lycan or not?"

I feel like I can't breathe. "I– I hadn't even thought of that."

Noah gathers me into his arms, settling us on our sides. I relish his grounding squeeze, huddling into his protective scent until I droop into his chest.

"There you go," Noah whispers. "I'm sorry, I should've–"

"Steven," I say. Noah tenses beneath me, not daring to take a breath. "Steven Barrett."

42

I'm met with silence, which I'm relieved about – our emotions speak for themselves, burning my chest as Noah's anger dances with mine. I take a steadying breath, and Noah rubs my back.

Unfortunately, I haven't told him the worst of it. I peek at him, unsure how he'll react. "I was denied a restraining order since we were dating when 'the thing' happened."

Noah's wolf is set ablaze, burning through his yellowed irises.

But I can't stop talking. "I have no idea if he's a Lycan, or how I'd even know. God, he could track me so easily no matter where I went if he is. You think he could be here? That he'll–"

"No." Noah tucks my head against his chest. He frantically kisses my mark, soothing the petrified, sour scent emanating from me. "No, he's not in the pack. I just checked."

I droop into Noah, swimming in overwhelm. It's a relief, but at the same time, it's not. Steven still exists out there, and I've always been afraid he'd come back for me someday. The only thing keeping me in this state - no, this country - has been Amy.

But there's a tangible, creeping memory behind Noah's tense glances over his shoulders too. Is it his PTSD reminding him of a past event, or should I be watching out for Noah's well-being too, protecting him from something? Some*one*?

I bite my lip, struggling to keep my heart in check. "What about you? Do you feel safe here?"

Noah avoids my eyes. His thumbnail-picking morphs into an aggressive task. I sit in silence with him for a while, but as his breath picks up, I grasp his hands to stop his shaking thumbs before he makes himself bleed.

"Noah, you never have to tell me *anything*."

He furrows his brows, sucking in a short, sharp breath to speak. But he remains silent. Maybe he decided against speaking, or maybe the trauma he's plagued by stole his voice.

My gut aches for him, but it's nowhere near the pain seeping from the base of our bond as Noah recollects whatever this is. It kills me that Noah has been carrying this agony alone.

I give his hand a soft squeeze. "I mean it. You don't owe me any explanations, even if I'm your mate."

Noah shuts his eyes, letting out a slow breath.

I figure that's his answer - he can't talk about it right now - so I settle into him with my arm around his waist.

But Noah clears his throat. When he speaks, there's an unfamiliar darkness to his rumbling tone, lacing my body with goosebumps. "I don't know where mine is either."

Acidic anxiety surges through my veins. So Noah's trauma was caused by a *person*, not some freak event?

Noah is such a confident Alpha. But by admitting he doesn't know where his monster is, his wolf bristles in our bond - doubling in size and morphing into a furious, drooling beast. This intimidating display would scare anyone, but I can feel the emotions tied to it.

He's terrified. Noah feels small, insecure, and way too exposed. Whatever happened wasn't just horrendous but felt deeply personal.

A growl escapes my chest, my arms locking around my mate on instinct.

I understand Noah's fears about me now. What if *his* abuser comes back? If Noah is this afraid, does that mean his monster is as strong as him? Even stronger than him? In what world could my part-human flesh be strong enough to fight anyone of Noah's caliber?

A soft chuckle escapes Noah as he loosens my death grip. "My sweet Omega. Goddess, look at your little fangs extending again. How did I get so lucky?"

My shoulders soften as we meet eyes. Affection overflows from Noah's stare, the darkness I saw moments before dissipating by the second. He's okay. At least for now.

I nuzzle into his shoulder, letting out a grumpy groan. "I hate that I'm so little."

Noah's deep laugh rumbles through my chest. "You're not little in spirit."

I scowl, and Noah laughs again.

He kisses the top of my head. "You don't have to protect me. It's oka–"

"I will. I have your back now, just like you have mine."

Our thoughts swirl, filling the silence. After tracing my cheek with his thumb for a while, Noah mutters, "We are a pretty great team. Bad things could happen again, but they don't have to. Who knows - especially with this badass Omega by my side."

I smile, welcoming the uncertainty.

Uneasiness mills through our bond, but so does a satiating warmth. Noah huddles into me, scooting me closer by the hips.

As soon as I'm smushed against him, Noah nuzzles into my neck, kissing my mark. Every soft press of his lips floods me with endorphins, giddy, gentle waves of affection swirling in my chest. I squeeze him in as tight of a hug as I can manage, throwing my leg over his hip.

Noah chuckles, his heavy purr vibrating our chests as we relax into each other. The sound erases every ounce of fear I felt moments before. Noah didn't say it out loud, but his sense of ease proves it; no matter what's to come, we feel safe together.

I bury myself in him, forgetting all about our picnic as the blanket turns into an extension of our nightly cuddle ball. Noah grips me twice as hard until we scoot close enough to squeeze out all air between us, enveloping ourselves in one collective, sizzling body heat.

We share a toasty silence. The stone's chill seeps through the picnic blanket, keeping us from overheating. I fall into the rhythm of Noah's heartbeat against my ear, my eyes drooping in delight.

But Noah takes a shaky breath. "This used to be where I'd go to hide."

My eyes snap open. My focus races over the dark, damp walls of the cave - the place that held Noah's trust when no one else could. Since I'm here, it dawns on me just how much Noah trusts me. I can't imagine how risky sharing this den must feel for him.

Or maybe I can, and I just hate that we've had to experience such pain to be able to relate.

Noah's trust is pure and raw, opening his soul up to mine in our bond. I'm struck with a momentary fear: am I worthy of being trusted by this sweet soul?

But as his shy stare gazes at me with absolute faith in who I am to him, one thing is certain; I want to be this special, trusted person for Noah. I want it too badly to care whether I deserve it or not.

I grab his hand to roll us over, but Noah grabs all of me. Rubbing the entire length of my back, he nuzzles me into the picnic blanket until his weight settles over me. I cup his scruffy jaw in my hands, giving it a gentle scratch and loving how it softens the remaining tension around his eyes. We lean in to trace each other's noses, kissing every time our lips pass one another with aching, tender slowness.

"Thank you," I say. "For allowing me into your life."

Noah's shyness hits harder than I've seen it in a while - raised shoulders and an irrepressible grin rendering him speechless.

Putting his forehead against mine, Noah mindlinks, *I love you.*

I break into a smile. *I love you so much.*

But as I spread my thighs, deepening our cuddle ball, his limp weight over me melds our hips together. Passion strikes even lower, my pelvis tilting for more attention. Noah's blinking softens as he strokes my head, giving my hips a gentle nudge.

God, I don't just want him, I want to love on his body in every way I can - drive him wild with bliss. I bite my lips, vivid fantasies whirring across my mind until I settle on one: Noah's satiated, open lips, dissolving into pleasure as I lick the bulge forming against my lower abdomen.

As lust pools between my legs, craving to summon Noah's primal side, I offer something I never thought I could want again.

"Can I spoil you?"

Noah's gaze zips to mine. Desire emanates from his eyes, but this is new for both of us; he's usually the one asking for requests. My hips squirm, unaccustomed to taking charge.

Noah clears his throat. "O-okay. As long as you enjoy it too."

We settle onto our sides, taking a clearer look at one another now that we're not nose-to-nose. I trace a line down his torso, stunting his inhale. The sound squeezes my knees together, nudging my swelling clit.

Noah's relaxed, wide shoulders tell me how comfortable he is around me, lying in full view despite my full focus on him. I massage his chest, dragging slow, sweeping pressure over the broad muscles until his nipples harden through his shirt.

"Would you like my mouth on you, Alpha? Or my hands?"

His shirt's hem is already rolled, drawing my eyes to a sliver of skin showing at his waistband and dark hair trailing to his belly button. But when I speak, my eyes drop even lower; his sweatpants warp from a silhouette of his shaft to a rigid view. If I can make Noah's cock flex in his sweatpants like that from a mere suggestion, what can I do to him with my lips?

But the sweet man can't even look at me, still unaccustomed to being taken care of no matter how much I nurture him. He works his bottom lip between his teeth, hiding his eyes behind his hair. "I-I'd– I'd like both too much, but–" He takes a heavy, shuddering breath, flexing his abdomen and tenting his pants in the process. "T-the way you use your mouth feels good."

With my exploding, mischievous smile, Noah breaks into giggles. The heavenly sound is cut off when I dive for his sweatpants, whipping the elastic down and dragging my tongue over the bulge in his boxers.

Noah gasps. "Oh, *Goddess*–"

He's on his back for me now, just how I'd like him. I douse every angle of his clothed shaft with my tongue until the fabric is soaked. Within thirty seconds, his hips lift, pressing this hot erection against my tongue.

I peek at Noah. Flustered cheeks intensify those ever-golden eyes I always tease out of my mate during sex. It creates a sense of pride in my wolf like no other.

Burrowing my fingers beneath his boxers' waistband, I stare at his heaving chest above me as I slowly expose his cock. I kiss and nuzzle it, waiting to add tongue until his back arches and his hands find my cheeks in desperation.

Is this what you like, my love? I mindlink.

Noah can't respond as I drag my tongue along the sensitive

underside of his shaft; by the time I reach the tip, a soft, needy gasp escapes his lips. It's beautiful - so honest. Fire envelops my veins, a full heat threatening to take force.

But as my licks grow frantic, Noah brushes my arm with his fingertips. "H-hang on."

I lift my chin, worried I did something wrong, but I'm met with desperate, ravished eyes.

His voice is raspy with pleasure. "Can you turn around?"

I sit up. "Turn around?"

"Yes, please. I'm dying for you to feel this good with me."

My heart flips. He means we'd lick each other senseless at the same time, right?

"I've never tried that position before," I say.

Noah's eyes sharpen as we lock stares. "D-do you want to, or–?"

"Yes," I blurt out. I turn myself around before I can overthink it, my skirt skating over his exposed cock. As I position myself on my hands and knees, Noah flips the loose fabric over his head, sending my stomach into my throat.

I can't see him, but I shudder as hot fingertips trail up my thighs. They dig in when they reach my hips, drawing me to him. I try to refocus, shaking on my knees as I grip his flexing shaft. But when his lips brush a soft kiss over my clothed clit, my lungs hitch.

Just my breath lifts Noah's hips, his tip bumping my bottom lip. I taste the salty fluid he left behind, my heart hammering as Noah plants kiss after kiss between my legs, warming my cold, wet panties.

Circling my tongue around his tip has Noah breathing twice as fast. I can't get enough of the grateful hum in our bond to be nestled into each other's pleasure. Its sweetness settles into my core with every tender lick between my legs. I breathe harder than I mean to, stirring Noah's hips into jerking again. Nerves pound my pulse into my ears, but I dip my head, suckling off the new droplet forming on Noah's tip. He hisses behind me. The sharp puff of air clenches my pussy so tight that I whimper.

Having tasted Noah, I want more. When I slip his tip deep into my mouth with shaking hands, Noah yanks my panties out of the way. A jolt of pleasure zaps up my spine with the introduction of Noah's wide, hot tongue. My chest heaves, but I bob my head, slinking over him. He drags a gentle, wet wave of pressure up my entire core.

My hips dip, and Noah purrs, vibrating my pelvis. Without meaning to, I suck his cock hard, swallowing the heavy warmth blooming in my belly. Noah's breath blasts against my wet pussy, clenching it over his prodding tongue.

Every vein in me throbs, warning of an incoming climax. Noah's fingers dip into the grooves of my hips, thrusting me back into his tongue. I flex my tongue down his shaft, dousing the length in saliva. The next time I taste the entire length, I slink my mouth over him as far as I can until his hips jerk, brushing him against my soft palate. This time, I swallow him, staving off my body's panic at such a large object in my throat.

One deep swallow is the end of Noah. He whimpers, breathy and weak against my pussy. The pleasure it induces courses through me so strongly that I swallow again, moaning between deep suckling over his shaft. With rapid, frantic breaths, Noah erupts in my mouth. His body attempts to fill me so heavily that seed spills from my lips.

"Oh, *fuck*," he whimpers.

He's still squirming below me as I swallow every drop I can before sucking in a desperate inhale.

But Noah isn't done with me. Moaning through residual pleasure, Noah licks me faster, startling such heaving, rapid breaths from me that his tip pops from my mouth. My hips buck in the air on the verge of climax, so Noah swirls his tongue in wider and wider circles until I'm so open for him that he enters me.

When he slips his tongue out of me and down my clit, it's his nose that does me in, nuzzling into my core. I can't stop myself from coming all over his face, dropping my hips back for deeper attention as he flicks every bit of my orgasm from my swollen clit. My shaking legs threaten to give out, but Noah's grip keeps me pressed to him, riding out every delighted swivel of my hips.

By the time he comes up for air, I melt over him, dropping my chest flat against his abdomen. His cock already rehardens against my cheek from how deeply he satisfied me, but Noah pays it no mind. His big hand rubs the entire length of my back, soothing my eyes into closing.

His whisper is roughened with sleepy bliss. "There you go, gorgeous. Seeing you like this spoils me more than anything."

When I open my eyes to find such an earnest, doting smile, my core flexes, desperate to have deep, cuddly sex with him.

"Do you have a condom nearby?" I mumble.

43

Noah's eyes widen, and I erupt into giggles.

But when I lift my head to give his shaft a soft kiss, we grow startlingly serious. Noah fetches a condom. I spit into its tip, massaging saliva over him until his breath deepens.

There's a tense, forward pull in Noah's shoulders, aching to cuddle with me. Twisting over my shoulder, I lean into his lips.

I'm surprised by the eager force I'm met with. Noah kisses me hard, throbbing into my hand as I stroke him. He drags his fingertips in tantalizing circles over my entrance, lengthening my desperate breath between our heavy makeout until his tongue glides over mine, drinking up my greedy moans.

Within seconds, my pussy drops over his fingers, gaping for his deeper touch.

It feels too good too soon, so I pull away. Surprise ripples through our bond, confirmed by Noah's searching gaze.

He doesn't know what secrets the mirror told me: that he comes harder watching himself slip in and out of me. With my back to him, I settle his palms on the sides of my ass as I raise it - giving him plenty to grip.

My voice shakes with nerves. "Yesterday, I was thinking– i-in the shower–"

Noah sucks in a raw, unrestrained gasp as I tilt my hips, allowing his swollen shaft to enter me in full view.

My eyelashes flutter as he stretches me to my limits. "A-about how you might like this position."

"*Like* this?" He rasps. "Like isn't– isn't strong– strong enough–"

Noah's brain melts, and I can feel it in how plump he's become.

I'm thrilled I was right; he's more aroused than usual, so engorged that we have to take our time. That allows me to wiggle my hips, settling him into me bit by bit until Noah's feet squirm in front of me.

"Fuck— *Fuck*, feisty Omega—"

Noah squeezes my ass hard as he fights a battle for patience beneath me, his hips struggling to keep from bucking beyond light thrusts. But with how good he feels in our bond, my pussy can't stop clenching over him in a needy stronghold, forcing us to freeze. Even as we hold still, Noah's cock responds to my squeezes with deep pulses inside me, dropping my jaw with its sweet massage.

When my muscles finally relax, Noah groans as I thrust my hips back, pushing him deeper. His tip finally breeches my pelvic opening with a sweet, popping sensation in my belly. Fluttering tingles shoot up my torso, swirling over my breasts until it teases a whine from my lips. Noah moans just as hard as I do.

"Fuck, I love you," he breathes.

I can only whimper, gripping his wrists as we settle into a slow, crawling thrust. We leave no corner of my insides untouched. Fluid spills between my legs as he settles against my cervix - an ache hitting my heart so deep that my back arches, squeezing Noah into stopping.

When I can finally catch my breath, my breathy whisper shakes. "I love you too."

I drop my weight onto my palms between Noah's legs. Rolling my hips back in a slow, snapping dip, I lead us. Noah's groans liquify into breathy whimpers.

And I'm craving deeper pressure. I play with my clit, and my eyelids flutter as Noah's hands roam to my waist. When he hesitates there, his desire to drop me hard onto his lap is barely restrained beneath twitching fingertips.

I drop my hips until my ass squishes against that deep V between his hip bones. Noah prods so deep that I whimper.

I haven't heard another peep from my usual potty-mouthed mate, but that's probably because of his hard, racing breath. I stay sitting on him, circling my hips in a wide arc.

His knees raise in front of me at the end of every circle, jerking upright until I'm leaning farther and farther back, the new angle thrusting him deeper. We moan in unison - except mine comes out like a choked gasp, the stimulation he's piling into me making my thighs quiver beside his hips.

He can barely choke out his words. "F-fuck. Are you– Okay?"

My hair is curtained over my back, so I gather it into a sloppy bun, peeking over my shoulder. My breath is stolen by how totaled Noah looks behind me: heavy-lidded eyes and red cheeks gracing his golden skin.

"*Yes*," I breathe.

I widen the circle of my hips, dragging the counterpressure of his throbbing cock against every corner of my inner walls. Noah's hips jerk into the air, sending me off balance and reaching for his hands. But there's no need to worry; Noah stabilizes my hips with blazing palms.

His chest heaves as we restart my hips together. Noah matches my movements, but I roll or wiggle when he least expects it, leaving him guessing what's next.

I don't realize how deep his pleasure overcomes him until his legs squirm beneath me like mine just before I come - and then the sensation hits. Raw, unfiltered pleasure shoots up my abdomen, amplified by the aching delight in Noah's side of our bond. I've somehow left him edged on the precipice, and now I get to feel it too.

I cry out, tipping my pelvis back into his thrust as Noah's hips bounce me over him. Once we've both had a taste, that's all we want to do. As his hands grow hungry for my reaction, lifting and dropping my ass until we speed into a slapping rhythm, I can't stop whimpering with soft, pleading whispers that only increase in pitch.

But Noah suddenly gasps. "Fuck. No, no, stop–"

I lift off of him on instinct.

But Noah shakes his head, rubbing my back with weak, trembling fingers. "I need to see your face. I need to hold you."

A blast of emotions spread goosebumps over every inch of me, so turned on by his words yet so flustered that I can only stare back in awe.

This is worlds different from the "needs" I've heard ordered over me before. There's pure love staring back; these "needs" are an overwhelming yearning to bond with me.

But my next, deeper reaction surprises me. Pain courses through my chest, leaving me empty. Tears pool in my eyes.

At first, a blast of fear shoots through my ribcage - why would I be crying again during sex? But then I recognize what's wrong.

Every inch of me is magnetized to Noah, begging to merge myself with his polar draw. He's too far away when our bond melds us closer than ever, physically hurting us to be separated. I need to hold him just as badly as he's aching to hold me.

When I turn around with desperate, outstretched hands, Noah tackles me into his embrace. In one breath, my legs are thrown around his waist, our chests compressed as we squeeze each other like we're reuniting after a painful year apart.

I nuzzle our noses, cupping Noah's cheeks as I absorb every second of his eyes on me. Noah dives for my lips, and I kiss him back twice as hard, wincing from the impact when I get a little too eager. But Noah doesn't mind; he soothes me with massaging, cuddly precision, working my lips just as tenderly as his arms squeeze me closer.

Our breaths tangle, interrupted only by sharp moans and hard squeezes of each other's bodies. We're unable to morph ourselves into one, no matter how hard we try.

Noah slips his palms beneath my thighs. I freeze, catching my breath.

As if I could. I'm met with ravenous, yellow eyes, searching my eyes and swollen lips.

"Do you still want more?" His whisper vibrates my chest, clenching my core tight.

I nod, feeling more ready for him to be inside me than ever.

When Noah re-enters me, the sensation hits straight into my heart muscles from how deeply it blasts our love coursing through us. My loud, unrestrained moan pushes a raspy breath out of Noah, his arms wilting beneath our pleasure. But without him holding me up, his cock plummets as deep as he can reach in one breath. My nails grip his shoulders, and Noah curls over me, hugging my hips as we acclimate to each other's warmth.

But then he opens those gorgeous eyes, letting them loose on me. The way he witnesses me turns me on more than anything we do together. Noah cups my face as it contorts in pleasure - jaw dropped, eyelids drooping, and swollen lips encasing my needy whimpers - and I let him watch, hiding none of it. He absorbs every second, pumping his hips harder the heartier I gasp.

Noah's embrace tightens until I'm flat against his chest as I bounce on his lap. When I fist handfuls of his gorgeous hair, he pants so hard that there's hardly any oxygen left between us, the air permeated by a flood of his flowery, adoring scent.

Noah crumbles into my chest, sputtering his words. "Fuck, I– I can't knot already."

"Enjoy yourself," I breathe.

But with one look into my eyes, Noah lifts my hips off him, leaving me empty and aching. He pants hot air against my sweaty chest, sending an icy, rousing shiver through me.

Noah shakes his head, only a hard swallow interrupting his rapid breath. "No, I want to wait. I love seeing you feel good."

My back arches, overcome by my pulse's hard throbbing between my legs. "I love seeing you feel good more than anything."

"Fuck, you're so fucking brave. Sometimes I want to cry, thinking about everything you've overcome to let me see you unraveled like this." He peeks into my eyes, flipping my heart with his burning, red-rimmed stare. "I would've loved you just as you were the second we met, but you keep surprising me. And somehow, I keep loving you even more. I don't know what to do with myself around you."

My neck flushes. I'm unsure how to respond.

But Noah softens into a rumbling whisper. "Can I spoil you back?"

I bite my lips, my eyes burning with affectionate tears. "O-okay. Yes. Please, yes."

As Noah dips back into me, I'm surprised at how slick I am. He's holding me so close, but I'm melting in his arms, forcing him to broaden his hold on me to keep me from spilling apart. I smash my open lips against his sweaty cheek, my chest heaving through him stuffing me with pleasure. It aches even stronger than when we started, tingling, thick pressure blooming in my abdomen the deeper he fills me.

But I know Noah hasn't even started with his spoiling. He doesn't bounce me over him anymore, opting to tilt my hips in a slow roll. The action drags my clit against his pelvis, sharpening my breath.

"There you go," he whispers against my lips before kissing them. "That feel good?"

I whimper. "Yes. You feel good."

A flare of heat flashes through Noah's eyes.

But he takes his sweet time with me. I droop against his chest, too weak with delight to hold myself up, but Noah nuzzles against my forehead. After planting a tender kiss on my head, he rocks his hips as he rolls mine, increasing the pressure he drives into my cervix. My knees raise to our sides with my hearty moan.

His stare flashes with the same uncontainable desire, its yellow fire growing into an inferno. God, he's stretching me to my limits, even though I'm more lubed up than ever. Is he enjoying my pleasure this much?

The more I react, the more stimulation he layers over me - roaming over my breasts, ass, back, and neck until I'm a blubbering puddle in his arms. The rising pressure he builds in my belly feels so intense that I can't hold it in much longer, but I'm desperate to, smitten by Noah's delighted stare.

But as desire mounts our bond, Noah's thrusts are disrupted by his own uncontrollable jerking. Its unpredictability stuffs me in random bursts until my legs shake.

Noah hitches me closer in his lap, our hips colliding hard. I clench over him hard enough to shove him out of me, but my loosening muscles between my pussy's desperate pulses suck him right back in. The sudden speed it creates between thrusts pushes wispy, rising moans from my lips, my pussy massaging him so hard that it fills the cave with wet, colliding slaps of our hips.

Noah whimpers against my forehead, his breath quivering. I'm desperate for him to lay me down and pound into me, but my satiated muscles are too far gone to fully drop myself over him to help. I squirm in his lap, my feet slipping behind his hips as I lose my rhythm to the fuzzy warmth spilling over my pelvis.

I know Noah might ask me what I want like he always does; that primal glaze over his eyes tells me he's aching to make me come. But instead of waiting for his prompting, my true desires erupt from me in airy, pleading whispers against his cheek.

"Harder– Harder– *Harder–*"

"Fuck." Noah grunts. "I can't believe how *proud* I am of you." As if that wasn't torturously sweet enough, he pumps his thickening shaft into me until my every inhale and exhale are breathy, rapid cries of pleasure. "What a good girl–"

With a hard jerk of my hips, I squirt between our bodies, dousing our thighs. But I'm left a moaning mess, clinging onto the edge with desperate, digging squeezes of his back. Noah groans into my mouth, his gaping lips eating up my needy breaths as I relish in his heightening pleasure in our bond alongside mine.

Judging by the widening I feel at the base of his shaft, Noah is seconds away from knotting me, only adding to the delicious fullness he's burrowing inside me.

Noah wheezes. "Oh, *fuck*, I'm–"

My eyelashes flutter as Noah's incoming climax hits just the right spot. My knees drop open wide, granting Noah unrestrained access as I come in his lap. With a growl, Noah dives for my mark. Scraping his fangs over my neck, Noah pumps as fast as he can, riding out my orgasm as my legs twist through its satiating ache.

I cling to him, suckling over his mark in return. He moans against my neck, jamming his hips into me as he orgasms. His shaft jerks against my cervix with his short, choppy breaths, shaking the last bits of pleasure from my thighs.

I drag my hands and head over him, overwhelmed by the love coursing through our bond. Noah clings to me, holding my head to his heart like I'm the most precious being he's ever held. I can't stop moaning with every breath, squirming through the leftover bliss of his knot filling me up. Noah holds my body through it, but it feels like he's holding my heart through it too - healing another old wound.

By the time we slump into each other on the ground in an exhausted heap, every atom of my body and spirit feels so loved that our bond's strength surges beyond what I knew was possible.

Noah is right. I've changed. As I kiss him, I'm not afraid of the unknowns in our future together anymore; I'm afraid of not cherishing every minute left of the life I have with my mate.

Losing out on each irreplaceable second is far more terrifying than any horrors we could face together. Now, we have each other to pull us through.

Easing myself into Noah's arms with utmost trust, I feel so alive. I feel like me.

To Be Continued in Book 2

Aliya craves every good, bad, and uncertain task that comes with becoming Noah's Luna - and hopefully, the mother of his children. But danger sprouts from every corner, and unresolved trauma derails Aliya and Noah's plans. Healing can't be forced, no matter how hard they love each other through it.

Desperate to regain her bearings, Aliya sets her sights on conquering everything that once plagued her. As Noah and Aliya navigate an unknown future, trusting in each other's passion to carry them through, dark secrets come to light about their fathers' deaths. The fated mates search for the truth, but who they find lurking instead threatens to devour the entire Greenfield Pack's sense of safety.

RIVER KAI

Freeing My Alpha

Book 2 of *My Shy Alpha*

THE STEAMY SHIFTER ROMANCE SERIES

Acknowledgments

This book was terrifying to write. For the same reason, I loved writing every second of it.

I used to feel like I needed an instruction manual that I was never given. In June 2022, I sought Exposure and Response Prevention therapy after a lifetime of struggling through what I concluded might be OCD. Sure enough, I was diagnosed with OCD to go along with my diagnosed PTSD, social anxiety, depression, and a laundry list of physical chronic illnesses.

Knowing I was an avid reader and writer, one of the first homework tasks my ERP therapist suggested was to read Everyday Mindfulness for OCD by Shala Nicely, LPC, and Jon Hershfield, MFT. I had never been so emotional over a non-fiction health book, but with every page, I found anecdote after anecdote that explained my whole life. I didn't need to come with instructions; I just had a brain with Obsessive Compulsive Disorder.

Their work inspired a deep need to write again - translate the thoughts I finally puzzled together into a separate, fictional story, hoping it could resonate with at least one reader. I pushed my boundaries, creating something I wasn't comfortable writing but wholeheartedly needed to.

I was indescribably nervous to share Book 1 with an editor, but Kayla Vokolek edited My Shy Alpha without judgment, digging back to the core of what I wanted to express after I compulsively buried some of the best elements. Thank you, Kayla, for your generosity, impeccable analytical and critiquing skills, incredible sense of humor, and for always bringing out the best writer in me.

My family has been equally warm throughout the writing process, even when I initially described my book in the vaguest yet weirdest way possible (it's like a werewolf-y, romance thing, but, uh, *too* romantic) and then banned most of them from reading this book (sorry, Grandma).

Thank you, Mom, for encouraging me through every step of my "sexy book" and consistently saving my sanity during my worst plot holes.

Thank you, Dad, for your generosity in keeping me afloat during treatment and supporting my art endeavors no matter what they en*tail* (enjoy the dad joke).

Thank you, Blake, for your invaluable enthusiasm in supporting my passions and genuine, good-natured outlook on whatever life throws at us - you always inspire me to keep going.

To my ERP therapist, I can't thank you enough for your compassionate guidance through my worst fears. I'm so grateful for your inventiveness in working with this novel as part of my healing, as it made otherwise uncomfortable work immensely fun and twice as rewarding.

A huge thank you to Shauna Pichette, Licensed Therapist, LPC, LPCC, NCC, for generously donating your time and expertise around Exposure and Response Prevention and Prolonged Exposure. I know your work is crucial to countless lives.

I made some of the best author friends I could ask for through this book.

Julia Aniella, fellow Steamy Romance writer and one of the most empathetic, engaging, and compassionate friends I've ever met, stuck by my side from day 1 of My Shy Alpha's creation. With early morning phone calls despite the long distance, giggling over Omegaverse anatomy, and writing power hours, it's been a joy to write alongside you. Thank you for your tireless support, and for being the first to fall in love with my characters.

Ariadne Tay, thank you for laughing with me over intrusive thoughts just as much as diving into serious, cathartic discussions about mental health.

Yulia Harper, thank you for bringing my witchy, weirdo side back out of me and always knowing how to laugh, even in the darkest situations.

My close friends have pulled me through so many intense stages of my life, and this one was no exception.

Thank you, Layla, for joining me in forgetting TMI exists and always cheering me on (and cheering me up). I adore you and am so lucky to have you in my life.

Thank you, Jamee, for hyping me up and always believing in my work's potential, even from its sketched stages.

Thank you, E, for taking the time to comment, read, and encourage me to keep writing despite life's tremendous challenges.

Thank you, Lukas, for not only beta-reading, but also showing up to support every story with absolute kindness, no matter what I've created thus far.

A huge thank you to every Patron on Patreon - Lukas, Katy, Phoebe, Anonymous, Stacie, Cass, Bella, Annie, Courtney, Drask, Mitchie, E the Cat Caterer, Rob, Jennifer, and Leyth - for believing in my work enough to generously support me during My Shy Alpha's creation.

Thank you to everyone who tipped me on Tapas and every reader who left the most beautiful, heartfelt reviews on Inkitt. Your generosity amped me up beyond words.

A special thanks to readers who read the original visual novel edition of My Shy Alpha, as well as web novel readers on Tapas, Wattpad, and Inkitt. Your enthusiasm for Aliya and Noah's well-being still amazes me and gives me hope.

Thank you to every pop-up market visitor in Portland who has stopped by with a bright smile and boundless enthusiasm for my small business. You've taught me it can feel safe where I live.

And lastly, thank you, reader. My Shy Alpha gave me a million exposures to practice, rolled into one book. It has always been a book with way more sexual content than my OCD was comfortable with. It addresses heavy topics I'm terrified of getting wrong because of how deeply I care about them, and it exposes PTSD realities I'd rather avoid sharing (thanks to PTSD, ha). So, reader, while I've been terrified to share this story with you in all of its stages, it's been one of the most rewarding fictional experiences to write. Thank you for giving Aliya and Noah the opportunity to be heard.

You matter to me. If you or someone you know is struggling, please flip to the following page for mental health resources.

Resources

You deserve support and free access to knowledge. Please utilize the resources below whenever you need them. The world needs you here.

International OCD Foundation
https://iocdf.org

International Society for the Study of Trauma and Dissociation
https://isst-d.org

RAINN (Anti-Sexual Violence Nonprofit)
https://www.rainn.org

Psychology Today - Find a Therapist (International)
https://psychologytoday.com/intl/counsellors

Trans Lifeline
https://translifeline.org

The Trevor Project
https://thetrevorproject.org

International Association for Suicide Prevention
https://www.iasp.info

More by River Kai

BOOKS

Freeing My Alpha: Book 2 of My Shy Alpha, the Steamy Shifter
Romance Series (Summer 2024)
Book 3 of My Shy Alpha (Winter 2025)
Unraveling with You: A Steamy Contemporary Romance

GRAPHIC NOVELS

Resonance: Space Gays Vol.1
What-Sexual?? Vol.1
What-Sexual?? Vol.2 (2024)

For current updates, follow River Kai on social media

@riv_kaii
@riv_kai
River Kai
River Kai Art

or sign up for the River Kai Art newsletter at
riverkaiart.com

About the Author

As a bisexual and transgender creator, River Kai specializes in LGBTQ+ Romance, Sci-Fi, and Fantasy with mental health and disability representation, creating stories for readers like him to see they're not alone. While he writes in multiple Romance sub-genres, his stories share three recurring themes: empowering character arcs about healing from trauma, authentic representation of transgender or bisexual main characters with depression, anxiety, PTSD, and OCD, and a sweet-but-spicy emphasis on consent.

Made in United States
Troutdale, OR
10/14/2024

23717448R00192